EVERY STEP OF THE WAY

KIT DOMINO

Second Edition published 2016 ISBN 9781909734272
www.thornberrypublishinguk.com

DEDICATION

This novel is dedicated to all those people who died during the Great Smog of 1952 and to those whose lives were wrecked and altered by this monumental event.

It is also dedicated to Dave, whose love, support and encouragement allowed me the time to devote to this work, and who has never stopped believing in me. And to Jane, without whose friendship, enthusiasm and moral support I would have given up long ago.

ACKNOWLEDGEMENTS

To Avis, Tricia, Rosemary P, Rosemary E, Brenda, Chris, and absent friends of the Ivy Writers for all their advice, suggestions and support, but most of all, for our wonderful evenings together. Thank you for inviting me to be part of the group. My heartfelt thanks especially go to Tricia, for patiently working through the final draft seeking out my mistakes and making such valuable and helpful comments.

DISCLAIMER

With the exceptions of those clearly in the public domain, all characters depicted in *Every Step of the Way* are fictitious, and any resemblance to persons living or dead is purely coincidental. All the events and incidents portrayed are, however, entirely real.

COVER DESIGN

kitdominoart.com
makedonskii Dreamtime.com

PRAISE FOR EVERY STEP OF THE WAY

"A richly evocative saga depicting a period of the twentieth century that few writers have attempted. ... This is one author to watch for the future." Lizzie Lane

"This has been the best read I have had in a long time ...I was transported back to London in the 50s; the sounds and smells and the atmosphere are all there, in this book, a great read."
Janet Cross

"Bringing to life West London in the 1950s beautifully!"
Bookbabe

"Who knew fog could be so dangerous.... A great historical fiction read." The Kindle Book Review

"A true page turner. ... A great read and one I would definitely recommend." Jo Lambert

FOREWORD

Shortlisted for the 2004 Harry Bowling Prize, *Every Step of the Way* brings to life the social history of West London during the 1950s. A time witnessing the rise of teenage culture, and where Teddy Boys rule the coffee bars and play the jukeboxes. An era that sees the birth of the *New Musical Express* and the British pop charts. It is in this brave new world, where rationing has almost ended, central heating a pipedream for most families, and where men still rule the roost in a country fighting to recover from the devastation of the Second World War that, upon the afternoon of 5th December 1952, a killer smog descends over England's capital.

London was well known for its frequent fogs and smogs (it wasn't called "The Smoke" for nothing) but none had ever seen smog of such magnitude as befell the city that winter's afternoon. Lasting for four days, the Great Smog became one of the worst man-made air pollution disasters the world had known at the time, and probably since, given the sheer number of people who died as a result. Reaching 4,800 in the following weeks, during the next few months the human death toll rose to figures over 12,000, although exact numbers have never been confirmed. To these figures must also be added the vast numbers of wildlife that perished.

No one realised the ramifications this dramatic event would leave behind when it lifted or how it would change the course of history for millions of people. Some of those changes are well documented: the burning of smokeless fuels and the beginnings of the Clean Air Act that finally came into force in 1956, for example. But many more went unrecorded; countless legacies the official records failed to mention or chose to ignore.

Beth Brixham's battle to hold her family's lives together in the aftermath of the Great Smog is one such story.

Chapter One

5th December 1952

Head bent, mindful to watch out for uneven paving slabs, Beth Brixham groped her way along the high wall of the gasworks, her only guide through the ever-thickening fog. The pavement along this part of Brentford High Street was narrow, barely wide enough for two people to pass and she feared wandering out into the road. The rough, yellow London bricks snagged at her knitted glove, pulling at threads.

The fog had descended swiftly; within minutes turning from a damp, misty haze into one so dense, it blotted out all familiar landmarks, the old gasoemeter, and the tapering tower of the Victorian pumping station near Kew Bridge soon lost from sight.

Clutching her coat collar to her throat with her other hand, Beth put on a spurt; she mustn't be late. She *had* to keep going. If only she could run the rest of the way. But that would be stupid; it was impossible to see where she was going. She might trip over. No way could she turn up for an interview with holes in her stockings and grazed knees, let alone late. That just wouldn't do.

Somewhere across the street stood St George's Church with its stubby, hexagonal bell tower. Had she passed it yet, she wondered. From the church to the pumping station and Green Dragon Lane, her destination, took a good ten minutes' brisk walking. But with the church shrouded from view, she had no way of judging how far she had come, how much further she had to go.

Shivering inside her coat, she couldn't ignore the dampness from the cold, December pavement seeping

1

through the thin leather soles of her black boots.

"I need a new pair," she muttered. "These ones won't see the winter out. I have to get this job."

In an effort to keep at bay the sulphurous stench filling her nostrils, she pulled her knitted scarf up over her mouth and nose, pressing it closer. It did little to prevent the acrid odour filtering through. The air around the gasworks always stank of rotten eggs, but today it had a most peculiar smell. It made her eyes sting, and had a ghastly, foul taste. Of tar and carbolic. The scarf's coarse, woollen fibres irritated her cheeks, tickled her nose, made her sneeze. When she inhaled again, she realised the smell came not from the towering gasometer; it was the fog itself that reeked.

Behind her came the sound of heavy footfalls approaching. These gave way to the noise of a man's hacking, persistent cough.

The church clock bell chiming out suddenly through the murk stopped her in her tracks. In her head she counted… Two. Three. Blast, I'm already late! I'm supposed to be there by now.

"Hey, watch where you're going, kid," the man behind grumbled, bumping into her. Face hidden behind a trilby pulled down low over his forehead, he sidestepped into the road, coughing and spluttering into a handkerchief as he hurried on.

"Sorry," she called out, but he had already vanished into the fog, the air falling silent. No footsteps. No coughing.

Just eerie silence.

Stamping her feet and rubbing her hands together in an effort to keep warm, she peered into the strange half-light. Hidden by a veil of shadowy unnaturalness, the street had taken on a strange, unworldly perspective. She listened, expecting to hear the occasional car or lorry, the sound of an engine, the crunch of a missed gear, a sporadic trolleybus trundling along. There should have been drays going back and forth from the brewery yard. Not even the sound of a pair of high-heels tapping on the pavement.

Only minutes earlier the street had been packed with people rushing to and fro, cars zooming past. And surely it wasn't more than five minutes since she'd waved out to the rag-and-bone man with his cart pulled along by Delilah, his lumbering horse, clip-clopping along on the other side of the road? Where had everybody gone?

Two faint lights glowed ahead, slowly growing larger, getting closer. With it, the muted rumble of a car's engine. From the gloom, a black Ford car emerged, its dim headlights casting misshapen shadows across the pavement. As it crawled along towards her, the driver wiped at the inside of the windshield with his hand as if waving. She recognised the car; Uncle Donald owned one just like it. Perhaps it was him? Her heart lifted. He'd give her a lift.

Waving out, she took a step closer to the kerb.

As the car drew parallel, her shoulders sagged. It wasn't him. She doubted the driver even noticed she was there such was the intent look on his face as he stared straight ahead, gripping the steering wheel as if his life depended on it. As the vehicle drove on, its chugging engine noise fading, she thought how much its rear lights looked like a pair of devil's red eyes receding away to nothingness.

The sense of isolation returned, with it the unnerving feeling she were the only person left in the world, just like Bill Masen in *The Day of the Triffids*, the book she had been reading in bed last night. How, upon removing the bandages from his eyes, he found not one single soul about. At least he could see, she thought wryly. She could hardly see her hand in front of her face.

She stared at her gloves. A small hole had formed in the right one, on the third finger. It would need darning when she got home. Hopefully, there would be some of the wool left over from the old pullovers Gran had unpicked and reknitted into the colourful matching set she wore.

The fog turned a dirty yellow-brown colour in the winter twilight. There was something falling within it too. Black sooty specks that drifted down slowly. Other particles seemed to hang there, motionless. Unease gripped her chest; made her shudder. There was something about this fog that didn't feel right; a sense of foreboding hiding within its murky depths.

How on earth was she going to find the offices of Wicker & Sons in this? She didn't even know how far up Green Dragon Lane she had to go once she reached the pumping station. If she continued, she'd be even more late. Hardly creating the right impression. Who would want to hire someone who couldn't even arrive on time? There were bound to be other girls waiting to be interviewed as well, so what was the point in going on? She might as well turn around and go back home.

Disheartened and disappointed, she shoved her hands into her coat pockets. Coins clinked.

"Don't walk home in the dark, love." The words her mother had spoken, thrusting the loose change into her pocket before leaving the house, reverberated inside Beth's head. Money meant for the bus ride home. The next bus stop couldn't be that much further on, she told herself, and a bus must surely be due along soon.

She plodded on, anxious now to be home safe and

secure, and settled in the warmth thrown out by the coal fire.

Up ahead, a woman slowly materialised through the fog. Beth saw she stood next to a tall, concrete post, its square, red bus-stop sign at the top barely visible. Behind the woman, Beth spied another person. Then another emerged. And another. A red glow from a cigarette flared, outlining the silhouette of a tall man also waiting for the bus.

Squeezing her way passed everyone in the line along the narrow pavement, Beth couldn't avoid knocking into a couple of people. Elbows collided.

"That's all right, love," said one woman, armed with two heavy-looking shopping bags.

"Don't mind me," said the other in a supercilious tone.

Beth took her place at the end of the long queue. The woman immediately in front of her turned, gave a half smile. Hair rollers peeked out from beneath a white headscarf tied tightly under her pointed chin, accentuating her thin, over-rouged face.

"Been stood here a good half-hour, I have. Ain't been no buses. Don't know what's happened to 'em all. A right pea-souper this one's turning into."

Beth couldn't help but notice the smudge of bright red lipstick smeared across the woman's teeth, and was about to reply that it was certainly the worst one she'd ever seen, but the woman continued, talking non-stop, not letting her get a word in.

"Lord-love-a-duck, I ain't seen nothin' like it since I don't know when. It ain't doin' my chest no good niver, I can tell you. And she in front," she nodded towards the lady in question who coughed persistently, "she's been barkin' her guts up like nobody's business. I'd swear she's hackin' up a gold watch. It ain't healthy, it ain't. Be glad to get back indoors wiv me feet up for half hour before I has to come out again. I was supposed to be home by now gettin' changed into me gladrags, ready to be back at the Wagon in time for openin' at six. Don't seem much point goin' 'ome, does it? My old man'll be doin' his nut 'cos I ain't back to get his tea. I could murder a cuppa, meself, I can tell you."

Behind her scarf, Beth licked at dry lips. They felt chapped. She could do with a cuppa herself to warm up. Take the chill from her bones.

A few yards beyond the bus stop, bright lights from a café shone out like a beacon. Could she wait in there in the warm for a while, she wondered. After all, the bus when it did arrive would no doubt be full. Standing room only. Last in the queue, not a hope in hell's chance of getting on it. But did she have enough money for a drink and the ride home? She couldn't very well just go in and sit down and not order anything.

She pulled off a glove, plunged her hand into the coat pocket, and retrieved a thrupenny bit, a tanner, and a silver florin. Just enough for a cup of tea and the bus fare home to Busch Corner.

Pushing open the door to Maisie's Tea Room, loud chattering, bursts of laughter and rattling china were fighting for air space over the unmistakable voice of Al Martino singing out *Here In My Heart* from some unseen wireless. The till clanged with a loud ding, money clinked. Above the noise, the tantalizing aroma of fresh coffee, hot food and warmth beckoned Beth in.

Spying the only empty table, near the counter, she made her way to it quickly before somebody else claimed it. Once seated, she yanked the knitted beret from her head and shook free her tousled auburn hair before ramming the beret into one coat pocket, the gloves into the other.

The camel-coloured coat, sewn by her mother from an army surplus blanket, bought from the Army & Navy Stores in Chiswick, was two years old and getting far too small to wear for much longer. The cuffs were worn and beginning to fray, there was no more hem to let down, and the buttons strained across her chest. She undid them, longing for the day when she could afford to buy a new one. Not getting that job today meant that time was now even further away. Likewise her new boots.

Trying to catch the attention of one of the busy, white-aproned waitresses, she looked around Maisie's, taking in the modern, clean décor. One of many new teashops opening up everywhere now tea rationing had ended, its bright ceiling lights reflected on shiny, wood-effect Formica tabletops.

Swagged between the light fittings were colourful paperchains, just like the ones she had spent last Saturday afternoon making at home. All that licking and looping the sticky, coloured paper strips Mum had bought in Woolworths with some of the Christmas Club money. Beth ran her tongue over her top lip, still able to taste that peculiar, sweet-flavoured glue.

On a glass shelf behind the counter a tinsel garland wove in and out of upturned drinking glasses. The thin silver strands sparkled and shimmered as light and air played across them. Christmas was but twenty days away. Fast approaching.

She loved Christmas. All the decorations, the crackers with silly jokes and paper hats and plastic little daft toys and trinkets. Most of all she loved the tree. There *had* to be a tree. It wouldn't be Christmas without one. Mike would bring it home from the market on Christmas Eve. And they would have lots of balloons pinned to the ceiling in the front room and hanging from the picture rail. She liked balloons but didn't like the noise they made when they burst. Mike always blew them up too much on purpose, just to make them go bang because he knew she didn't like it.

But this year, David would be there, on leave from the army. He would stop Mike's teasing. A warm glow filled her insides. She was so looking forward to seeing her eldest brother again. He'd not been home for over a year. She smiled. Yes, it was indeed going to be a lovely Christmas with all the family together again.

Near the other end of the counter she could see a group of schoolgirls. They wore the dark green uniform of her old school. Huddled around the table, they were leaning close together chatting. Laughing. She watched them whispering, hands at sides of mouths telling secrets, all the while thinking that it hadn't been that long ago she'd been just like them. Now here she sat, sixteen and out in the real world. A world apart. And lonely.

Since leaving school back in July, she'd lost touch with most of the girls in her class. She missed them all. Even Elaine Newans, her once best friend, hardly ever called at the house nowadays, certainly not since Elaine started going steady with that pimply Ricky Hopkins from the youth club.

The girls were giggling now, all eyes staring at the tall, good-looking waiter who had just appeared behind the counter from a curtained doorway.

The sleeves of his white shirt were rolled up to his elbows, the muscles of his arm flexing as he pulled on levers on a shiny metal contraption with some foreign name emblazoned over its front that she couldn't quite make out from where she sat. It let loose a loud hiss of steam as he filled two white coffee cups. His black quiff of hair curled slightly to one side, swaying as he moved. She guessed him to be about nineteen or twenty, and bet all the girls swooned over him.

He looked up, and seeing her watching him, gave her a wink. Embarrassed, Beth darted her eyes back quickly to the schoolgirls. They were still giggling, and no doubt talking about him. How she envied their innocence and freedom.

"You looks like you've lost a guinea and found tuppence. Been stood up, 'ave you? Never mind. There's plenty more fish in the sea."

Seeing a smiling waitress, not much older than herself, with a notebook and pencil in hand standing by her table, Beth hurried to explain.

"Oh no, it's nothing like that. I was supposed to be at an interview for a job, only I never got there. I'm just killing time until the next bus comes along to go back home."

"Crickey, haven't you 'eard? They've stopped all the bloomin' buses 'cos of this smog. They just said so on the wireless. Apparently the whole of London's like it."

Beth noticed several of the tables were clearing rapidly, their occupants hurrying out of the door. People who must have had the same idea as her to wait in here until the bus came, and who were now scurrying off, forced to walk wherever they were going.

She sighed heavily. "Blast. That means I'm going to be late home as well as not making it to that interview. Dad'll be livid with me when he finds out. Likely he'll knock my block off. Tell me I'm stupid, and that I should have caught the bus there in the first place."

The waitress laughed. "You'll be all right. There'll be

other jobs. There's plenty about now with everythin' back to normal after the war. Everywhere's cryin' out for people. Right, wot'll it be? We've got tea, coffee or 'ot chocolate. And lovely 'ot toasted teacakes. Or toast, eggs on toast—"

"Just a cup of tea, please," Beth interrupted before the waitress tempted her further. A thought struck. She wouldn't be needing any money now for a bus.

"No, I've changed my mind," she said. "I'll have a toasted teacake as well, please. I shall need something to keep me going. It's a long walk back home." She sighed again. "This day really isn't going well at all. I really needed that job, you see. Any job. Anything to stop my dad's constant grumbling. He's always on at me it's about time I got up off my backside and found something. It's not as if I'm not trying my best. After all, this is the third interview this week." She hung her head and mumbled, "Well, it would have been... Dad can't work, see, on account of his disability. It's all right for my brother, Mike. He's just turned eighteen. He works down the road in the veg market. He doesn't have to pay much housekeeping to Mum because he brings home bags of fruit, or trays of veg, and sacks of potatoes to eke out the rations. Whatever's going begging. Falls off the barrows, he says. Most of his money seems to go on his motorbike. Dad's always going on at him about it. Mike's going out with Janet Collier. I don't like Janet much. I knew her at school, she was in the year above, and she's a troublemaker. It's only a matter of time, I keep telling him, before her true colours are out, but Mike won't hear none of it, of course. 'What do I know', he always says whenever I voice my opinion." She looked up at the waitress.

"A lot of you at 'ome, is there? There's nine of us. All

squashed into a basement flat down Waldecker Road."

"No. Just Mum and Dad and me and our Mike. And there's Gran. She's bedridden and has to share my room. She's got a bad hip, see. She had a fall. Can barely walk more than a few steps so she had to move in with us. Then there's my other brother, David. He's twenty-two and serving with the Middlesex Regiment. They were stationed out in Hong Kong and got sent in to help the Americans fight the war in Korea. He's due home next week. Mum'll be so pleased to see him."

Beth didn't know why she was telling all this to the waitress; it just all seemed to come tumbling out of her mouth in a rush, unable to stop herself.

The waitress tore the page from her notebook. "Crumbs. Don't seem right, does it? One war ends and then they call up our poor boys to go and fight in another. Can't say as I even know where Korea is, let alone understand what it's all about. Right, one 'ot teacake and a pot of tea comin' up. Only one lump of sugar, mind. It's still on ration."

She seems nice, Beth thought, watching the waitress take the order to the counter.

A few minutes later the waitress came back to the table, carrying a wooden tray. From this, she set down a china cup and saucer, a stainless steel pot and a small jug of milk.

"'Ere you are, then. Tea for one. Careful mind, that pot's 'ot. One teacake to follow. Terry's doing it now. So, wot sorta job were you goin' for?"

"A secretary at a solicitors."

"Blimey. You must be clever, then?"

"Not really," Beth laughed. "I can type well but I'm not much good at shorthand yet. This job offered further training at night school. To be honest, I don't want to spend my life in some dreary office typing-pool day in, day out."

"Well, if you really needs somethin' quick, perhaps I can 'elp. I know we needs more girls 'ere in the week leading up to Christmas. Apparently it's always extra busy then, Christmas shoppers an' all. Mrs Pilkin'ton, she's the boss, she told me she's goin' down the Labour Exchange in the morning to put in an ad. If you're interested, come back tomorrow afternoon. She'll be 'ere then. Tell her Kate Whitchurch told you. That's me. It's hard work, mind. Me legs and feet are killin' me stood on 'em all day. But Mrs Pilkin'ton's all right. She's a bit of a dragon some days, but well, who ain't? Still, there are some perks." She tossed her curly head towards the counter. "Like that Terry over there. He's worth comin' in for any day. Anyway, best go. More customers to serve."

"Thanks, Kate. I'll think about it."

Beth watched Terry working at the counter and agreed heartily with Kate. Yes, he certainly was a dreamboat of the first order.

When she left Maisie's half-an-hour later the street lamps were on, the sodium-yellow lights casting weird, green haloes along the street. Beth wrapped the scarf tighter round her face so that only her pale blue eyes showed, placed the beret back firmly on her head and began the long trudge home.

Chapter Two

Alfie Brixham, a tall man in his mid forties graced by a receding grey hairline, stood by the foot of the stairs, a newspaper tucked under his arm.

"Where the ruddy hell 'ave you been?" he bellowed the instant Beth opened the front door.

"I had to walk home, didn't I," she snapped back. Cold, tired and with aching legs and feet, the last thing she needed was the third degree from *him* the moment she got in.

The hallway, illuminated by a single light bulb halfway down the narrow passageway, could do little to brighten the drab colours of the paintwork, or her mood. Tossing her coat over the newel post, she glanced up the dismal stairwell. A light glowed from her bedroom.

"Where's Mum?"

"Up changin' your gran's bed. She's gone and messed 'erself again."

"Isn't it about time you got that commode you keep going on about? Better still, move Gran down here. It'd save Mum having to run up and down the stairs all the time, and avoid these accidents which, let's face it, can't be nice for either of them."

She watched his face, sensing his reaction at the mention of the never-ending argument in the Brixham household, that of moving Gran down into the front room.

He shifted his weight, looked uncomfortable.

"Don't you bloomin' start naggin', girl. I have enough of that from your mother. It'll all get seen to in time."

"Huh, I believe that when I see it. Like everything else in this house. Just look at this place, Dad. You've been promising Mum for ages to do something about it. Four years it's been like this, ever since we moved in. That red paint down the middle and up the centre of the stairs doesn't fool anyone it's carpet."

Dark-brown bottom half, dark-green top half; colours so dull and unwelcoming for a new house, nothing could convince her it wasn't leftover camouflage paint from the war, bought as a job lot on the cheap by the council.

Sitting on the second stair, she heaved off one boot and wiggled her toes, glad to be free of its tight grip. Pulling off the other, she was dismayed to find a hole the size of a two-bob bit in the sole. She poked a finger through, all the while thinking how little effort her father made around the house. Despite being at home all day, he never did so much as mow the front lawn. It was always left for someone else to do. Normally Mike or her mother.

"I'd best go and see if Mum needs a hand with Gran then."

"Make us a cuppa rosie before you go up, there's a pet. I'm gaspin'."

No doubt Mum could use one too, and Gran, she thought, but would *he* ever think to put the kettle on? Oh no, not on your nelly. She doubted he even knew how many sugars he took.

"It would have been nicer if you'd offered to make a pot for once." She couldn't resist the dig.

"That's women's work."

She sighed, hearing the same old excuse he always made whenever he didn't want to do anything around the house. She'd have been shocked if he'd said anything different. It wasn't his fault, she supposed, pulling on her slippers. It was how *all* men had been brought up. Indoctrinated since birth to believe women kept home and men brought home the bacon. Except in this house, that is.

"Things will certainly be different when I marry. My husband will be far more housetrained." Not that she'd given much thought before to being married. She certainly didn't want a replica of Dad, that was for sure.

Ignoring his derisive snort and the draught from under the front door blowing about her legs, she wrapped her arms around her knees, smiling at the image forming in her head of the sort of man she'd like to marry. Someone tall and handsome and strong. With sexy eyes. A real man. One who didn't mind making a cup of tea or rolling up his sleeves to help with the washing up. Someone like that Terry in Maisie's teashop earlier. He was certainly gorgeous. A real hunk.

"Wot you grinnin' at like a bloomin' Cheshire cat?" Her father's voice interrupted the daydream. He stood over her, a finger wagging. "Fought for king and country I did, so as the likes of you young lot can live happy, safe lives. Just as our David's doin'. Now it's all your turns to look after me. I've done my bit, my girl."

"Yes, Dad." She shook her head, unable to keep away the sarcasm in her voice. "We've heard that story often enough." So many times, she knew it verbatim.

Staying on in Germany at the end of the war, Dad's regiment had been part of the Allied Forces taking stock of what was left of Germany's assets. On the very day they were leaving to come home, the troop lorry he was driving got a puncture. All the soldiers in the back jumped out to help replace the tyre, but the lorry slipped off its handbrake, rolled forward, and knocked over the jack. One soldier hadn't dived out of the way fast enough. The truck rolled over him, crushing his legs under the heavy wheels, and running over her father's foot as he, too, had tried to leap out of the way. Compared with the other soldier, who had to learn to walk on two artificial legs, Dad had escaped lightly, and ever since used that accident as a means to doing nothing.

"And now he gets under me feet all day long. Do you have to stand there, Alf?"

Beth turned at the sound of her mother's voice as she came down the creaking stairs carrying a pile of soiled sheets. A slim woman in her early forties, she looked old before her time, Beth thought, reading the exhausted, worn out expression set behind her mother's smile of greeting.

"Honestly, he does nothing but sulk about the house all day listening to that stupid *Dick Barton* programme on the wireless or that gardening chap. Claims he has an interest in chrysanthemums and growing parsnips, yet out back's nothing more than a patch of weeds and brambles to catch on the washing." Although the tone was lighthearted, Beth knew her mother was, in her own way, chiding her father's laziness.

Her father shuffled from foot to foot. "Come on, Connie, you knows I can't helps me limp, can I? I didn't ask for the ruddy brakes on that lorry to fail and break my foot. Lost a toe, I did."

"That's your stock answer to everything, Alfie Brixham. Never changes. You've seen how he spends the day, Beth. Reads the newspaper from cover to cover, then sneaking out to the betting shop when he thinks I'm not looking. Limp doesn't stop him then, does it? No. Nor going to the pub. But give me a hand hanging out the washing…"

"Gawd blimey, 'ere she goes again," he moaned. "Change the flippin' record, Con."

Beth stifled a laugh; they were always at it.

Connie turned to her. "You were a long time, pet. I was getting worried, you out in that smog."

"It's horrible out there, Mum. It came down so quick. I couldn't see my hand in front of my face; it stinks something awful too. And I had to walk home as they'd stopped all the buses."

Alfie shook his rolled-up newspaper in their direction, tutting. "I don't know. This country's gone to the flamin' dogs, if you asks me. One flake of snow and everythin' grinds to a halt. One heavy fog and London Transport stops the bloomin' trains and trams. What on earth do they think we did in the war, I ask you? Buses never stopped then because of bombs droppin'. Makes me wonder why we even bothered fightin' one."

"Oh, do put a sock in it, Dad, you're always grumbling. You don't know what it was like. You weren't here for most of it."

"And I want to hear how our Beth got on at her interview," her mother intervened. "Go and do your businesses, Alf." She ushered him away towards the lavvy across the hall before asking, "So, how did it go? Do you think you've got the job? Were there many others being interviewed?"

Beth gave a nonchalant lift of her shoulders. "It was all right, I suppose. They were interviewing lots of girls. I think I did okay. They'll let me know in a week or two."

Staring at Connie's hands Beth couldn't help noticing how swollen and sore her mother's fingers looked. Worse than usual. Perhaps when she finally found herself a job, Mum wouldn't have to take in so much other people's dirty laundry, she thought. Meanwhile, she hoped she hadn't blushed at fibbing about the interview, but what else could she say with Dad stood there listening? Whilst Mum might understand, even sympathize and agree she'd done the right thing by coming straight back home when the fog came, he wouldn't be so amiable. More as like he would start on at her, going on and on about it all night. She'd never hear the last of it.

Alfie, standing outside the lavvy door, had the fingers of one hand clamped tightly over his nose, the newspaper waving back and forth in the other.

"Phew, take those bloomin' sheets away, Con, they stink."

"Well, if you'd move your mother down here, closer to the toilet, I wouldn't have all this."

"Oh, come on, Con. You knows how I feels about that?"

Shaking her head, Beth left her parents to it and went to make the tea. To her, the solution about Gran was so obvious. So simple. Yet he would hear none of it. Lifting the kettle off the gas stove, she gave it a shake. Empty.

They had been living in a small terrace in Half Acre, just off the High Street when Gran first moved in, she recalled, stepping towards the kitchen sink. Dad was still in Germany so Gran shared Mum's bed. Mike and David shared one room, whilst she had the small box room all to herself, where she could be untidy as her mother would allow, which wasn't really that much, she thought now, upon reflection. Just a few clothes scattered here and there. The odd *Girl* comic or *True Romance* magazine tossed under the bed.

Gran had only been with them a week when the house had been blown out of existence. A bomb, fallen during the air raids, had lain lodged between the coalshed and the back wall of the house; no one knowing it was there until the morning it decided to explode. Beth still found it difficult to believe no one had been killed. Any earlier or later in the day they would all have been at home. Mum was out shopping, David already away in the army, and she and Mike were at school. It was only her parents' heavy double wardrobe falling across the bed that had saved Gran. Everything else had been wrecked. Now tall, rosebay willowherbs grew amongst the rubble where it had once stood. Bombweeds, Gran called them when she had described the vibrant pink spikes to her. Gran said they always sprang up wherever the bombs had dropped and set fire to everything.

Lost in thought, wishing for her own room again, not that she begrudged sharing with Gran, she loved the old woman dearly, she reached out for the tap and let out a loud scream.

Alfie shuffled through the kitchen doorway at the sound of her shriek.

"Now what's flippin' up, girl?"

Pointing to the stone sink, she screwed up her face in repulsion. There, slithering and sliding at the bottom were coiled half-a-dozen large, fat brown eels. As much as she enjoyed eating them, live ones made her squirm.

"I see Uncle Don's been. You could have warned me."

One eel was making its bid for freedom by escaping up the side of the sink and on to the wooden draining board. Alfie limped across the kitchen, reached out with his rolled-up newspaper and knocked the renegade eel back down to join his slippery mates.

"They won't hurt you, you daft bugger."

The paraffin heater at the top of the landing hadn't long been ignited. The fumes it emitted couldn't overpower the odour of disinfectant laced with an undertone of excrement emanating from the bedroom. As she climbed the stairs, Beth could hear her grandmother's knitting needles clacking away. The dexterity and agility in the old woman's bony fingers always held her in awe. Gran was always knitting something.

"Here, I've brought you a cuppa."

Beth set the cup and saucer down on the makeshift bedside table, in reality an upended wooden crate covered by an old cotton tablecloth. On it, her grandmother's teeth occupied a half-filled glass of water. Seeing them there like that always bemused her, half-expecting them to start chomping away on their own.

"Ah, there's a pet. Glad you is 'ome safe."

Propped up by three feather pillows in her double bed behind the open door, Gran's thinning, silver hair looked freshly combed. Her yellow wyncette nightdress still sported the crease marks from being folded away in the drawer. She stopped knitting the half-completed sock for David, wound the brown, fuzzy wool around the three wooden needles a few times, to prevent the stitches slipping off, then put the whole lot down on the bed.

Squeezed into the largest of the three bedrooms, the room felt cramped with the two beds, two wardrobes and an old walnut tallboy standing in front of the window, blocking out most of the natural light. Behind it now, the pink brocade curtains, a secondhand pair from Auntie Val, weren't quite drawn properly, a black chink showing where one of them had caught on a nail at the back. Beth went across and pulled the curtains together, blanking out the dark, smoggy night.

"You're in the best place tonight, Gran. I've never seen anything like it out there."

"Did your mum tell you? 'Fraid I've gone an' spoilt meself again."

Patting the old woman's cold hands, Beth sat down on the bed, ignoring the springs creaking in protest. Until that moment, she'd never noticed how much Gran's green silk eiderdown had faded, the quilting stitches broken in many places. It's getting old like Gran, she thought sadly.

"It's not your fault, Gran. You should be downstairs nearer the bathroom. We keep telling Dad it makes more sense."

"Your dad's too proud to let his front parlour into a room for me. Says it ain't the done thing."

"No, because he'll have to get up off his backside and help if you're down there. If the boot were on the other foot he'd have his bed in there quicker than you could say Jack Spratt."

Gran laughed at the unintended pun. "Now, now, girl. 'Course you're right, but it is his house. And after comin' home from the 'orrors of the Rhine and findin' your 'ome's been bombed to bits, he's more than 'appy 'avin' this new one off the council. We could've been given one of them 'orrible prefabs, like those down in Mogden Lane, near the sewage works, instead of this place. Leastways we've a garden and an inside karsie instead of that old stinky thunderbox at the bottom of the back yard, like back in Half Acre."

"Yes, but if you were downstairs you could benefit from it as well. Perhaps if he had to change your bedding he'd change his mind pretty quick."

"Then we'll just have to keep workin' on him then, won't we?" The old lady chuckled and winked. "Now, tell me all about your afternoon. I do looks forward to our little chats. Your dad only ever bothers to put his 'ead round the door to toss me the paper when he's finished readin' it. And your poor mum's up to her armpits in soapsuds and flat irons all day, she don't have time much to stop and natter when she brings up me meals. It gets lonely up 'ere, confined to me bed all day with nothin' but the wireless for company."

She told Gran all that had happened that afternoon, including how good the tea had tasted in Maisie's.

"Not like the weak, dishwater brew we're used to having thanks to rationing. This was proper tea. Apparently, the owner of the teashop is looking for more waitresses so I'm going back tomorrow to see."

"But what about your job interview at Wickers? How did that go?"

"Oh, Gran, I never made it there."

She never could lie to Gran. There was no need to because the old woman understood everything. Her closest friend and wisest of teachers, calmer of the most angriest of arguments, especially when Dad was involved. Best of all, she could share confidences with Gran she couldn't with her mother.

"Now I shall have to send myself a fake letter telling me I haven't got the job. Just to keep Mum and Dad quiet. It's a good thing we had to type out lots of self–addressed envelopes as part of our typing lessons at school." She giggled a little. "I saved them all. I must have known they'd come in handy one day."

Gran looked disappointed. "You really ought to tell your mother, you know, girl. It ain't right to be dishonest. She'll understand."

"I know that. But you know Dad, he'd never let it rest until he found something else to find fault with. It ain't worth all the hassle."

"Why not takes the offer in the teashop, if that's what you want to do, leastways for the time bein'? It'll give you some money an' gets you away from 'ere durin' the day."

"But the money's nowhere near as good as working in an office. By the time Dad takes my housekeep into account, I'll have none left."

"Then don't tell him how much you earns."

"Gran, how could you suggest such a thing? He's a right to know. Telling the odd little white lie is one thing, but deceit—"

"Poppycock. Listen to an expert, girl. Tell him only three-quarters as much you earns. One third of that is your housekeep. You keeps a third of the rest as your spenders. You know, for clothes and makeup and fun. The last third you saves for the big things. The other quarter you keeps stashed away. Keeps a tin locked in your knicker drawer, likes I does. He'll never look in there. Your grandfather didn't."

"But surely Granddad knew how much money you earned. Didn't he have to for the taxman and things?"

Gran smiled slyly as she tapped the side of her nose. "Takes it from me, girl. Always keeps some money back for yourself. Savings that no one knows about, only you. That way you'll never be be'olden to any man."

"Didn't Granddad even suspect you—"

Gran laughed, interrupting. "What 'im? No. The daft old so-and-so didn't have a clue. Every Friday without fail he would 'and me his unopened pay packet. I'd 'and 'im back his spenders for the week, just enough for his fags and beer. The rest was 'ousekeep. And what I earned from me job at the soap factory, he only knew half of."

"Oh Gran, you are a one."

"Beth, I need a hand please. Can you come down and peel the spuds?"

With her mother's plea beckoning, Beth reached across the bed and passed her grandmother back her knitting.

"I'd best go. It's stewed eels and mash for tea tonight."

Gran smacked her gums together and gave a wide, toothless grin. "Me favourite. Puts plenty of vinegar on me liquor. I likes it like that. Mind, I'll be glad when summer's 'ere and the winkle man starts comin' round on his bike again. I misses me winkles an' cockles for tea."

Chapter Three

Huddled under the blankets, reluctant to get out of the warm bed to go to the bathroom downstairs, Beth hoped the pressure in her bladder would go away.

How she loathed these dark, winter nights. The cold that penetrated down to the very bone no matter how many layers she wore. Windows that froze on the inside into frosted, swirling leaf patterns. It might look pretty but it was no wonder she was forever getting colds and Gran suffered with arthritis. The cold seemed particularly relentless this winter. A bitter wind had blown for months, almost non stop since the early snowfall in September. A lazy wind Dad called it, on account it went straight through you instead of around. The heatwave they'd all enjoyed back in June seemed so far away she could hardly remember what the sun's warmth felt like.

It was no good; she had to go.

Shivering uncontrollably in the darkness, she scrambled into her candlewick dressing gown before groping on the floor for her slippers. The brown linoleum felt cold, almost frozen, such was the chill seeping through her knitted bedsocks. Her hand touched something rubbery, making her recoil back in surprise, then realizing with relief it was only her hot-water bottle fallen from the bed. Only it wasn't hot now. It was cold and clammy to the touch. She picked it up. Underneath it, she found her slippers.

From downstairs came the muffled sound of the clock in the front room chiming the half hour. But which half, she wondered, no idea of the time. Gran didn't like having a clock in the bedroom. Said the ticking drove her up the wall, said it reminded her too much of her time ticking away.

Sidling past the cast-iron double bed by the door, trying hard not to disturb her snoring grandmother, she almost tripped over Gran's old, black coat slipped from the bed.

In the depths of winter, a dressing or overcoat on top of the eiderdown and a hot water bottle between the flannelette sheets was the only way to keep warm in bed. There were no spare blankets other than borrowing those off David's bed, and Mike had already purloined them. They would have to be put back when David arrived home.

She gathered up the old coat and laid it gently back over her grandmother. In her sleep, Gran sucked on her gums, muttered something incoherent then rolled over onto her side. The snoring ceased.

Whilst the aluminium kettle shook and clicked as it came slowly up to the boil on the gas stove, Beth set about raking out the clinkers from the grate. It would save Mike the task of lighting the fire when he came down, apart from which moving about was preferable than standing freezing, waiting for the kettle. The clinkers in the grate were still warm. She held a few of the larger clumps, enjoying the sensation of gentle heat warming her cold hands.

Upstairs, Mike's alarm clock suddenly burst into life, its trill ringing disturbing the quietness of the house. She heard her brother's curse, followed by a dull thud. The alarm clock stopped its dreadful din.

The final bundle of kindling in the grate, she struck a match and held it to a corner of scrunched up newspaper beneath the wood. The bright, yellow flame caught a corner of paper, spreading rapidly.

Bedsprings creaked, followed by footsteps padding

across the ceiling.

Poor Mike, she thought. Fancy having to get up at the crack of dawn in summer, the dead of night in winter to go to his job in the vegetable market. Four o'clock he had to be there, which meant he usually left the house without a warm drink or any breakfast inside of him. Was it any wonder Mum frequently nagged him to find something better? Something with more normal hours.

Mike said it was because the pay was too good to toss aside and they would miss the supply of fruit and vegetables he brought home if he changed his job. Which was more than true, even she had to admit. He also said working at the market was a good crack. That they had lots of laughs and that every morning at nine they would all trundle off to a café for a good breakfast.

Mike's bedroom door squeaked. Another creak from the stairs. A moment later, he appeared, stretching and yawning, in the doorway.

"What are you doing up so early, kid?"

Over his green and grey striped pyjamas he wore a navy pullover. It was on inside out and sported a large hole in the armpit. She made a mental note to darn it for him when she repaired her glove.

"I needed the bathroom," she told him. "And as I was already down here, I thought I'd make some tea and refill my bottle."

"Fill the kettle right up then, so I've got some hot water to wash in. Gawd, I hate getting up this early in winter." He turned and headed for the bathroom across the hallway.

"Don't pull the flush or you'll wake Dad."

"Like I need reminding," Mike grumbled.

She watched the flames licking at the splinters of wood in the grate. Early starts also meant early bedtimes for her brother. It couldn't be much fun for him knowing all his mates were out of an evening enjoying themselves, she thought. In that respect at least, she knew Mum was happy. He wasn't out every night, riding that big, noisy motorbike of his goodness knows where. Or getting drunk or into fights. Causing trouble, like lots of other boys his age did. But those early starts also meant he finished at lunchtime and so had all afternoon to please himself. What other job could be better, he often boasted. She only hoped she would be able to find a job she enjoyed as much as he obviously liked his.

Mike snatched the double broadsheet from Tuesday's *Daily Mirror* out of her hands.

"Here, give me that before you set the bloody house on fire."

In an attempt to draw the flames up the chimney more quickly, she had been holding the newspaper across the belly of the fire. Mike screwed the paper into a tight ball then cast it onto the flames. She stood back, watching how he blew on the wood then placed further lumps of coal in the right places so the burning pile wouldn't collapse and put the whole thing out. He's so much better at this than me, she thought. She always made a mess of lighting the fire, whereas he always made it look easy.

"By the way, did you get that job?" he asked, in between blowing on the flames.

"I didn't go."

He shot her a disappointed look. "Why ever not?"

"Because I was late, wasn't I? I got caught up in all that smog yesterday. Anyway, I'm going for another interview today, in that new teashop by Kew Bridge. Only don't say anything to Mum and Dad, as I haven't told them yet."

"What, in Maisie's? You don't wanna be working

there." He shrugged. "Up to you, kiddo, but you know the old man. He wants you to have a decent job, not serving cups of tea all day like some skivvy. He wants you to be a nurse or scientist or a secretary. Anything to make him proud."

"More like anything to give him something new to crow about to his mates in the pub. 'Our Beth's a brain surgeon. My Beth works at thingamabobs. Our youngest is matron at the West Mid hospital. Didn't you know my girl runs the typing pool at Gillette's?' Can't you just hear him bragging, Mike?"

"Yeah, but nor do you want to be working on a counter in Woolies or stuck in some factory for the rest of your life either. He only wants to be proud of you."

"And what's so wrong with doing any of those things? I know for a fact Coty's up on the Great West Road pays good money. According to Elaine, who works there, you even get cheap cosmetics and perfume at discount prices. I could earn flippin' good wages too, at the soap factory or in Brentford Nylons on their production lines."

"For shift work. Look, kid, there's nothing wrong in doing that kind of thing but it would bore you to death doing the same thing over and over again, day in, day out. You're too clever for that."

"Of course it would *bore* me. Anyway, working at Maisie's will only be temporary until I find an office job."

Mike stepped back from the fire. "If you say so. There, that's got it now. That tea brewed yet?" He put the flimsy metal guard around the hearth. The flames were going well, the wood beneath the bank of coal cracking and popping as they burned.

Still shivering despite the warmth already thrown out from the fire, she watched Mike gulp down his mug of tea.

He smacked his lips. "You can do this for me every morning," he joked. "Right, must go. See you later, kiddo."

Zipped up in his leather jacket, he opened the back door into the yard where he kept his motorbike, and peered out. It was still pitch dark but, worse, the fog hadn't lifted. She could even see the brick wall not three feet from the door. Thick wisps trailed through the kitchen in a stream of sooty smoke, evil-smelling like a witch's chimney.

"You can't ride your bike out in this," she pleaded.

"I haven't a choice. How else am I supposed to get to work?"

Beth watched him wheel the machine down the alleyway leading to the front of the house before closing the door. It jarred against the frame where damp had swollen the wood, forcing her to shove hard against it with her shoulder. The resultant noise seemed to shake the whole house.

Running to the front room window, she pulled aside the heavy curtain to peer out. Barely visible, Mike stood by the front gate, kick-starting the bike into life. When he switched on its lights, the headlamp cut a dim orange beam through the murk. Worrying for his safety, Beth watched him go, the bike soon swallowed up in the fog. Then, clutching the freshly filled hot water bottle tightly to her middle, relishing its comfort, she hurried back to bed.

The sound of the kitchen tap running followed by the clunk of the kettle being put on the stove, brought her back from the edge of sleep. Mum's up early, she thought. She heard a mumbled curse.

"That's not Mum," she said half-aloud, diving out of bed and reaching for her dressing gown. "That was

Mike's voice."

He was drying his hands on the roller towel on the back door when she entered the kitchen. A quick glance up at the clock showed it was only ten-to-four.

"What's up, Mike? Did you forget something?"

"That smog's a real killer, kiddo. I couldn't see where I was going. Complete wipe out. No way could I ride anywhere, I wasn't going to risk it. Cor, and the stink too. Worse than that coal tar soap Mum insists on us using."

In a way, she was glad he'd come back home. She hadn't been at all happy about him riding off earlier. It didn't look safe out there, and Mum would only fuss and fret when she got up and saw how dreadful things were outside.

"Will they mind at work? Will you get into trouble?"

Mike shrugged. "If I haven't made it in, no doubt others won't have either. What can they do? I'll lose a day's pay but, so what? Better than losing me life out there."

Chapter Four

Beth studied her family seated around the blazing coal fire in the front room. Her father occupied the armchair nearest the hearth, hogging most of the heat the fire threw out, as he reread yesterday's newspaper. Since getting up, he had done nothing but moan about the paperboy failing to deliver today's paper. Every few minutes he would shake and rattle the pages, illustrating his continued irritation.

Mum, seated on the settee opposite the fire, was busy sewing a button onto one of Mike's shirts as she hummed along to the music of Joe Loss playing on the wireless. After getting up and seeing the smog and hearing from Mike how bad it was, she had forbidden them all from going outside except as far as the coalshed to refill the copper coal scuttle.

Beth felt trapped, hating the idea of being cooped up indoors all day. Apart from which, she wanted to get back to Maisie's to ask about that job. By the time she got there now, it would probably be too late.

Feeling Mike staring, she looked across to him seated at the dining table shuffling a deck of cards. He beckoned her to come join him for a game. She shook her head. It was always draughty by the window, and she wasn't really in the mood for playing whist or brag, Mike's favourite.

Her book nestled in her lap, she tried to pick up where Bill Masen had just found a little girl running through a deserted street amongst crashed cars and vans, but she couldn't concentrate. Her thoughts kept drifting to her oldest brother.

"I wonder what our David's up to at this precise moment," she said to no one in particular.

"I expect he's fast asleep, pet," Mum answered, breaking a thread of cotton with her teeth. "They're on a different time zone out there."

"Knowing our Dave, he's tucked up warm with some little Korean bird and—"

"Michael! David's not like that. After all, he is engaged." Mum put down her sewing, worry evident on her pale face.

"That don't stop a young lad when he's far from 'ome and wants some comfort, woman," Dad chipped in, turning over another page of the newspaper, rattling it far more than Beth felt was necessary.

"Oh aye. And you speak from experience do you, Alfred?"

He rattled the paper again. "I'm only pullin' your leg, Con, you daft bitch. Of course David's not up to any hanky panky. He's in a war, ain't he? Don't have time for no shenanigans when you've the enemy looking down your rifle."

Connie's tight lips showed her discontent. "I just hope this stupid war doesn't escalate further and prevent him coming home. Pattie's been as high as a kite since his last letter saying he was getting some leave and should be home for Christmas."

Beth fiddled with the edge of the linen arm cover. "Does she have to keep barging through this house like she lives here? Ever since she and David got engaged she just lets herself through the back door and waltzes straight in like nobody's business. Why can't she knock on the front door like anyone else? Don't get me wrong, Mum, I like Pattie, but it's so irritating the way she keeps asking if we've heard the latest news on the war over the wireless. Have we received any letters? Have we had a telegram? Was he still coming home the week after next?"

She mimicked Pattie's squeaky-pitched London lilt, which made Mike grin, before reverting to her normal voice when she added, "Doesn't the stupid girl realize talking about the war always upsets you, Mum?"

"She's only worried, like all of us. And she *is* almost family."

Mike stacked the playing cards, pulled the brown chenille tablecloth back in place and said, "Knowing the Yanks, they'll drag the rest of Europe into this war. Retribution for Pearl Harbour."

"You don't know what you're talking about, son. It wasn't us that dragged the Americans into the last one."

"No, Dad, but it was us that started it with Hitler. That's what I mean. Give up else we're at war. We did it to them; they do it to us. Tit for tat and bang bang, you're dead."

Despite reading about the Korean War in the newspapers and listening to her father's diatribes on the matter, she still didn't fully understand about communism, or why the Americans were involved in this stupid war in the first place. This was one discussion she was staying well out of. All she did know was she hated each day that kept David away from the family, and how her mother constantly worried about him, always fretting. The patchy news that did filter through was not enough to keep them satisfied he was okay.

Wasn't it bad enough they had all suffered with worry about Dad throughout the war years without having to worry all over again if David was safe? Mike had said David only joined the army to get away from Dad, but she liked to think that wasn't true.

She leaned back in the armchair, bringing her legs up underneath her. Her hands were cold, as was her back, although her face and front were roasting from the roaring flames. She fidgeted. She just couldn't get comfortable. Having lost all interest in the book, she tossed it down to the carpet.

The carpet didn't fully fit the room. Well worn in several places, the worse bits were hidden beneath the settee and sideboard. Strips of linoleum, off-cuts from the upstairs bedrooms, skirted the edges of the room, but at least it looked like it covered the whole floor. The carpet had also come from Gran's house in Walthamstow, fetched along with most of the other furniture by Uncle Don on a borrowed lorry. It was lucky her grandmother still had it all, else they'd have ended up sitting on orange crates, she thought with a silent chuckle.

The only things in the room that were not secondhand or someone's generous donations or castoffs following the explosion at Half Acre, were the red plush curtains. Mrs Hooper, Gran's old neighbour, had kindly given them a remnant of a bale of fabric. Between Gran, Mum and herself they had sewn them by hand because Mum's ancient treadle Singer sewing machine had been reduced to sheared, twisted metal in the explosion. Gran's old three-piece suite didn't look too bad in here, she supposed. It was a bit threadbare on the arms, but the cream antimacassars and matching arm covers hid the worst of the wear.

Alfie shook the newspaper yet again. "'Ere, I hopes you're goin' to pick that book up and not leave it for your mother."

"No, Dad. I'll do it when I go upstairs in a minute." She pulled herself from the chair, picked up the book. "In fact, I'll pop upstairs now and see how Gran's doing. It must be awfully lonely up there for her all day long, don't you agree, Mum?"

The question was posed more for her father's benefit

but he appeared to take no notice. Her mother opened her mouth to speak but instead coughed. A chesty bark that sounded painful.

"Sounds to me like you're getting a cold, Mum."

"Just this damp, foggy weather. It always gets on me chest, pet."

The newspaper rattled again.

From the wireless on top of the walnut sideboard, in centre place amongst silver-plated frames holding sepia photographs of her and her brothers as babies, prone, naked and bare-bottomed, and Gran's best china flower vase, the announcer's voice crackled and hissed as it faded in and out. It had drifted off the BBC Home Service signal. Mike got up and gave the knob a tweak.

Beth sat down again, clutching the novel close to her chest, wanting to hear the news to find out whether there was any sign of the smog abating. Whether there was any chance of getting back to Maisie's today.

The newscaster's voice came through crystal clear.

"*...just been announced that this afternoon's football match at Wembley has been cancelled due to the bad weather. Organizers say this is the first time since the stadium opened they have been forced to do this...*"

"Oh bugger. I was gonna go to that with Stan. He's got tickets." Alfie sighed heavily. "I don't know, if it's not snow, it's fog and this whole bloody country comes to a standstill."

"Shoosh, Dad, we wanna listen," Mike snapped. "Can't hear a flippin' word with you prattling on all the time."

"*...unconfirmed reports of flocks of pigeons crash-landing out of the sky after losing their way. Yesterday's Smithfield Show was brought to a halt after several cattle dropped dead. The RSPCA said the unusual weather conditions are to blame. In Leytonstone, a*" man has died after being crushed by a dustcart when the driver became lost in the fog and mounted the pavement. Investigations are continuing into…"

According to the news, the whole of London was trapped beneath a choking, yellow-black cloak. All normal life put on temporary hold, as if caught in suspended animation. Nothing could function properly, despite the apparent concerted efforts of people trying to continue as if nothing out of the ordinary had happened.

Alfie shook the newspaper yet again. "It'll all be gone by tomorrow, you mark my words. A lot of bloomin' fuss over nothin'."

"If he does that once more, I'm going to take the dratted thing away and throw it on the fire," Beth said through gritted teeth to her brother.

"You wouldn't dare," mouthed Mike.

True. She only wished she had the nerve. Just to see the look on Dad's face.

Monday dawned with the smog remaining as thick and foul as ever. Alfie poked at the fire and put on a few more lumps of coal.

"You'd better ease up on that, Dad, we're nearly out of it. The bunker's almost empty again and the next delivery ain't due for another two weeks. If we carry on using it at this rate, we'll run out long before then."

Alfie waved away his dismissal of his son's concerns.

"There's plenty of wood stacked up in the shed, Mike. We'll survive."

The wood for the fire came from the crates Mike used to bring home the vegetables, balanced precariously across the petrol tank of his motorbike. Broken-up, they made good kindling.

Mike looked towards his sister dusting the sideboard,

and raised his eyebrows as if to say, "There's no telling Dad, is there?"

Beth lifted up the willow patterned vase carefully in order to dust underneath with the cleaning rag. She was nervous of dropping it. Gran had told her it was worth a lot of money, a family heirloom. It already had a chink in the base and a crack on its lip. She turned to Mike.

"We might not freeze, but we might starve waiting for this smog to lift. If it doesn't clear soon Mum won't be able to go out and get any fresh meat. It wouldn't do her any good standing in the queue at the butchers with that cough of hers."

The stock of vegetables had diminished as rapidly as had the coal. Having to create meals from almost nothing had been common practice during the war, but the thought they might now have to return to those ways was not a prospect she welcomed. She hoped it wouldn't come to that.

"Then you'll just have to go do the shoppin', won't you," her father uttered with an agitated shake of the paper.

Goodness knew what he still found to read, Beth wondered. He must have read every single word at least three times.

Straightening up from pushing the carpet sweeper across the floor, her mother patted Alfie's knees. He raised them in the air so she could clean under his feet.

"Do you have to do that *now*, woman?"

"Yes, I do. Listen, I'm worried. How are we going to manage with Mike not being paid? People have stopped bringing round their washing. Mrs Jones from number seventy-four was supposed to bring her old man's shirts this morning. And your pension ain't gonna go far, Alfie."

He lowered his newspaper, rolled his eyes. "Oh, do

stop fussin', for gawd's sakes. It's only been a couple of days. We've had worse pea-soupers than this. Anyways, can't say as I miss havin' the neighbourhood's sheets and shirts hangin' about me kitchen all the flippin' time."

He banged his pipe against the edge of the hearth. A small pile of black debris fell out onto the rag hearthrug. He rubbed it in with his foot. "Makes the whole place stink, bloomin' washin' dryin' everywhere. It ain't healthy. You watch. This fog'll be gone by tomorrow. Mike will be back to work, and madam over there," he pointed in Beth's direction with his pipe, "can get up off her backside and find herself a job. How do you think we managed during the war?"

"We didn't," Beth responded tersely. "You were all right. The army made sure you had plenty to eat. And when it didn't, you rifled those poor Germans' food. Stealing their scrawny chickens and pigs, like you're always boasting about."

"Bully beef was all we had, me girl. Bully beef for breakfast and bully beef for tea. Sick of it, we was."

"Well, bully for you, because bully beef's all Mum's got left in the cupboard."

Annoyed with her father's constant gripes, she wished she had her mother's patience with him. Most of the time Mum seemed able to ignore his banal remarks, whereas she bit. At times she could swear he did it on purpose, just to wind her up.

"Switch the wireless on, pet, while you're there," her mother asked. "The eleven o'clock news should be on. Let's hear if it's getting any better out there."

"This morning the Government has issued instructions for everyone to hunt out their war-issue gas masks from cellars and cupboards. People are strongly urged to stay indoors and keep all windows and doors shut..."

"Bloody too late for that! Typical of the flippin' government," Alfie grouched, turning a page.

"Hush, Alf, we can't hear."

"...*continuing inquiries into the death of a man leading a funeral cortege on its way to the cemetery. The man, whose name has not been released yet, was waving a hurricane lamp in front of the hearse to help the driver see where he was going through the smog when the tragedy occurred.*"

"Bloody hell," uttered Mike.

The newsreader spoke of policemen having to force their way into a house in Marylebone, a family of ten found perished in their beds. People dying everywhere, choking and coughing themselves to death all across London; the undertakers unable to keep up with it all, the morgues running out of space. Grave diggers couldn't see where the empty plots were in the cemeteries because the smog was so thick. There was talk they might have to open up some of London's Victorian catacombs in order to store the bodies until they could be buried.

"God, how long can all this bad weather go on?" Beth uttered, fearful of what else the newsreader would announce next. It was so unfair. Hadn't they all suffered enough during the war, with all the fighting and needless deaths? Never knowing if your husband or father or sons were coming home again. Praying at night that the bombs wouldn't drop or, if they did, that they would miss your house, your air-raid shelter. Life was just getting back to normal again. And now this. The Fifties were promised as the new age, a time of prosperity and optimism. A time for the nation to regenerate and grow in peace, not have it all snuffed out again because of smog.

She wiped the mushroom-coloured painted windowsill with the piece of rag, thinking how depressing all the news was. Staring out through the starched net curtains, she could see the gate. The hedge. She pulled the net aside and looked out intently.

"You know, I think perhaps this smog's finally lifting. You couldn't see to the end of the garden path earlier." She could just make out a hearse pulling up outside number twenty-seven. "Something's happened across the road, at the Reades."

No one seemed to be listening to her. Silently, she continued watching in saddened concern as Jimmy and Jack, the Reades' two strapping sons, clumsily carried a coffin inside the house. There was no sign of Mr Reade or his nice wife. She wondered which one of them had died.

She tidied the curtain. "I'll go up and see if Gran's all right. Do you want me to dust upstairs, Mum?"

"Please, pet."

"Whilst you're at it, you can fill my cup up again. And your mother's. Make yourself bloody useful for a change," Alfie ordered, his head still engrossed in his four-day-old newspaper.

Whatever was he going to read when the paper was needed to light the fire in the morning, heaven only knew, Beth thought, snatching the cup from his proffered hand and flouncing out of the room, piqued by his remark.

"Do you have to keep on at the girl, Alf?" she heard her mother say. "The poor kid's doing the best she can. For goodness sake, leave her alone."

The newspaper rattled.

"Got any arsenic, Mum? We're fresh out of sugar," Beth called from the kitchen.

"Yes. In the tin under the sink. Put three spoonfuls in your father's tea; give us all some peace."

Enjoying the tune being played on *Music While You Work*

on her grandmother's bedside radio, Beth put away the last of the freshly ironed clothes into the top drawer of the tallboy. She pulled back the net curtain and looked out of the window again. Filthy smuts of soot covered the outside of the panes.

Above the rooftops opposite, a weak sun filtered through in a smoky, blurred haze. For the first time in almost a week, she could see to the end of Busch Lane. There were cars driving by, a milk cart parked outside number five. She could see Mrs Graham across the road gossiping to Mrs Freeman, her neighbour, over the garden hedge. Life in the street was beginning to return to normality.

"Five days it's been like it, Gran. Five whole days. Can you believe it?"

Gran looked up from her knitting. "You know, it's been nice 'aving you all 'ome for a change. Like a string of Sundays."

"I'll be glad to get outside for some fresh air. Mum and Dad have been driving Mike and me bonkers. Dad still won't hear of you coming downstairs; we've been on at him all week. 'Where are we all supposed to sit', is his latest excuse."

Gran sighed. "It's more your mother's coughin' that concerns me at the moment, girl. Barks better than that bulldog next door."

Her mother's coughing was a virtual constant in the house. Beth could hear her even now, downstairs in the kitchen. Cough, cough, cough, cough, cough.

"It certainly isn't getting any better, Gran."

"I blames all this smog. I heard on the wireless this mornin' that the Government's gone and decreed this pea-souper the worst ever to descend over the city. And that housin' minister…," she hesitated a moment, "…oh, you know the one. Old whatshisname…"

"Harold Macmillan?"

"That's 'im. Well, he's gone an' ordered three million cotton masks to be handed out. The newsreader was tellin' everybody where they could get 'em."

"I heard. It's a bit late now though, isn't it? Anyhow, Mum hasn't been out in it. Now me, if I started coughing like that, I could understand."

She was more than worried as to the cause of her mother's distress. It seemed far worse than the coughs and colds she normally caught. A horrible thought struck. She turned to her grandmother in a panic.

"You don't think she's gone and caught TB, do you?"

What would they all do if she had? Mum'd be sent away. Taken to the isolation hospital. People rarely came home from there. The more Beth thought about it, the more worried and fearful she became.

"Good Lord, no, girl. Perish the thought. It's a totally different cough to that tuberculosis one. That's what your granddad died of. 'Course, I don't expect you to remember much about it, you was only little."

Gran's words were reassuring, but doubt still hung in the crevices of her mind as to what was wrong with Mum.

Beth had been awake for some time, snuggled up under the blankets and eiderdown listening to Mike getting ready for work. As the back door shut with a judder, she realised it wasn't her brother's movements about the house that had woken her, it had been her mother's incessant coughing.

Later, wrapped up against the cold, Beth made her way to the Labour Exchange. Although the worst of the smog had lifted, she could still detect the lingering smell in the air, as if a thousand bonfires had been burning the night before. The morning held a strange light. Misty and yellow, like twilight in autumn.

"We've nothing at the moment," the tweed-suited lady behind the counter in the Exchange said when she enquired if there were any secretarial vacancies on offer. "But I'll make a note of your details."

"You've already got them," Beth informed her with a sullen frown.

The woman shuffled some papers. "So we have. Well, come in again in a few days' time. There's sure to be something in by then."

Disheartened, Beth tied her headscarf tightly under her chin to keep out the keen wind that had sprung up, and walked back down the steps of the grey building. By the time she'd reached the pavement she had made up her mind. Before going home, she would first call back into Maisie's, just on the off chance…

Chapter Five

The sound of the espresso machine fascinated Beth, marvelling at the way Terry kept the steaming contraption under control. As he worked, he whistled, pursed lips emphasizing his high cheekbones. He seemed always happy. And always smiling at her, another of his charms she secretly admired. He must have sensed her watching him for he looked up and winked. Beth felt herself blush, and tore her eyes away again. He'd been doing that all afternoon, seemingly unable to take his eyes from her. Watching her all the time.

Seeing what was going on, Kate nudged her arm.

"You gotta watch 'im, mind. He's a real charmer, that one. He asked me out once, but I said no."

"Well, you have to admit he is rather good looking."

"Trouble is, he knows it. Aye up, look busy. Here's Mrs Pilkin'ton comin' back from the stockroom. She don't like it none if we chatter."

Beth turned to the bald-headed, pinstripe-suited customer seated at the table, waiting patiently.

"What would you like, sir? We've tea, coffee, hot chocolate and..." After two days she knew the menu by heart, rattling off the list to perfection, able to make each item sound irresistible.

"'Ere, Beth. You've gone an' slopped somethin' all down your pinny," Kate pointed out a short while later. "You'd better go change it quick before Mrs Pilkin'ton sees."

Beth looked down in alarm at the brown stain. "I haven't got another one. This is my second this week. Mrs Pilkington said she'd only wash two a week for me. Oh heck, what am I going to do?"

"Borrow one of Jane's. She ain't in 'til Saturday. She won't even notice it's missin'. Just make sure you washes it and brings it back in time."

Thanking Kate, she slipped through the small kitchen area and into the dingy stockroom where, amidst wooden shelves stocked with boxes of crisps and crates of Coca-Cola and milk stacked on the floor, the staff could hang up their coats. She untied the dirty apron, rolled it up in a ball and rammed it into her wicker shopping basket hanging underneath her coat.

Jane's two aprons hung on a peg next to her own. She lifted one down. It didn't feel right, borrowing it without the owner knowing. She didn't even know Jane yet. And how was she going to sneak it into a load of washing at home? Mum was bound to notice it.

The double knot was tied tight on the apron strap, the thin cotton fabric beginning to fray. Frightened she might tear it if she pulled too hard, she sat down on a wobbly chair to attack the knot methodically.

Of course, if she had told her parents straightaway, she wouldn't be in this particular predicament now, she scolded herself. After all, it wasn't as if she was doing anything illegal by working in a teashop.

"What if someone we know sees you?" Mike had asked her the night before. "What if they tell Mum and Dad before you do? You'll narf cop it one. Better tell them before someone else does. I've seen Mrs Scott from number eighteen in Maisie's. You know what a gossip that old cow is. Remember how she grassed on me to Mum, when she caught me playin' hooky from school that time I was fishin' in the Thames down by the London Apprentice? No, best get it out into the open. No more pretense. It will only lead you into more trouble with the old man."

He was right, of course. She should have told Mum and Dad from the start. She would do it tonight, she decided. After tea. When the old man would be more amiable on a full stomach of scrag-end and dumpling stew Mum was cooking for tea. Mike would be there then, too. He'd back her up as there was bound to be a row. Mum would be okay about it, she was certain of that, once she explained how this job is only a stopgap until a proper one comes along. But Dad? Well, he would probably blow his top.

She fiddled with the knot on the apron. It wouldn't budge.

"Oh, bugger this wretched thing."

But being a secretary or working in an office wasn't her ideal job either. Her future had to be better than typing and filing and making tea all day for a couple of years, then finding a man she loved enough to marry. Keeping house. Having a gaggle of babies. Watching them flee the nest eventually. Growing old. Was that all there was to life? Surely there had to be more?

She had always wanted to travel. See the world. Take fancy cruises on that new liner, the SS United States, like she'd read about in last week's *Woman's Weekly* magazine. Marry a rich man. Huh, she laughed out aloud. There would be more chance of coming up on the football pools than finding a rich man around here. Certainly not one she'd want to marry. Well, with the exception of Terry, that is. Just the thought of him made her feel all tingly inside.

It hadn't been that long ago, she remembered, she'd had visions of becoming an air-hostess. Of flying off to far-flung, exotic locations. Only she wasn't tall enough. That and failing her French oral exam – a major requirement. When Wendy Cartwright in her class at school had commented air-hostesses were nothing more than glorified flying waitresses, she'd changed her mind rapidly about doing that as a career, despite her parents' protestations. They thought it a very glamorous career. One to be proud of. The next best thing to being a model.

So, here she was now, waiting on tables. There wasn't much difference really, except here both her feet were firmly on the ground, she thought with an ironic smile. She had hoped by now the Labour Exchange would have found her something more suitable, then her parents need never know she worked here and she wouldn't be going through all this agony now.

"Beth? Beth, are you all right in there?" Terry called out from the kitchen. "Hurry up, it's getting busy out front. Kate's rushed off her feet."

Tweaking and teasing at the knot in the apron, it finally unravelled.

"I'm just coming," she shouted back, jumping up from the chair.

An idea crossed her mind. Perhaps when she found a real job, she could carry on working for Mrs Pilkington on a Saturday. Earn some extra money to scuttle away like Gran told her.

She liked the thought of having money of her own at the end of the week. Mrs Pilkington didn't pay much, but it did mean she would have enough to give some to her mother to help out with the extra expense of Christmas, and every little helped. But what she would earn here this week wasn't going to be enough to buy those new boots yet. There'd been a pair she liked in Lilley & Skinners that very morning, tempting her from the window to go in, try them on, ask if they'd keep them back for her.

She looked down at the clothes she wore. They were

drab. Her old school blouse, once brilliant white, was now a yellowish-grey with age, and getting so tight across the chest she could barely do up the buttons. It gaped open in places, exposing her bra, not that she had much to fill it. She wasn't what she would call exactly busty, but it was lucky the apron had a bib to cover her decency. And as for her narrow-pleated, black old school skirt? It had long taken on a faded, washed-out appearance, and so old-fashioned compared with the full skirts everyone wore nowadays. She hankered for the one she'd seen in a shop window yesterday. White with bright red roses.

The yearning to be able to buy her own clothes tugged harder than ever at her heart. It would be so nice to be able to afford to buy a new dress instead of making do and mend. No more trimming with remnants from old skirts in order to extend a frock's wearability. None of that adding a bit of ric-rac here or a trim of lace there to change the look. No more altering of Mum's old dresses to fit, a once best frock taken in at the seams and shortened, or made into a blouse or headscarf. No more topping and tailing of sheets wearing thin in the middle or turning worn-out ones into pillow cases. Fed up, too, of ripping up those that were beyond repair to use as rags, thinking it would be wonderful not to have to scrimp and save any more.

"Ah, there you are."

She spun round at the sound of Terry's voice. He stood behind her, one hand around the back of his neck, smiling broadly. A wide, infectious beam. She couldn't help but smile back.

"Sorry it's taken me so long, only I had trouble with this knot. See?" She held the apron up to show him. "I've just got to put it on then I'm all done."

As she moved to step by, he caught hold of her arm.

His grip was strong. Warm on her cold skin.

"Hang on a mo', don't rush off. I wanted to ask you something. I wondered if you might like to come for a drink later with me after we're finished here?"

Surprised by his sudden invitation, she wasn't sure whether she should accept. Was he asking her for a date or was he just being friendly? Kate's earlier warning echoed in her head. She tried to ignore it, thinking maybe Terry hadn't really asked Kate out at all. Kate was probably only jealous observing what was going on between them.

"Look, you don't have to if you don't want to," he continued when she didn't answer. "I won't mind. Only I normally go across the road to the Wagon and Horses for a pint before I go home. I thought perhaps you might like a drink as well." He pulled out a metal comb from his back pocket and began teasing his black hair back into shape.

"I can't, I'm afraid," she told him. "I'm not old enough to go into a public house."

Not that being underage had stopped her before, she recalled with a pang of guilt. She'd been in pubs many times with Elaine during the summer holidays. At first for a dare, then more and more often they would saunter gaily into the White Hart in the London Road, where hopefully they wouldn't be recognised. She would bag the nearest table to the door, so they could make a swift exit if anyone they knew should come in, Elaine always went to the bar, ordering the usual two port and lemons.

Terry's look of surprise seemed genuine. "Never? I would have said you were at least nineteen."

"Really? Do you think so?"

Did he really mean that, she wondered, flattered. Or was this his normal chat-up line? But a drink after work?

There wasn't enough time.

"I can't. Honestly. I have to get home by six to help my mum get the tea ready. I daren't be late back."

He shrugged. "No problem. I'm borrowing my mate's car at the moment while he's away. I can take you home after, if you like?"

Looking up at him, she saw for the first time how dark his eyes were. A deep, chestnut-brown reflecting tiny green and golden flecks from the glare of the bare light bulb hanging above them. A thrill of excitement ran through her at being asked out for the first time. So tempting. Oh, what the heck, she thought. What harm could it do?

"Okay, but just one drink mind, then I really must get home."

"One drink it is. Here, let me tie up your apron. Turn around."

"And just where do you think you're goin', young lady?" Dad yelled out.

Poking her head around the kitchen door, Beth saw him seated at the table eating a spam roll. Her mother stood at the gas stove, trying to strike a match to ignite the burner under the kettle.

"Just out with Terry, like I told you and Mum," she reminded him.

"Oh aye. Then why are you all dressed up like the dog's bleedin' breakfast?"

Surprised by his comment, she stepped into his full view and looked down at herself. She couldn't see anything wrong with the black and yellow, geometric-patterned flared skirt, made from one of her mother's old dresses, her yellow jumper finished off with a wide, white belt. Perfectly respectable for a Saturday, she thought.

After the heated discussion a few nights ago, following her admission of working at Maisie's, she was shocked he'd even agreed to let her go out, expecting to be grounded for a week. Not for taking the job at the tea room but for not owning up about it at the start. All the secrecy. She'd kept Maisie's quiet on account she didn't know at first whether she really liked the job, she had told them, on account of not wanting to disappoint them if she didn't like it there, if she couldn't stand the pace. They had seemed to accept this.

"Not on about that," Dad said, pointing to her skirt with his knife. The knife moved up a couple of inches. "I'm talkin' about all that muck on your face. You're not goin' out of this house lookin' like some flippin' Soho tart."

"It's the fashion nowadays. All the girls wear it. It's only a bit of rouge and a touch of lipstick." And a hint of blue eye-shadow and a brush of black mascara that she thought wise not to mention.

"I don't care what it ruddy well is; you ain't wearin' it. Go wash it off. *Now!*"

Wide-eyed, she looked to her mother, pleading silently for her intervention. Mum shook her head and nodded in the direction of the bathroom. The tight curls, from the home perm Mrs Coombes from next door had given her mother's fair hair that morning, shook.

"Your hair looks nice, Mum." But not the pale face, she thought, thinking her mother didn't look at all well.

Connie patted the top of her head. "You don't think it makes me look too old?"

"No. It suits you. Doesn't it, Dad?"

He didn't answer.

Giving up any hope of winning this battle and with little choice but to comply with his order to wash off the makeup, she headed for the bathroom, only to collide with Mike, racing down the stairs two at time as he pulled on his leather jacket.

"Hey, watch out, Mike."

"Oops, sorry." He lowered his voice to a whisper. "You should know by now, kiddo. Do what Janet does. Put your makeup on after you goes out. That way, the old man doesn't see. And what he can't see, he can't moan about, can he?" He grinned and ruffled the top of her head.

Angrily, she pushed his arm away. "Oh buzz off, Mike. I've spent ages getting my hair right. Now I've got to backcomb it again. I always did say that Janet was deceitful."

Arms folded across his chest, legs crossed at the ankles, he leaned against the hallway wall.

"Oh, and you're the expert?" There was a sarcastic edge to his voice. He nodded toward the kitchen door. "Have you told 'em yet?"

"Told us what?" Alfie hollered.

"Nothing, Dad. Mike's just winding you up."

"Will you be back for tea?" Her mother's voice.

"I've already told you, Mum," she said, going back into the kitchen. "I'm meeting Terry at the end of his shift in Maisie's, and we're going to the pictures. That new Gene Kelly film is on up town, at the Odeon. Afterwards, he's taking me for a meal."

Mike followed her, his eyes fixing on the remaining food on the plate in the centre of the table.

"That roll anyone's? Dad? Beth?"

She shook her head. "It's mine but have it if you want, I'm not hungry." There were butterflies in her stomach at the thought of seeing Terry and they were dancing with the toast and dripping she'd eaten for breakfast, the resultant mix making her feel queasy.

Mike pounced on the roll as if he hadn't eaten for a week. Turning a chair, its strutted back leaning against the table, he cocked a leg over the seat, sat down and began chewing noisily. After a couple of hurried mouthfuls, he then picked at a crumb wedged between his teeth with his fingernail.

"I don't likes the sound of this Terry fella," Alfie announced, spraying crumbs everywhere.

Beth turned away. Speaking with his mouth full was a habit of his that repulsed her. What was it with the men in this house when they ate? Like father, like son. She didn't know which one of them was worse.

"Gawd, it's the first time the girl's been out with him," snapped her mother, coming to her defence. "You've never met him, Alf."

"Nah, an' nor 'ave you. What do we know about 'im, eh? Some greasy, long-haired apprentice mechanic, I suppose, who's just left school and still wet behind the ears."

Connie slammed the flap of the blue kitchen cabinet shut. The patterned glass in the top part of the cabinet rattled. "And what if he is? What's wrong with being a mechanic? You were one once, remember, you silly old goat?"

Ignoring the question, he gesticulated at Beth with his pointed finger. "Just be home by nine, mind. Or else."

She was horrified. "Nine o'clock! Oh, come on, Dad, I'm not a schoolgirl any more. I do go out to work now."

"Yeah, and you're still only sixteen. No daughter of mine's goin' out gallivantin' the streets at that time a night with some boy you hardly knows."

With a sullen sigh, she slumped down on a chair at the table. If she had to be back home that early there was

little point in going out at all. And she just had to see
Terry today, she just had to. What would he think of her
if she had to be home by such a time? Likely as not to not
ask her out again.

"Anyway, Terry's not a mechanic," she countered.
"He's at college, studying. He only works in the teashop
to help pay his rent."

"What about his family then? What do you knows of
'em?"

"Oh, for gawd's sake, Dad, I don't know. I've only
known him a week."

"'Ere, I hope he ain't one of them Cosh Boys? All a lot
of no-good, bone-idle layabouts that would stitch up
anyone who crossed their paths they don't like the look
of."

His bigotry incensed her. According to him, every
burglary, every fight, every bit of thuggery could be laid
firmly at the feet of Cosh Boys. All teenage boys painted
with the same brush, the same derogatory name.

Mike winked at her from across the table, sharing her
frustration. Say something, Mike, she pleaded inwardly.
Defend me. Help me out here.

As if hearing her silent cry, Mike said, "Come on, Dad,
give a bit. Beth's seventeen after Christmas. She's growing
up whether you likes it or not. This Terry's okay, I've met
him. And she won't be out walking the streets, Terry's got
a car."

Alfie spluttered on his tea. "Even bloody worse. And
stops sulkin', missy, or you won't go out at all."

"Thanks a million, big mouth. Lot of help, you are."
She hoped the glare she shot her brother was enough to
tell him to shut up and not say anything else, in case he
spilled the beans that Terry was also twenty-three. Not
some teenage boy as Dad wrongly assumed. Not that it

mattered to her one iota that Terry was seven years older than she was. As far as she was concerned, it made him more mature, more responsible. She knew Dad wouldn't approve of the age difference and would forbid her to see him.

Mike raised his arms in a gesture of innocence. "What have I said now?"

The tea pot thumping down on the table with a force strong enough to make the brown brew slop out of the spout and splatter across the gingham tablecloth, made her jump, as did Mike. Dad, she noted, never even flinched.

"*I* said she can stay out this evening, Alfie. It's Saturday, all right? I'm fed up with all this. She's not a baby any more. Nor a schoolgirl. She deserves a night out. God, what's wrong with—"

Her mother's next words were lost as she began to cough again; a loud choking sound emitting from her mouth, making her catch her breath. She sank down swiftly onto a chair, pulling a man-sized handkerchief from the pocket of her wraparound pinny, coughing hard into it. A hoarse, chesty cough that made Beth wince.

"Are you all right, Mum?"

Looking up at her through watery eyes, her mother nodded. It took a few moments before she recovered her breath enough to speak.

"I'm fine, pet. Phew, don't know what brought that on." She dabbed her mouth on the handkerchief, and with her forearm wiped away the tiny beads of perspiration breaking out across her brow.

Alfie glared at Beth, the scowl on his face showing he was more irritated than concerned at the obvious discomfort Mum was suffering.

"So how comes a so-say college boy can affords to

'ave a car, if he's havin' to work in a cafe to pay his rent? That's what I'd likes to know," he grumbled.

Beth groaned. "Gawd, if I thought going out my first proper date was going to cause such an inquest, I wish now I'd never mentioned it in the first place. I'd have gone to meet Terry in secret instead."

"Aye. Full of little secrets you are lately, missy. What else haven't you told us about?"

"Nothing, Dad. Anyway, it's not Terry's car. He's only looking after it for a friend while he's away doing his national service."

Terry had never actually said this to her, she had just assumed this was the case, but she certainly adored the little, cream Ford Popular. It made her feel all grown up and posh climbing into it the other night when he'd driven her almost home, dropping her off at the top of Busch Lane after they'd been for that drink after work.

Alfie pushed the last piece of his food into his mouth. "I 'appen to knows what 'appens in the backs of cars, that's all."

Her mother tucked the soiled handkerchief back into her pocket. "Is that so, Alf? And I expect there's even a name for it. It can happen anywhere if they're so inclined, not just in cars. Remember? And stop yapping with your mouth full, crumbs are going everywhere."

Beth darted her eyes from one parent to the other then up to the clock. Time to get going if she was going. At least she could have some time with Terry at the pictures. Better than nothing. Better than staying here and listening to Dad harping on all afternoon.

"Right, I'm off. See you later." She kissed her mother's cheek.

"Give you a lift on the bike, if you like," Mike offered, getting up.

"No thanks. I'd rather walk than risk getting my hair messed again."

"Ten o'clock then," Alfie relented. "Just watch yerself, that's all. I only goes on 'cos I cares."

Relieved, she raced around the table and gave him a hug. "Thanks, Dad."

He pushed her away. "Get off me, you daft bugger. Just don't be late. Or else…"

The sinking sun had transformed the muddy waters of the Thames into a wide ribbon of liquid gold swirling beneath Waterloo Bridge, the buildings stretched out along the Embankment bathed in a deep orange glow. High overhead, thin, pink-tinged clouds streaked the late afternoon sky. Slowly, almost imperceptibly, the first pinprick speckles of stars grew steadily brighter.

"It's beautiful," Beth whispered, a single tear escaping down her cheek.

Terry lifted her chin gently with his finger, tilting her face to his.

"What's this? Sadness? Am I that depressing to be with?" With a delicate, tender touch he wiped the teardrop away.

"No, on the contrary, I'm so happy. It's been so lovely just wandering about, strolling through St James's Park and along the river. It's hard to believe it's so mild after that dreadful smog last week. A pity we couldn't get into the pictures, though. I never expected a queue like that. It went all around Leicester Square."

"We can always go another time. If you want to, that is."

He cupped her face in his hands and lowered his lips slowly to hers.

Her first real kiss. She didn't know whether to shut her

eyes or keep them open so she could gaze into his. No idea how to respond. Should she open her mouth or keep it closed? Put her arms around him or keep them firmly at her sides? What was she supposed to do?

A brief kiss before he pulled his mouth away from hers, the corner of his mouth curling slightly.

"I'm sorry, I shouldn't have done that," he said softly, almost a whisper.

Feeling her heart pounding rapidly, beating wildly against her ribs as if trying to get out, she smiled back.

"I'm not."

It was the truth, but a feeling of shame swept through her. Nice girls weren't supposed to kiss on their first date, but she wished he would kiss her again.

Chapter Six

Hearing her mother's relentless, wheezing cough as she bent double, caught in another coughing fit, reminded Beth of the man who had bumped into her the day the killer smog had first descended.

Over the last few days she'd watched helplessly as her mother's normal chirpiness faded. Nor was there any sign of the normal rosy glow about her cheeks, even if that was usually caused by being stooped over a hot, steaming copper or a flat iron in front of the kitchen fire all day. Instead, sucked into her sallow face, Mum's bloodshot eyes showed the strain of constant coughing and gasping for breath, and the pallid colour of her face told all was not well. She'd been like this for over a week now but today, the coughing fits seemed to come more and more often.

All this coughing couldn't be right, Beth worried. Something more serious had to be wrong with her. As her mother recovered from this bout, Beth stirred the homemade cough remedy; mixing sliced onions and brown sugar together gently until all the sugar dissolved into a thick, caramel-coloured syrup. Yesterday's batch was all but gone. This one needed to steep overnight before it would be ready to drink. The mixture didn't seem to be doing much good. The time had come for some proper medicine. From the doctor.

Studying her mother's face and bare arms, checking anxiously for signs of the rash she'd heard supposedly appeared, one of the symptoms of sickness from the poisonous fog, she helped Connie to a chair.

"Sit down, Mum. I'll finish in here."

Connie smiled weakly, pushing a strand of hair out of

her eyes.

"That's not fair, pet, you've been on your feet all day in that teashop. I do wish you'd find something more fitting."

"Don't you start, you're getting as bad as Dad. I've told you, it's only temporary until I get something better. Just until Christmas."

Beth returned to the stove to remove the pan from the heat before it boiled over, frustrated she could do nothing to help as her mother began coughing again, face screwed in pain as she clutched at her ribs.

"We should get the doctor in, Mum."

"Doctor for what?"

At the sound of her father's voice, Beth spun round, warm syrup pan in hand.

He was standing in the doorway, leaning against the jamb, a newspaper tucked under his arm. "Nowt wrong with her that won't go away in time. Ain't that right, Connie?"

Her mother shrugged meekly as she continued coughing.

"See, she's okay. It's only a cold."

"Oh, come on, Dad, she's ill. She needs a doctor. Don't you care?" What was up with the man? Didn't he realize Mum could die? He'd heard all the stories on the wireless just as much as everybody else had; all those people dying because of that smog, and not just of the accidents out on the streets. The smog may have disappeared days ago but people were still falling ill all over London. Dying in a rampant epidemic with no discrimination, affecting the young and the old and the well. No mercy. She looked down at the pan she held, wanting to lash out at him, knock some commonsense into his thick skull that Mum's coughing wasn't something to be shrugged off as if it were nothing.

"I don't need no quack to tell me what's wrong with your mother. She always gets poorly when she's up the duff."

Syrup slopped over the edge of the saucepan. Beth realised then she was shaking as the enormity of his words took a few moments to sink in. The sudden realization.

"You mean she's having a baby? Bloody hell, Dad. How could you?"

"You watch your tongue, me girl. You're not too old to be put across me knee, you know. Show some respect."

"You dirty, selfish—" She slammed the pan back down on the cooker before she threw it at him. "Didn't what the hospital told you last year mean anything? They said then, when Mum lost the last baby, falling for another could be fatal."

She stopped herself before she swore again. He wasn't past clipping her around the ear or slapping her face. Once, he'd washed her mouth out with a bar of soap and she'd never forgotten that experience. Having vowed she'd never make the same mistake, she now guarded her tongue.

Connie spat a large, green globule of phlegm into the fire, watched it hiss and steam on the hot coals then lifted the hem of her pinafore to wipe at her mouth.

"Stop it now, both of you. Alfie, you go and sit in the other room and read your paper. Beth, you sit down here and listen to me. I won't have—" The next words never formed as she began coughing yet again.

Gran stroked Beth's hair as she snuggled against her on the double bed. She liked the warm, soft feel of her grandmother, swaddled in her hand-knitted bedjacket, a tartan blanket wrapped around her shoulders. Although Gran felt huge, it felt deliciously warm and comforting cuddling into her.

"Don't be too 'arsh on your father, girl. He's a man and 'as manly needs. It's normal for a married couple."

"Then he should have controlled them. Or been more careful."

"If you asks me, you're more put out at the thought of 'em still doin' it."

Wide-eyed, Beth tilted her chin to look at her grandmother's face, surprised but not shocked to hear her talk of such things.

"It" was never a subject discussed in the Brixham household. Mum had never spoken to her about the birds and bees and the things that married people did to make babies, and it had been to Gran she had run the day her first period arrived, when she had imagined she was dying of some dreadful disease. Gran had explained it all, shown her how to keep herself clean, explained why the old sheets were never really used as dusters, but torn up to use for protection against "The Rags", as they referred to that particular time of the month. That was also the day she learned her mother had another name for it, that her mother's "Little Visitor" wasn't the four-year-old kid from up the road who liked to pop in sometimes when Beth wasn't there.

"Well, you just don't like to think of them doing that. It doesn't seem right."

"Sweet'eart, it's the most natural thing in the world for married people to do, even your parents. There ain't nothin' dirty or sordid about it."

She sniffed. "I know you're right, Gran, but he makes me so cross. Especially when he won't have the doctor in to take a look at her. He says he won't be paying no quack to tell him what he already knows. But he doesn't know, don't you see? That cough of hers isn't no ordinary cold. I'm really worried about her."

"So'm I, girl. I've heard 'ow she is, especially at night. Look, fetches me me tin. It's in the bottom drawer of me tallboy. At the back."

She found the battered, old toffee tin with its picture of some idyllic cottage with faded red roses climbing around the door, under Gran's best cotton nightie. She handed it to her grandmother, who promptly began pushing and straining at the top. The lid would not budge.

Gran handed it back to her. "'Ere, see if you can prise it off for me."

In one last final effort, Beth succeeded, the lid falling to the linoleum floor with a clatter before rolling away under the bed. The tin was full of money, notes of all denominations spilling out over the edge at their sudden release.

She gasped. "Gran, there must be hundreds of pounds in here. Where did you get all this?"

"It's me savings, girl. In there's enough to bury me and gives me a good send off, with enough left over to 'elps all of you. And listen, me girl," she beckoned Beth closer to the bed. "Only you, me and your mother knows about me tin. Okay? And I knows precisely how much is in here."

"I won't say a word, I promise."

"I knows you won't, girl. Now, takes what you need and go fetch Doctor Williams. Tell him it's urgent."

"But Gran, we don't have to pay for a doctor to come. Not any more. Like I keep telling Dad, we've the Health Service now. I don't need this. I'll put it away again." She put the tin down on the bed.

Gran snatched it up into her arms. "Leave it 'ere, girl. I've somethin' else I wanna put in." She shooed her away with a sweep of her arm. "Off you goes then. No point hangin' about. Perhaps on your way out to fetch the doctor you'd call next door to Annie Coombes. Ask her to pop in and see me. Oh, and before you does, you'd better get down on your hands and knees an' find that lid, there's a ducks."

The seriousness of the situation was evident in the expression on Doctor Williams's face as he spoke to her father.

"I'll put this to you straight, Alfred. You and I have known each other a long time. I brought you and your brothers into this world, and all three of your children, so you know me well enough to know I don't mince my words." He inhaled deeply. "Let's cut to the quick. If you don't get Connie out of London, and soon, she may well lose the baby, or die. Perhaps both."

For the first time in her life, Beth saw tears welling in her father's eyes. He shook his head, seemingly lost for words. Tears formed in her own at the sight of his distress. She flicked a glance to her brother who stood with his back against the stone sink, arms folded across his chest, his face set in a sombre frown.

"Is she really that bad?" Mike asked.

"Yes. Both your parents knew the risks involved. Your mother's lungs and heart just aren't up to carrying a baby to term. Her defences are down and she's got a nasty infection on her chest. Now, the penicillin I'm prescribing will clear the infection I hope, but the strain from all that coughing could be the final straw. If pneumonia sets in... well, you know what happens. You'll need to keep the camphor oil burner going day and night for the time being. It'll help clear the air."

She saw her father grimace at the mention of the burner, knowing how much he hated the smell. She turned back to the doctor.

"Was it that smog that caused the coughing?"

"Most probably. Your mother's always had poor lungs. That fog was nasty. Caused by pollution, a toxic concoction of smoke and diesel fumes and chemicals being constantly pumped into the air. Although no one has actually admitted the rise in deaths are a direct result of the unusual weather, to me it is obvious the two are connected. These things can't all be put down to a bad spell of influenza."

"So the protesters at Battersea Power Station were right in trying to get it closed down?"

The doctor shrugged in response to Mike's question. "Who's to say? Nothing's proven, but… well… a lot of questions are going to be asked in the House. People will want answers. *I* want answers. We need to know the truth."

From upstairs, another rasping cough from Connie could be heard. Mike turned his back to everyone, thumping his fist hard on the wooden draining board, venting his anger and frustration.

"And if we get Mum away, she'll be okay?"

Doctor Williams met Beth's anxious gaze and shook his head. "I can't say that for certain, but it is her only chance. Clean, fresh air through her body will help, but I don't know how much it has affected the baby. We've no way of knowing what will happen until it's born."

Alfie looked up, his face white with anguish. "Be sensible, man; how can I affords to take Connie away? And where?"

"There are one or two sanatoriums that might be able to help, but everywhere's full to overflowing." The doctor gave a sympathetic smile. "I'll see what I can do for her, but I can't make any promises."

Beth reached into her pocket for the ten-shilling note she had put there earlier. "How much do we owe you for the medicine?"

He waved it away and rose from the chair. "Nothing."

Making his way around the table towards the back door, he stopped and patted her father's hunched shoulder.

"I'll do what I can for Connie, I promise. Now, I must be off. I've still seven more calls to make before tonight's surgery. If she gets worse, fetch me immediately. I'll call in again, let's see, the day after tomorrow, and see how she's doing. Meanwhile keep her warm and plenty of fluids. A bottle of Mackeson wouldn't go amiss of an evening either. Plenty of iron in it. It'll do her good. And make her stay in bed, she needs all the rest she can get."

After the doctor left, Beth turned to face her father, anger surging towards him for putting her mother in this precarious situation. She wanted to shout and scream and beat him on the chest that this was all his fault, but the look of sadness on his face, the sagging jowls replacing his once proud chin, and the lost look in his eyes, took away any notion of blame. Instead, she rushed across the room and threw her arms about him.

"Oh, Dad, don't worry. Mum'll be okay. Something will turn up."

He patted her head lightly, sighed heavily. "Your mother could die, pet. And all because of me."

"Don't go blaming yourself, Dad," said Mike. "You didn't make the fog."

"No, son, but I did make her pregnant."

With that, Dad pushed away her embrace and reaching for his demob jacket from the back of his chair, swept out of the back door, slamming it behind him. Every other door in the house shook.

Beth turned to her brother. There were tears in his eyes too.

"Something will turn up, Mike, you'll see. Mum'll be fine. We'll sort something out."

"I wish I had your faith, kiddo."

Chapter Seven

Relieved for the opportunity to sit and enjoy a refreshing cup of tea during a lull in customers inside Maisie's, Beth stifled a yawn, rubbing her eyes with her fists.

"How you copin' with your mum?" Kate asked from the other side of the table.

"You know, it isn't until your mum's laid up you appreciate just how much she does. I never realised how exhausting running a house is, and I've only been doing it a week."

"Well, at least it's the weekend tomorrow. You can have a break. You doin' anythin' nice?"

"More housework. It's never ending. I'm going to have to set about changing and washing the sheets on all the beds. I feel I could curl up into a little ball and sleep from here to next Thursday, I'm that flippin' knackered. Don't get me wrong, I don't mind helping at home. There's no question of it being otherwise, but all this constant running up and down stairs. Now I knows why Mum always moans about it. And Dad still hasn't got that commode like he promised so I have to clean up after Gran *and* Mum. Still, at least my nose has stopped twitching now when I empty out and scrub the soiled chamber pots."

Kate flicked her a glance. From the way her friend constantly looked about the tea room, keeping an eye out in case one of them was needed, Beth had the impression Kate was only half-listening but she chatted blithely on, glad to have someone to talk to about it.

"Last night, I had to help Gran wash her hair over a bowl of warm water balanced on the bed. From what the doctor said, Mum's going to need constant help all the way through this pregnancy. So help every which way I will, for as long as necessary. Mum *has* to get better. I don't know what we'd do if we lost her." She fought back welling tears, not wishing to blubber in front of everyone.

"Don't your brother help?" Kate asked, taking a sip from her cup.

"He does his bit. Always has all the veg prepared for tea, ready for when I get in, and he doesn't think twice about taking food or cups of tea upstairs, helps with the washing and drying up of an evening. He does what he can, but there are some things only a woman could do for another woman, if you know what I mean?"

"Don't your dad help none?"

Beth shook her head. "You have got to be joking. He's totally unwilling to help. Never has. He just mopes about the house all day, same as ever, expecting to be waited on hand, foot and finger. He can't even be bothered to lug in the coal scuttle. Whether it be making a pot of tea or spreading a few slices of bread with marg, he won't even go out for a loaf of bread, and the baker's only at the top of our road." She rubbed a hand across her forehead where a headache was forming.

"You know, Kate, I'm beginning to begrudge doing things for him. He doesn't appreciate anything I do. Has to criticize all the time. And no matter what I cook, it's wrong."

"Perhaps he's cut up about your mum?"

"Take Wednesday, for instance. I'd managed to persuade the butcher to let me have some lambs' hearts the day before. They're one of the old man's favourites. I stuffed them with some leftover bread and a bit of sage and onion, just how Mum told me to do, and put them on slow in the oven all day. Even put a touch of ale into the stock. And all the ungrateful sod could do was moan I hadn't put enough salt in. I'll tell you, I could have chucked the whole lot over him. I feel as if I just can't win. On Monday, I'd fried up a nice slice of liver, but according to him, it was overcooked. And last night, I'd done egg and chips."

"What could possibly go wrong with *that*?" Kate asked, aghast. "Eggs an' chips is easy."

"The eggs weren't runny enough to dip his bread in, that's what. So bugger him and his comments. As to the idea of him lifting a dishcloth or helping with the washing, that day's never going to dawn. Just as I know we'll never be able to afford to get Mum away from the dirt and smoke of this stinking city."

"So why don't your mum or brother say somethin' to 'im then?"

"It wouldn't make a blind bit of difference if they did. He'd take no notice. If it weren't for Mrs Coombes popping in mid morning, Mum and Gran wouldn't even get a cuppa until Mike gets home at lunchtime." Beth stared into her empty cup, frightened and helpless to prevent the inevitable happening at home.

Kate twiddled with a strand of her black hair, pulling the curl straight then letting it go. It sprung back into a long ringlet. "Don't you think you've taken on too much, what with workin' 'ere all week an' all?"

"I have to work. With Mum unable to take in washing now, we need the money. Christmas is almost here and our David's due home any day."

She watched Kate fidgeting on her chair, biting her lip, green eyes downcast. Something gave her the feeling Kate wanted to say something but didn't quite know how to.

There was a silent pause for a minute before Kate said, "I'm surprised Mrs Pilkin'ton took you on here full-time. When I asked her a couple of weeks back for extra hours, she told me the shop weren't busy enough during the week to warrant it. Said she only needed extra help on a Saturday."

Guessing Kate's nose was more put out about Terry taking an interest in her than with Kate than by the hours Mrs Pilkington allowed her to work, Beth said, "Perhaps she thought the extra week will give me a chance to get used to things around here before the Christmas rush."

Kate sniffed without answering.

Terry joined them at the table, stroking Beth's cheek softly as he sat down. "You look worn out. Never mind. I'll take you dancing tomorrow night. Up the Palais. That'll take your mind of things. We *are* still on, aren't we?"

"I don't know, Terry," Beth said, amazed at how he could make her feel a whole lot better by just being so close, the gentlest of touches on her skin. "I don't think I'd be up to much dancing. My feet are killing me."

On them for most of the day waiting on tables, as well as having a daily three mile walk to and from Maisie's because she couldn't afford the bus fares, it was small wonder her legs throbbed and her feet ached.

"How about the pictures instead?" he suggested. "We could try and get in to see that film we missed last week."

She smiled. "All right. I'd like that." She could feel Kate's cutting stare.

"Good. Fancy a quick drink after work?" he asked.

"I'd love to, only I won't have time. I have to stop off at the fishmongers on the way home. Mr Sims promised to put back a couple of pints of sprats for our tea." Then a quick dash in to David Gregg's to buy some cheese or eggs before hurrying across the road by the Half Acre to the Frank Frizzel, the butcher, Hoping to catch him before he closed, praying he'd been able to keep something back under the counter for her.

It had been the same mad rush each evening on her way home, grabbing a bit of shopping here, a few necessities there. Meat was still on ration, coupons needed for bacon or a pound of belly pork. There wasn't time of a morning to stand and wait in the queue, especially on Tuesday when the lamb and mutton came in. Without the butcher's help, she didn't know how she would have managed this week. As soon as he had heard her mother was sick, he'd gone out of his way to help, suggesting things she could buy, what was more value to get the most from her coupons, and giving her advice on how to prepare and cook it. She thought she'd done rather well, considering she'd never shopped for food or cooked before. Not proper meals.

"I've got the car tonight," Terry told her, his eyebrows rising. "We can stop off for your fish and I'll run you home."

The tinny sound of the bell above the shop door announced the arrival of another thirsty customer. Terry got to his feet.

"You two beauties stay here and finish your tea. I'll see to this one."

"Ta, Terry," Kate said. After Terry had moved away safely out of earshot, she leaned across the table and half-whispered, "You and 'im goin' steady then?"

Beth shrugged. "Not really. It's nothing serious."

"Then why are you blushin'?"

Because she wanted it to be serious with Terry, that's why. She longed to be his steady girlfriend. His sweetheart. She loved his company, the way he made her laugh, the cute way his lip curled up slightly on one side whenever he smiled. And that kiss... She wanted more of them. Lots more. Only she didn't want to admit it to

Kate, not wanting to rile her friend.

Wasn't it time to go yet, she asked herself for the umpteenth time, looking up again at the clock on the wall behind the counter. Still another twenty minutes before the end of the shift, she saw glumly. The last extra half-hour seemed to be dragging by. The bell over the door sounded again.

"Afternoon, Henry. You're early today. You don't normally come in at this time," she heard Mrs Pilkington say.

"Aye. But it is Poets' Day," a male voice responded loudly followed by a hearty laugh.

Turning from the table she had just wiped clean of spills and crumbs left by its last occupant, she observed the owner of Maisie's talking to a tall, tubby man in his mid thirties. He wore wire-rimmed glasses and an expensive-looking, navy pinstriped suit. She watched as he made himself comfortable at one of the tables by the window. It was a tight squeeze between his chair and that of the customer seated behind him.

"What's Poets' Day?" she whispered to Kate, squeezing by carrying a tray stacked with dirty teacups and plates.

"Piss off early, tomorrow's Saturday. Cor blimey, Beth, ain't you never 'eard that one before? Shift your bum."

"So who is he? Do you know?" She breathed in to let Kate through then nodded in the direction of the poet man unfolding a newspaper, making a fuss of shaking out its rustling pages, reminding her of her father.

"That's Henry Chisel'urst. Don't know what he does but he comes in 'ere every evenin' 'bout half-five. You've normally gone by then."

Mrs Pilkington beckoned Beth across to the table.

"Take this gentleman's order please."

"Yes, sir. What can I get you?"

"A large pot of strong tea, double eggs on toast and one of your delectable doughnuts."

"I don't think we've got any left, sir."

"Oh, there will be. Maisie always puts one back for me, don't you old girl?" he called out to Mrs Pilkington talking to another customer a few tables away. She waved a hand above her head, acknowledging.

Beth scribbled down the order in a short series of squiggles and marks on her notepad, aware of his eyes running up and down her body. His gaze made her feel slightly uncomfortable.

"I haven't seen you in here before, lass. New, are you?" he asked.

"Sort of, sir. I've been here over a week. I normally finish at five."

She looked at the clock again. There was still another fifteen minutes to go. "It's nearly time for me to knock off."

"Well then, you'd best be getting your skates on and fetches me my tea. I'm that thirsty I could swallow Loch Ness in one mouthful. I haven't had so much as a drink all afternoon, what with my secretary doing her vanishing trick this morning."

Beth ripped the page from her pad. "Oh dear. Was she taken ill?"

"Eileen? No, bloody worse. She phoned in this morning and tells me her fella's back from the army, so she's going off with him for the weekend and will see me on Monday. I told her, if she didn't get her backside down to the office toot-sweet she can kiss her job goodbye. So here I am, up to my armpits in work with a mountain of letters to get out and no one to do them.

The blasted girl only started with me a fortnight ago. I'll have to ring up the Labour Exchange on Monday to get another. I don't know what these young women think they're doing, leaving a darned good job like mine at the drop of a hat. I won't have her back, I can tell you."

Her ears pricked. Was this the golden opportunity she was waiting for?

"So does that mean you're looking for a secretary?"

"Oh aye, lass. Someone reliable I can trust. One that can do shorthand and who's good on the phone. And one who isn't liable to run off with sailors, soldiers or tinkers."

What was it Gran was always saying? Those that don't ask, don't get. Those that don't ask, don't want. This was definitely too good a chance to miss. The worse he could do was say no. Go for it, girl, Gran would say.

"I could work for you, sir. I've been looking for an office job for weeks." She thrust the piece of paper towards him. "My shorthand's not perfect yet, I'm still learning, see? But I can type forty words a minute. I haven't had much to do with telephones but I'm sure I could learn. I'm a hard worker and quick on the uptake, and I know how to do filing, and I'm good with figures. I'm honest and I'm—"

He waved a hand up and down. "Slow down, lass, slow down. Okay, you've convinced me."

She couldn't believe her ears. "You mean it? Just like that? Don't you want to interview me or anything?"

He laughed. "I think I just have. Look, lass… sorry, I didn't quite catch your name."

"Beth, sir. Beth Brixham. Well, actually my proper name is Elizabeth but everyone calls me Beth."

"Well, Beth, if you were good enough for Maisie to take on here, that's good enough for me, I trust her integrity implicitly. That woman has a shrewd eye for honesty and doesn't tolerate shirkers. I'll tell you what, I'll give you a week's trial…" He hesitated as if calculating in his head. "No, I'll be fair to you as I likes the look of you. Let's see how you cut it between now and the New Year. That's what, not quite a fortnight? And if we're both happy, we can make it permanent."

"Oh, thank you, sir." She wanted to throw her arms around him in appreciation but resisted the temptation, thinking he probably wouldn't approve of such a show of gratitude.

He pulled out a wallet from his inside jacket pocket and handed her a white card.

"Here. Report at my office Monday morning, nine o'clock sharp, and we'll take it from there."

Professor Henry Erskine Chiselhurst, Accountant, she read on the business card. It sounded very posh.

"Thank you, Mr Chiselhurst. I won't let you down."

"No, I don't think you will," he replied with a twinkle in his eye.

Still unable to believe her own audacity with Mr Chiselhurst, or her luck, she ran down the garden path. Now perhaps Dad would get off her back. She reached through the letterbox to retrieve the string with the key attached. Oh, but they hadn't discussed wages yet. Or hours. She shrugged. Oh well, what did that matter?

Mr Chiselhurst had seemed such a nice man, she thought, happy for the first time in weeks. He was, after all, a businessman, and an accountant at that. All the finer details could be sorted out on Monday. And if she didn't like what he was offering, she would put up with it whilst looking out for something else. In any case, the money had to be better than what Mrs Pilkington paid. And she wouldn't be on her feet all day long; she'd be sitting instead. What joy.

Dumping the newspaper-wrapped bundle of sprats onto the draining board, the house seemed abnormally quiet. Gran's wireless was silent. Nor could she hear the usual sounds from the other room, that of Mike and her father talking or arguing over something and nothing. A difference of opinion Dad always called it.

Pushing open the door to the front room, she found her father asleep in his armchair, snoring loudly, a newspaper spread-eagled across his lap.

The room felt chilled. In the grate, a small pile of whitish-grey coals burned with a weak flicker of pale orange. Not caring if she disturbed him, she stomped towards the fireplace and began raking around the coals with the poker.

"Oh, you's is 'ome then. 'Bout time. What's for tea?" Alfie muttered, stirring himself. He stretched his arms, yawned widely. The newspaper slid to the carpet in a crumpled heap.

"I can't believe you sometimes, Dad. How can you let the fire get so low? It isn't as if you had lots to do all day. You're so thoughtless at times. This room's freezing. You know Mum wants to come down for a few hours this evening." She began piling lumps of coal into the grate with the brass tongs. She felt more like throwing the black lumps at him.

"Don't you start naggin' the moment you's is in, me girl. You're gettin' too big for your boots. I purposely lets the fire go low of an afternoon. We can't afford to burn coal all day like it's goin' out of fashion. I dozed off for a while, that's all. I normally banks it up before you gets back."

She wedged another lump of coal into the grate.

"Where's Mike?"

"He went off out in a huff the moment he got home from work."

Straightening, she faced her father, hands on hips. "Please don't tell me you two had another argument. What over this time? I bet you started on him the moment he walked through the door."

Alfie heaved himself from the creaking armchair. "Just hold your bloomin' horses, girl. He had a letter this mornin'."

"What letter?"

"His call-up papers for his national service. Neither he nor your mum's very happy about it. She's frightened he'll be sent straight out to join your brother in Korea."

"They won't do that, will they?" She dropped her angry stance immediately, all elation at her good fortune crushed by this blow. She knew it was coming, they all did. Waiting out the inevitable that before long Mike would be sent off for two years' square-bashing and yomping across the moors. But surely they didn't send new recruits straight into a war? She thrust the tongs into her father's hands.

"Here, you get on with it. Make yourself useful while I go up and see Mum and Gran."

She blew out a hard breath of air, composing herself with calmness before climbing the stairs. Perhaps her good news would cheer everyone up.

"Put the kettle on first, there's a pet," he called out after her. "I'm gasping for a cuppa."

"Aren't we all. You know where the kitchen is."

Her mother's eyes opened immediately Beth entered the bedroom.

"Oh. I didn't hear you come in, pet. I must have dozed off a bit. You're looking pleased with yourself."

Beth picked up a magazine from the floor and placed it on the bedside table, hardly able to contain her excitement.

"Mmm, I am. You'll never guess. This man came into the teashop today, just as I was finishing, and offered me a job. A proper secretarial one. Can you believe it? I start on Monday."

"What, just like that? Came up to you and said, 'Do you want a job?'"

Beth laughed. "No, don't be daft. He was telling me how his secretary decided to take the day off to go somewhere or other, I can't remember where. And he told her, if she didn't come in she needn't bother coming back. Left him right in the lurch, she did. So I said I could do it and, well, I got the job. He's an accountant. Up in Morley Street. You know, in those posh houses on Richmond Green."

Connie stretched out her arms, beckoning her daughter for a hug.

"Oh, love, I'm so happy for you. Look, pop in and tell Gran your news whilst I'm getting meself up and dressed. She'll be so pleased. Did Dad tell you about Mike?"

Connie tossed the eiderdown and blankets aside and swung her thin legs out. The effort brought on another coughing fit. Beth hated the sound, the wheezing, the strained effort to breath a constant reminder of the frail condition her mother was in, so ushered her back under the blankets.

"I should wait a little while before you come downstairs, Mum. Dad's let the fire go low and it's going to take an hour or two before it warms up down there. Let me get tea sorted and come down then." She tucked the blankets in. "I'm not so sure you should be getting up at all. You sound dreadful. And I know you. The minute you're downstairs you'll be fussing with things. Trying to do everything."

"But it's about time I made an effort. I'm feeling so much better. I want to get David's bed aired and made up. He'll be home any day now."

"I can do that. Tomorrow. You stay here for now. Doc Beth's orders."

"Yes, but it's boring up here all day. There's a limit to how much reading or ripping and stringing squares of the *Radio Times* for the lavvy one can do. I don't know how your Gran puts up with it, having to stay up here all the time. I know we can natter to each other through the wall, but I can't leave you to do everything, especially now as my girl's going to be a real, proper secretary."

She wiped the hair out of her mother's face, noticing how clammy her forehead felt. "I'll bring up a cup of tea in a minute. Kettle's on."

"You're a good 'un, Beth. I don't know what I'd do without you. Do one for Gran too. We haven't told her yet about Mike. She's been that quiet this afternoon, I'd swear she's been asleep since Annie Coombes fetched us up some soup at dinnertime. I haven't heard the wireless on all afternoon, either. She didn't even put on *Mrs Dale's Diary*. I likes to listen to that meself. She never misses an episode."

The instant she walked into her own room, Beth knew something was wrong.

Propped against three pillows, Gran's head was tilted to one side in a position that looked most uncomfortable. Her toothless mouth was wide open, eyes staring vacantly at the ceiling. On the bedside table, a white china bowl of untouched tomato soup.

"Gran?"

She touched her grandmother's hand. It felt cold. Icy

cold. Gran didn't move.

"Oh no, Gran. No. *Please no!*"

Chapter Eight

On what should have been a happy day, her first day in her first proper job, any excitement Beth should have felt had been lost in grief over Gran's sudden death. She'd been only too glad to leave the house, anxious to be away from its heavy, depressing atmosphere, and normally enjoyed the pleasant, riverside walk into Richmond, but today it was all spoilt. She just couldn't stop thinking about the awful last two days.

The weekend had passed in a blur of constant comings and goings at the house. An endless stream of neighbours and friends calling in to offer their condolences. The vicar arriving to say his bit and reading a passage from the Bible over Gran's lifeless body. The endless tea brewing. Plans being made.

Uncle Frank had come over to take charge of all the funeral arrangements, declaring himself Head of the Family on account he was the eldest of Gran's eight sons. This pronouncement had sparked a heated argument between him and her father. For once, she agreed with Dad, seeing as how Gran had been living with them these last four years. Dad should have been the one organizing it all and deal with the undertaker, not Uncle Frank, who had rarely bothered taking any interest in Gran's wellbeing.

By the time she reached the footbridge at Richmond Weir, it had started to snow; large white flakes floating down silently about her in swirling abandon before pitching, her booted footsteps leaving their trace behind where she cut across the park.

From the address on Henry Chiselhurst's card, she had envisioned one of the grander, porticoed, three-storey houses that surrounded Richmond Green, imagining a large bay window flooding a plush office with light. All high ceilings with chandeliers, and thick red carpets underfoot. A modern typewriter, one of those new-fangled electric ones like she'd heard about. Walking into number six Morley Mansions came as a huge let down.

The office she pushed open the door on was over a betting shop, up two flights of steep, narrow stairs at the side of the building, reached by a back street off Brewers Lane. The pokey room smelled musty. There were no carpets, just plain, bare wooden floorboards that had long since lost their varnish, as had the two desks that took up most of the space.

On one, assumingly hers, was an ancient Olivetti typewriter, its workings and mechanical bits in an open-cast frame of the type that always reminded her of skeletons. No doubt it would shake like billy-o when she struck the heavy keys, she thought with disappointment.

Mr Chiselhurst sat on the edge of the other desk, reading. He looked up.

"Well, lass, you're going to have to put on a better smile than that if you're going to work for me. That sour face will put off my clients."

It was all she could do to smile meekly and nod.

She pulled off her gloves, shrugged out of her coat. The room felt icy cold. A single-bar electric fire burned in the corner, throwing off little heat. She hoped it wouldn't take too long to warm up or else her fingers wouldn't be able to work properly.

"Don't look so scared, lass. I don't bite. Here, let me have that." Henry took the garment from her hands and hung it up on a coatstand by the desk.

She could no longer contain herself, the full force of her misery issuing forth in a flurry of tears.

"Bloody hell," he yelled. "Now what's up? Don't tell me I've gone and got myself a bloody sniveller. I can't stand tears, lass."

Recovering her composure swiftly, fearful she wasn't making a very good impression on her new boss, she dried her eyes and wiped her nose quickly with her handkerchief.

"I'm so sorry, sir. It's just that… well…" She took a deep breath before continuing. "You see, my Gran died on Friday. She lived with us, and my mum's very ill. And then coming here this morning and—"

He rushed across, pulling her into his arms and giving her a gentle squeeze.

"There, there, don't take on so, lass. Here, sit yourself down a moment."

Ushering her onto a chair, she could detect the odour of stale tobacco and sweat on his suit amid an overpowering, strong waft of Old Spice aftershave, making her empty stomach heave.

"The funeral's on Wednesday, sir. We're lucky to be able to have it so quick, what with all the problems over the smog and so near Christmas. There's still a waiting list for burials, would you believe? But there's so much to sort out, I didn't realize."

"You mean, you had to make all the arrangements yourself? What about your parents? I thought you said—"

She sniffed. "One of my uncles saw to all the paperwork and legal stuff. It should have been Dad. Dad's crippled… well, a war wound. Sort of. And our Mike's just got called up to do his national service. Our mum's ever so upset. He got the letter the same day as Gran died. Then there's our David. He's out fighting in Korea. He's supposed to be home on leave for Christmas, but we haven't heard from him for weeks and my mum's getting worried. She's having a baby and is poorly. I have to take care of her and do all the housework."

Beth realised she was blabbering on but she couldn't help herself. Once the words started coming out, she couldn't stop them. Words were better than tears, she thought, wiping her nose again.

Leaning against the other desk, Henry stroked at his chin.

"I expect then you'd be wanting Wednesday off?"

"If that's all right, sir. It's not a good start is it? I'm sorry, Mr Chiselhurst, I didn't know this was going to happen."

"Happen you didn't, lass. Now go and tidy yourself up and make us both a cup of tea, and then perhaps we can get down to some work. A few hours here and you'll soon forget all your woes."

She felt touched by his concern. "Thank you for being so understanding."

He pointed in the direction of another door flanked either side by a rank of tall, green, metal filing cabinets cluttered on top with piles of paper and box files.

"Through there is my office. Kettle and such are in the top drawer of that cabinet on the left." About to open his office door, he turned. "As a matter of interest, just how many grandmothers have you got?"

"Just the one, sir. Well, none now, I suppose," she responded, thinking it a most peculiar question to be asked.

"Well, that's all right then. You'd be surprised how many girls I've had here with at least three, some even four or five." He grinned and winked at her then disappeared into his inner sanctum.

How odd, she thought. How can anyone have more than two grandmothers? She got the impression suddenly that secretaries didn't last very long with Henry Chiselhurst and wondered what she had let herself in for.

*

Out in the kitchen, she could hear her father pulling the stopper from another quart of beer. He appeared in the doorway of the front room, holding up the brown bottle of India pale ale.

"Right. Who's for another then?"

"Over here, Alfie. We've given 'er a good send off. She'd 'ave been proud," said Uncle Bert, draining his glass.

"Is there any more of that sherry goin'? This Emva Cream's a nice drop of stuff, it is, Alf."

"'Ere Vera, don't you go gettin' pissed on that stuff."

"Oh shut your cake'ole, you miserable devil, Bert. I'm entitled to a few drinks at me muvver's funeral, ain't I?" Aunt Vera protested loudly.

"Over 'er, Alfie. Don't forget my glass," Uncle Mitch shouted out above the din.

"I'd rather have a cuppa rosie. Go see if that pot's brewed, Beth. And chase up my Joannie while you're about it. She's only out there gassin' to Maggie," ordered Uncle Frank.

Uncle Bert laughed. "Yup, they're probably discussin' who's gonna get the old girl's diamond engagement ring."

"Won't they have a bloomin' shock when they finds out it's only paste."

A roar of laughter went up.

"Got a dash of lemonade to go in this beer, Alf?"

The crowded room was hot and thick with cigarette smoke. Beth became increasingly aware of the steady rise in volume as everyone became more relaxed and equally more merrier as the beer and sherry went down rapidly. The Brixham family always did love a good booze-up.

Even though most of the family lived in close proximity, some only streets away, they rarely visited each other, only coming together at weddings, Christmas and funerals. The trouble was, all the family get-togethers Beth could remember usually ended in a fight. Punches being thrown between uncle and uncle. Hair-pulling and screaming matches between aunts. She dreaded how this one would end, and wished they would all just go home now and leave them in peace.

A glance across the room to her mother's pale, drawn face as she sat by the roaring fire, told her Mum felt the same way too, but it would be hours before everyone took themselves off home, leaving her to clean up the mess.

The Brixhams were a large family, but until that morning Beth hadn't realised just quite how many relations she actually had.

Amongst aunts who had aged considerably since she'd seen them last were uncles who'd grown fat or bald, some both, all come to pay their respects to the matriarch of the family they all had practically ignored during the last few years of Gran's long life. As had the cousins she vaguely recognized.

She couldn't even remember the last time she'd spoken to Maxine, considering how close they'd been as young children. Even Gran's sister, Ellen, a slight woman with white hair in a tight bun and who used a stick to walk, had made the journey from Dartford to be here. She didn't even know Gran *had* a sister until she had turned up on the doorstep that morning. Unfamiliar faces introduced as cousin Wendy or Great-Aunt Alice or Uncle Jim; strangers that seemed to crawl out from the woodwork as if in some Bela Lugosi film, all come for a share of the spoils.

She stood watching them devouring the sandwiches Mrs Coombes and Pattie had helped prepare earlier. Everyone eating *their* food, *their* precious rations. Everyone stuffing their faces as if they hadn't eaten for a month. Where were they, she wanted to ask them, when Gran needed help getting out of bed? Where were they when Gran soiled her sheets or needed a bed bath? When had they ever called in and offered to rub lanolin into her bedsores or change the bandages?

Go home, she wanted to shout at them. Leave us in peace now, you've said your goodbyes.

Forcing a path around bodies wearing black mourning suits or coats with fur-trimmed collars that only came out once a year, judging by the smell of mothballs, proved difficult. At least there were no young ones running amok, getting in everyone's way, she thought thankfully, squeezing her way through to reach Aunt Alice on the other side of the room. Her mother wouldn't have been able to cope with kids screaming and crying and getting under everyone's feet. Not today. Bringing children to funerals was never a good idea any day.

"I'll have another of those sandwiches, pet? That's a right tasty bit of 'am, that is. Oh, and I'll 'ave another pickled onion. Ta. Gives me wind, but what the 'eck."

"Our butcher gave us the bacon after he'd heard about Gran's death," her mother said as Aunt Elsie reached for a triangle of food.

"Right generous, that." Aunt Elsie spoke as she chewed, nodding to Mrs Finnigan seated next to her. Mrs Finnigan, a neighbour from a few houses further along the road, agreed then helped herself to another sandwich.

"Yes. He came round the house with it the night before last. Three hours it cooked for. I got Beth to pop in a muslin bag of split peas nearer the end and chuck in a few spuds and carrots. It made us a nice pease pudding and tasty stew for our tea last night."

"Bet that was nice, Con." Elsie crunched noisily on the pickled onion then belched loudly. "Oops, pardon me, I'm sure." She patted her enormous stomach, her black skirt rucked tightly across the bulge and straining at the seams.

Beth offered her another. "Mum made all the pickles. They were meant for Christmas, but well, we won't be having that now, in the circumstances. We were going to take them to Maggie and Don's on Boxing Day."

She had looked forward for weeks to spending the day with her favourite aunt and uncle, from the non-Brixham side of the family, who hadn't been able to come today. Huh, Christmas, what a merry one theirs was going to be now, she thought gloomily, catching sight of Mike. He had Janet propped up against the wall, whispering into her ear. Janet, looking a little more than tipsy, was giggling loudly.

"Beth, bring us them sandwiches over 'ere, there's a ducks," Aunt Betty called out. "'Ere how's your David doin'? He ain't 'ere then?"

She was about to respond but her mother answered first, tears evident in her eyes.

"There hasn't been any word from him. He doesn't even know his grandmother's dead yet. We had thought he'd be home by now. We don't quite know what's happened."

Beth gave her mother a smile and mouthed, "You okay?"

Connie smiled tightly back and nodded.

Poor Mum, Beth thought. It's been such a long day for her. The sooner this lot sling their hooks the better.

Pattie appeared in the doorway carrying a tray of

Gran's best cups and saucers. The thin, white china with gold rims and painted with bright red and yellow roses had been fetched down from the loft especially for the occasion.

"Right then, who's 'avin' wot?" she called out.

"Tea for me, ducks," a voice answered.

"Not for me, I'd rather have a coffee. Got any of that instant stuff?"

"Got any whisky stashed away?"

"Trust my George to ask," commented Aunt Betty with a laugh, taking yet another sandwich.

Uncle George, whom Beth hadn't seen since last Christmas, and whom she disliked bitterly, since that time at cousin Jeffrey's wedding two years ago when he'd cornered her alone on the landing and run his hand up her skirt, wandered in from the kitchen behind Pattie, glass in hand. He looked drunk. Very drunk. He could hardly stand without swaying.

Beth avoided his eyes searching round the room, sensing he was looking for her. She tried to look busy, keeping her back to him, but he sidled up behind and patted her bottom. Glaring, she brushed his hand away brusquely.

"'Ere, our Beff." His speech was slurred, his breath reeking of cigarettes and beer. She turned her face away in disgust.

"You've done grand, you 'ave. But, well, I've 'ad a word with Alfie likes, and 'e agrees. You don't wanna be 'avin to cooks Christmas dinner tomorrow. An' seein' as 'ow that chicken our Effal's gone an' bought is enough to feed the whole bloomin' street, you's all comin' to us. Ain't that right, Con?"

Beth's heart plummeted to the floor. She didn't mind Aunt Ethel's company, she was good fun, and knew her mother always enjoyed their company. Ethel was also a good cook. The thought of a well-roasted chicken with chestnut stuffing oozing out made her mouth water immediately. A real treat in the offering. But that didn't compensate for having to spend the day in Uncle George's lecherous company. But what could she say, seeing as how her father had already agreed to the invitation? There was no point in arguing about not going.

If only she could explain to Mum and Dad the real reason why she didn't want to go, but she daren't. If she did, there would be such a fight and rumpus Dad would kill him. So would Mike. And David when he got home.

"That's good of you," she answered, trying to sound enthusiastic. She would just have to make sure she was never alone in the same room as him.

Her loathsome relative gulped down the remains of his beer.

"That's sorted then. Effal says to bring the veg like, seein' as 'ow your Mikey gets it for free. Perhaps you could sort somethin' out now for Effal to carry 'ome, save messin'. Oh, an' bring a couple of those Christmas puds your muvver's got stuffed in 'er wardrobe. She told me she's got some left from last year."

From the hallway, her father beckoned her. He held up two empty beer flagons.

"Looks like the last one, girl. Perhaps you'd better take 'em empties back to the Coach and Horses and get 'em refilled." He pulled out a ten-bob note from the top pocket of his demob suit jacket. "Here's the money. I want change mind. And take Janet with you. That girl looks pissed out her brain. Fresh air and a walk will do her good."

"Oh, Dad. Can't Mike go? I've been on my feet since

before dawn. I'm not the hired help, you know. Even Cinderella got a better deal than is. Do this. Do that. Run upstairs and fetch this. Make a pot of tea. I'm worn out, Dad."

His expression changed instantly to one of fury.

"No. I asked you to bloody go and that's the end of it." A roar of laughter issued forth from the front parlour. His face softened. "Sound's like I'm missin' all the fun. Now don't be long about it, girl."

She rushed upstairs and flung herself onto her bed. She shouldn't have spoken to her father that way, she knew, but she was tired, she was hurting, and she missed Gran.

During all this, not once, even today, had anyone asked how she was coping. It was as if her feelings and pain didn't matter. All she wanted from any of them was a hug. A kind word. Was that too much to ask?

Instead, she'd been the one to hold it all together, left to her to make sure there was enough plates and cups to go round. She'd been the one to ask the landlord of the Coach and Horses for a loan of glasses and sweet-talking him into not having to leave a deposit. Checking this and that and everything was done, the wreath ordered, enough food in the house. An endless, unhappy list.

Another roar of laughter carried up the stairs and drifted through the floorboards.

How *dare* they all be laughing? How dare they all be enjoying themselves when not an hour ago they had gathered around her grandmother's graveside, watching and weeping as they lowered the coffin into the cold, dark ground?

She heard the sounds of Uncle George's deep, drawling voice cracking yet another bawdy joke, Aunt Joan's high-pitched chatter coming from the kitchen.

How can they be so heartless? She buried her face in the pillow and wept uncontrollably.

Mrs Coombes had said it would be like this, the sadness followed by anger, said it was a natural part of the normal grieving process, but Beth had never expected it to feel this painful. She missed Gran so much. Who was there for her now with her gone? And with Mike going soon, there wouldn't be anyone to help fight her seemingly endless battles with Dad.

More tears fell, tears of loss and tears of exhaustion as she wondered what had happened to David. Mum needed him. What if something had happened and he wasn't coming? She didn't think she could bear it if he didn't come. Nor Mum.

There was a gentle tapping at the bedroom door. It opened slightly, Pattie's face peering round.

"Are you all right? May I come in?"

Beth sat up, sniffed loudly and rubbed at her eyes. "Yeah, sure."

Pattie joined her on the bed and wrapped her arms about her.

"It's hard, I know. It's been a long day and a difficult week for you. You should have let me help more, not take it all on by yourself."

There was comfort in Pattie's presence, her kindly words, her warm body holding her. She sniffed back more tears.

"It's just so unfair, Pattie. I wish David were here. I know Mum feels the same way. I've watched her all day looking round for him, hoping to see him come striding down the street in his uniform. He should have been here by now."

Pattie's eyes clouded, filling with tears as she pulled an envelope out from a pocket in the black skirt she wore.

"This was delivered when you were all at the cemetery. It's... it's a telegram. Addressed to your dad. I didn't think it right to mention it when you got back, what with everyone here."

The buff-coloured enveloped edged in a narrow black band had the regiment's insignia stamped in the corner. It meant only one thing, as no doubt Pattie had already surmised. She took it from Pattie's shaky hand and stared at it, knowing the awful message its contents would say.

Chapter Nine

Killed in action, the telegram had stated matter-of-factly. The only comforting solace Beth found was in the fact that Gran hadn't lived to learn of her grandson's murder, for that was surely what David's death was. A mindless, needless murder, no matter how fine a word used for war.

It was only today, after almost three weeks of enquiries, her father had finally been able to find out from the war office that her brother had been out on patrol with three members of his battalion when they had been surprised in an ambush. The other soldiers with him had also been killed.

It was hardly surprising her mother looked worse these last few weeks, despite the brave face she tried to put on, Beth thought. The coughing fits still came but at least Mum had regained her sense of humour although most times it was a false, nervous laughter that issued forth from those pale lips. A brave attempt to put on an act but the sallow complexion and frequent bouts of being sick told a different story.

Even the whisky Mr Chiselhurst had sent home with her on New Year's Eve, as a gift for Mum to put some colour back into her cheeks, failed to live up to its promise.

Mum had lost weight too, she had noticed, her dresses hanging loosely from her waist where they should have been getting tighter and tighter, and slightest effort tired her. Believing her mother was slipping further and further downhill, despite any protestations to the contrary, Beth was at a loss what to do.

Mike's impending departure hadn't helped the situation either. Due to report at the end of January, she clung to the hope her brother would fail his medical. Hardly likely, considering he was as fit as an ox. Hounslow Barracks might only be two bus rides away, but that didn't stop her worrying, or Mum constantly fretting about his going.

Dad carried on as if everything was normal. Mike avoided discussing the current crisis in the family, leaving her as the lynchpin holding everything together. Under the load she carried on her shoulders, feeling herself bending under its growing weight, she felt scared she would break completely. For her mother's sake, she knew she had to be strong.

"Did you hear me, Beth?"

Henry's voice brought her thoughts crashing back into the office, to the pages of paper curling out of the top of the typewriter.

"Sorry, Mr Chiselhurst, my mind was elsewhere for a moment."

He sighed heavily, perching himself on the edge of her desk.

"Look, my lass. I know things have been tough for you lately but you really must concentrate. Life goes on. Business goes on... Now, I asked if you have finished that letter yet. I have a report I need to get done today."

"Just finishing." She typed the closing swiftly, pulled the paper from the typewriter then carefully separated the original and two copies from the carbon paper in between each sheet, before handing him the top copy.

She watched him as he read the document through. She liked working for Mr Chiselhurst, and he had seemed genuinely pleased with her progress over the past few weeks. Always typing or filing, dealing efficiently with telephone call and visitors to the offices, running errands to the post office. The hours flew past, and busy all day, she rarely had time to think about things back at home.

So why today she had difficulty in concentrating, she didn't know. There probably weren't many bosses as kind and considerate or as understanding with her as he had been, she thought, even if at times he sat a little too close for comfort, such as he was doing now.

"Perfect. Well done," he congratulated. "Fresh paper in the typewriter please, three copies. I'll dictate and you type direct. It will be quicker. We have much to get through."

Her stomach knotted. "I've never done that before, Mr Chiselhurst."

He laughed. "You'll soon get the hang of it."

As he dictated and she typed, she found she could keep up with him with little effort. Before she looked up again it was almost time to go home. Another week over, another weekend of cleaning and washing to look forward to.

"That's it for today, lass. You've done well. Oh, and by the way, I'd like you to stay on permanently. You're a good worker."

"Why, thank you, Mr Chiselhurst." Her heart and head lifted. It had been what she had been hoping for these last few weeks.

"Aye, lass. You've proved you're a good worker considering the circumstances. Now, if you could manage it, I'd like you to come in earlier of a morning, at half-past-eight for the next week or two. We've a busy time ahead."

"Oh." Her elation evaporated. The prospect of doing extra hours filled her with exhaustion just thinking about it. And what next? Expecting her to work later, too? But what if she refused? Would he change his mind about keeping her on?

"Well, I'll do my best, sir, although getting here earlier might prove difficult with all I have to do at home of a morning seeing to Mum."

"Just do what you can, lass. I'll make the time up to you."

He patted her shoulder, leaving his hand resting there for what she thought was far longer than necessary.

Terry chatted with the chestnut seller about this and that and nothing in particular as she stood silently by, warming her hands over the brazier, waiting patiently for the next batch of chestnuts to turn black on the hot coals.

Half-listening to their lighthearted banter, deep in her own thoughts, she realised Saturday evenings spent in Terry's company were becoming more and more precious to her.

His little jokes always made her laugh and forget her woes for a brief while. He was fun to be with and made her feel special, creating a warm, wonderful feeling deep inside her.

When the chestnuts were ready, the roasted smell scenting the chilly night air, Terry bought a half-pound for them to share.

"Let's walk along the Embankment."

She nodded, taking a nut from the proffered paper twist. Wearing gloves, she found it difficult to peel.

Terry took the hot nut from her and tossing it from hand to hand, blew on it to cool it down enough to tear away the burnt shell, passing back the sweet-tasting kernel inside. He dealt with one for himself in the same manner, then prepared another for her. By the time they reached Waterloo Bridge, the newspaper twist was empty.

He hurled the screwed up paper into a litterbin then put his arm around her shoulder as they walked on. A little further along he stopped suddenly and turned her to face him.

"What's wrong, Beth? You've been quiet all night. I thought you'd be pleased your boss has kept you on permanent. It's what you wanted, wasn't it?"

A large teardrop ran down her cheek. She sniffed. "It isn't that."

"Tell me."

"I'm so scared, Terry. It's Mum. I swear she's getting worse, and there's nothing we can do but watch her suffer. I'm not worried about the baby so much, it's her I care about. I don't want her to die. Then losing our David. I don't think she'll ever get over that. I catch her sometimes just staring out like she's on another planet. Like she's not with us. And Mike's off soon. What with Gran, all this upset isn't doing her any good at all. I just wish there was something more I could do to help. If only I knew what."

She fought back the tears threatening to cascade in a torrent down her cheeks. She'd done too much crying lately, she thought, and whilst it made her feel better, all that weeping hadn't solved anything.

He pulled her to him, holding her tightly, comforting.

"I'm sure the doctor will sort something out for her soon." His words were gentle.

She snuggled against his shoulder. In his arms she felt safe. An anchor for her to cling to.

"But she could die before then. We're totally helpless unless we can get her away from London before this rotten, stinking city kills her. Trouble is, we can't afford to take her anywhere. It wouldn't be so bad if Dad got himself a job. He isn't that disabled he can't do anything. There must be *something* he could find, but he doesn't want to. He doesn't make any effort. It's as if he wants her to die."

"I can't believe that. I expect he feels just as powerless."

Unfolding her from his arms, he turned, resting his elbows on the parapet of the bridge, staring out into the swirling, rising water of the Thames lapping noisily against the stonework of the Embankment as the tide flowed back in. She copied his stance.

"I don't want you to ever go away, Beth." It was almost a whisper.

Under the yellow glow of the streetlamps she studied his profile, his taut expression, and thought she could understand the emotion etched there. She felt the same way. If she couldn't go on seeing Terry she would just die, she knew she would. He was everything to her. If this was how love felt she knew she would love him forever. She slipped her arm through the crook of his.

"That's hardly likely to happen," she told him. "No way can Dad afford for us to move. The house belongs to the council, and he's only got his war pension. If only we could get her away for just a few weeks somewhere. Down to the coast or something, it might help. Dad's useless around the house. He's incapable of looking after himself, let alone Mum, and now that Mike's got his call-up papers, I'll be left to do everything. I don't think I can cope much longer."

It was all beginning to weigh her down just when her life should be looking up.

He turned his head to her, the gold and green flecks in his eyes flickering from the streetlight.

"You will. You're strong. Resourceful. And do you know something, Beth Brixham? I'm proud of you. Lesser girls would have given up, but not you. You battle on. A bit like me, really. We're both fighters, and us fighters will always find some way of coping."

"I keep telling myself something will turn up. I know this must sound awful, Terry, but in some ways I wish Mum would lose the baby then maybe she'll have a good chance of recovering. Am I wicked to think that?"

He shook his head. "No more than anyone else. I expect your mum's thought the self-same thing. It's a natural reaction."

She placed her hands on the cold stonework, wondering why Waterloo Bridge was the place they always seemed inexplicably drawn to whenever they came up town, as if pulled by some unknown force.

She noticed then they were standing at the exact same spot where they had watched the sun go down on their first date together. The place where Terry had first kissed her. In that moment recognizing that, for her, Waterloo Bridge had become their special place, knowing that whatever happened in the future, no matter what paths their lives might take, she would never be able to walk across this bridge again without stopping to look across the river and think of him.

"I blame Dad for all this," she said, breaking their silent contemplations. "It's all his fault. He's a bigoted, self-opinionated, lazy, selfish pig. He doesn't think about our mum. Or anyone else, for that matter."

He pulled her to him. "Hey, calm down. Remember, it takes two to make a baby. Your mum must have known what could happen. I'm sure deep down he's suffering and just as worried as you are."

"Then he's got a funny way of showing it, that's all I can say."

But Terry was right. It was all to easy to brandish blame when frustrated by a hopeless situation. Just as it was easy to give up when the going was difficult. No, she wasn't going to give up, she told herself resolutely. Never.

He uttered a muted laugh. "Your dad sounds a bit like my old man in some ways. Only not quite as bad."

"Don't joke, Terry. I'm not in the mood."

"I'm serious. You haven't met my dad. Why do you think I don't live at home? Why do you think I rent a room off Chiswick High Road and work all the free hours I can in that teashop when I'm not studying in order to pay my rent? Certainly not out of love for hard work."

She hung her head. "I'm sorry. I'm so wrapped up in my own misery I forget everyone else has their problems too. What makes me so mad is that Gran had a tin stashed with money. Full to the brim, it was. There must have been hundreds of pounds there. Enough surely to buy a house elsewhere. But Gran never offered the money to help get Mum away. I know she meant that money for me and my brothers, but Mum's needs are far greater than Mike's or mine. Even after we paid out from it for the funeral expenses and the booze-up afterwards, there must have been loads left, but Mum won't hear of us using it."

"Then she must have her reasons. Have you asked her why?"

Beth tutted. "Of course I have. She says she's not using our inheritance to pay for her own mistakes."

Terry raised her chin with his finger until he was looking directly into her eyes.

"If your grandmother left that money for you and Mike, then your mother's right not to use it. It couldn't have been an easy decision for her to make, but I admire her for it. She has your interests and future at heart. That's important. Look, let's go grab a drink before the pubs shut, and see what we can come up with. There has to be some way to sort all this out."

She fell into step with him as they turned their backs on the river. He surprised her a few steps later by pulling her round into his arms again.

"You could always marry me, you know. Solve all your problems."

"Was that a proposal or another of your silly jokes? Because either way, it doesn't help."

"I mean it, Beth. I'm in love with you. We could run away to Gretna Green."

She pushed him away. "Don't be stupid! I'm far too young. And I hardly know you, Terry Gibbs. Plus, neither of us can afford to get married. And then there's Mum to consider. I couldn't leave her and—"

"I can wait, Beth, but... well, there's nothing to stop us getting engaged, is there?"

"Yes. My dad, for one thing. He'd kill me." She shrugged off his arms, half-laughing, half unsure if he was in all seriousness asking her to marry him.

He pulled her back to him, lowered his lips to hers and whispered, "Kill me, more like."

Chapter Ten

A loud rat-a-tat-tat on the front door knocker interrupted Connie, mid sentence.

"Who the 'ell is that on a Sunday evenin'?" grumbled Alfie.

"I'll go," offered Beth, putting down her half-eaten slice of bread and homemade bramble jam, and wiping her mouth of crumbs with the back of her hand.

"If it's those bloody Jehovah Witnesses again, tell 'em to bugger off," her father's voice boomed out from the kitchen.

Her heart leapt with surprise and joy as she opened the front door.

"Terry! This is unexpected. Don't say we made a date last night and I've gone and forgotten? Are we supposed to be going out somewhere?"

"I've not come at an inconvenient time, have I? I can always call back later if you're still eating."

"No. No, it's okay, we've just finished."

He bent to kiss her. She moved swiftly out of his reach.

"Not here. The old man's liable to come out. Look, come on inside, into the front room."

She opened the door wider to let him in, hoping her father would stay put in the kitchen and leave them be.

"Only, it's your dad I've come to see," Terry explained. "I was hoping to talk to him."

He seemed nervous, judging from the way he fidgeted with the collar of his leather jacket as he wiped his shoes on the doormat.

The kitchen door opened. Alfie came out into the hall, saying, "Who the 'ell is it? Whatever he's sellin', we don't want none."

Terry thrust out his hand in greeting. "Mr Brixham, the very man. How do you do?"

Alfie eyed him suspiciously. "Who wants to know?"

"I'm Terry Gibbs. Beth's boyfriend. I wonder if I might have a word with you?"

Ignoring Terry, he glared at Beth. "You didn't tell me he was comin'?"

"I didn't know. It's you he's come to see."

"Well, me lad, I don't know what you wants, but let me tell you, I don't want no fly-by-night messin' about with our Beth 'ere, see? She's a good girl. And if you thinks you're askin' for her hand you can go and takes a runnin' jump. She's too young. I ain't havin' it."

Beth stared at her father, then back to Terry. Surely he wasn't going to ask him that, she thought. He was only joking last night when he proposed, wasn't he?

"Mr Brixham, I have a proposition to put to you. It concerns your wife."

"There ain't nothin' you've got that I'm interested in," Alfie snarled.

Beth rolled her eyes skyward. She knew this was going to happen, that he would start on Terry the moment he clapped eyes on him.

"Dad, will you *just* listen a moment. Hear what he has to say."

"If you didn't know he was comin' here, how comes you knows what he wants to talk to me about, eh? Been hatchin' plans, have you?"

"Oh for goodness sake." She shook her head despairingly under his accusing glare. Now perhaps Terry could see why she always suggested they meet elsewhere whenever they had a date, instead of calling for her here.

Terry, however, seemed undeterred by her father's

hostility.

"Look, Mr Brixham will you just hear me out? If you don't like what I have to say then fair enough, I'll leave and that'll be the end of it."

After several long moments of hesitation her father finally acquiesced, much to her relief.

"I'll give you a minute, boy, although I can't honestly—"

"Who is it, Alf?" Mum called from the kitchen. "Hurry up and shut the front door, it's letting one hell of a draught through."

"It's this Terry geezer of our Beth's," Alfie shouted back over his shoulder. He glared at Terry. "You'd best come in then."

The front room felt cold, the fire not lit yet, they were low on coal. Beth went to the window and drew back the curtains to let in more light, although the dismal grey of a winter afternoon could do little to lighten the tense atmosphere in the room.

"Well, lad?"

Beth leaned back against one wall, hands clasped behind her back, eager to hear, but at the same time anxious over what Terry was so keen to say to her father.

"Beth tells me her mother's very ill," Terry began.

"Happen that's our business."

"She says she needs to get away from London, into the country."

"So?"

Terry licked at his lips and drew breath. "My uncle owns a farm in Gloucestershire. He's looking for help as most of the men from the village were either killed in the war, or still in the army. Most of the lads there are on their national service."

This was all news to her. Terry had never mentioned

anything about his family, other than the fact he didn't get on with his father.

"So what's all that got to do with my Connie? She might need fresh air but she ain't no good at ploughin' fields."

Her father's tone told he was becoming increasingly annoyed by this conversation. He didn't like discussing family affairs with strangers. Airing dirty linen in public, as he called it.

"No, but you could drive a tractor. Help with the harvest. Do odd jobs about the farm that Uncle Tom never seems to have time for. There's a cottage that goes with the job too. There's even work for Mike if he wants it. It might help prevent his conscription, working on the land."

Her father kicked off his slipper and raised his leg up onto the dining table, trying to wiggle his toes for Terry's benefit.

"Dad!" Beth cried out, embarrassed.

"How can *I* work? I'm pensioned out on account of me foot. See? This is all twaddle you're speakin', boy. If your uncle's so desperate for labourers, then how comes you ain't there workin'? I mean, a big, strong lad like you, you looks like you could 'andle a plough or milk a cow."

The sigh her boyfriend gave sounded defeated. Poor Terry. It couldn't have been easy for him to come here with his suggestion, knowing how much of an ogre her father is. Hadn't she told him often enough the man was unreasonable? Now perhaps he could see for himself she wasn't exaggerating.

Terry made a move towards the door. "Will you at least think about it, Mr Brixham?"

She knew her father wouldn't, so added, "Look, Dad, Terry's offered a perfectly good solution, one I think you should let Mum consider before you dismiss the whole thing out of hand. I think it's a wonderful idea. *You* haven't come up with anything else."

Her father's silence was unnerving. Eventually, he spoke, a triumphant look upon his face, as if he'd thought of something to scupper Terry's little plan.

"There's this 'ouse, see? The council will takes it away from me if we moves out."

Terry's eyebrows rose slightly. "Well, that's the other part of my proposition."

"Oh aye?" There was renewed suspicion in her father's voice.

Terry looked at her. She held her breath, staring back at him with raised eyebrows, wondering what he was going to come out with next.

"Beth stays here."

Her jaw dropped. Terry couldn't be serious? Did he honestly think her father would agree to that? Not a hope.

Alfie glared at Terry before turning on her. "Is this your flamin' idea?"

She shook her head rapidly, knowing he wouldn't believe when she mumbled, "I didn't know anything about it, honest."

Glowering at Terry, Dad put his worn slipper back on. "And just who, I might ask, is goin' to look after us? After Connie?"

"My aunt," Terry replied. "And then there's also my two cousins, Sally and Freda. Freda's a midwife. Sally's… well…," he hesitated. "Well, Sally's just Sally."

Alfie scratched his head. "So what's in it for you? There has to be somethin', else you wouldn't be botherin'."

Suddenly, the door swung open and Mum backed in

carrying a tray of crockery.

"Terry's not stoppin'," Alfie announced.

"What, already? No, you musn't go, I've made us all tea. Do stay, Terry. Now, for what do we owe the pleasure of this visit? Oh, do sit down, lad. Alfie, offer the poor boy a chair, what's up with you?"

Beth watched Terry seated nervously on the edge of an armchair, sipping his tea, whilst her father recountered the offer. She wished Terry had discussed this with her first, so it hadn't come as such a shock. She avoided his gaze whilst she tried to take in all he had said, all the ramifications. As much as she loved surprises, she knew her father didn't, nor did he take kindly to decisions being made about his family by others, no matter how well meant those intentions were.

"The whole idea's flamin' ludicrous, if you asks me," her father suddenly shouted having finished explaining Terry's proposal.

"But I think it's a wonderful idea," her mother exclaimed, clapping her hands together. "A little house in the country, it's just what we've always dreamed of."

"You don't understand, woman. He wants our Beth to stay 'ere and I ain't 'avin' that. No way. I'll put me foot down. If we goes, and it's a big if, I might add, she comes with us. Don't look at me like that, Beth, it ain't open to discussion. And we have this 'ere house to think about. I imagine if we gets our lodgings as part of the deal I won't be earnin' much money, so how is we expected to pay the rent whilst we're away? You tell me that."

Terry put his cup and saucer down onto the tray. "I do have another idea."

"Too many flippin' ideas from the sound of it," Alfie grumbled. "I ain't listenin' to any more of this claptrap. Send the boy—"

"Oh, do shut up blithering, and let him finish, will you?" Connie said. "Let's just hear what he has to say."

Terry wrung his hands nervously. He looked uncomfortable. Beth wanted to run to him, hold his hands in her own and tell him it was a wonderful idea, her staying in London, but she knew better than to upset her father even more. One wrong word, one false move and any hope would be quashed quicker than a fly under the fish-slice.

"Look, at the moment I'm in digs, renting one shabby room and sharing a bathroom on the floor below, and paying a fortune for the privilege."

She hadn't been to Terry's flat yet, but he had described its dilapidated condition to her.

A dingy bedsit where the wallpaper peeled away because the walls were so damp, the permanent smell of cooked cabbage throughout the house, the constant tang of mildew on the air. The bath that had no enamel left on its grubby inside and supported a ring of verdigris around the plughole and taps. He'd told her of the cracked toilet bowl that leaked over the floorboards and didn't flush properly and was so badly stained even the flies had stopped coming in. Walls so paper-thin every sound could be heard from the adjoining rooms. It sounded a dreadful place to live.

"Why don't you live at home?" her mother asked.

"I don't because my father doesn't approve of what I'm doing. He and I don't see eye to eye, on many things. My idea, if you were in agreement, is that I could stay here whilst you're away. I mean, we're not looking on this as a permanent move, are we? I presume once the baby is born you'd be wanting to come back home. But this way, you'll have someone keeping an eye on the place while you're gone. I'll be paying the rent so you wouldn't have to worry about the council. When you're ready to come back, I'll move straight back out. How does that sound?"

Absolutely wonderful, Beth nearly said, but controlled her exuberance. Her father, however, looked anything but. He tapped on the table with his finger.

"If you's is only a student, likes our Beth says you is, then 'ow comes you can affords the rent on this place, on any place come to that, *and* drive a car to boot? You kids is always pleadin' poverty. I can't see how—"

"Dad, I've told you," she interrupted. Dad wasn't being fair to Terry. It wasn't any of his business how Terry came by the car. But Terry seemed unperturbed by the question.

"The car isn't mine, Mr Brixham. I'm only looking after it while my roommate is away. Keeping it running to stop the engine seizing up. As a mechanic yourself, even you can see the importance of that."

Seemingly satisfied with his answer, Alfie leaned back in his chair, arms folded across his chest. "So, what does your father do?"

Beth looked to her mother, pleading with her eyes to make him stop giving Terry the third degree. What did it matter what Terry's father did? It was totally irrelevant.

"My dad's a boatbuilder on the Thames. Well, repairer's more correct. He overhauls the barges and lighters."

"So why ain't you workin' with him, learnin' a proper trade instead?"

She rolled her eyes again. Perhaps Terry could see now she wasn't making it all up about her father, that he really was such a difficult man who always thought he was right and everyone else didn't know what they were talking about.

Terry stiffened and said indignantly, "You don't think

training to work in the legal profession is an honourable job then?"

Her mother came to his defence. "I think it's a very worthwhile profession, Terry. Solicitors can make a lot of money."

"Yeah, by screwin' the likes of us into the ground when we're in trouble," came Dad's caustic reply. "Kids nowadays don't want to work. Most of 'em are too frightened of gettin' their bloody hands dirty."

Terry coughed. "Well, I'm not. I'm used to having mud and rust and grease in my nails, scrubbing the ingrained dirt off my hands until the skin's raw. I've helped on the boats often enough, have done since I was a kid. I'm trying to carve out a career as a barrister so I can help the working classes, the kids who don't have a decent education, and who get squashed and put-upon because they don't know any better and haven't got the means to do anything about it. I've read how fat cats in factories, especially up north, treat their workers. There was this one cotton mill up there I read about, the largest in the country, at least it was until the factory owner laid off all the workforce, sold all the machinery, and put the factory up for sale."

"I expect there was money troubles. It always comes down to money and if trade had fallen off, what else was the owner supposed to do?"

"Hush, woman. You don't know what the bleedin' hell you're talkin' about," Alfie growled to Connie.

Terry shook his head. "Quite the contrary, Mrs Brixham. During the war, this particular company made army uniforms. Couldn't churn them out quick enough. The looms and presses and sewing machines were running twenty-four hours a day. They couldn't get enough material to keep up with demand. Then, after the war, cheaper imports started coming in from abroad and they couldn't match on prices. The Government wasn't prepared to pay a premium to keep the factories running, so the owner was forced to lay off the workforce. Those women had been loyal to him for years, worked like Trojans during the war, and many were widowed because of it. Now, not only don't they have their husbands and sons, they also don't have an income to keep their families. I didn't agree with what that factory owner did. He should have diversified. He could have saved the workforce and the factory."

Alfie clapped slowly in mock applause. "Very noble speech, son. Sounds more to me you should be in politics. But if you stand by what you's pontificatin' now, you'd be doin' precisely what you're arguin' against, by makin' a livin' at the expense of the workers. You'd become one of those fat cats. Barristers and solicitors makes a fortune, I know. They charges an arm an' a leg."

"Someone has to side with the workforce, with those women. They have rights to a decent standard of living, to a decent job," Terry countered.

"Hear, hear," Beth enthused then sank back into the settee under her father's steely glare.

"But there's plenty of work about now. Factories are springing up all over the place. Everyone's got money in their pockets and bread and butter on their table," her mother interjected.

"We ain't. Women should step back and let the menfolk have all their old jobs back. Give them back their dignity. They've done their bit for the war effort; they should go back to their kitchen sinks and children and let the men get on with runnin' things. Get back to the way things were before the war."

"That's good coming from you, Dad." Beth couldn't

resist the dig.

Terry gave her a sympathetic look then turned back to her father. "This isn't about giving men their jobs back, Mr Brixham. You see, there were no jobs left when that mill owner closed the factory, no jobs at all. For men or women. Nothing. But women have as much right to jobs as men. Don't you think even men on production lines need protection? All workers have rights, but it seems this country doesn't believe that women workers have rights too. A right to equal pay and equal terms and conditions. They need someone to stand up for them. Something or someone more powerful than unions."

"You can't change the world, son."

"No, but I can at least try to change the lot of the workforce of this nation. Do something worthwhile."

Her mother stretched out and patted Terry's hand. "Your father ought to be proud of you. Perhaps when he realises what you're trying to do, he'll come around."

Terry sighed wearily. "I doubt it. He's too concerned with himself to worry about me. I'm the spanner in the works. An upstart and not worthy of the family name, according to him. That's one of the reasons I don't live at home."

"So what you really mean is your old man threw you out?" There was a look of self-satisfaction written across her father's face.

Terry fell silent. Beth felt sorry for him. He'd been so brave to stand up to her father, but he now looked forlorn and dejected. She glanced back and forwards. To Terry. At her parents. Then back to Terry. Waiting for somebody to speak. The only sound she could hear was the steady tick-tick-tick of the clock on the mantelpiece.

Finally, Terry looked up. "You haven't got a clue what it was like at home, Mr Brixham. Not a clue. I left home because I hated him. He was a bully. A brute who didn't give a damn about us kids or my mother. You know nothing of the terrible beatings he dished out when he stumbled home from the pub drunk every night."

"Clip round the ear never hurt anyone. I expect you deserved it."

"*Dad!*" She couldn't believe her father could be so spiteful.

"You think so?" Terry came back at him. "You honestly believe he was right to take his belt off and thrash the backsides of my brothers and three sisters or me until they were raw and bleeding? You think giving your wife a black eye because your supper's cold because you've come home late, is a justifiable reason? You're saying he put my younger brother in hospital with three broken ribs and a cracked arm was well deserved?"

Beth looked on horrified. Terry had never spoken of this. Dad might have annoying habits and grouch a lot, but he wasn't cruel. He didn't beat them. He'd never actually hit any of them. He'd threatened it often enough, but never carried out any of his threats.

"I've lain in bed and wept for my family," Terry continued. "Heard them screaming out in agony and been unable to do anything to stop him. Believe me, Mr Brixham, I wanted to kill him, and if I'd have had the guts, I would. Have you any idea what it's like to lay out your own mother in a coffin, looking down on her blackened, bruised face, knowing it was your own flesh and blood, your father, the man she'd married and had six kids by, had done this to her?"

Terry rose, pushing the chair angrily out of the way, and stood before the window, facing away from them all. Beth rushed to him, putting a comforting arm around his waist.

"I'm all right," he murmured without looking round, "but it makes me so angry that I couldn't stop him. The memory of those beatings. I can still hear my sisters' screams when no mercy was spared. You know, we were unable to go to school sometimes because of the red welts and cuts across our legs and backsides. I can almost feel the weight of that belt across the cheeks of my arse even now. Sorry, but it's just brought all the hatred and venom back to the surface." Tears formed in his eyes.

She turned on her father. "Now look what you've done."

"I was only askin'. I didn't mean to upset the lad."

Connie coughed. It came as a single noise at first, then in uncontrollable barks that made her face turn red, her eyes water.

"Excuse me a moment," she whispered and ran from the room, her hand over her mouth.

Looking calmer and composed, Terry returned to his chair.

"Sir, this looks a warm, nice place. Big. We lived in a damp, cold house with mould climbing up the walls. A two up-two down by Isleworth Ait. Most days it was only bread and dripping for tea. Eight of us cramped into a small terrace. We all got on top of each other. After we buried Mum, I had to get out."

"Huh. There was ten of us when I grew up, I'll have you know. We all managed. So, you just buggered off out of it and left your brothers and sisters at his mercy? Very gallant. Only a coward would do that."

It was obvious by his snub her father was never going to understand. She was about to give him a piece of her mind for being so demeaning when Terry thumped his fist down onto the table, making the cups rattle in their saucers.

"I'm no coward, Mr Brixham. I had to get out because the authorities came and put the rest of the family into care. Except Joe that is, my elder brother. They took my sisters and our Billy away. Oh, they were glad to be away from him, have no doubts about that. Joe and I, we tried to keep in touch with them but they're scattered between three different orphanages. Joe's a river pilot further down the Thames."

"Where's your dad now?" Alfie's manner was subdued. Beth hoped it was because he was ashamed of himself for being such a pompous pig towards Terry.

"I haven't a clue, and I don't want to know. After they took my sisters and Billy away, that's when I decided to study law. I'm hoping we can all get back together again once they're old enough to leave the homes. I couldn't stay in that house and I need somewhere quiet to study. That's why living here while you're away would be so ideal."

Connie came back into the room, her face flushed, her eyes moist.

"You know, Alfie, I've been thinking. A little cottage in the country could be the answer to our prayers. How else—"

"I think it's a wonderful idea, Dad," Beth interrupted, her head held high. "We haven't come up with any other solution."

"There's still all that money of me mother's. We should be usin' that, not havin' to take charity off the likes of him." Alfie nodded in Terry's direction.

"This isn't charity, Mr Brixham. I'm doing this for your wife. And for Beth. It's the perfect solution. If, on the other hand, you decide you like the country life better than London, then I'll be moving out anyway. What have you got to lose?"

"He's right, you know," Connie said, putting a hand on her husband's shoulder. "And I've told you, I ain't using Queenie's money. She left that for the kids. And surely if it means Mike doesn't have to do his national service, it has to be worth it to keep him safe? I couldn't bear losing another son." Her eyes filled with tears. She pulled a handkerchief out from her pocket, and began coughing again.

Terry stood. "I do beg you to reconsider about Beth, Mr Brixham. There's little for her in the country and the farm's miles from anywhere. She's found herself a good job here with prospects. It would be a pity if she had to throw all that away. Even you must be able to see the sense in her staying here, Mrs Brixham?"

Beth was disappointed but not surprised by her father's response when he said, "She'll soon get another job when we returns. Jobs are two a penny round 'ere. And if she stays, which she won't be doin', it means you wouldn't be movin' in here, me lad, and so I'll still be 'avin' to pay the rent."

"Yes, but you'll also be earning a wage, even if it isn't a lot, Alfie. Think on that," said her mother. "But Terry, I'm afraid I must agree with my husband. I really wouldn't feel happy about Beth staying here all on her own. My daughter's too young for that. It's too much responsibility. I'd worry far too much."

Alfie rose, pulling himself up to his full height. He was shorter than Terry by several inches.

"She comes with us, or we don't go at all. We'll think on it, me lad."

Before opening the front door to let Terry out, Beth touched his shoulder.

"I'm sorry he put you through all that."

Terry smiled and brushed her cheek lightly. "I don't

think your dad likes me. Still, I've said what I came to say. We can only wait and see what happens next."

She nestled her cheek into the warmth of his fingers, experiencing the tender security in his touch.

"I don't hold out much hope to him agreeing to go. But thanks, Terry. I know Mum appreciates the offer. And so do I. But what happens if they make me go with them?"

"We'll worry about that then." He stooped to kiss her. This time she didn't prevent him.

As she closed the front door, she overheard her parents' voices in conversation in the front room.

"...that Terry's a lovely lad you know, Alf. There's not many kids would try to help like that."

"Bah! He's far too bleedin' old for our Beth. The sooner it's put a stop to, the better. I ain't havin' it."

Beth's last evening with Terry found them returning to their special place, where they had shared their first kiss, but standing now in the twilight on Waterloo Bridge, watching the pigeons flying in to roost on the buildings along the Embankment, brought little pleasure to her heavy heart weighed down by sadness and gloom. Whilst Terry may have solved her parents' problem, in so doing had created an even larger one for her. One that couldn't be resolved.

She had been given no choice. She must go to Gloucestershire. To a strange world where she knew no-one but her parents to live in a cottage that wouldn't be home, miles from anywhere. No shops. No cinemas. No life. Nothing but empty fields and vast acres of alien sky. She would have to leave behind her job, all her dreams. Worst of all, she would be leaving Terry.

"I don't want to leave you, but what choice do I

have?"

She had begged her father, pleaded with him to let her stay. Arguing and cajoling, thinking of any and every reason and excuse she could to make him change his mind. But he had been adamant. Her duty lay with her family and his word was law, he had told her.

Terry ran his hand through her wind-tousled hair. "You're of legal age to get married. Marry me and stay here."

"I may be old enough," she said through tears threatening to break, "but not old enough by law to make my own decisions. Not old enough to even buy a drink to drown my sorrows. By law, I'm not classed old enough even to see an A-rated movie unless there's a grown-up with me to put their hands over my eyes at the naughty bits, or block my ears at the swear words, let alone adult enough to see a horror film. But those self-same laws regard me old enough to suffer the pain of childbirth. I can walk out with my babies but by our stupid laws, I'm too young to be able to buy anything for them on hire purchase. Nor am I of age to be able to vote for their future, even though by law, I can work every hour God sends and pay income tax to the wretched Government that makes these crass laws. Where's the sense in all that? And even if we wanted to get married, I still need my parents' consent. No way would Dad give it, you heard what he said. So what's the point in talking about weddings, Terry? It's just making me more and more unhappy."

He kissed the tips of her fingers gently, a sensation that always made her squirm inside with pleasure, and she believed he could sense it as well. He squeezed her hand tighter.

"It's not like it'll be forever. You'll be back long before

you know it and everything will be all right. At least in the country there are no young fellows about who will steal your heart away from me."

"No, but there'll be plenty of temptation for you whilst I'm gone."

He looked hurt. "How can you say that? You know I love you. You know you're the one for me. I've known lots of girls. Had my chances with plenty, but it's you I care about and want." He pulled her into his arms and gave her a long, lingering kiss.

"I'm gonna miss you like hell," he whispered softly into her hair. "Still, at least we have tomorrow together."

"Me too, Terry. Oh, what are we going to do?"

Chapter Eleven

It was dark when Terry steered the Ford Anglia off the single track lane at the brow of the hill. The car bumped, bounced and weaved along a rutted, muddy track.

Sitting in the back next to her mother, Beth gripped tightly to either side of the driver's seat in front of her, holding on for dear life.

"It can't be much further, can it?" she asked, hoping they wouldn't have to endure the cramped conditions in the car for much longer.

"Almost there," Terry replied cheerily.

"Thank goodness, I need to spend a penny again," said her mother.

It had been a long drive from London. The two stops on the way, to stretch their legs and relieve themselves and fill up with petrol again, weren't nearly enough. She could feel an attack of cramp coming in her calf muscle and needed the loo herself; the shaking and bumping wasn't helping.

Wiping the condensation off the window with her coat sleeve, she peered out into the blackness. It all looked so bleak, so barren and lifeless, as if they had arrived at the end of the world.

Shifting uncomfortably, she twisted to look through the back window, checking that Mike was still there.

Following them all the way, Mike drove an A40 van he had borrowed from a friend in the market. Its headlights danced and dipped through in the darkness as he battled the wheels against the ruts and numerous potholes. She could make out the outline of her father seated next to Mike, keeping him company.

"He's done nothing but moan from the moment we've

left the house," Mike had told her during the last stop. "The road was too bumpy; wasn't there another way we could have come? There was too much traffic about. Couldn't the van go any faster? Didn't the heater work any better? Why did Terry have to be there at all? We could have all squeezed everything into the van, according to old misery guts."

"No way," she'd exclaimed, relieved Dad wasn't in riding in the car with her and Mum. "The van's loaded to the hilt as it is with all our cases and boxes of linen, as well as the groceries and cartons of baby things. The only things we didn't bring are the pram and big cot from the loft. Mum says she won't be needing those until after the baby's here, and we'll be back home by then. Poor you, but at least you only have to tolerate him for today. I've got to listen to him moaning all the time."

According to Terry, there were no convenient shops near the farm in which to buy a newspaper or a packet of soap powder, so for days beforehand she had done extra shopping, stockpiling toiletries and dry groceries.

This had entailed begging from the man behind the counter in David Greggs for several months' supply of sugar and flour, and other bits and pieces, sometimes having to plead with him to take extra ration coupons in payment. He'd asked her on one visit if there was another war on because, if so, no one had told him about it. His sarcastic comment still irritated her, thinking of it now.

In her head, she went through the endless list her mother had written out during the days leading up to this exodus. It had grown longer and longer. Packets of dried peas and haricot beans, yellow lentils for pease pudding, tins of baked beans, tinned ham and bully beef. Blocks of Wrights coal tar soap and washing powder, bottled fruit and tins of Euthymol toothpaste – all the familiar things

Mum thought she might have difficulty finding "out in the sticks", as her parents referred to the West Country.

Had they remembered everything, she wondered, staring at the lights of the bobbing van behind them. Images formed in her head of the boxes inside shaking and rattling and slithering around inside the van.

The car slewed sideways sharply as Terry swerved to avoid a large puddle, throwing her against the door.

"I hope the old man's beer's okay, else he'll be like a bear with a sore head if any get broke," she said, thinking of the things in the van being tossed about.

"Did you pack them like I told you?"

"Yes, Mum. I wrapped all the bottles carefully in towels and stood them upright inside one of the crates." For weeks, Mike had been bringing wooden fruit crates from the market, carrying them precariously on his shoulder as he drove his motorbike home.

The lights from the car lit up a row of cottages looming out of the darkness behind a row of tall, leafless trees.

Not a single light showed at any window. They looked nothing more than run-down, ramshackle hovels and were probably cold and damp inside. Terry finally brought the car to a halt on the verge and switched off the engine. He left the headlights on so they could see what they were doing.

"Yours is the one on the very end," he said, pointing. "The other four are empty. They're normally only used by casual workers who come onto the farm to help during the harvest season. My uncle's thinking about doing them all up to rent out for holidaymakers."

Beth wiped the condensation off the window with her hand and stared out at the dismal buildings.

"Who in their right mind would want to come here for

a holiday?" she muttered.

She felt her mother shudder underneath the tartan blanket stretched across their laps, and wondered if she was feeling just as apprehensive. Had they done the right thing?

The cottage door was unlocked. The tantalizing smell of something good cooking wafted out as Terry pushed it open.

"You all wait here a moment in the doorway whilst I light the lamp," he instructed.

The bright glow from a match flared briefly, then a pale-yellow flame from an old oil lamp on the table flickered on whitewashed walls around the small room. It created just enough light to see by.

"Blimey, it's hot in 'ere," Alfie said, stepping inside, taking off his cap.

To Beth's amazement and relief, instead of smelling dank and musty as she had expected, the cottage felt warm and welcoming.

The heat emanated from an enormous cooker, the likes of which she'd not seen before. On top, a large cooking pot sat, steam escaping from its lid. Her mother lifted the lid and peered cautiously inside, sniffing.

"It's a rabbit stew, with carrots and potatoes and even dumplings."

The table was set for five persons, a loaf of bread placed in the centre. Next to that stood a tall, white jug of milk, and a pie of some sort on an enamel plate. A piece of folded paper was propped against a covered butter dish.

"Looks like my Aunt Edith's thought of everything," Terry praised, picking up the note and passing it to Connie. "Here, it's addressed to you."

Alfie lifted the china lid, smiled at the slab of bright

yellow butter beneath, dipped in his finger then put the finger in his mouth.

"*Alfred!*" Connie admonished.

"Mmm, that's real proper butter, that is. Cor blimey, I was beginnin' to forget what it tastes like."

Beth watched as her mother held the paper nearer the lamp in order to read it.

"It says the beds are made up and aired. There's candles in the top drawer of the dresser by the Aga, and that she and the girls will be over in the morning with fresh eggs and to say hello."

Connie looked up and smiled. "Well, what a lovely welcome. I was dreading this all the way here."

Alfie licked his finger again before giving his wife a gentle squeeze round her waist.

"We can pretends we's on 'oliday, old girl."

Beth shot her brother a look of disdain. Some holiday, she thought miserably, and began removing her gloves and undoing her coat.

"Shall I start dishing up the food, Mum?"

"Nah, we'll unload the van first," her father ordered. "Let's get it over with. I don't wanna be doin' all that humpin' and carryin' on a full stomach."

"'Ere Alf, you sure you loaded that box from the kitchen table, the one from Annie Coombes?" Connie asked. "She'd packed it full of cakes and baking and homemade biscuits. Used up most of her month's rations on us she did, and wouldn't take anything in return, insisting we take it, bless her. She's a good neighbour, that woman. I'm going to miss her popping in for a cuppa and a natter."

"Oh, do stop fussin', woman. Mike put it in the van. We've got enough to survive a bleedin' atomic bomb, the amount you've brung with us. Anyone would think we were gonna be snowed in or goin' to the North Pole, the amount of food we've got. How do you think the people that live round 'ere manage? They do have shops in Gloucestershire, you know."

"Yes, but we don't know when we can get to them. I don't want to be reliant on other people all the time, particularly strangers."

"You won't be strangers, not with my aunt and uncle. They're a right friendly bunch," Terry reassured her.

"Wonder you didn't want the copper and kitchen sink loaded as well," her father continued his gripe. "Why on earth you had to bring all that other stuff with us is beyond me. Terry said there were plenty of sheets and towels and blankets we could use. We didn't have to bring all our own."

Her mother's nose creased in distaste. "Arrgh. You know me, I can't bear the thought of sleeping on someone else's bedding. No offence to your aunt, Terry. I'm sure she keeps everything spotless."

"None taken, Mrs Brixham. I know what you mean."

"I'd still like to know where your George rustled up that bundle of notes for petrol he gave us, Alf."

"That's what families is about, ain't it? If we can't helps our own, who can we? We'd have done the same for any of 'em. Come on, lads. Jump to it. Me tummy thinks me throat's been cut. Soonest done, soonest finished and soonest we can eat."

Both Mike and Terry looked exhausted, but neither complained and obediently followed Alfie back outside into the darkness.

"They could at least have had a cup of tea first," Connie said as she walked around the room, trailing a finger over the shelves on the dresser, inspecting for dust. "Well, it's all nice and clean. I wonder what upstairs is like. Shall we go and see?"

Beth nodded in agreement and went to fetch the candles in the drawer. She lit two, handed one to her mother then, shielding the flame with a hand so it didn't blow out, ventured behind her up the narrow stairs, stooping to avoid the low ceiling.

There were two bedrooms leading off either side of a tiny square, uncarpeted landing. In one, a large cast-iron, double bedstead with a brightly coloured quilt looked exceedingly comfortable after such a long day. In the other, a much smaller room, a single bed was made up which looked equally inviting. Underneath it, Beth spied a china chamberpot and pointed it out to her mother.

"I wonder where the bathroom is."

Connie pulled a face. "Probably isn't one."

Beth groaned. "This is like taking six steps backwards in time. How are we going to manage without having a bath once a week? Worse, how are you going to cope with no convenient lavatory?"

It was going to be dreadful here, she could tell. She wanted to go back home. Now. Perhaps she could make one last ditch attempt to persuade her father to allow her to go back with Mike and Terry. The chances of that were about as much as waking up and finding the whole journey had been one terrible nightmare.

The shouts and calls of the men's voices outside told her it was no dream, this was reality and she had better get used it. There was no going back. Not yet. Not for months.

The meal Terry's aunt had thoughtfully prepared was delicious but eaten in silence. When nothing but crumbs from the blackberry and apple pie remained on the enamel plate, and the pot of tea almost empty, Terry rose from the table.

"It's time we left, Mike."

Her mother grimaced. "I'm not happy about this idea. It's too much driving in one day, especially in winter and in the dark. I won't settle. I'll be worrying all night about you two. You must be tired out. Can't you drive back in the morning? We can always make room."

"Give over, Mum. You know I've got to get the van back in time and report at the barracks by noon tomorrow," said Mike, slipping back into his jacket.

Despite all Alfie's arguments with the authorities, Mike had to do his national service. There was no way out of it unless he had two left feet, was blind or sick, or had some terrible, contagious disease, according to the Adjutant. He'd passed his medical with flying colours, despite trying to walk with a limp like Dad's and faking a cough like Mum's, he'd told Beth afterwards. She still wasn't sure whether her brother had been joking or as serious as the look upon his face at the time. It was, after all, typical of the sort of thing she knew he might do, if only for the prank of trying. Something to boast about later to his mates.

"Yes, and I've got to be in college first thing in the morning. Don't worry, Mrs Brixham. We'll be just fine," Terry added.

"But what if it starts snowing?"

Alfie banged out his pipe on the edge of the table, a trail of ash falling to the flagstone floor.

"It ain't gonna snow, woman. It's too cold for that."

"And since when did you become an expert on weather?" Beth scorned.

He tapped the side of his nose. "Experience, me girl. You'll learn."

Standing by the door to the cottage, Connie cried as she hugged Mike. Beth saw a glistening in her father's eyes as he shook Mike's hand and then pulled him closer and gave him a hug.

"Take care, boy. Don't let the buggers get to you. I knows how it is in the army with you squaddies. Show 'em you won't put up with no messin'."

Mike seemed reluctant to break from this rare show of affection.

"All sorts keep going through my mind about this national service lark, Dad," he said. "Signing up of your own accord is one thing, but being forced into it is something else. It ain't right. I keep wondering what's it going to be like taking orders, polishing boots, and having to say sir all the time, and all that saluting lark. I'm bound to get it wrong."

Beth really felt for her brother, sorry for all the lads forced to do their time in the army.

Dragged away from their homes as boys during the war, and now, even in peacetime, as soon as they were old enough, they were dragged away to be trained to fight in case another Hitler reared his ugly head over Dover. Sent away as boys and so-say coming home as men. Boys who have no choice in being trained in warfare, yet too young to have their say in how the country's run. If the Government says jump, they have to jump. Let's have another war, kill all the boys off as canon fodder and send in the land army with their pitchforks and spades, plough the enemy into the ground. Where was the sense in it? For all they knew, the Government could be plotting at this very minute to send girls into enforced army training. Heaven forbid it might come to that, she thought. She was certainly going to miss Mike about the place.

Alfie slapped Mike across the back. "You'll soon get used to it, son. At least you's is used to gettin' up early, so that bit won't come as a shock. You'll be all right. Just keeps your eye on your fags, and a lock on your Brasso and boot black. Come on, let's get you goin'. Your mother don't look too perky and I'm freezin' me balls off out here."

Mike came over to Beth, ruffled her hair and gave her a tight hug.

"Don't worry, kiddo, you'll be all right. It'll all look so much better in the morning, you'll see, after you've all had a good night's sleep. This place ain't so bad, and I'll be home before you know it."

She doubted if she'd sleep even though she felt tired; like her mother, she'd be worrying all night if he and Terry got back home safely.

"When's your first leave?"

"Not for eight weeks, but once the initial training's over I think we get almost every weekend off, so you'll be seeing a lot of me around here."

"Depends where they send you to, son. You could get billeted up north, or even abroad," Alfie chipped in. "There's no saying where you'll be sent after your training, mind. You could even be sent abroad like our David."

Seeing the sudden horrified look on her mother's face, able to well guess what was going through her mind, Beth felt like kicking her father for making such a thoughtless comment.

"You're not helping, Dad. Do you have to keep reminding us? You know it upsets Mum," she snapped.

"I was only sayin'."

"Yeah, I know you were, but it ain't helping none."

The smile her mother was trying to keep up slipped when she hugged Mike again.

"Don't fret, Mum. I'll be okay," Mike said.

"Come on, Mike," hurried Terry. "Best we get going."

Mike turned to Terry and Beth. "I'll leave you two lovebirds alone to say your goodbyes." With that, he ran to the van, jumped in and started its engine, sending out billowing clouds of exhaust fumes that hung on the cold, damp air.

Slowly, arm-in-arm, footsteps crunching on the mud still frozen despite the countless treks across it the men had made unloading the vehicles, she accompanied Terry down the path to the gate. Each step she took was an effort. Not because of the rutted ground but because each step meant another footstep pulling Terry away.

A faint red glow from inside the van caught her eye as Mike drew on a cigarette. She knew he was watching them through the windscreen.

Trying desperately not to cry, she turned to Terry. "I do wish you could stay. I'm going to miss you so much."

"And I'll miss you, but I have to finish my studies. And you have to stay here and look after your mum. She needs you. It's only for a few months then you'll all be home again. The time will go so quickly, you won't even notice it. And I'll come down and see you. At Easter, perhaps? And then it will be summer. Then before you know it, it'll all be over and you'll be back in your own bed again. Or mine."

She shuddered with pleasure at the idea of spending all night wrapped in his arms, sharing his bed, knowing that time would come eventually.

"You will write to me, won't you? You promised me you would."

Terry laughed and ruffled her hair as Mike had done. It was annoying whenever her brother did it, but Terry's touch was gentler. A gesture of affection, not torment. She liked the feel of his hand on her head and nestled against it.

"I'll write every week. God, I'm gonna miss you." He pulled her into his arms and gave her a long, passionate kiss, holding her tightly as if he never wanted to let her go.

She shook with sadness and longing, never realizing saying goodbye would hurt so much inside. She clung to him, holding him so close she could feel his heart beating through his thick grey overcoat. Eventually, they drew apart.

"Time to go," he whispered.

As he walked to the car, she followed in his footsteps, keeping a tight hold on his hand until that final moment when she had to let go to let him open the car door and climb inside.

"Goodbye, my sweet. Be brave. And don't cry. You promised me you wouldn't cry."

She wiped her wet eyes with her hands, blew him a last kiss then watched, arms wrapped around herself, as first the van and then the car reversed into the gateway of the field opposite and drove off down the lane.

She stood waving as their lights flooded out across the fields like a beacon before they vanished over the brow of the hill. As the sound of the two engines faded, silence fell over Clackett's Farm.

A bright, full moon hung low in the sky, held up, it seemed, by bare skeleton branches of the trees skirting the edge of the furrowed field. It seemed so close, so large, the craters and shadows across its surface clearly visible. She'd never seen it so near, appearing almost as if it were about to collide with Earth.

Across the dark field the frost glistened and sparkled as if someone had shaken glitter about and not knowing what to do with the remainder in the packet, had thrown up the rest into the black field of the heavens.

The sky looked so vast, the stars so much closer. Even during the blackouts of the war, the night-time sky had never seemed this brilliant, this full of twinkling lights from a myriad stars.

But it was the stillness that captivated her the most. In the cold, she shivered, never knowing such complete quietness.

In the far distance beyond the hill, a mass of yellow lights shimmered. Some were moving. That must be Bristol, she reckoned, and wondered if she'd have the opportunity to visit it. She hoped so. Living out here in the middle of nowhere was going to take some getting used to. At least if a town was near she might be able to get out to the cinema once in a while.

"Beth, come on in now, you'll catch your death of cold out there. Come and 'elp your mother to bed." Her father's voice bellowed from the cottage doorway, shattering the silence around her.

"Coming." She turned and ran back inside, her footfalls crunching on the frozen ground.

"I still don't know why that boy's done this," he said as she warmed her hands over the Aga. "I don't trust him."

"Does there have to be a reason, other than the fact that he wanted to help? Gawd Dad, why do you have to be so cynical all the time?"

"Because people in this world don't do nowt without an ulterior motive, that's why. Always 'as to be somethin' in it for them, else why do it? Like I says, I don't trust him."

"Did it ever occur to you Terry's done this out of love for me?"

"Love? Twaddle. You's is both too young to know what love is. 'Ere, I hopes you two ain't be up to nothin' you shouldn't have. He hasn't tried—"

She cut him off. "Oh, for goodness sake, Dad. What do you take me for? Terry's not like that. He respects me."

"He's too flamin' old for you, me girl. Boys of his age are only interested in one thing. I know, I was one meself."

"And you've got a dirty mind." She picked up a lighted candle and shielding its flame, headed for the stairs.

"I'm going to bed. Perhaps by morning you'll see all this for what it is – the only way Mum's going to get through things because you couldn't come up with a better idea. You ought to be grateful to Terry and his family, not putting him down all the time."

Upstairs, Mum was already in bed. As she bent to kiss her goodnight, Beth could see how pale and tired she looked. Her eyes were red and puffed, as if she'd been crying.

"Are you all right, Mum?"

Connie shook her head and pulled a handkerchief from the sleeve of her flannelette nightdress. She sniffed, her cracking voice unable to hide the fact she was on the brink of bursting into floods of tears when she said, "I can't help it. I don't like leaving our house. I know we'll be going back an' all, but when you're poorly or pregnant, you want your own home and things about you. People and places that are familiar."

Getting out of London was a hard decision for her mother to make come the end, and Beth knew she was putting on a brave face, despite voicing her misgivings about the entire thing. It had been an exhausting and traumatic day for her. For everyone.

Beth hugged her mother, giving what little support she could, trying to be strong for both of them.

"Please don't cry, Mum, you'll start me off again. It'll be all right. A good night's sleep and you'll feel much better tomorrow, and then we can go exploring proper in the daylight."

"Oh, I don't know about any exploring, there's everything to unpack and, and... well... everything. It's all so quiet here, and so dark. But at least the beds are clean and aired. And warm. Mrs Clackett's put hot bricks wrapped in a towel in the bed. Isn't she lovely? We'll have to make sure we thank her properly tomorrow. I still wonder if we've done the right thing." Connie sniffed again.

Beth patted her mother's cold hand. "Of course we have. Look at it like Dad says, a holiday. A holiday on a farm in the country. What could be better?" She could think of plenty of things.

Connie laughed. "Some holiday for your father. The lazy so-and-so's gonna have to pull his finger out and do some work for a change. We ain't living here for free so he has to earn our keep. Still, won't do him no harm, will it?"

"I 'eard that," said Alfie coming up the stairs.

Chapter Twelve

In the cold morning light, the cottage and its setting felt far less depressing than it had first appeared under last night's darkness. Dawn had only just broken, the western skyline a deep cobalt blue with a single, straggling star on the horizon waiting until the last moment to go out. To the east, red-hued, high clouds scudded towards the hill when, true to her note, Edith Clackett knocked at the front door.

The elder daughter looked about twenty-five. She held out a small wicker basket of brown hens' eggs.

"Hello, I'm Freda. These were fresh laid this morning, and Sally here's got some milk for you," She nudged the younger girl forward.

Sally stayed half-hid behind her mother, her freckled face and wide, green eyes peering sheepishly around Mrs Clackett's broad hip. The girl looked to be in her early teens but acted more like a frightened six-year-old.

Beth, surprised when Mrs Clackett announced the child was only ten, stepped forward and, smiling, held out her hand for the churn.

"Hello, Sally. Have you brought that for us? Why, thank you."

The child shied away completely, winding herself in Mrs Clackett's voluminous green skirt, obviously hoping no one could see her hiding there.

"You'll have to excuse our Sal, me dears, only she's a bit nervous with strangers. She'll soon get used to you. By the time we goes you won't be able to stop her chattering. Come on, Sal. Hand over the milk to the nice lady. She won't bite."

Mrs Clackett spoke with a funny accent, Beth thought,

the words as rolling as the countryside around them, but at least she could understand what she said as Mrs Clackett's pace was slow and relaxed, as if she had all the time in the world.

Her mother came to the door. "Come in, won't you? I'm Connie Brixham. We can't thank you enough for taking us in like this. And such a lovely welcome last night." She looked towards Beth for confirmation.

"And you must call me Edie," said Mrs Clackett.

Beth beckoned them all in so she could close the door. It was blowing a chilly draft through the cottage with the front door wide open, threatening to overpower the warmth from the Aga that had burnt all night, keeping the cottage cosy.

"It certainly was. It was so nice this morning putting a foot out of bed and finding it wasn't freezing cold, but warm enough to stop the shivering and shakes as I dressed."

What Beth really wanted to tell Mrs Clackett, but refrained because she didn't want to appear ungrateful to this kindly woman, was that she thought the cottage poky, the bed so hard and lumpy that she'd hardly slept. And as for that excuse for a lavatory outside, it was a horror. She'd swear if she had constipation for the rest of her life, it wouldn't bother her one bit. It couldn't be any worse than having to brave the spiders and creepy crawlies she'd seen lurking in there last night.

The lavatory, such as it could be called, was a narrow, wooden shed at the bottom of the garden. Nothing more than a rickety shelter over a bucket sunk into the ground over which straddled a rough, wooden bench with a gaping hole upon which to sit. There was no flush. Just a bucket of sand alongside, a handful to be thrown in each time it was used. Whose job was it to empty the soil bucket when it became full, she'd wanted to know, but didn't like to ask. As long as she wasn't expected to do it, she didn't care, but the thought of how it must smell in the heat of summer, all the flies that must get in there, was enough to make her stomach do a triple somersault.

"You needs to toughen up, girl. You've had it too soft," her father had chided when she'd first complained about it. "Livin' in the countryside will soon sort you out. Be the makin' of you, it will. That lavvy's nothin' compared to the latrines I had to put up with in the war."

But she wasn't in a war, so why should she have to put up with living in the Dark Ages? If only she could find one thing that was good about the place, but for the life of her she couldn't.

Yet her mother appeared to find nothing but praise for the cottage; at this very moment extolling the virtues of the Aga with Mrs Clackett, who stood listening, arms folded across her heaving bosom.

"...it's so good not having to rake out the fire, nor waiting hours for the copper to heat up, or having to boil a kettle so I could have a swill. But you're gonna have to show me how this cooker thingy works. It looks complicated."

Mrs Clackett's grin spread across her chubby face. "All in good time, me dears. But first I have to tell you that Tom, he's me husband, is expecting your husband down in the tractor shed. Says to be there at ten o'clock sharpish. He's plenty of work to keep him occupied. Now, our Freda here wants to have a little chat with you to discuss the bubby."

Sally, who had remained hidden behind her mother's skirt the whole while, suddenly appeared, grinning like a Cheshire cat, all shyness seemingly evaporated.

"What bubby? Where? Show me, I wanna see." She

skipped over to Beth. "Is you havin' a bubby? Ooh, I loves bubbies, I do, don't I, Mum?"

Beth laughed and nodded towards her mother. "No silly, not me. My mum here, she's the one having the baby."

Sally skipped across to where Connie was seated and stared hard at her tummy, her nose pressed so close to her mother's middle Beth could swear the child was trying to smell it. Then Sally turned to her own mother and, pointing to Connie, said, "No she ain't. She ain't got no big belly."

Beth giggled. Mrs Clackett blushed, clearly embarrassed by her daughter's rudeness.

"Come away with you, Sal. Mrs Brixham's not showing yet. It's too early. I'm so sorry, me dears. 'Fraid me young'un gets over-excited with things, especially bubbies, though if truth be told, she's more used to seeing chicks and lambs."

Connie stroked the little girl's tumbling, ginger ringlets. "I am having a baby, Sally, but I've been poorly, which is why your parents have kindly let us come and stay here until I'm better."

There was visible excitement in the girl's wide green eyes. "Will I be able to hold the bubby?"

Connie laughed and put an arm around Sally's waist, pulling her closer. "Of course you'll be able to, once it comes."

Sally wiggled free from her grip and backed away slightly.

Freda took hold of her sister's hand, holding tightly. "We'll have to see about that when the time comes. My sister here's more inclined to squeeze them to death, Mrs Brixham. Hugs things too hard, she does. Doesn't know any better."

Beth hoped Freda was only joking with them, but the young woman's face was serious.

"Oh, don't worry, Mrs Brixham. It's just she hasn't learnt things are fragile. Last time we gave her a chick to hold, she clamped it so tight in her hands to keep it warm, the poor thing died, didn't she, Mum?"

"Hush up, Freda. You're frightening the poor woman. You see, me dears, sorry but... well, my Sal's a wee bit heavy-handed, but she don't mean no harm by it. She's a good girl really."

"I'm sure she is," said Connie, smiling, "and I'm sure we're all going to get along fine."

Edith Clackett nodded in agreement. She seemed a homely, likeable character, thought Beth, most unlike her two daughters.

Freda... well, Freda seemed the complete opposite – starched and straight-faced, a matter-of-fact person. Sally was too young and, well, not to put too fine a point on it, simple minded. Freda appeared more like a maiden aunt in starched petticoats, but at least it looked like her mother had found a friend in Mrs Clackett. That was good.

Freda looked at her watch. "I'm going to have to go soon. Is there somewhere private we can have our little chat, Mrs Brixham?"

"Oh please, call me Connie." She ushered Freda up the stairs. "We'll talk in Beth's room as my Alfie's still in bed, no doubt keeping well away from a house full of women."

When they were gone, at Beth's beckoning Mrs Clackett made herself comfortable at the table. Immediately, Sally climbed on to her mother's lap, stuck her thumb into her mouth, and began sucking noisily.

"Our Freda works in the cottage hospital, over in the

town you can see from here. Not that one in the far distance, that be Brizzel. The town at the foot of the hill, well that's Chippin' Sodbury. Or just Sodbury, as we says around here. That runs into Yate a bit further on. The two places are slowly merging into one the way things are going. Leave that, our Sal."

Mrs Clackett stopped talking a moment to pull the thumb out from Sally's mouth.

"Like I was saying, there's rumours they're going to expand the town," she continued in her West Country drawl, "and build lots of new homes and shops, but I reckon it's all just gossip. The town's small but it's got a cattle market, and there's an aircraft factory nearby that was bombed during the war."

Hope upon hope, Beth offered up a silent prayer. "Does much happen in Yate or Sodbury? Are there nice clothes shops or a cinema to go to?"

"Oh no, me dear, there's nothing like that around here. You'll have to be going into Brizzel for that, but if you likes reading an' all, there's a library comes round once a month. I don't much meself. Don't have time, see, and they do have a dance in the village hall once a month."

Oh dear, thought Beth, this place really was the pits. What were her parents thinking of, dragging her away from London to the depths of no-man's land where nothing happened but a monthly military two-step or the occasional barn dance? With only a backward child and a starchy matron for friends, and a karsie that one good gush of wind and the whole thing would probably roll away down the hill. They must be mad to want to stay here.

Sally fidgeted and wiggled her way down to the floor and headed straight for the stairs, peering up.

"Now where you going to, Sal? That'll do. Come away," Mrs Clackett ordered. The child did as her mother bid.

Looks like young Sal's going to be a bit of a handful too, thought Beth.

With so much to do, the unpacking, filling the few cupboards and the larder with tins and packets, hanging away clothes, finding where everything was kept and a place for everything, the hours rushed by. But every now and then Beth stopped what she was doing and thought of Terry, wondering where he was at that precise moment.

Less than twelve hours since they had said goodbye but already she missed him. Missed the feel of his touch, the warmth of his kisses. Aching for sight of him. How was she ever going to bear this time apart? By keeping busy and not letting it get to her, that's what, she told herself sharply, folding the last of her underwear into a drawer. The time would pass. Best to make the most of it.

When darkness enveloped the cottage, she carried a candle upstairs, and by its flickering light reflecting in the dressing-table mirror, began the next best thing to talking to Terry, by writing him a letter, telling him about her day. Light-hearted in her words, she told how nice they all thought his aunt and uncle and two cousins were, not that she'd met Mr Clackett yet, and how happy they were all going to be here, telling of all the things they had already planned to do and see.

But it was all lies. Lies because she didn't want Terry to feel guilty. She was too grateful to him for arranging all this for her mother, even if it was in the back of beyond. And it was all for her mother's sake, she kept reminding herself.

As she signed the letter with a row of crosses for kisses, she made a decision. For her own sanity, she would greet each new day as being one day nearer to their return to London. Her life and future had been put on hold temporarily, but that's all it was. A detour. Eventually everything would be back to normal when they returned home. The thought reminded her of all she'd left behind. Her home so far away on the other side of the country.

A hundred doubts and a thousand questions seemed to pop into her head all at once. How much would have changed when she returned? Would Terry be waiting for her with outstretched arms? Would Maisie still be running the teashop? And would Mr Chiselhurst really give her her job back?

He'd been so understanding, if disappointed, when she'd handed him her notice last week. He told her she must look him up when she returned, that she would be more than welcome back, as long as she kept up her typing speeds. How she was supposed to do that buried in the middle of nowhere with no typewriter to practice on, she had no idea. Unless Mrs Clackett has one. The sudden hope raised her spirits. She would have to ask her.

The sound of her mother's laughter filtered up the stairs. A good sign. Even if the small cottage might not be perfect, its facilities basic, it was at least warm, she thought as she climbed into bed.

The next morning, she trudged down the mud track that dissected the back garden to the gate at the bottom. The path led to the farmhouse. She was anxious to catch Freda before she left for the hospital. She wanted to give her the letter to post on her way to work.

Apart from the GPO van calling in at the farm every now and again with packages and parcels, the entire farm's mail had to be taken into Sodbury by Freda. Once a week, Freda would call at the post office to collect any letters that had been sent, so Mrs Clackett had told them yesterday. The farm was apparently too far out for the postman to deliver to, and the hill far way too steep for him to cycle up, although it must be great fun to free-wheel down, thought Beth gleefully.

She heaved open the wooden gate and stopped. It was then she noticed the wind. It hit her full in the face like a back-hander. A cold, biting gale that blew full force across the Atlantic, with nothing to stop its flow before it hit Clackett's Farm situated high above the river.

Although it felt cold, the air was crisp and sharp. It was air like she had never known. It smelled clean. Pure. A vitality in the atmosphere that made her face tingle. On her lips she could almost taste the saltiness of the Severn estuary and Bristol Channel stretched out far below in the valley, a silver slither in the distance. She could even smell the earth beneath its frosty covering, smell the bark on the naked trees, sense every scent of nature in its rawest form.

She took a deep breath, drinking it in, filling her lungs. It felt good. Doctor Williams would approve. This was just what her mother needed. What they all needed.

Sally pounced on her the moment she walked into the warm kitchen of the farmhouse.

"Are you come to see our hens? I'll show you." She pulled on Beth's hand.

"Give over, Sal," said Freda, pinning a navy, narrow-brimmed hat on her head. "There's plenty of time for that. I don't expect Beth's had her breakfast yet."

"That's right, Sally. I'll come over later when I've cooked ours and you can show me then."

"Oh goodie. I likes the hens, don't I, Freda? Mum says

I'm ever so good with the hens. I got names for them all."

Freda held out her hand. "Is that for me to post?"

She handed across the white envelope. "Yes please. You won't forget, will you?"

Freda placed the envelope on top of the wicker basket now perched on her arm. "Never have yet. Right. Cheerio for now. I'll be back at four, Mum," she called out and disappeared out the back door.

"Okay, me lover," Mrs Clackett's voice answered from another room.

Beth ruffled Sally's hair. "Tell your mum I'll pop over again later."

Chapter Thirteen

Beth's days fell swiftly into a routine of cleaning and washing and dusting but, being tiny, the cottage didn't take long to tidy. She made her mother stay in bed out of the way of a morning so she could get on with things without being under her watchful eye.

The worst daily job, apart from keeping up with the clothes washing and seemingly impossible task of getting everything dry, was having to scrub down the flagstone floor inside the cottage where mud and filth seemed to be forever trodden in.

Impatiently waiting for Terry's reply, she went about her chores, yearning to hear his voice again, if only in her head as she read his return letter. After a week had slipped by and still no letter from Terry, she was disappointed, but not really surprised.

But when a fortnight was nearing its end and she hadn't heard from him, she couldn't control the niggling seed of doubt growing inside her. Had he forgotten her already? She couldn't believe that. They were engaged, after all. Well, sort of. She'd never actually said "yes". Despite her efforts to keep cheerful, the seed grew into a stiff stem of resentment at being forced to come here. It wound its bitter way through her veins, strangling her heart until she felt weighed down like a full-bloom rose sodden with rain. It made her moody and irritable.

"Why hasn't Terry answered my letter, Mum?"

"Give him time, Beth, we've only just got here."

"But what if he's found someone else? Another waitress at the teashop or someone at college, perhaps?" She turned on the hot tap to fill the washing-up bowl and dissolve the soda crystals she'd sprinkled in before putting in the used plates and cutlery.

Connie handed her another dirty plate left on the table. "Then he isn't worth your worrying over. There's plenty more fish in the sea."

Whilst that observation might be true, she didn't want other fish. She wanted only Terry, or at least confirmation that he hadn't swum off with some other young mermaid. She swirled the water around again, dispersing a thin layer of grease clinging to the edge of the enamel bowl.

"Perhaps Freda's forgot to post my letter?"

"Don't be daft, pet. She wouldn't forget. How could she, with you pestering her every day, running across to the farmhouse as soon as you hear the sound of her little car chugging up the hill? Here, pass me the tea towel and I'll start drying up. I don't like seeing the washing up left to drain on the board."

"It's healthier that way than being wiped on a cloth full of germs. You need a clean one anyway. I saw Dad wipe his hands on it earlier."

Her mother stared at the tea towel then screwed it up into a ball, tossed it into the basket of dirty washing on the floor, and took a clean one from the dresser drawer.

"I don't know, the ideas you picked up at that teashop. That Mrs Pilkington seems to have filled your head with a lot of nonsense?"

All the things that might have gone wrong or prevented Terry from receiving the precious letter raced around in her head. Stupid, irrational thoughts they may be, but something must have happened to her letter else why hadn't he answered?

"Maybe the postman dropped my letter and it's been lost. His van might have caught fire and my letter burned. Or stolen?"

"Perhaps he don't want to write, pet."

Beth turned from the sink. "Oh thanks a bundle, Mum. That's really cheered me up."

Facing up to the fact that the inevitable may have happened was the one explanation she would not accept. The one that said Terry had indeed dumped her, well and truly and in both ways.

Yet, somehow she knew he wouldn't have done that to her. Not like this. Not without letting her know, even if it was by writing to his aunt and asking *her* to do the dirty deed.

The clearing away of lunch complete, Connie settled herself in the only comfortable seat in the cottage, an old leather armchair whose brown fabric was faded and torn, and picked up her knitting.

"I d'narf miss my wireless, Beth. If I'd known we had no electric here, I wouldn't have bothered to bring the wretched thing along."

Beth joined her mother at the table and began flicking through a magazine Freda had brought across that morning. It was full of knitting patterns.

"Mrs Clackett said you could always go across there and listen to hers. Dad said he was going to have a look at that old generator out back when he had time. He reckons he could get it going again.

She looked at the half-finished pink matinee jacket slowly growing row by row, the clack-clack of the needles reminding her immediately of Gran. "Mum, are you sure it's a girl?"

"Positive."

"But how can you tell?"

"After carrying as many as I have, believe me I know."

"But how?"

"By the way it's laying. And I've done the needle test."

Beth was both intrigued and horrified. "You mean you

stuck a needle in your belly? Didn't it hurt?"

Connie laughed. "No, silly. You swings a needle and thread over the bump. If it swings back and forth it's a boy. If it goes round in a circle, it's a girl."

"But that's just an old wives' tale, isn't it?"

"Been right every time with you three kids."

"Blimey," was all Beth could think of to say, and went back to scanning the magazine.

"That Tom's certainly keeping your dad busy. He's trying to straighten out those blades on the furrower today, the ones Tom said he'd knocked out of line by a large stone when he last ploughed the fields. He's even managed to repair that ancient tractor. Alf said it had blown a gasket and had a split con-rod, whatever that is. It's a good job your dad's mechanically minded."

Beth looked up. "Working here certainly has seemed to agree with him, that's for sure. Who'd have thought it?"

Early each morning she would watch him set off for the farm buildings, whistling as he walked along. Even his limp was less pronounced.

"There's a cake mix here, Mum, that comes with everything included in the packet, even little red and green glace cherries to put on. Shall I see if I can get some next time I go shopping with Mrs Clackett?"

"You know Edie's offered to teach you how to bake proper, not out of those packets? Goodness only knows what's in them things."

Beth turned another page. "Oh look, there's a lovely pattern here for a jumper. What a gorgeous shade of red. It's got fancy crocheting around the edges. Look." She turned the picture in *Woman's Weekly* towards her mother.

"Why don't you knit one for yourself? Give yourself something to do instead of moping about here all day."

Beth shook her head. "I haven't got the patience like you or Gran. Holding them needles for hours makes my fingers cramp."

"Read out my horoscope then, let's see what that says."

"Oh Mum, you don't believe in all that mumbo-jumbo, surely?"

There was a light tap on the back door. It was Mrs Clackett coming to join them for an afternoon cup of tea and a natter, a habit she'd fallen into several afternoons a week. Beth was grateful she came visiting regularly as she knew her mother enjoyed the company. The two women would chatter away for hours.

Mrs Clackett always brought Sally along. The child plonked herself down on the cold stone floor, content to play with her dolly. After five minutes she became restless, wandering about the cottage, looking at things. She never touched anything, just peered at it, lost in her own world of what Beth could only imagine.

"Does Sally know how to read?" she asked Mrs Clackett.

"Oh no, me dearie, she don't know how to do *that*."

"Don't they teach her at school?"

"She don't go to school, on account the one in the village can't cope with her. She gets fidgety like, and disturbs the other kids. The nearest other one is too far to get her to, so I teaches her meself when I gets the time. Freda reads a bit to her sometimes, but she can't read, oh no. She don't seem to be able to recognize the letters. She can't even tell the time yet."

"Would you like me to try to see if I can teach her?"

Edie looked at Beth, then to Sally before turning back to Beth and shrugged.

"Well, you could have a go I suppose, me dear. Won't

do no harm, would it? There's a copy of *Alice in Wonderland* at the farm that Freda reads her, it's Sal's favourite."

"Mrs Clackett, I was wondering," Beth began, hesitant. "I haven't heard from Terry since we got here and I was wondering whether you have?"

Edie shook her head. "We haven't heard from him, me dearie, but, then again, that ain't unusual."

"Boys don't like writing letters. Don't you remember how bad our David was at writing home?" her mother added.

Beth pondered on this a while. "I suppose that's true when I think back. You were always going on about it, Mum." She turned to Edie and said, "She used to get really upset when he didn't write. And our Mike's only written once since he's been gone."

Mrs Clackett smiled knowingly. "There you go, see. Or perhaps you sent it to the wrong address?"

Realization of her stupidity dawned. "Of course. Why didn't I think of that? He'd be living at our house now. Fancy me forgetting that. But he could have at least written to me first, not waiting for it to be the other way around."

"You have to give men time, me dearie. Be patient with them. Don't keep chasing or they'll run even faster. I expect Terry'll write when he's good and ready."

"But what if he's had an accident in that car of his, lying at this very minute in some hospital bed with his legs in plaster? What if the coffee machine at work exploded and he's scalded so badly he can't write?"

"We would have heard," said Mrs Clackett. "A letter'll come soon, you wait and see."

That night Beth decided waiting wasn't the best policy.

Against Mrs Clackett's and her mother's advice she wrote Terry another long, chatty letter, telling him how anxious she was to hear from him, just so she could sleep at nights, rest easy knowing he was okay. This time she was mindful of putting the address of their own house in Busch Lane on the envelope, the one she wished she was back in now.

Next morning, walking back across from the farmhouse where she'd left her letter for Freda to post, the heavens opened. By the time she reached the cottage she was drenched through. In the kitchen she stripped out of her soaked clothes. Connie handed her a towel to dry her hair.

"Thanks, Mum. According to the news Mrs Clackett heard on the wireless this morning, the whole of Britain's been battered by strong gales and torrential rain. Apparently there's been a major flood in East Anglia. A surge came down the North Sea and swamped whole villages. Loads of people have been drowned. It's sunk ships and wrecked countless homes. Apparently London's on permanent flood alert."

Her mother looked shocked. "Oh my goodness. Well, at least up here on the hill there's no danger of us being flooded out."

The back door suddenly burst open to reveal Alfie returning from a trip down the garden to the lavvy. He, too, was soaking wet. The two-day-old newspaper he'd been reading in there was folded in half over his head, dripping wet and making a puddle on the floor.

"Bloody rain! It's like a bloomin' quagmire out there."

He crossed to the Aga, leaving dirty footprints in his wake, where he kicked off his muddied boots and leaned them against the Aga to dry.

Beth felt tears well up inside. Suddenly, everything

about this place was depressing. Cut off from a world of vibrancy and life she knew existed back in London, her whole world now revolving around her parents and the farm. She hated it.

"For Christsakes, Dad! I've already washed this floor down once this morning. Now look at it. I'm fed up with mud splattered everywhere. This place really is the pits. All it ever does here is rain. Whatever possessed you to insist I come as well? I'm fed up, I'm lonely and I'm bored. There's absolutely nothing here for me. I want to go home," she yelled.

"Stop your 'ollerin'. You're here because your mother needs you," he reminded. "And don't you start snivellin' just because lover boy's done a vanishing' act on you. Don't expect us to mop up your waterworks. I told you he was no good."

His cutting words along with her frustration made her burst into floods of tears. She ran up to her room and threw herself down onto the bed, sobbing into the feather bolster.

So what if she was being childish? She couldn't help it, she told herself. It was the way she felt. Forced to do as she was told like a child despite being a grown woman. She hated Gloucestershire, hated being away from London. Hated her father and she hated Terry. She hated everyone.

Seated at the dressing table she wrote a letter to Mike, knowing he'd appreciate hearing from her. He'd be disappointed to learn how things had turned out with Terry. He'd understand her unhappiness.

There's no opportunity to meet anyone here, she wrote, telling Mike how much she missed her friends, not that she had many back home. Here there was no-one she could relate to. Even Terry's two cousins hadn't turned out to be the friends she had first hoped for; she had nothing in common with either of them.

Freda was seldom around the farm during the day. Apart from passing each other occasionally as they both went to and fro about the farm, her asking if there were any letters, Freda shaking her head and saying, "Not today" she'd rarely exchanged more than one or two sentences with the young woman. Certainly not someone she could share gossip with or talk about make-up or fashion, music or film stars, Beth added. Even Mum said Freda didn't talk to her much either. Hardly the sort of person to get close to.

She felt sorry for Sally, she told Mike. There wasn't going to be much of a future for her, being so slow, and she would always need Mrs Clackett's constant supervision. What would happen to her when Mrs Clackett's no longer around, was a question she often pondered. Who would look out for Sally then apart from her older sister? What future was there for a young girl here in the middle of nowhere, surrounded by nothing but fields and trees and mocking crows.

If only Gran were still here, she continued. But Gran was gone and she would just have to cope as best she could for the time being, resign herself to the fact that this was her life now, revolving around taking care of Mum and the chores in the cottage.

And it seemed she had to forget Terry; push him away from her mind. He didn't want to know her any more, that much was obvious, she told Mike, so she might as well get on with life in the best way she could. The decision didn't help make things any easier or her heart feel any lighter, but there was little point in dwelling on what might have been, because it was never going to happen now. But if only he would write…

When Mike's letter was securely enveloped and propped against the mirror ready for taking over to Freda in the morning, she made up her mind to write to Terry one final time. She addressed the letter to Maisie's, in the hope he would receive it there. If this goaded no response, then the answer was very clear in her mind – he had indeed ended their relationship and had given up on her.

That thought hurt, the reality too dreadful to contemplate and so hard to bear, and she didn't want to believe it. Buried deep in her heart, she carried the hope she was wrong, for the grip he still held wouldn't loosen no matter how hard she tried to ignore it.

Curled up with Sally nestled against her on the old sofa in the farmhouse kitchen, Beth read aloud from *Alice*.

Sally turned her face to look as Beth and asked, "What's a nobby?"

"It's the top end of a new loaf of bread. What you would call the topper. Why?"

"Oh." Sally sounded disappointed. "Only this morning your dad said I was a nobby short of a loaf when I asked him to say hello to my dolly, too. He wouldn't."

Beth pursed her lips. "Did he indeed?" She pulled the child closer. How was she supposed to explain this in a way Sally would understand? "You probably misheard him, Sal. I expect he was carping on about Mum cutting off the crusty end to make a bit of toast. The end bit's always my Dad's favourite. I expect he was a bit cross."

Sally wriggled free. "I don't think it was that because he had that funny look on his face when he said it."

"What funny look?"

"The one he always has when he looks at me. He don't

look at you or Mum and Dad like it. I don't think he likes me."

"Of course he does. I shouldn't worry about it. Now, what's this letter?"

Determined to draw Sally's attention back to the task in hand, Beth pointed to the capital of the next sentence in the book, thinking *just you wait until I get home, Dad, then I'll give you what for. Whatever were you thinking saying such a thing?*

Sally studied the character above Beth's finger. "That's a... a... a 'T'." There was triumph in her voice.

"Good girl. Now, try reading the whole word."

The child looked at the word for a long time. Finally, she announced with some hesitancy, "The."

"Well done."

Sally grinned widely at the praise, clearly pleased with herself.

Although Sally was making definite progress, the pace was slow and at times Beth found the process painful. It was hard teaching her and often she regretted offering to help, but at least it passed the time doing something more constructive than washing and cleaning. In those hours poring over the white rabbit, she was able to forget Terry for a while.

"Right, Sal. Let's try the next word. What's this letter?"

Return to the cottage, the reading lesson over, Beth heaved off her muddy wellington boots and shrugged off her sodden raincoat. *Bloomin' rain. Everything around here lately is always damp, including me,* she thought glumly, shaking off the worst of the rain. Even the kitchen felt damp thanks to the never-ending pile of wet washing hanging over the line above the Aga. *It's a wonder Dad's not complaining. Funny that,* she thought, *seeing as back home he constantly moaned about wet* washing drying about the house.

She hung up her coat behind the door and turned on her father, sitting at the table chomping on a doorstep sandwich. Mum sat opposite him, drinking tea. Perfect.

"Here, Dad, tell Mum what you said to Sally this morning."

Alfie spluttered crumbs. "Wot you on about, Beth?"

"You know. About saying Sally's a nobby short of a loaf. I didn't know what to say when she told me." She watched her mother's face, wondering what she'd have to say about his carelessly tossed remark.

Mum put down her cup, and glared at him. "Oh Alfie, you never did? You should be ashamed of yourself."

"Well, she is, Con. No good trying to pretend any different. It's all this inbreedin' that goes on in these here out of way places."

"That ain't the point, Alf. Sally can't help it if she's a bit retarded. Trust you to open your fat gob. I don't know what gets into you at times."

"The wretched kid makes me nervous, always hoverin', always askin' questions," he retorted.

"Then you should be used to her by now. It's only because she's curious and interested in what goes on around her. You of all people should know better than saying things like that in front of kids. What's Edie and Tom gonna think?"

"The daft brickbat will probably have forgotten by teatime. Two of 'em wouldn't understand neither. They's is country folk. They knows us from up the smoke says things differently. It ain't gonna do no harm."

Beth shook her head. "You really don't get it, do you Dad? Upset them, and we could be back where we started, and Mum in a worse state than before. Think on that next time you open your mouth."

*

Mrs Clackett stood at the farmhouse door waving a brown envelope in the air, a big smile across her face as she waited for Beth to pick her way over the puddles and mud.

"Looks like your letter's come, me dearie."

At last! Beth held her green beret down tightly on her head and ran the rest of the way down the path. Gleefully, she snatched at the envelope then recognised the laboured writing across its front, part smudged, part obscured by the postmark. Her shoulders sagged.

"Oh. It's only from my brother."

"What a shame. Sorry, I don't mean about it being from your brother." Edie flushed.

"It's all right, I know what you meant." Beth looked up and clicked her tongue. "Oh, Mrs Clackett, what am I going to do about Terry? Why hasn't he written to me? He promised me he would."

Edie patted her on the shoulder. "Don't fret so. He'll write soon enough. I expect he's busy and working every other hour God sends to pay his dues."

Despite Mrs Clackett's attempts in trying to appease, she wasn't persuaded that was the case. In fact, the more she studied Edie's expression, the more convinced she became the woman knew more than she was telling. To her, Mrs Clackett seemed almost afraid to look her in the eyes. Did she know something about Terry but was afraid to say? Beth stared back at her, willing the woman to speak out, imploring her to be truthful.

"If you do know anything about Terry, you would tell me, wouldn't you?"

"Of course I would, me dearie."

She didn't believe her. Terry had let her down, and the pain she felt was harder to bear than if she had been dropped from the top of the tower of Big Ben. She was convinced Mrs Clackett knew something. What was she hiding? After all, she only wanted to be put out of her misery. It wasn't a lot to ask, was it?

Mike swept her into his arms and spun her round and around.

"Put me down, you nutter, I'm feeling dizzy," Beth begged, laughing. "I love the hair cut."

He put her feet to the ground then ruffled her hair. "Great, ain't it? All the rage back in the barracks. So, how's it going, kiddo?"

She kissed his cheek then let him go to greet Mum and Dad standing inside the front gate watching them, Dad with his arm around Mum's blossoming waist.

Connie side-stepped Alfie's arm to let Mike through the gate, before giving her son a hug, holding him close for what to Beth seemed ages. Finally, she loosened her embrace, ruffled what little was left of her son's brown hair where the army had shorn it to almost nothing, then pushed him to arm's length, studying him up and down.

"You've lost weight, son. Are they feeding you properly? Come on inside, there's some pie left from last night. You must be hungry."

Alfie held out his hand in greeting. "All right, me lad? Army lookin' after you okay? When you goin' back?"

Aghast, Connie turned on him. "Alfred, that's not a nice welcome. The poor boy's only just arrived. Sounds like you can't get rid of him quick enough."

"It's all right, Mum," Mike said, laughing, unbuttoning his fatigue jacket. "I know what Dad meant. What he really meant to say was, 'Good to see you, son. How much leave do you have before you have to go rushing off again?' Didn't you, Dad?"

Alfie scratched his backside and followed everyone indoors. "Yeah, course I'm glad to see 'im."

Later, Beth and Mike walked across to the farmhouse so Beth could introduce her brother to the Clacketts. She stopped and caught hold of his arm.

"Mike, I need you to do me a favour? I need you to find out what's happened with Terry. Go round home and check he's all right, please."

"Why? What's happened?"

"Nothing, that's just the point. I haven't heard from him and I'm worried."

"You mean he still hasn't written yet?"

She shook her head.

"But surely he's been to see you, regular like? Like he promised."

"Oh, Mike, he's never been. Mrs Clackett's not heard from him either. I just need to know he's okay."

A cold wind blew over the hillside. Mike pulled his collar up.

"Cor, it's a bit bleedin' bleak around here, isn't it? How do you stand it?"

"You get used to it. It's quite pleasant when the sun's shining. Look, about Terry—"

"Don't worry, kiddo. I'm sure he's just busy. But I will call in. I'll leave earlier than planned tomorrow and go round and see what's going on. Check he's paying the rent like he promised. Are you sure he's moved in?"

"I'm not sure of anything. Speak to Annie Coombes. If he's there, she'll know. Just check it out for me, please. Perhaps you can drop me a line to let me know what's going on. If he's got another girlfriend, well then fair enough. Just as long as I know."

"I can't believe that's the case. That fella was nuts on you. Big farmhouse, ain't it? Right, is me cap on straight?

Are me boots clean enough?"

She looked down at his feet. His shoes were shiny if a little mud splattered.

"You'll do," she laughed, rapping on the door then opening it, ushering Mike inside.

Chapter Fourteen

Clean, fresh air and simple living appeared to work, for Beth could see how much better her mother was just by looking at her. Putting on weight, her belly swelling with each passing week, and even though she still tired easily, there was colour in her mother's cheeks and that old familiar sparkle of life shone in her blue eyes. Beth couldn't even remember the last time she'd heard that dreadful cough.

But the biggest change of all was not in her mother, it was in her father. He showered caring and tenderness upon her mother constantly, kissing her for no apparent reason. A cuddle whenever he came home or giving her a gentle squeeze about her waist. Forever telling her mother how beautiful she looked as he rubbed his hand over her ever-swelling bump.

It was if they lived with a different man. A different father. One who whistled constantly and seemed content. She'd never seen him like this, let alone heard him give compliments to anyone before, least of all to her for her cooking.

"That's meltingly good pastry you've made there, our Beth." This after a mouthful of steak and kidney pie. "The cabbage's cooked to perfection, not all limp and soggy." At her first attempt at a spotted dick, he had commented, "This 'ere suet puddin's as good as your mum's. Got any more custard?" And as for her homebaked bread. "Cut us another slice of bread there, girl. It's got a proper crust on it."

Seemingly endless hours learning how to knead dough properly, finding out the correct mix of shortening to use in pastries, had paid off. Now, her fatless Victoria sponges were equally good as either her mother's or Mrs Clackett's, especially when filled with Edie's sweet jam made from last autumn's wild blackberries or rosehips.

Whilst it might be heaven for Mum and Dad, she thought, peering out the window, the incessant rain dampened any spirit she felt for their temporary home.

The early spring crop sowing on the farm had begun, but the sodden fields were making it difficult for Mr Clackett and her father to get the seeds into the ground, always under threat of being washed away or rotting before they had the chance to germinate. The farm vehicles readily became bogged down in mud, which meant Dad and Mr Clackett had to haul them out with the tractor, which itself often became stuck.

The grand plan for when the weather improved was that her father would give all the cottages a lick of new paint inside and out. There were lots of running repairs also to be done. Broken guttering to be made good, chimney stacks needing re-pointing, as well as fixing all the twisted, rusted hinges on the garden gates.

There was talk of laying down proper paths with flagstones and concrete to the front doors and to the farmhouse, instead of everyone having to pick their way across the muddy ruts for fear of turning an ankle. Always dodging puddles that often were so deep, the water sloshed into hobnail boots and wellingtons. Soaking feet and socks and trouser legs. Almost daily, it seemed, more jobs were added to the list of things to be done. So many in fact, Beth doubted he would have time to complete them all before they moved back home to London.

The back door swung open. Soaking wet and covered from head to foot in red mud, Dad stood in the doorway grinning. Beth frowned, seeing the mess he was in. More washing.

"Whatever have you gone and done now?"

"I lost my footin', didn't I. Me wellie got stuck firmly in the mud in the top field and we parted company. When I tried to heave it out, I fell over. It all happen'd in slow motion, too. Tom was pissin' hisself, he was," he laughed, pulling off his mud-caked socks, nearly falling over again in the process.

Why he thought it was at all funny, heaven only knew, thought Beth. It would take ages to washing all that dirt out.

He began stripping off his clothes down to his string vest and underpants and, rolling the sodden trousers, jacket, socks and pullover into a ball, throwing them to the draining board with a well-practiced shot.

"You've heard of the tar baby, ain't you? Well, just call me the Mudlark," he bellowed heartily on his way upstairs.

Connie and Beth couldn't help but laugh at his silly joke.

"It's good to hear him laughing again," Connie said, after Alfie had put on a clean pair of overalls and an old sweater and disappeared back out again into the driving rain.

"Certainly makes a change from hearing him moaning all the time," Beth said, filling the stone sink with hot water and pouring in the soap powder, adding an extra handful of Omo. She whipped it up into a froth with her hand then gathered up the pile of muddy garments and dropped them into the sudsy water to soak for a while.

"It's because he feels useful again. It wasn't easy for him coming home from the war to a house he didn't know, his mother under his roof and his foot injured to boot."

"But if only he'd found himself a job. I mean, Mum, it

wasn't as if he was that crippled. I never could understand why he never applied for a desk job. One where he didn't have to stand on his feet or do a lot of walking all day. There were plenty of things he could have turned his hand to, the last few months have proved that, but he never made any effort. Yet now, when the pay's abysmal and our surroundings dire, it seems to me he can't get enough work to do. He's always off on some errand for Mr Clackett, full of himself about the next one Tom has lined up for him."

"Beth, you have to understand that what your father needed was time to adjust to normal life again. Time to recuperate. We can only imagine what it was like for our men away fighting. He's never talked about it much. Men don't."

"Gran said it was because he'd given up on life."

"Your grandmother didn't know everything, girl. I know she kept comparing this last war with the one before, but there *was* no comparison. And believe me, she knew even less about the First World War than she'd liked to make out. Gawd, but I miss the old girl."

Beth nodded slowly. She missed Gran too.

"Sally told me the other day that Dad was trying to tell Tom the best way to chit potatoes, and how to tell if a chick's male or female."

Her mother laughed. "That's your father for you – knows it all. It's a wonder Tom didn't clock him one. But it is so good seeing Alfie like this again."

"Again?" Beth lifted the scrubbing board into the sink and began to pound the soaking clothes against it.

"You never knew your father before, when we first met. Oh, but he was a handsome young man. All us girls were after him. He was charming. Courteous. He'd courted me in the old fashion way, you know with flowers and chocolates, even though he couldn't really afford such luxuries on his mechanic's wages. And he was always so kind and polite to my mother. He used to take me dancing. Yes, don't look so surprised. Your father was a marvellous dancer once upon a time. No one could waltz or foxtrot better around the Lyceum, where we used to go."

"But Dad's always had two left feet. There ain't an ounce of rhythm in his body."

This was all news to her. She couldn't imagine him all dressed up and gliding across a ballroom under a glitterball. It wasn't the father she knew.

Her mother's smile was wistful. "Your father has medals for his dancing, I'll have you know. I'll show them to you when we get back home. They're the only ones now he'll ever likely own, poor man. There's a lot of things about your father you don't know or understand, Beth. The war changed him. And with his injury even his dancing days had been wrenched away from him, let alone all his mates he saw killed or injured."

"But he was only an engineer in the army, and a driver. It wasn't as if he actually did any fighting."

Connie looked up from the needle she was trying to thread with white cotton. "No, but he drove the ambulances, ferrying the injured away from the killing fields, helping to dig his friends out of bomb craters and all sorts, and having to help bury many of them, that much I do know. At least here, he's got something worthwhile to get up for."

"I would have thought *we'd* have been enough for him to get up for, Mum, instead of feeling sorry for himself all the time. He hasn't been fair to you. Or us. You shouldn't have to be making excuses for him all the time."

"Let's look forward, pet, not backwards. Things

change. People change. It's a fact of life as much as the certainty of death. Be nice to him. Life's too short and precious to be bickering. He only wants what's best for us all."

"Huh, he should have thought of that before he put you in the club again."

Beth began scrubbing at the collar of the workshirt with a bar of carbolic soap, thinking if only he'd spoken more about the war, perhaps then she might have understood him a little better. "I'll try, but he's only got himself to blame."

"I know he's not the easiest of people to get along with. He can be a cantankerous old bugger at times but, in some ways, you're just as stubborn and headstrong as he is."

Beth plunged the shirt into the soapy water again, swished it around and around before lifting it out of the sink and twisting it in her hands, wringing out the excess water, before starting on the next item.

"Right, all done," she said when the last sock sat on the wooden draining board waiting with the other things to be rinsed.

It wasn't the actual washing bit in foamy, hot water Beth minded so much. In fact, she enjoyed the sensation of the hot water on her hands and fingers instead of them feeling cold and chapped all the time. It was the constant plunging into cold water to rinse and all the wringing out business she hated.

"Not quite, pet. Don't pull the plug, these need doing as well." Her mother pulled at the cotton thread with her teeth, breaking it before throwing the longjohns she'd just finished repairing towards her daughter.

Beth pulled a face as she caught the grubby undergarment and tossed it into the sink of by now cold, scummy water.

"It's no good, Mum, we're going to have to save up and buy one of those fancy washing machines like I saw advertised in the *Sodbury Gazette* last week. One that has two tubs. One to wash in, the other that spins the water out. What a luxury that would be, because I dread the thought of having to help wash dirty nappies as well when the baby comes."

Whilst the change of lifestyle might have been a blessing to her parents in their own individual ways, she loathed living in the country. The alien smells she could never get accustomed to, the emptiness of the fallow fields where the fresh air no longer held that tingle of magic she had felt that very first morning when she'd walked down the garden. She still felt like she was sinking beneath a sea of mud and mire. How she missed the feel of solid pavement slabs under her feet, and the sight of row upon row of brick houses holding up the sky that here seemed to fall in on top of her.

Of all the things she disliked about farming life and the countryside, it was the sense of isolation and loneliness that bothered her most. The feeling she was living a life that wasn't really her own, viewing it as if detached from her own body in a bad dream that wouldn't end. Forever hoping she would wake up and find she was back in her own bed in Busch Lane. She felt trapped at the farm, with no means of escape. A prisoner in the wide open spaces of England. Try as she might, she couldn't help feeling homesick. And still, there was no word from Terry.

By trying to stay busy and keeping occupied, she hoped she would be able to push all thoughts of him away, consigning him to her history. She found it easy not to think of him during the day, but of an evening and at weekends when there was simply nothing for her to do here once the daily chores had been done, her thoughts constantly turned back to him.

As if the days weren't bad enough, darkness brought more horrors. At night, the foxes barking chilled her spine. Strange snortings and snufflings coming from outside from creatures she never saw. Worse were the bats swarming about the farm at twilight. Scary little creatures escaped from some horror movie about to become tangled in her hair, or sink their fangs into her neck as she slept.

In bed, she would wrap her arms about her feather pillow for comfort, sobbing gently into it before falling asleep, waking up red-eyed and tear weary. The knowledge her mother's confinement was getting closer and closer each day helped her cope. Soon they would be going back, she kept telling herself. Soon. Soon. One day less.

One day nearer to going home.

Mike's latest letter couldn't bring any light to the Terry situation. Someone was obviously in the house occasionally, he'd written, as the post had been stacked neatly on the kitchen table. None of it looked important so, he said, so he'd bring it all with him next time he was on leave. Mrs Coombes hasn't seen hide nor hair of him although she had heard movements in the house sometimes. I've checked the bedrooms. Terry's clothes aren't there, so as to where Terry is, I've no idea, Beth read.

Mike told her someone he'd met at the barracks knew of Terry apparently, and hinted that he'd gone away for a while, but didn't know where. All Mike could suggest was that Beth was probably right in her assumption that Terry had indeed finished with her. When he finally caught up with him, he intended giving him a piece of his mind for treating his little sister so cruelly, he had added as a postscript. Beth smiled at that. So like Mike.

His news was disappointing but somehow not unexpected. She tucked the letter away in a box in the dressing table, where she kept all her private, special things – old birthday cards and photographs, her autograph book from schooldays, an old diary, cinema ticket stubs. Her little box of treasures she couldn't bear to leave behind, although why she was hanging on to them, she had no idea.

She could feel a headache coming on so hoped some fresh air might blow away the cobwebs inside her brain.

She hadn't noticed it at first, but now saw that slowly but surely, the tips of the tree branches were beginning to green, reluctant leaf shoots unfolding in the April sunshine.

The muddy fields were blanketed in a short, lush green swathe of new barley shoots and the spindly hedgerows were bursting into life with shiny, swollen mahogany sticky-buds. Some had already erupted into silvery, downy-soft pussy willow and pale yellow catkins, and the sickly-sweet perfume of hawthorn blossom filled the air, bees busy droning from white flowerhead to flowerhead.

She turned off the lane that ran in front of the cottage and headed towards the high bank of trees at the far end of the field that marked the entrance to Clackett's Wood.

She'd seen paintings and pictures of bluebell woods but the swathe of blue now carpeting the woodland floor was a scene she would never forget. It was truly the most awe-inspiring sight she had ever seen. Amazed and beguiled, she stopped in her tracks to gaze at the spectacle.

Gaily, like a child possessed, she danced and skipped through the flowers, inhaling the subtle scents filling the air, before stopping to gather a large bunch of the blue nodding heads to take back home for her mother, where in an empty jam-jar they would brighten up the tea table.

"Well, are you goin' to tell her, or shall I?" Beth heard her father say when she pushed open the back door to the cottage. Her parents were seated at the kitchen table drinking tea. Connie wiped her hands down her apron.

"Come and sit down, pet. Your father and I have something to say. We've come to a decision."

Anxiously, Beth looked from one to the other. What monumentous decision had they reached, she wondered. Had they finally decided to go back home? Now. Not wait until after the baby was born. Her spirits rose. Please let it be so, she inwardly prayed.

Connie pushed a freshly poured cup of tea towards her, saying, "Despite the shortcomings of this little place, we've really become quite attached to it. We've talked it over, and your father…"

Dad coughed. "Look, wot your mother's tryin' to say is that we've decided we likes it 'ere. Who wants to go back to smoky, smoggy London when we can 'ave all of this? Mr Clackett, he's offered me a permanent job on the farm, and I've accepted. We're stayin'. For good."

"You can't be serious?" Beth couldn't believe what she was hearing. But her parents' expressions told that her father had indeed meant every word, that they had every intention of remaining at Clackett's Farm.

This was disastrous. She pushed the chair back and stood, hands holding firmly to the table.

"Well, I'm not staying here. I hate it. There's nothing here for me. No life, no friends. Nothing! At least in

London I had a decent life and a decent job. This place is dead. The pits."

Connie reached out, grasped her hand. "Listen. Once the baby's here and things get back to normal, you'll see things differently. You'll be able to find a job around here, I won't need you to look after me then. Edie says the factory in Yate is always looking out for staff. She's sure you'll get a job in the office there, especially with the experience you've had working for that accountant fella and how well you can type."

"Mum, I only worked for Mr Chiselhurst for three weeks. I'd hardly call that experience. No, I don't want to work in no factory. It's miles away. I want to go home. Anyway, you can't force me to stay here in the back of beyond. I'm seventeen now, I can do as I please."

She looked at the bluebells she still clutched in her hand, drooping like her own crushed hopes. She threw them angrily to the floor.

"I won't stay here. You can't make me."

She heard her father's chair scrape against the flagstone as he pushed his chair back and stood, fists slamming down on the table.

"You'll do as you're ruddy well told, my girl. I'm not havin' you livin' on your own back there. It ain't safe and it ain't right."

She turned to her mother. "*Please*, Mum. Surely you can understand how I feel? I'm not cut out for this country living lark. Crickey, we haven't even got a proper bathroom or toilet in this house. We're worse off than when we lived in Half Acre. And what about Mike? What's he supposed to do when he leaves the army? Have you considered him?"

"The boy can make his own mind up. Tom says there's work here for him if he wants it. Or he can go where he pleases. It's up to him what he wants to do."

"But that's not fair, Dad. I'm—"

"Life's not fair, missy," he cut her off. "Mike's a man. He makes his own choices now. You're still far too young to be left doin' as you please. Likes I say, it ain't safe in London for you on your own."

Knowing there was little point in arguing with her father when he was in this mood, she shook her head in utter despair and disbelief.

It wasn't supposed to turn out like this. They were all supposed to be going back home when the baby came. That was the plan. They couldn't just change their minds like this, not without consulting her and Mike. She straightened up, head held high as she made up her mind.

There was only one thing for it. She would just have to go back to London under her own steam, whether her parents liked it or not. Run away if necessary. They couldn't make her stay. She had to escape from never-never land, the place where things never-never happened. Somehow she would think of a plan.

"You'll get used to it, you'll see, pet. It's for the best," her mother appeased. "I don't want my baby growing up in fog that can kill you, and all that dust and dirt back home. There's a whole world here full of fresh, clean air and fields to run and play in and explore. What more could any mother want for her child?"

"But what about your other children, Mum? What about me? I don't need fields to go skipping in and fresh air to bring colour to my cheeks. I'm entitled to my own life. I'm not a child any more."

Alfie thumped the table. "Then stop acting like a spoilt one. We've decided and that's that."

Not to return to London was too awful a thought to contemplate. Going back home was the only reason that had given her strength to cope with everything during this enforced evacuation. Perhaps after the baby was born her mother would be able to see she could cope without need for her to stay. She'd only be in the way.

If she just kept on at them, nibbling away around the edges, maybe she could eventually convince them she was a grown woman who wanted her independence. Give them enough time, she thought, and maybe they would come to understand how life in the country wasn't for her. She was a town girl.

If only her brother were here. He would know how to persuade them to change their minds, but Mike's visits had become less and less over the past few months. He seemed to prefer to spend his weekend leaves with his mates and his girlfriend, Janet. Always making excuses not to come. She couldn't blame him.

Chapter Fifteen

May turned into flaming June and summer had arrived with unseasonally high temperatures, the sun beating relentlessly down from dawn to dusk. Rooks argued in the treetops of Clackett's Wood, swarms of starlings swooped low over the barley field before descending *on masse* to the ground to peck and root through the swaying green crop.

Looking up into the clear blue sky, Beth watched a flock of swifts, their incessant calling filling the air, swirling and weaving in a graceful, orchestrated flight overhead as they fed on millions of insects rising from the ground.

But she would have been happier listening to the sound of sparrows twittering from the plane trees along Busch Lane, the rattling of the milk float in the early hours, the call of the rag-and-bone man, or the steady trundle and tooting of traffic. Sputtering lorries backfiring. Normal sounds. London sounds.

Her parents had let her down by wanting to stay here but, then again, she thought, reaching up to pull the remaining wooden clothes peg off the other corner of her father's flannel shirt on the washing line, even she had to agree that on days like today, when the sun was shining and the birds were singing their hearts out, the Gloucestershire countryside was certainly a nice place to be in. But not permanently.

Slowly, a distant rumble invaded her hearing, the brrrr-brrrr-brrrr of an engine labouring up the steep hill. As the sound came nearer, she recognised the noise. There was only one thing that could make that sound. Mike's motorbike.

She dropped the shirt into the laundry basket, picked it up hurriedly and dashed back through the house to the front garden, calling, "Mike's coming, Mum. Mike's here," as she went.

Her brother pulled the bike to a halt outside the gate, eased the Bantam over onto its stand, pulled off his gloves, and ran towards her, arms outstretched.

"Hiya, kiddo!"

"Mike, what a lovely surprise! What are you doing home? We weren't expecting you."

"I've got a short leave before they sends us to some camp out on Salisbury Plain, so I thought I'd come and see my favourite sister. And Mum and Dad, of course," he said, smiling at his parents who'd come out to greet him. "Thought I'd surprise you all."

"Glad you got that old bike going again, son. We was ever so disappointed when you couldn't make it last time. Your mum was really lookin' forward to it. Got herself worked up in a right tizz when you never showed up. Didn't you, old girl?" Alfie gave Connie's waist a gentle squeeze.

"Yeah, I know. Flippin' chain broke and buggered up the crankcase. I had to persuade the engineers back in the barracks to fix it for me. Cost me a month's fag ration an' all, it did."

Dad opened the gate wider to let Mike through. "Never mind, son, you's is here now."

Upon hearing there was an extra, unexpected mouth to feed, Mrs Clackett had sent Sally across with a freshly plucked and drawn chicken and with a large bowl of the first of the season's crop of garden peas. Grateful and looking forward to their meal, Beth was seated crossed-legged on the back doorstep, enjoying the warm sunshine as she shelled the peas.

"I'll just finish these then I'll make us some lemonade, Mum. You look as hot as me," she said, suddenly feeling thirsty.

Connie, seated on a stool by the back door, preparing freshly-dug new potatoes, able to wipe off the thin, papery skins with her fingers before dropping the white potato into the saucepan of cold water at her feet, wiped her brow with the back of her hand.

"Phew, I am a bit. I'm getting very uncomfortable carrying junior about in this heat. It don't help having no thin clothes to wear, especially me knickers, they're getting too tight and are cutting in. I'd have gone without but I don't trust that wind around here. It catches you out, and I wouldn't want to be caught with no drawers on in my condition." She laughed.

Beth did too. "Not a pretty sight, I have to admit. Honestly, Mum, I swear all this fresh air is blowing away your sensibilities. Still, not wearing knickers in this warmth is rather tempting. We'll give it a go one day when the old man's out the way. Wouldn't want to embarrass him, would we?"

"That'll be the day. There ain't much your dad hasn't seen that would make him blush. You lose all your inhibitions in the army and the war. We should have brought some summer dresses with us. But then, we weren't expecting it to get as warm as this. The Queen's going to be scorching in all that regalia she has to wear for her Coronation. Pity we won't be there to see it."

"Knowing our weather, it'll probably rain. Least we'll be able to hear it over on Mrs Clackett's wireless. And to think, only a few weeks ago we were all huddled up in double layers of cardigans and jumpers." Beth scrambled to her feet, brushing down the back of her skirt. "Perhaps we can persuade Freda to drive us down into the town so as we can buy you some decent underwear. She says there's a good haberdashers there that sells them. Mrs Clackett always buys her stuff there."

"I'm glad you're getting used to the idea of staying here, pet. Can you imagine peeling spuds like this back home? We'd have been coughing up petrol fumes all day long. I swear that road was getting busier and busier, what with more people having cars nowadays. The washing always had smuts on it, no matter how careful I was about checking which way the wind was blowing before I hung it out. And look at all these lovely vegetables. Picked in the morning and on your plate by dinner time. You couldn't get them any fresher. Your dad says he's going to have a go at growing his own next year. Could you ever imagine him lifting a spade back home? He couldn't even handle a cake fork, let alone a gardening one. Or a hoe."

She could well understand why her parents didn't want to move back to their old way of life in London. There was no mistaking the changes the move had brought about in her father, and country living had certainly done her mother the power of good, Beth thought with a smile. Good old Doctor Williams had been right. She looked so much younger too. And happier. If it weren't for the shortness of breath Mum always seemed to have, she'd swear her mum was a thousand-fold better. Cured.

Her mother's innocuous comment about summer clothes and the impending Coronation planted a seed of an idea in her brain, one that grew stronger by the second. Suddenly, there was a way out for her after all. A way back to London.

She stooped and kissed the top of Connie's head, as she squeezed between the stool and the back door.

"Would you rather a bottle of Mackeson instead of lemonade?" she asked.

"No thanks, not now, pet. I'll have a Mackie tonight, when we have a drink with Mike after tea. He's going down to the village later when the pub opens, to get some more beer in. I just hope he'll be okay driving back up that hill. I don't like the idea of him riding that motorbike carrying glass bottles. It's a pity he has to go back tomorrow, though. A forty-eight hour pass just isn't long enough."

No, thought Beth, but long enough for her to persuade her brother to take her back to London with him. She crossed her fingers and hoped he would agree to her plan.

"Never mind, Mum, there'll be other passes. He'll be back before we know it."

Later that afternoon, Beth and Mike were seated on the back doorstep, a half-drunk, brown bottle of ale in his hand, a glass of shandy in hers. Dad was down at the bottom of the garden in the thunderbox, their mother upstairs taking a rest on the bed. She watched her brother take a long swig of beer from the bottle before saying what was on her mind.

"Mike, you've just got to help me. You've got to make them see sense. I can't stay here, not forever. It's awful. And I'm so lonely."

"But what about Mum if you go? She needs you here. I mean, she still isn't well. We don't know how she's going to be after the sprog's born. She might—"

"Mike, she's bags better. You've only got to look at her to see that. Anyway, Mrs Clackett's here, and Freda, to keep an eye on her, so it's not like she'd have no other women about. She won't need me. Then there's Sal. She's a bit backwards but she reckons she loves babies, and I'm sure she'll be more than enough help for Mum. Probably better than I would be, if truth be known. Don't you see? It's different for them. Mum and Dad have the Clacketts for company, and Dad's a changed man in a lot of ways. Have you noticed he doesn't even limp now? But me, well, I've got nothing. No one. Apart from which, I don't want to end up as a glorified babysitter for the rest of my life, because that's what I would be, at Mum and Dad's beck and call for goodness knows how long. I'd be the one who has to take the baby for a stroll in the pram, the unpaid mother's help. The child's nanny."

Mike hesitated. "I don't know. She'd be awfully upset if you're not here. You know how Mum worries about us. Imagine what she'd be like if you're up in London. She'd be beside herself fussing about you."

"She'd have to get used to it sometime. What if I was married? I'd be away from home then, wouldn't I? They can't keep me here forever, so what's the difference whether it's now or later?"

"That isn't the same. If you were married you'd have a fella looking out for you. She'd know you'd be okay then. This is different, and even I don't like the idea of you on your own. Even I'd be wondering all the time if you're all right."

"Please, Mike," she pleaded, begging him with her eyes to understand. "I'll go as doolally as Sally if I have to stay here much longer."

He shrugged, shaking his head and then reached across and ruffled her hair.

"I dunno, kiddo, what we gonna do with you? I know you're all grown up and that but the old man doesn't see it that way. To him you're his baby. You're a girl, and to dads girls is special. Different."

"If I have to wait until I'm twenty one, when I become of age and they can't stop me, I'll simply die here if I stay much longer. It isn't fair, Mike. They can't force me to stay."

"I don't like it none but I can see your point of view. Even I'd be stifled livin' out in the sticks like this. But I think they can make you." He fell silent, his gaze falling across the stretch of grass that passed for a lawn.

"Then listen to me. Help me get away. I've an idea that might work, but I need your help."

She told him what she had in mind and watched him mull it over in his head.

He took another swig of beer. "I don't know, Beth. It sounds good but surely there's another way we could persuade them?"

"There isn't. Believe me, I've tried."

The wooden door on the thunderbox opened and Dad stepped out, pulling up the flies on his trousers. They watched him as he walked slowly back up the garden flicking away a wasp bothering him.

"He does walk better, doesn't he?" Mike said quietly. "Makes you begin to wonder how much he was putting on all that limping lark." He turned to her and keeping his voice low, said, "All right, I'll try and help you, but you know Dad. Once he's made up his mind, there ain't no way you or me or Uncle Tom Cobbley's gonna change it."

Alfie approached. "What's you two whisperin' about? 'Ere, Mike, I hopes you left some of that beer for me?"

"There's plenty in the pantry, Dad. We're just enjoying a drink and admiring the view."

Mike pushed his empty plate away, a look of satisfaction upon his face.

"That, Mum, was the best meal I've had in ages. Better than all that muck they feeds us in the camp sometimes."

"Told you they weren't feeding you properly. There's some potatoes left if you want more, and meat on the chicken if you want to pick on it. I've saved you the parson's nose."

Mike rubbed his belly. "No thanks. But, cor, what a treat that chicken was. No, I'm saving room for that there apple tart Beth's getting out of the oven."

Alfie winked. "Yeah, I'll give our Beth her due, she's turnin' into a good little cook. But then again, she has a good teacher. She's settled down now she's got that Terry bloke out of her head. He was too old for her anyways, apart from all that mess he'd gone and—".

"Ssshhh." Her mother flapped at him to be quiet.

Beth wondered what he had been about to say and slammed the hot enamel pie plate down on the table. "And don't talk about me as though I'm not here; it's not nice."

"I was only sayin'. Gawd, girl, you're turnin' into a right old nag before your time."

"Is it surprising when I've only you two old 'uns for company?"

"There'll be other fellas, kiddo. Once you get a job down in that factory you'll meet hundreds of fellas. You'll be fighting them off at the door," said Mike.

She gave her brother a sarcastic smile before handing him the cream. Mike poked his tongue out to her as she sat down, his signal to her to bring up the little subject matter he had earlier reluctantly agreed to go along with.

With one hand behind her back, fingers crossed, all the while looking at Mike opposite for moral support, she took a deep breath.

"Mum, you know what you were saying earlier about

us bringing no summer clothes with us? Well…, I've been thinking. It would be daft to waste what little money we have on buying new stuff when back home we both have a wardrobe full."

"What's back there wouldn't fit me, pet. I'm too fat with this here bulge at the moment. But I'm going to have to do something, even if I just buy a few yards of material and make us some."

Beth shuffled nervously on her chair and looked at Mike again. His eyes widened, willing her on as he nodded slightly.

"Yeah, but I'm not, Mum. I can still fit into all my summer things. So I was thinking… what if I go back with Mike when he leaves tomorrow, and fetch them back here? And whilst I'm there, I could stay and see the Coronation."

"And how do you suppose you's is gonna get back here?" Dad demanded, spraying pastry crumbs across the table as he spoke.

Their father may have improved in some ways, thought Beth, but his table manners still left a lot to be desired.

"The boy's gotta get back to camp on time or he'll be in the glass'ouse. He can't go swannin' off for a couple of extra days just so as he can lug you and a suitcase back 'ere now, can he? Bloody stupid idea, girl."

Mike came to her defence. "But she could get the train back from Paddington. And Freda's already agreed to collect her from the railway station in Bristol."

Alfie put down his spoon. "I see. Looks like you two 'ave this all worked out. So how's she gonna pay for the ticket? She ain't got no money. And I certainly don't 'ave enough in me wallet, especially as seein' you talked me into buyin' the booze today." He tapped his half-drunk glass of beer with his finger before picking up the glass and gulping down several large mouthfuls.

"*I'll* pay for her ticket," said Connie suddenly. "I've a few quid put by. The train can't cost that much. No, the girl's right, Alf. It is cheaper than paying out for two lots of new clothes when they ain't needed. Can't say as I agree to the whole idea, mind, but what the heck. The girl deserves a break from all she does here. I can't see no harm in it."

Dad shook his head resolutely. "I can, and I tells you, I ain't havin' it. No. Surely Freda or Edie's got somethin' the two of you can borrow for the time bein'? The whole idea is bloody daft. Never heard of such malarkey."

All Beth's jubilation plummeted as she watched him pick up his spoon again, pushed the last slither of tart onto it and put it into his mouth. As he chewed, far more than was necessary on such a small morsel of pudding, she thought, he made a big play of placing his spoon back down on his empty plate. Precisioning it at six o'clock exactly across its face. It was a game he liked to play when major decisions needed to be made, to show he was deep in thought, concentrating on his answer, when in fact they all knew that's just what it was – a game. Keeping them on tenterhooks to show them who was still boss.

Finally, he looked up at her. "All right then. Perhaps your mother's right, but you'd better be careful, me girl. And don't go speakin' to any strange men while you're up there. It's gonna be bleedin' chaos in London, wot with the Coronation an' all. And I suppose you can see if there's any post for us, though Mrs Coombes has been sendin' everythin' on. You can fetches me back one or two things as well, all me shirts and that. We'll have to go back ourselves at some point, to sort the house out and things if we's is stayin' 'ere. And I suppose it would mean there'll be less to cart back when we clear the house out."

Beth ran round the table and hugged him, planting a huge kiss on his stubbly cheek.

"Thanks, Pops. I'll be careful."

Nice one Mike, she Beth, looking at him, smiling her thanks.

The only problem now was that she had to think of a way to sneak her case out with all her things from the cottage without her parents seeing or suspecting what she was really up to.

Dawn had only just broken fully, in the west the pale blue sky was streaked with high bands of wispy clouds.

Where the top barley field dipped over the brow of the hill, out of site from the farmhouse and cottages, Beth stashed her battered old suitcase into the hedgerow, ready for her and Mike to collect as they went by later on the motorbike. She'd been so engrossed in what she was doing, she hadn't noticed Sally coming along the lane.

"What's you doo-in'?"

The child's voice made her startle. "Sal! What are you doing up and about so early? You should still be asleep like the rest."

Beth tried to hide the offending case, pulling the withered grass and dried leaves hurriedly around it so no one else would accidentally spot it, not that anyone was likely to come by this way.

Sally tried to peer over Beth's shoulder to get a better view. "What's you got there? May I see?"

"No. It's a secret."

"Ooo, I like secrets, I do."

Beth's mind raced, frantically searching for a response to the girl's inquisitiveness. "Ah, but I bet you don't know how to keep a secret."

187

Sally nodded rapidly, her tangled, uncombed hair bobbing up and down. She wasn't properly dressed either, Beth noted as Sally squatted on her haunches next to her. The child had on odd shoes, the buckles undone, and her food-stained red dress, which she had worn for the past three days, was unzipped at the back.

"Course I do," said Sally, indignantly. She crossed herself over her chest and grinned innocently. "See. I won't ever tell. Never, never, ever. Why? Is it a surprise?"

"It certainly is, Sal. It most certainly is."

"What, for your mum? Is it her birthday present? What's you got her? Is it nice? You can show me. I won't tell."

But she couldn't show Sally what was in the suitcase. Not all her underwear, the several pairs of precious stockings she hadn't had the chance to wear since coming to this god-awful place. Nor her hairbrushes and toothbrush, or the rose-scented bathcubes still in their pink-coloured box; a Christmas present from Mike she hadn't been able to use yet.

She was so looking forward to having a bath tonight, even if she would have to wait ages for the copper to heat up enough water. Whatever had gotten into her mother, wanting to stay here living in the dark ages with no bath, no inside toilet and no neighbours, apart from the Clacketts? No shops nearby. No nothing. She must have been mad!

If the child saw those things inside the case, she knew Sally wouldn't be able to help blabbing to Mrs Clackett the first moment she was able to. She would undoubtedly skip across to the cottage with the breakfast eggs and let slip what she had allegedly bought for her mother's birthday, which wasn't until September anyway. If her parents caught wind of what she was about to do, she knew her life wouldn't be worth living. They would put a stop to it with more than a slanging match and a heavy foot down.

"My surprise is already wrapped up, so I can't show you. I would have to tear the wrapping paper off and I haven't got any more."

Sally shrugged. "Well, can I just see the paper then? Just a little peek. I won't touch it, I promises. I likes pretty paper, I do. Has it got flowers on it?"

Exasperated by all her questions, Beth stood, reached out and pulled Sally up from her crouched position.

"No, Sal, it hasn't got flowers on. It's plain. Plain red, like the dress you're wearing. Come on, let me take you back to the farmhouse else your mum will be wondering where you are."

Sally gripped Beth's hand tightly, making her wince. The strength of the girl always amazed her. She'd heard it said before that what a person lacked in one department, they made up for in another, like the deaf rarely needing to wear glasses, or the blind having extra-sensitive hearing. In Sally's case, what she didn't have up top, she more than made up for in brute force.

"Oh, it's all right. Me mum's used to me getting up early. I always wakes up before she and Daddy does. I even gets my own breakfast."

Beth doubted that was true, knowing Mrs Clackett always cooked a full and hearty breakfast for her family before Mr Clackett and Freda went off to work, Freda in one direction down the hill, Tom in the other towards the worksheds.

She pulled the child round suddenly then squatted down to look at Sally directly, at her level.

"Look Sal, I've something to tell you, but you must promise me not to breathe one word. I'm going away for a little while and whilst I'm gone, I want you to look after my mum for me. Do you think you could do that?"

Sally squinted, her brow furrowed as she contemplated this. "Will you be coming back?"

"Of course, but I need you to pop in every day and see that my mum's okay, that she's not needing anything. You know she's been very ill, that's why we came here, but I need you to keep an eye out for her, and if you think anything, the slightest little thing, is wrong with my mum, you must rush over and get your mum or Freda straightaway."

"I can do that, Beth. I'm good at running, I am. But *why* are you going away? Where are you going?"

"I'm going to London to visit the Queen." Which was true, she thought lightheartedly, but she didn't dare risk telling Sally she wasn't coming back.

"Does you really know the Queen?"

Under Sally's questioning gaze, Beth told her, "No, of course I don't. Actually, there's something I have to do in London. In secret. Now, promise me you won't tell anyone what I've told you, especially about the present. Promise me?"

Sally grinned, a wide, gappy smile where some of her teeth were missing. "I promises, Beth. Crosses me heart and hopes to die if I should ever tell or lie. Is the Queen pretty?"

She laughed and hugged Sally, and wondered whether the child had really understood anything at all she had said to her. She doubted it. In a funny way, she was going to miss her little friend.

"Come on then, let's get you back home. I can smell the bacon frying from here."

"Race you," said Sally, pulling away and running off in her ungainly gait.

Chapter Sixteen

Mike reached inside the letterbox, pulled up the string on which was tied the front door key, and then let them both into the house.

"Hello. Is anyone here?" he called out.

Following him inside, quite what she would have done if someone had answered, Beth didn't know, but deep down, she hoped Terry was there. She pulled off the scarf tied around her head and ran a hand through her tousled hair. It might not have looked very attractive, but the scarf had helped to keep the wind out of her ears.

"I'll put the kettle on. Gawd, my legs are stiff sitting on that bike for so long, they feel all shaky. Don't yours, Mike?"

"Nah, you gets used to it. Don't worry about tea for me, kiddo. I've got to be on me way. I'm meetin' a few of the lads at The Bell in Hounslow for a couple of jars before we go back to the barracks, and it's half-one already." He put her suitcase down on the hall floor and made a dash for the bathroom. "It's a pee I need."

She was crestfallen. She had hoped he would stay for the rest of the afternoon because now she was actually here, she didn't want to be left on her own. Not straightaway.

But boy, it did feel good to have escaped, and having imagined it would feel strange and cold back here, surprisingly the house had maintained its lived-in feeling. A warm, comforting atmosphere that immediately enveloped her in its familiarity. It was great to be back.

She heard the cistern flush then the tap run. Moments later Mike re-emerged from the lavatory, pulling up his zipper.

"Right, I'd best be on me way. Now, are you sure about all this? You do know there'll be hell to pay for us both when they realize what you've done? Don't forget to drop Mum a line. Let her know what's happ'nin'."

"Don't worry. I know what we did was wrong, sneaking away like this, but you saw what it was like there."

"Well, don't say I didn't warn you. Now, I'd best be off. Come here, sis, and give your big brother a hug. I don't get many of 'em in the barracks."

"I should hope not," she laughed. Signs of affection were scarce in the Brixham house but there was no hesitation in cuddling him tightly now. "Is it really awful in the army?"

"No worse than expected. Some of the sergeants are bastards but us lads have a good crack. Just hope we don't get sent to war. Not like our poor Dave; he copped a rum 'un there."

She hugged him a little tighter at the mention of their brother.

"You know something, Mike? All the while we've been buried in that wretched farm, Mum and Dad haven't once spoken about him. I can't understand them. I wanted to talk about him. Tell them how much I miss him, and yet they wouldn't even mention his name. It's as though he never existed."

Mike stroked her hair. "It's just their way of coping, kiddo. Old folks like them think differently to us. Me, I talk about him all the time to me mates. Probably bore the pants off 'em. I miss him terribly at times, and thankful myself they don't send me off to fight in some rotten foreign bloody country nobody's ever heard of. Mum's probably blocked him out because she's got the little one to worry about now, as well as me. As for Dad, well, who knows what he's thinking half the time. But you know the old man, buries his head in the sand and bottles it all up. Never shows emotion, but I bet he hurts too. Don't be harsh on them, Beth. They hurt and grieve for David just as much as we do, if not more, I expect. It's just they do it differently, that's all. Mum's been through a tough time, what with Gran an' all. I expects she opens up to that Mrs Clackett when you're not around. Now, I really must be off. I'm gonna have to push it as it is or I won't have time for a pint before closing. Look after yourself now. And don't forget, if it all gets too much, catch the train back like we said. Mum and Dad will get over it soon enough."

"I do hope you're right."

She watched as he started up the motorbike again, thinking how smart he looked in his khaki uniform, his cap always tilted at that jaunty angle. Mike turned and waved before disappearing around the corner. He was lucky, she thought jealously. He had plenty of friends in the army. She only had him and now he was gone again, leaving her all alone.

She closed the door and leant against it, unprepared for the wave of guilt that swept suddenly over her, followed by a sense of impeding doom. How could she run off and leave her mother at a time like this? What had she done?

Trying to shake off the feeling, knowing coming home was the best thing for her even though for selfish reasons, she ran the cold tap at the kitchen sink for a few moments before filling up the kettle; she didn't want rust and dust to make her tea with. As she fiddled with a match to light the gas stove, she thought she heard movement upstairs.

Standing at the bottom of the stairwell, she called up.

"Terry? Terry, are you up there?"

No answer came. Convinced she'd heard something, she ran up the stairs and burst into her bedroom.

Inside, it looked so bare, so unlived in with both beds stripped of sheets and blankets. At the window, she pulled back the curtains, noticing the patch where the sun had faded the pretty, flowered pattern. She pulled aside the greying net curtain and flung open the window wide to let in some fresh air, gazing out at the familiar view of the street below. At the road with cars and lorries rumbling by. At the red brick façades of the houses opposite, dirty from all the smoke and grime, each house a copy of its neighbour. At the dark-green lampposts standing tall like sentinels along the pavement. Oh, how she'd missed all this, she thought, glad to be back in all that was familiar.

Seeing the old gentleman who lived several doors down riding past on his bicycle, she waved from the window and called out.

"Ooo-oooh, Mr Rogers. How are you?"

He looked up and waved back, the bicycle wobbling under his single-handed grip.

Across from the house, she could see a man up a ladder at one lamppost, tying up bunting. She watched as he climbed carefully down, holding the bundle of red, white and blue under one arm as he crossed the road. He then fetched the ladder across and positioned it against the lamppost just outside their front gate, and climbed up. As he reached the top, he noticed her watching him, and waved out. Recognizing Mr Allison from number twenty-six, she felt frightened for him, afraid in case he lost his grip and fell.

Another man approached. "'Ere mate, want me to 'old your ladder?"

"Cheers, mate. If you could," Mr Allison called down. "'Ere, catch this bundle of buntin'. Your kids joinin' in the street party?"

"You try and stop 'em. It's drivin' me nuts in the house with 'em chasin' around gettin' all excited. We can't move in the kitchen what wiv our Elsie makin' jellies like they was goin' outta fashion."

"Knows what you mean, mate. Mine's just the same. Says she can't cook today as she's got 'undreds of bloomin' sandwiches to make. House stinks of farts with all the eggs she's been boiling." He climbed down to the pavement. "Still, good excuse for a drink, ain't it? She can't moan at me drinkin' all day to the Queen, can she?"

"Too right. We has to drink to her good 'ealth, don't we?" The men laughed as they crossed to the other side of the road again.

Beth turned at the sound of scraping that seemed to emanate from her parent's bedroom and went to investigate. Tentatively, she pushed open the door.

"Terry? Are you in here?"

"Oh shit," a female voice mumbled.

Beth recognised the voice. "Janet! What the hell…?"

With the covers pulled coyly up to her chin, Janet's embarrassed face stared towards the door. Her hair was dishevelled. And she wasn't alone. Underneath the blankets Beth could tell someone was very definitely hiding. She stormed into the room.

"Get out of there. How dare you? And how could you, Te—"

She yanked the covers out of Janet's hand, pulling them back, expecting the other form to be that of the elusive Terry, but the naked body and shocked face looking up at her belonged to a young lad with a spotty face, his black hair sticking up in rumpled spikes.

"You said we won't be disturbed," he hissed to Janet.

"Shuddup, Ken and go. I'll sort this out," Janet ordered him. She was already out of bed and reaching for her underwear scattered on the floor, and hopping into her knickers. "Beth, let me explain."

"Explain what? How you've been two-timing Mike?" Angry as she felt, Beth was enjoying this. She'd been telling Mike for ages what a devious little cow Janet was and now, at last, here was the proof.

She turned to the boy still wrapped under the sheet and blankets.

"This little bitch is our Mike's girlfriend, didn't she tell you? My brother Mike, who's doing his national service, and who was in this house not five minutes ago."

Ken scrambled from the bed, reaching for his trousers and underpants. "Bloody 'ell. I weren't to know. You said this was your nan's house, Jan."

Swiftly, Beth turned to the window to look away, not wishing to see more of Ken's naked flesh than she already had.

"Look, I can explain. It's not wot it looks like," Janet stammered.

"Oh, but I think it is," Beth said without looking round, hardly able to believe that these two people had the audacity to be using her parent's bed like this. The nerve of it. "So this is how you treat Mike, you bitch? And my parents, after they've made you so welcome here in the past. I've always warned Mike you were using him."

"We didn't know you was comin' 'ome yet, else we wouldn't 'ave." Janet's voice was shaky.

"Tell me, Janet, how long has this been going on?"

"Wot, Ken? 'Bout six months, not that it's any of your business."

She spun on Janet, now fully clothed and about to step

into a pair of scarlet stiletto shoes. "I meant, using our house."

"Oh, it's the first time, 'onest. Me parents 'ad a change of plan today. We normally goes to my 'ouse like."

Beth didn't believe a word of it. Not from Janet. Not now, having been caught out. It was all too easy to walk into someone's home when you knew they were away, especially one you were familiar with, knew where things were kept, like door keys. Particularly if you were someone as devious as Janet Collier.

Ken stood by the bedroom door, combing his hair down into place. "Right, I'm out of 'ere. Will I see you later, Jan?"

"I dunna know yet. Just get out of 'ere, will you?"

"I expect the little trollop will," Beth all but spat at him.

He fled down the stairs. A moment later the front door slammed.

"'Ere, who you callin' a trollop?" Janet's voice was indignant, but Beth didn't care.

"*You*, because that's what you are. A cheating, two-timing slut who should be ashamed of herself."

Janet took a couple of steps nearer. "Now look 'ere."

Without stopping to think of the consequences, Beth lashed out and slapped Janet's face. Janet tottered backwards on her high heels, her hand clamped to her cheek where Beth's hand had struck, tears forming in her eyes.

Beth knew she'd hurt her, but felt no remorse. Only satisfaction. "That's nothing more than what you deserve. Now, pick up the rest of your things and get out of here. I don't want ever to set eyes on you again, else I'll make sure the whole flaming street knows what you've been up to. And your mum and dad, as well as Mike."

As Janet regained her posture, Beth expected her to retaliate so side-stepped to the window, deciding putting the bed between them to be a prudent move. Instead, Janet remained still, rubbing where a red mark in the shape of Beth's fingers had formed on her flushed skin.

"You're not goin' to tell 'im, are you?"

"No, Janet. *You* are. When you tell him it's over between the two of you because you've found someone else. I'm not going to let you string him along any longer. He's enough on his plate. I'm sure you'll put it eloquently in the letter you're going to write him tonight. Do it, or I'll tell him everything I've seen here. Now, get out."

Head held high in defiance, Janet strutted from the room.

"Just one more thing," Beth shouted after her.

Janet stopped and turned. "Wot?"

"Have you seen Terry? Does he know you've been sneaking in like this?"

"Who the ruddy 'ell is Terry when 'e's at 'ome?"

"My boyfriend. The bloke that's supposedly to have been staying here, keeping this house safe from intruders like you."

Janet shook her head. "Nope. No one's been livin' 'ere. Always been empty when we've…" She blushed then hurried on down the stairs, her pace quickening with each step.

"So, it wasn't the first time then, you lying, cheating little cow," Beth called with a chortle.

The whole house shook as Janet slammed the front door shut, the key dangling from its string banging against it a couple of times before coming to a halt. That key's definitely not staying there, Beth decided, and ran down the stairs and into the front room, in search of a pair of scissors so she could cut the wretched thing off.

She couldn't find her mother's sewing box in the sideboard. Frantically searching through the drawers, she remembered Mum had taken the box to Clackett's Farm. She would have to borrow a pair from next door.

"There, there, don't take on so. You've had a bit of a shock, that's all. Nothin' that a nice cuppa tea won't cure."

Mrs Coombes stroked Beth's hair, trying to comfort her distraught visitor after Beth had blurted and blubbered out the whole story. "But as for your Terry, can't say as I've seen 'im, like I told your Michael. We've heard noises of an evenin' like, seen a few lights on but, well, you don't see much of anyone durin' the winter, wot with it bein' so dark all the time, do you?"

Beth wiped her eyes and blew her nose loudly on the proffered handkerchief.

"I just don't know what to do, Mrs Coombes. He hasn't written, and no one's seen him. I'm worried sick in case he's had an accident or something. And if he's not been staying here, who's paying the rent?"

"Perhaps 'e's found someone else, ducks, and didn't know how to tell you. Men are like that. All cowards."

Beth twisted the handkerchief about her hands. "But why couldn't he have just said? I can accept he's got another girlfriend, and I can't say as I blame him, what with me moving away, but I just need to know he's all right."

"Men are funny creatures. They don't think logically, the way us women do. Do you know where 'e was livin' before?"

"Yes, yes. I have the address. I'm going to have to go round there and see. I just want to know one way or the other. I'll go tomorrow."

"'Ere, ducks, you can't do that, not tomorrow, like. Not with it bein' the Coronation. Not with it bein' so crowded everywhere. People is blockin' off streets left, right and centre. It's gone bloomin' crazy out there, accordin' to our Stan. Haven't you been listenin' to the wireless, girl? No, I don't suppose you have, livin' out in the sticks. Hang on a day or two, let everythin' get settled again, and then go huntin' for 'im. More as like people would have seen 'im about durin' the celebrations."

"I'm really not interested in the Coronation now," she confessed to Mrs Coombes. "I had hoped Terry would be here and we could both go off and see it all, but there doesn't seem any point now."

"Wot, and miss all the fun? A Coronation might never 'appen again in your lifetime, girl, least of all mine. I'll tell you wot we'll do. You and me can put on our gladrags tomorrow, and we'll both go up on the Underground to the palace. And there's a street party in the road 'ere later. You don't wanna be missin' all the fun now you're 'ere."

"Oh, I don't know, Mrs Coombes. I don't think I'd be much company, but thanks for the offer."

"Nonsense, girl. It'll do you good." She nodded in the direction of the front door. "It'll take your mind off buggerlugs. And just you wait till I see that young Janet Collier next. And her mother. I'll give 'er what for, takin' liberties like that. I don't know wot's got into young people nowadays. It was never like that in my time."

"I'm afraid the war's changed lots of things, Mrs Coombes. Loose morals all round in some that seem here to stay."

Annie Coombes walked her to the door. "Now, you knows where I am if you wants anythin'. Just knock. And don't you go frettin' none, neither. I'm sure there's a logical reason for Terry's disappearin' act, you'll see.

You'll be all right."

But back in the sanctum of the home she had missed so much, she was far from all right. How could she have been so foolish as not to see what was going on with Terry? Well, she had learned her lesson, and no one, not any man, was going to hurt her again.

Perhaps her going away was the cause? Perhaps if she'd stayed here and not gone off to the cold, rotten, boring countryside, Terry wouldn't have dropped her like this? But it was his idea, after all. Surely he realised her father would never have allowed her to stay here? She hung her head. Maybe he just wanted her out of the way.

The more she dwelt on it, the more hurt and angry she felt. Suddenly, the real answer for all her troubles was there, right in front of her, and wondered why she'd never seen it before. The only justifiable conclusion she could reach – that *none* of this was Terry's fault. He'd *wanted* her to stay. He'd wanted to marry her, and pleaded with her father to allow her to stay in London.

No, this was all her father's doing. Dad who had insisted she must go to Gloucestershire with them. *He* was the one to blame for this whole sorry mess; not Terry.

He'd always disapproved of Terry. Right from the start. Perhaps he'd said something to scare him off. Oh, but that's cruel, she thought. Wicked and darned right mean of him. And if he hadn't got her mother in the predicament she was in in the first place, none of this would have happened.

It was raining the morning of the coronation of Queen Elizabeth the Second, the forecast dismal, so she and Mrs Coombes decided to stay at home, and instead bake extra cakes and cheese straws for the party

"The Government's issued everyone with extra sugar rations, so why not use it up," said Mrs Coombes merrily as she stirred another handful into the rock bun mixture.

She had already drunk a tipple of two of sherry, her cheeks flushed as she and Beth and Mr Coombes listened to John Snagge, Audrey Russell and Howard Marshall's commentaries on the wireless about all the pomp and pageantry. With the crowds described as being twelve-people deep, most having to watch through cardboard periscopes, Beth was glad they had stayed at home.

When the broadcast was over, they joined everyone else in Busch Lane, taking to the streets despite the drizzle, everyone dancing and celebrating until well after midnight and their feet ached. The street party was declared a major success, the food demolished with gusto and the beer free flowing. Even the rain hadn't been able to put a dampener on the day.

The following morning, after all the merriment was over, the trestle tables and chairs returned to various houses and kitchens where they belonged, the bunting removed and life in Busch Lane returned to normality, Beth nestled in her father's armchair beside the kitchen fire and wrote a long letter to her parents.

Somehow she had to try and explain why she had deceived them, and why she intended not returning to Clacketts Farm, that she just wasn't cut out for a country girl. Would they ever understand how much she hated the muddy boots? The smells. The wind. How much she had missed London. She wanted to live her life her way, she wrote in her neatest handwriting, saying she knew she would never find fulfilment living in the country. She would come and see them, of course, but they mustn't blame Mike at all as it was all her doing, and hoped they would forgive her, even if they couldn't understand all her motives.

Beth ended her letter by describing yesterday's events, the food they had eaten, how splendid it had all been, and what fun they'd all had dancing in the street to the records Mr Stanley from number ninety-two had played on his new gramophone. How Mrs Coombes had worn herself out and had blisters on her feet the size of florins, and was so drunk, Mr Coombes had to put her to bed long before the partying finished.

As Beth licked the envelope and sealed it down, there came a loud knock at the front door.

"Morning, Miss. Telegram for Mr Brixham."

With a shaky hand, she took the white envelope from the postman. It could only be bad news.

"Any reply," he asked.

She shook her head, and watched and waited as he walked down the garden path. As he closed the gate, he looked back and gave a semi-salute before walking away, whistling all the while.

After he had gone, she ripped open the envelope with panic in her heart and read the brief message.

Get back quick. Your mother's dying. Dad.

Over and over again she read the words, unable to believe them. Dying? Mum couldn't be dying, she'd been so well, so healthy. How could she be dying?

This was all her fault. If she hadn't been so wrapped up in her own selfish misery she would have seen all was not well. Perhaps it was the shock at finding out she had run away. Had Mum discovered she had taken all her things, never intending to come back?

Full of guilt and anguish, she offered up a prayer as she ran upstairs. "Oh Mum, please don't die. You can't die."

Hastily, she pulled on a cardigan, put on her shoes

then ran from room to room making sure all the windows were shut and the back door locked before letting herself out of the front door and running towards the bus stop at the top of Busch Lane.

Passing a telephone box, she thought to get hold of Mike, so ran back to it, relieved no one was inside.

"Do you have his rank and serial number?" asked the man on the other end of the telephone.

"Sorry, I can't remember it. He said he was being moved to Salisbury Plain."

"Six convoys went the day before yesterday, Miss, several more today. He could be anywhere. Without his details, I can't help you."

"But you must be able to do something, get a message to someone in charge? This is important. It's urgent. You can't have that many blokes called Michael Brixham there." She appreciated he wasn't being unhelpful on purpose, but the thought of her brother being reduced to nothing more than a rank and serial number was demeaning, and at moments such at this was more than frustrating.

"I do understand, Miss. Look, leave it with me and I'll do what I can. As soon as we locate him, I'll be sure he gets your message."

"Thank you."

Disheartened, her mind in a turmoil, she put the receiver down, pushed against the heavy door of the telephone box. Seeing a bus pulling up at the stop, she broke into a run, frantically waving out to the conductor to wait for her. With luck, she would make the twelve-thirty train at Paddington and be in Bristol by four o'clock. From there she could get the bus out to Chipping Sodbury. She only hoped she had enough money for all her fares.

Sitting in her seat upstairs at the front of the bus, she wondered if she should have rung Mrs Clackett in order to let Dad know she was on her way.

"I'm coming, Mum. I'm coming," she uttered, willing the bus to go faster.

Chapter Seventeen

The curtains to the cottage were pulled closed, the inside dark and gloomy, air heavy with grief. Her father sat at the kitchen table, his head in his hands. He looked up as she came in, his face white, his eyes red and sunken. His weary expression seemed to have aged him by ten years. He said nothing, but the look he shot her would have her dead on the spot if it were able.

She ran across the room and threw her arms around him.

"Oh, Dad. I just can't believe it."

He pushed her away. Never one for showing signs of affection, the Brixhams didn't go in for hugging and kissing each other, but his outward display of rejection hurt. She needed him, needed his comfort as much as he needed hers. Instead, he rose from the chair, shoved her aside and headed for the stairs.

After climbing the first step, he turned, eyes wet, and with a voice full of bitter hatred, snarled, "I blame you for this, you selfish little bitch. If you hadn't gone swannin' off like that, your mother would still be alive."

Beth's mouth dropped open in shock. "Dad! How can you say that? I was only gone a couple of days. She wasn't due yet. It wasn't her time. You can't blame *me*."

"If you'd been 'here, where you should 'ave been, Connie wouldn't 'ave been fussin' about tryin' to make the bed. You knew she wasn't to do any liftin' or strainin'."

"Tucking in a few sheets and blankets isn't straining."

"No. But all that bleedin' bendin' was."

The bedroom slammed closed.

Astounded by his outburst, her face crumpled, tears

uncontrollable as they poured out in a wretched flow. This wasn't her fault. How could he say such things?

The sound of the latch lifting on the back door made her spin round. Edie Clackett stood there, arms outstretched.

"Come 'ere, me pet."

Beth ran to her, grateful to feel support wrapping around her.

"There, there, love," Edie sniffed, sharing in her sorrow. "Don't take on so. He don't mean nothing by it."

"You heard?"

"Couldn't help but coming up the path. But he'll get over it soon enough. He's just hurt and angry. Leave him be for a little while to cry alone. Men don't like showing grief like us women do. They has to be strong and brave. Stiff upper lip, and all that twaddle. His world's torn in two and he don't know what to say or do. He feels all alone."

"But he's not alone. I'm here. So will Mike be when we can get hold of him. Dad isn't on his own, he has us."

"He is in his heart, dearie. Poor man, he can't even bring himself to look at the bubby. Doesn't want anything to do with the wee poor thing. Come on, come on over to the house and meet your little sister."

Beth's eyes widened in surprise. "You mean she's alive? I thought... I'd assumed that—"

"The scrawny little mite is as right as ninepence, with a set of lungs on her that would do Maria Callas proud. Come, I daren't leave our Sally rocking the cradle too long, she gets carried away. Over-excited. The bubby'll be tossed out the crib before you can say Bob's your uncle."

When they entered the farmhouse kitchen, Sally's face beamed the biggest smile Beth had ever seen. The child jumped up in jubilant glee from where she had been guarding the wooden crib, and ran to her.

"You've come back. You're back. Hurray. I didn't tell anyone, I didn't. I kept me promise, I did."

Mrs Clackett shot a questioning look to Beth, who only shrugged as she hugged Sally now clinging tightly around her middle.

Quickly satisfied, Sally dragged at her arm, pulling her towards the sleeping baby.

"Come and see the bubby. She's ever so lovely." Sally sat down again on the wooden stool and began rocking the crib to and fro gently on its wooden rockers.

Beth peered curiously into the crib. "Oh, she's so tiny."

The baby stirred, opened its eyes.

"Arrrh, you gone and woked her now," Sally cried out in alarm.

Beth turned to Edie. "May I take her out and hold her?"

"Of course you can, dearie, she's your flesh and blood."

Nervous, Beth pulled away the cream blanket. The baby was swaddled snugly in a cotton sheet, only her face exposed revealing chubby cheeks, a tiny button nose and the longest, fairest, curled eyelashes she'd have given her eyeteeth for. Carefully, she reached into the crib to lift the child.

"You gotta put one hand under her head, to hold it, see?" Sally instructed like an expert. "Be careful. She ain't a dolly."

Beth and Edie laughed. Sally was obviously echoing the strict instructions Mrs Clackett had given her.

In her arms, the baby seemed weightless, indeed like a doll. Tenderly, Beth moved the swaddling from the baby's head in order to gaze at this tiny miracle more closely.

The infant fidgeted against her confinement; she loosened the cotton sheet a little to allow the child to move freely.

"She's absolutely adorable," she exclaimed. "Look at her hands, her fingers, they're so tiny."

Jumping up and down excitedly, trying to see what Beth was doing, Sally asked, "What you gonna call her? She hasn't got a name. I wanna call her Susie, because that's my best dolly's name but Mum says I can't, on account she ain't ours. You aren't gonna take her away are you?"

Beth stared at Edie. "Hasn't my dad told you a name? Surely he and Mum had one in mind?"

Edie shook her head. "He hasn't so much as looked at the bubby. The best thing you can do is take her over there. Perhaps now you're back, seeing the little one might change his mind. He was in shock before, when it all happened. I'm thinking he might have calmed down a bit by now."

Beth had her doubts considering the cold welcome he had given her.

"Mrs Clackett, what happened with my mother?"

Edie nodded towards Sally, who was standing on tiptoe by Beth's side, cooing to the baby, and intimated with her eyebrows that it was not for discussing in front of her daughter.

"Bring the bubby into the kitchen and I'll show you how to make up her bottle and what have you. Sal, you go outside and find your father. He's probably up in the top field. Go tell him Beth's home."

Sally did as she was bidden without questioning, skipping out the back door as carefree as the wind. Beth knew taking the child away was going to break Sally's heart.

But, oh dear, what was she going to do with a baby?

Her little sister. She looked at the tiny infant, so fragile, so innocent. So… so motherless. She hadn't a clue how to look after it. She didn't even know how to change a nappy. Perhaps the Clacketts would keep her for the time being. After all, Edie was an expert with children, and Freda knew all about babies. She would help them of course.

"Mrs Clackett, I was—"

Edie interrupted. "It's a good job our Freda was here when Connie started having contractions. Her waters broke all of a sudden. It all happened so quick."

"But she wasn't due for several weeks yet."

"It happens like that sometimes, me dearie. The dates are only a guideline. Some come early, some late, and some comes bang on time. This wee one decided it was her time to break out into the world, and there weren't nothing gonna hold her back."

Edie twiddled with her apron, wringing the fabric in her hands as she tried to explain.

"Your mum was poorly, as you know, she didn't have a lot of strength and suddenly her blood pressure was way too high. Freda was very worried and dashed back here to phone for an ambulance. By the time she got back, the baby's head was already showing, next moment out she popped, bawling like a good 'un. But by the time it was all over, your poor mum was exhausted. She'd lost a lot of blood, see. Said she had a horrible headache and before you knew it, she'd slipped into unconsciousness. Apparently, she'd suffered a massive stroke. It couldn't have been helped. Oh, Beth, I'm so sorry." She reached out and took Beth's hand.

"So even if I had've been here, it would have still happened?"

"There was nothing none of us could have done,

dearie, whether you was here or not. It was God's way. This little one must have known and decided to make her appearance in the world first. Now, you mustn't go blaming yourself, mind. It wasn't anything to do with you, despite what your father says. He's only angry. That's a normal part of grief."

She remembered how she'd felt when Gran had died, and when they'd lost David. First the shock, the hollowness that comes with grief. Then anger had set in. Was this what it was like for Dad?

Holding this tiny bundle of life in her arms, the baby's tiny fingers clutching tightly to one of hers, she wondered how anyone could reject such a cute little thing. No, Mrs Clackett had to be right. Her father would see the child and fall in love with her, and all would be back to normal. Well, as close as back to normal as it could be in the circumstances, but things now would never be the same again, she realised sadly.

Her eyes filled with tears again, and for the first time since hearing the news of her mother's death, burst into loud sobbing. Through a veil of tears, she thrust the infant into Edie's hands.

"I'm sorry, Mrs Clackett, I'm not handling this very well. I need some air."

She ran from the house, down the Clackett's front garden, out into the lane that separated the farmhouse from the cottages. Oblivious to where she was going, she ran between the hedgerows of elder and hawthorn, running until she could run no more, a sharp pain catching her lower stomach. She flopped down onto a grassy tussock, buried her face in her hands, and sank deeper into misery and confusion as the tears kept coming.

How long she'd been there, she had no idea but when

her tears were finally spent, she looked up through sore eyes, her breathing calm. In control.

"Why's you crying? Don't you like your little sister?"

The sudden voice of Sally squatting beside her made Beth startle. She hadn't heard the child approach and had no idea how long she'd been there by her side.

She pulled Sally to her. "Of course I like my little sister. I'm crying because I'm sad. I've just lost my Mum and I don't—"

"But she ain't lost," Sally interrupted loudly. "I knows just where she is. My mum said she's down at the Co-op. In Sodbury. I thought at first she meant she'd gone shopping. Then Mum said she was laid out in a wooden box, asleep. I asked Mum if I could go and wake her up, but she said no."

Beth couldn't help but laugh at Sally's innocent remark.

"Oh, Sally, we all say that when someone dies. We don't mean we've lost them like a fallen penny or a mislaid handkerchief. We've lost them in the sense that they've gone away and because we know we're never going to see them again."

Sally nodded knowingly. "I found a ten-bob note once, I did. My mum let me buy whatever I wanted from the toy shop. I bought a new dress and blanket for my dolly."

"Then you were very lucky. The thing I've lost, I won't ever find again. My mum won't ever come back. When you lose people, they never do, and you can't ever find anyone to replace them. And I was crying because I've also lost Terry as well, and I feel as if my whole world has fallen apart. Every dream and plan I had for the future has been torn away from beneath my feet."

She didn't know why she was telling Sally all this, knew

the child wouldn't understand what she was talking about. To Sally, the world was black and white and told it like she saw. There were no shades of grey in Sally's mind. She lived in a matter-of-fact world where everything was simple, but talking nonetheless to this little girl made her feel better.

"Well," said Sally, straightening up and putting her hands on her hips, striking a pose of authority that mirrored Mrs Clackett's whenever she spoke knowledgably about things. "Cousin Terry ain't lost. And he certainly hasn't died. I know, 'cos I know just where he is."

Beth shook her head, her eyebrows furrowed. What on earth was the child on about?

Sally chatted on. "I heard Mum and Dad talking about him ages ago. They didn't know I was listening, but I heard them say Terry's in the best place for him. My Dad said something about if there was any sense or justice in this world, he'd be there for a long time. Said something about throwing away the key, he did, but I don't know which key he was talking about. He must have meant Terry's front door key, 'cos we've still got ours. It's on the dresser in the kitchen and—"

Beth jumped up from the tussock, took hold of Sally's upper arms and shook her wildly as she shouted, "Sally, what are you trying to tell me? Are you saying you all knew where Terry is? Why hasn't anyone said anything? Everyone knows how upset and worried I've been about him. Why all this secrecy, for gawd's sake? Tell me, Sally, tell me if you know. Tell me. Now!"

Seeing the fear in Sally's face, Beth pulled her into her arms and hugged her, repentant. "I'm sorry," she apologized softly despite the tension and anger inside. "Do you really know where Terry is? Did your dad say?"

Sally wriggled from Beth's arms. "I don't know where it is exactly. I keep asking Mum to show me in the atlas. Terry's gone to some place I've never heard of. I think they said it was called Prison."

"He isn't worth your time, me dear. Terry's no good. He's a bad one. Always one rotten one in every family," Edie defended herself when Beth confronted her with Sally's disclosure. "We didn't say anything because your dad asked us not to. We know you were cut up enough about being dragged here to the farm against your will. You had enough to deal with, what with your mother. Your dad thought it best."

"Thought it best?" Beth yelled. "Thought it bloody best!"

"Now, look here—"

"What's Terry supposed to have done, Mrs Clackett? Why was he sent to jail?" She still couldn't believe it.

"He got himself into a fight."

"But people don't go to prison just because they've been in a fight."

"Yes, well…this weren't no ordinary fight, dearie. This was serious. A landlord had his face glassed, and they wrecked his pub. Like something out of some wild-west film by all accounts. And someone got killed."

"Who? How? Surely they don't think Terry was to blame?"

"He got sent down. He's lucky he hasn't been hanged for it. The court was lenient because of his circumstances."

No! No! No! This couldn't be the same Terry she knew and loved. Her Terry wouldn't have got himself involved in some bar-room punch up.

"Then it *must* have all been a mistake. He must have

gone in to try and stop it. He must have been misidentified or something. He couldn't hurt anything, I know him. He wouldn't hurt a fly. He's kind, he helps people… Look how he sorted out for us to come here? He wouldn't have done that if he was no good. He's been studying hard for his exams, he's been working hard to get qualified and—"

"Terry admitted it." Tears swelled in Mrs Clackett's eyes, tumbled down her red cheeks, plopped onto her heaving bosom.

Beth had never seen her weep before and didn't know what to do. All she could think about was Terry.

"Mrs Clackett, who's Terry supposed to have killed?"

Edie dapped at her eyes with the corner of her pinny, and sniffed. "My brother Harold. His father."

"Then he probably deserved it," Beth blurted out, remembering that day in the front room at Busch Lane, the day Terry talked about his life at home as a kid. Yet somehow, deep inside, she knew Terry couldn't have committed murder. Not even of his violent father. Someone else must have done it and laid the blame on him knowing Terry had every motive. It all made sense.

In the ensuring silence, Edie bundled up the few bits and pieces of the baby's things, the feeding bottles and clean nappies, and handed them to her along with the sleeping infant.

"Take her home to her father, Beth, where she belongs. He'll come round. And forget Terry. You can do far better for yourself than the likes of him."

Beth tried to feed the baby from a bottle of formula milk she had prepared just as Mrs Clackett had demonstrated earlier, but the baby wouldn't suck. She wondered if the milk was too hot so shook a few drops out onto her wrist to check. It seemed okay.

Offering the teat to the baby's mouth again, trying to persuade her to take it, she wondered if the infant could sense the tense atmosphere in the room. Could one so fragile and so new into this world feel the rejection? Aware she hadn't even got a name yet? She held her sister tighter, lovingly, trying to convey the tenderness and love she felt for her, trying to make up for not having a mother, and a father who wouldn't even look at her.

"Come on, little one. Open your mouth."

The baby screamed and wriggled.

"Can't you make that bawlin' stop?" Alfie yelled.

"I'm trying my best. Your shouting ain't helping." She pushed the teat a little harder at the baby's lips, coaxing. This time her sister began to suck, much to Beth's relief.

The front door to the cottage burst open. Mike bounded in, the enormity and intensity of what had happened evident on his saddened face.

Immediately, Alfie pulled himself up from his chair and went to greet him with a large hug and a pat on the back.

"Am I glad to see you, son."

Mike held on to his father. "I got here as quick as I could. We were out on manoeuvres. The Sarge ordered me home. Said I had compassionate leave. I rode the bike flat out to get here."

From her chair at the kitchen table, Beth silently watched both men crying on each other's shoulder. Her own eyes stung with tears of pain and hurt that Dad hadn't welcomed her like that, hadn't offered her a shred of comfort. She didn't blame Mike; it was hardly his fault. But Dad's icy reception to her had driven a wedge between them at a time when she and Dad should have been supporting each other, not hurling accusations across the room.

Oblivious to the recriminations going on around him, Mike came and squatted beside her chair, put his arms around her shoulders, mindful of her burden, and hugged. Seeing the tears running down her cheeks about to fall on to the baby's face, he gently wiped them away.

"Don't worry, kiddo, we'll be all right." His soft words were choked and strained. He tugged gently at the blanket around the baby. "And who's this little one?"

So Mike could get a closer look at their new sister, she removed the bottle from the baby's lips. Eyes closed, the little one's tiny mouth searched for it again, wanting more.

He stroked a finger gently down the baby's flushed cheek then turned to his father.

"Had you and Mum chosen a name?"

Alfie shook his head.

Turning back to Beth, he said, "Looks like it's up to us then."

Placing the infant over her shoulder and patting its back gently, just like she'd seen other mothers doing, she shrugged. "I really think it's up to Dad."

Alfie remained silent.

Mike frowned. "Well, we've got to call her something. She can't go on without a name."

She thought of the name Sally had given her. "How about Susie?"

"No, I don't like that. I remember going out with a Susan when I was still at school at Smallbury Green. She was in the fourth form at Spring Grove Grammar. Only went out with her the once, to the pictures. She turned out to be a right stuck-up little bitch."

Poor Mike, Beth thought. He doesn't seem to have much luck with girls. What was he going to think when he learned about Janet?

From deep within her subconscious, a nursery rhyme suddenly filled her head; one she remembered learning from Gran.

Milly, Molly, Mandy, sweet as sugar candy. Milly, Molly, Mandy.

She repeated the names over and over in her mind.

Milly? No, that was short for Millicent and she didn't think much of that name. Molly, then? Mmm, better. A nice name. She couldn't think of anything it was short for. What about Mandy? She was certain that was an abbreviation. But of what? She thought a moment... Amanda? Yes, that was it. A pretty name but far too posh for the likes of them. The poor infant would never be called Amanda anyway; she'd always be a Mandy. No, that wouldn't do, either.

"Molly," she finally blurted out. "I think I like Molly."

Mike nodded, smiling. "Molly? Mmm, nice. I like it." He looked again at his father, who had seated himself on the backdoor step tapping his pipe out on the stone step. "Is that okay with you, Dad?"

"Suit yourselves," he mumbled then got up and walked away down the garden.

Mike shrugged. "Poor old Dad. He's completely lost without Mum."

"He's still got us," Beth snapped angrily.

"Give him time." He took hold of one of the baby's tiny fingers. She gripped his tightly in return. "Hello, little Molly. I'm your big brother Michael, and this is your big sister Elizabeth, and between the three of us we're going to take great care of you."

"Oh, Mike, that was really sweet." Again her tears welled, ready to fall. "I'm so glad you're here. Dad's being so difficult."

"Isn't it understandable?"

"Yes, but he blames *me* for Mum dying. He reckons it was my fault for running away."

"But, you didn't run away, not as far as he and Mum are concerned. He said you could go." He looked down at the baby. "For this one's sake as well as our own, we've got to stick together now. Dad'll come round in time. It's going to be hard, but once we get Mum back to London and the funeral over with, he'll be able to come to terms with things and move forward. It'll take time."

"She ain't goin' back to London." Alfie's bulk filled the doorway, blotting out the reddening setting sun sinking slowly beneath the distant horizon, casting a long, dark shadow across the floor. "Connie's bein' buried in the church down the hill. She's stayin' here with me."

Mike rose from his haunches. "But, Dad, you can't mean that. Mum wanted to be buried in Brentford, next to Nan and Granddad."

"She changed her mind. Said so not so long ago. We was happy 'ere, see, and 'ere is where she's stayin'. She'll be buried in the churchyard in Chippin' Sodbury and that's the end of the matter. I'm not havin' my Con hundreds of miles away where I can't go and talk to her or put flowers on her grave."

"But you're coming back to London, surely? There's nothing here for you now. There's no point."

"Everything's 'ere, boy. I've got a job. I've got friends 'ere too. I ain't budgin'. You lot can do what you flippin' well want. Stay or go, I don't care."

Eyes wide, Beth stared at Mike, a knowing looking passing between them that Dad wasn't thinking clearly. But if he had no intention of going back to London, where did that leave them? More importantly, where did that leave little Molly?

Mrs Clackett shook her head.

"I'm sorry, me dearie, but I can't take her in. I've enough here with the farm and Sally. If you stay on to look after the bubby, that's fine. That's what you should do. I'll help where I can, mind, but I can't take responsibility."

It had seemed the perfect solution, that Mrs Clackett look after the baby. That way, Molly would grow up close to her father, but Edie was having none of it.

"She's your kith and kin, Beth. And as I sees it, if your father wants nothing to do with her and you don't want to take care of your own flesh and blood, you only have one other choice. You'll have to put her up for adoption."

"Adoption! I can't do that. That's a ridiculous suggestion, giving her away. She has a father. A family."

"Then you has no other choice. You'll have to stay and look after her. Either way, I can't interfere. I'm sorry, but that's how it is."

Crestfallen that her hopes and ideas for her own future had been quashed, Beth sat down heavily on a chair, not knowing what to do for the best. She shouldn't have to be taking these decisions, not at her age. Discussing the baby's future was a decision her father should be making, not her or Mike. But putting Molly up for adoption? The idea was totally out of the question. No way could she and Mike do that to her. They'd never forgive themselves. They'd spend the rest of their lives speculating on what the child was up to, thinking about her all the time and wondering where she was. Constantly hoping she were being looked after properly, always asking themselves if she were safe. If she was happy. No, adoption was not the answer. She'd never let that happen, no matter what.

"But I've no idea how to bring up a baby, Mrs Clackett. It's one thing mixing up feeds and changing nappies, but the rest I wouldn't know where to start. I couldn't cope on my own."

"Nonsense. It's something that comes naturally to us women. It's what we were designed for, raising bubbies. It's our lot in the world. You do it by instinct, and it's not as if you won't have help. There's clinics you go to and have the bubby weighed and checked out regularly like. They give you free orange juice and rosehip syrup, and help put you back on the right track if things aren't going as they should. It's not so hard."

She didn't share Edie's opinion. She knew it was going to be exceedingly difficult. The prospect of her future, their future, hung dauntingly over her like a wavering, swinging sword ready to fall, but she was determined she would succeed. No one was going to take her little sister away.

She laid out her mother's clothes on the bed. Amongst them, Connie's favourite frock. An empire line, sleeveless dress in pale green scattered with tiny, pink rosebuds. Beth lifted it to her face. Her mother's favourite scent still lingered on the cotton. Four-Seven-Eleven. The small bottle with its blue and gold label, a gift Dad had brought back from Germany, on the dressing table, its glass glinting in a beam of sunlight.

It had been such a fraught few days filled with anger and pain. Tears formed in her eyes again. That's all she'd done lately, all this crying. It just wouldn't stop. Sorting through her mother's things now was the most difficult task she'd ever had to do next to standing at that cold graveside yesterday, as her mother's body was lowered into the ground.

The job seemed doubly difficult knowing that she would have to do it all over again in London, when she returned to the house in Busch Lane in a few days' time. Most things were to be burnt. It was such a waste of good clothes but the idea of someone else wearing her mother's things was one thing too many to bear. Edie had offered to do the task but that somehow didn't feel right. She didn't want anyone else going through her mother's possessions. It would be an invasion of her mother's privacy.

More than anything, she wished her father would put his arms around her and hug her. Just once would be enough. Even at the graveside, he had shrugged off her hand on his arm and turned away. A rejection that cut like no knife could ever do. She had turned to Mike for comfort and support, but he was too weighed down, staggering under his own grief and pain, and couldn't see what was happening between them.

Slowly now, she pulled open the drawers in the dressing table, lifted out the underwear and placed the bundle on top of the dresses. There weren't many clothes, they hadn't brought that much with them to Gloucestershire, just a few sweaters in the next drawer, and a cream woollen shawl that Gran had knitted years ago. She clutched at the shawl, burying her face in its soft fibres, remembering how Gran had shown her how to knot the fringe, using a crotchet hook and three strands of wool. So many memories. All the good times. The laughter they had shared.

Now all of that was gone. It was so unfair. Why was everyone in her life she loved being wrenched away so painfully? First Gran. Then David. Now Mum. And her father. She included him on her list, for even though he might not be dead, for his total spurning of her he might as well be.

With a heavy heart, she sat on the edge of the bed and pulled open one of the bottom drawers. Inside were bundles of papers, letters mainly. She flicked through them briefly before placing them next to the clothes.

Here, too, were her mother's box of knitting needles, a half-finished matinee jacket, and the white wicker sewing box with its padded rose-patterned lid. At the back of the drawer was an old shoebox full of new bars of soap, two green tins of Lily of the Valley talcum powder, bath crystals; Mum's stock of toiletries brought from London.

From the remaining drawer she lifted out a neatly-folded, cotton nightdress with its price tag still attached. What lay underneath it took her by surprise – Gran's old money tin. She'd forgotten all about it.

The lid was as stiff and tight as the last time she'd tried to open it. Pushing and heaving against the metal, it eventually came off in her hand. She gasped at the unexpectancy of seeing the tin still so full of money. Nestled on top of the paper notes and loose coins was a faded brown envelope, its top edge ragged from where it had been opened. It was addressed to her mother.

With shaking, nervous fingers, she removed the single page inside, curious to read what it said, and at the same time feeling guilty. It felt like prying. Glancing quickly over her shoulder to the bedroom door, checking it was closed, she slowly unfolded the letter.

Written in her grandmother's childlike handwriting, most of the words in capital letters, she realised she held Gran's will. Dated the fourteenth of December last year, it was signed by Gran and witnessed by Annie Coombes. She read it through, learning that the contents of the tin, once the funeral expenses had been taken out, were to be split three ways equally, one share each to Mike and

David, and her share to come to her on her eighteenth birthday. Next year.

Ten, eleven, twelve, she counted the last of the half-crowns into her hand then put them next to the remainder of the rows laid out on the bed. The notes had already been counted into tidy piles on top of the eiderdown. A single florin, four thrupenny bits and two silver tanners remained in the bottom of the tin. Nine hundred and forty-three pounds, fifteen shillings and sixpence. She could hardly believe how much was there. However had Gran managed to save such a fortune? She'd never dreamed it was so much the first time she'd seen the tin, the day Gran bid her fetch the doctor for her mother.

With David now gone, did that mean it was half Mike's and half hers? Did Mike know about it, or had he already had his share? What was she to do about it? Questions raced around in her head all at once. No wonder her mother refused to use the money to help herself. Mum obviously knew what the will said and intended keeping Gran's wishes.

In her head she offered up a silent prayer of gratitude.

Thank you, Gran. And thank you, Mum. I understand now.

The sound of her father's heavy steps on the flagstones downstairs resounded through the cottage. Hurriedly, she gathered up the money, sweeping it back into the tin before putting it back into the bottom drawer. Something told her he would be cross with her for finding it. Was he keeping it back until she was old enough, she wondered. What if he intended keeping the money for himself? She shook away the notion almost as soon as she had thought it. Even *he* couldn't be that selfish. That cruel.

Quickly, she bundled her mother's belongings into a tight roll then carried it downstairs. She would have to confront her father about the money tin; she couldn't just take her share, that wouldn't be right. Perhaps he didn't even know about the tin. After all, Gran said only she and her mother knew of it?

"Of course I bloody knew. What's you takes me for? No point in it sittin' stuffed up there, I kept tellin' Connie. It ain't doin' much good sittin' in no tin. Mike knows it's there, too. He wanted us to keep it safe for him until he came home for good. Just think yourself fortunate, me girl. By rights, that money should have come to your mum and me. It would have paid for us to move into the country, buy our own house, but your mum wouldn't hear of it." He shrugged his shoulders. "You might as well have your cut now, I suppose, now you know. Ain't no point hangin' on to it."

At least he's finally speaking to me, she thought.

Chapter Eighteen

Holding tightly onto the step ladder, Beth called up to her brother.

"Can you see it up there?"

Mike's head appeared at the open loft hatch.

"Yeah, but I'm gonna need a hand up here. Run and fetch Stan from next door. It's too heavy for me to manage on me own, and you're not going to be able to hold it when I pushes it through."

Box after cardboard box had already come down from the loft and were stacked in piles on the landing, leaving little room for Stan Coombes to manoeuvre. First the wheels appeared at the opening then the grey hood and finally, after much heaving and straining, Mike lowered down the chassis and carriage of the pram. It was dusty and smelled of mildew, but a good scrub down with Dettol and allowed to dry out in the sunshine would soon get rid of all that. And after Mike had cleaned and polished up all the chrome, the Silver Cross pram would look as good as new.

What was more daunting a task to Beth was the washing now to be done, for inside each box they found all the baby clothes Molly would need for several years to come. Knitted woollen matinee jackets, mittens and bootees, bonnets with pink silk ribbons, a shawl with a fringed edge, and cardigans with tiny ladybird buttons, no doubt all knitted by Gran's clicking needles. There were romper suits, frilly dresses and even frillier rubber-lined pants to wear over nappies.

It was a weird feeling, realizing she must have worn these things herself as a baby. Each item carefully packed away in case needed again, and each now smelling musty with damp. On some things she swore she could detect the faint, lingering odour of smog. A sulphurous, coaltar hint, a smell she would never forget. One box alone contained pile after pile of neatly folded terry nappies, still soft even if a little grey looking, but still serviceable. It was a good job the weather was dry and breezy otherwise the wet washing would be hanging about the house for days on end at this rate, she thought with wry smile, remembering how her father loved to moan about wet washing in the house.

She sighed. Oh Dad, I do wish you would come round. Whatever have we done to you to deserve this cold shoulder? It isn't poor Molly's fault she's here. She didn't ask to be born.

It hurt that not once had he mentioned Molly, let alone showed the slightest interest either of their wellbeing, not even when Beth announced she was bringing the child back to London with her. What would have happened if she'd not gone back when summoned? Would Mrs Clackett have taken care of Molly? Would the baby even be called Molly? Probably not, Beth realised, wondering what her name should have been, what Mum would have chosen. But Dad would have had to do something. He wouldn't have just wallowed in his own grief and let the child die.

Deep in contemplation, Beth carried a bundle of clothing downstairs, ready to make a start. From the makeshift crib, a drawer from Gran's old chest of drawers, Molly was kicking up a stink in more ways than one.

Nappy changing was the worst bit about babies, she decided, as she changed Molly's dirty nappy yet again. The sour smell of eau-de-poo still managed to make her heave, the way the sticky yellow faeces managed to cling to everything it touched. First thing of a morning, the reek of ammonia from the night nappy was so overpowering, she nearly resorted to fishing out one of the gas masks still hanging in the garden shed.

She had cleaned her grandmother up often enough after one of her little accidents, washed her soiled sheets and clothes, so she ought to be used to dealing with mess, she told herself, but all that was nothing compared with the stink or mess this little one made. How could such a cute bundle of human being produce such obnoxious odours? The sooner Molly was potty-trained, the better, but that would be several years hence, she knew. Would she ever get used to the smell? She very much doubted it, gritted her teeth and got on with the job.

"Do you have to go back so soon, Mike?" she asked when he came to say goodbye.

"You know I have, kiddo. Gotta do me time. Now, are you sure you'll be okay? It's a big thing you've taken on here, and I do feel as if I'm deserting you and running away. We both should be taking care of Molly."

"I'll be fine. Mrs Coombes next door will be looking out for us."

"Look, about the money. It's not fair that you should be spending all your share on looking after the two of you, especially when it's really Dad's job, so I want you to have my share as well. I've left it up in my room. Just help yourself."

Beth shook her head. "No, Mike. I can't do that. Gran wanted you to have it. It's yours."

"Gran ain't here to know. Anyway, if she was, she'd say the same thing. And considering the original split was three ways, it's only right Molly has David's share." He cupped Beth's face in his hands. "Listen, I'm sure in a few days time Dad will be back here as quick as a flash once he realises life has to go on, and that back here is where he really belongs. He'll see the error of his ways."

"I wish I could believe that. Dad never even said goodbye to me. His last words to me were about taking the money. He doesn't want to know me any more."

"I'll sort him out, don't you fret. Next leave I'll go up and give him a piece of my mind, if the Clackett's haven't already done so. Give him time then life will get back to normal."

She shook her head. "Life's never going to be back to normal, Mike, is it? It's all changed."

"Life now a nonstop routine of feeding, changing, washing; it was not the kind of life she had planned for herself when she'd made her bid for freedom from the farm, yet looking after Molly brought her great pleasure. Far more than she thought possible. That first smile, the gurgles of contentment. Often she would just stand and watch over the sleeping child, marvelling at that tiny thumb pushed into that cute, pouting mouth.

Molly was a happy child who rarely cried, content in her crib, or in her pram watching the clouds drift by.

"Where shall we go today, Molly?" she asked, putting the baby into the pram and fixing the white parasol to shade the child's face. "The sun's shining again and we have to make the most of what's left of summer."

Yesterday being Friday, Beth had walked up and down the High Street, buying a few bits and pieces along the way. The day before, she had pushed the pram around Syon Park, enjoying seeing the squirrels and birds, so it was a toss up today between Richmond Park or Kew Gardens. Kew Gardens it was; she hadn't been there all summer. The first push of the wheels and Molly was asleep.

At the far end of the High Street she found herself staring in at the window of Maisie's. No way could she go passed without dropping in and saying hello, see if Kate was still there. And she was thirsty. The day was hot; she could murder a cup of tea.

The idea of going into Maisie's brought with it thoughts of Terry. She hadn't thought about him for a long while, pushing him to the back of her mind, what with all the sorting and things that had to be done since her mother's death, and taking care of Molly. Now she wanted to see him again. Not because she wanted him back, that was impossible if he was in prison, but she did feel he owed her some sort of explanation for his silence, thinking he could have at least written, if only once to say what had happened.

Molly slept soundly on as Beth parked the pram by the window, checked the brake was firmly in place, then pushed open the glass door. The brass bell above the door sounded her arrival with a cheery, familiar tinkle.

"Well, I'll be blowed," exclaimed Maisie, looking up and smiling in surprise. "I never thought we'd see you in here again. Heard you'd moved away to the West Country."

"We did for a while, but I'm back now. Dad's still there. He didn't want to come home yet." She still clutched firmly to the hope her father would come back to London when he was over his grief; that he would make everything all right again. "Is it all right if I sit here by the window, so I can keep an eye on the baby?" Beth nodded towards the grey pram outside.

Maisie frowned. "You got a baby? Ahhh, I see. That explains it all then, your going away. I never took you to be the sort to get yourself into trouble. Terry, was it?"

"No, no, you've got it all wrong." Beth felt

disappointed that Mrs Pilkington could think that of her. "The baby's my little sister. Didn't Mr Chiselhurst tell you? We went away to get Mum out of London, away from the smogs whilst she was carrying, as she weren't so well."

Maisie looked physically relieved, and a little embarrassed. "Of course. I'd clean forgotten him telling me. I thought for a minute they'd sent you off to one of those mother-and-baby homes, like they did with our young Hilary a few years back. I thought that rogue Terry had got you into trouble. So... a little sister, eh? I expect you get left to babysit all the time. Not much fun, is it? So, how is your mum now? Is she better?"

It was a question that always brought tears to Beth's eyes, people asking after her mother. She took a deep breath before answering.

"Mum died giving birth."

Maisie blanched. "Oh, you poor thing. Come and sit down, love, and I'll fetch you a cuppa then we can have a nice little natter, and you can tell me all about it." Maisie dashed off behind the counter.

Whilst she waited, Beth looked about the tea room. It hadn't changed. The décor just the same. The steaming coffee machine still sat on the counter, hissing and puffing away, screeching out loudly as the tap was opened to let out the scalding milk. When the waiter behind it turned around, Beth felt her breath catch for a moment, but it was a stranger's face that looked across at her and smiled slightly, not Terry's. There was no sign of Kate.

"So, what happened?" asked Maisie, returning with a tray of tea things and a plate of digestive biscuits.

Beth told her all about her mother. The act of being able to unburden herself, being able to talk about it without interruption, brought comfort. A kind of release.

Whether that was because Maisie never knew her mother, or because she was about her mother's age, she wasn't sure, but when Mrs Pilkington patted her hand and asked how she herself was, she felt relief, like a weight had been lifted. It was the first time since the whole dreadful thing had happened that anyone had taken the time to ask, except Mike of course, but that was different. Everyone else just seemed to take it for granted she was coping okay. She *was* coping, she always had done, but it was a front she put on. People couldn't see that inside, her heart was broken in two by grief from the loss of her mother, and in shattered pieces from being dropped by Terry. She didn't think it would ever mend. Yet now, talking about all to Maisie was cathartic.

"When Dad shunned the baby, everyone kept telling me to have her adopted, but I couldn't. She's my sister; I couldn't just give her away."

"So how do you manage? For money and things?"

"Mike sends me some of his pay from the army, and my grandmother left me and my brother a fair bit when she died last Christmas, but it's difficult. There's the rent and electric and gas to pay for, and our food. Thankfully, Mum kept all my baby clothes from when I was little so I haven't had to buy anything yet for Molly, apart from milk and things, but the money won't last long at this rate. I'm going to have to find myself some sort of job before too long, although how I'm going to manage with Molly, I don't know. I'll have to take in washing like my mum used to do, I suppose."

Maisie tutted. "That's no life for a young girl like you."

Beth sighed, resigned. "I had such great plans, Mrs Pilkington. There's so much I wanted to do, places to see, but I can't do all that now as I have to look after Molly all the time. Mrs Coombes, my next-door neighbour, she's offered to look after Molly a few mornings a week, and to babysit on the odd Saturday night so I can go out, but where can I go to? I've lost touch with any friends I had since we went away. I was rather hoping Kate might still be working here."

"Kate left shortly after you went to work for Henry Chiselhurst. She got herself a job at the soap factory. But you were always more friendly with Terry." There was a nervous edge in her voice.

"Terry's let me down badly, Mrs Pilkington. You see, he arranged it all for us. We were staying at his uncle's farm, but he never once wrote to me while I was there. I was so worried for him at first, thinking he might have had an accident or something. Then I'd just assumed he'd found someone else when he didn't write. And then I hear he's in prison for killing his dad. I can't take it in. Do you know anything about it?"

Maisie flushed. "So you know then? Actually, Beth dear, I wasn't going to say this, but you're better off without the likes of Terry Gibbs. He's a bad one, that one. Gone and got himself into a whole heap of trouble."

Beth shook her head. "Terry couldn't possibly be guilty of anything so heinous as murder. Never in a million years. He wouldn't kill anyone, certainly not on purpose. Not even a man as despicable and spiteful as his father." Deep down, in the fragments of her heart, she knew it all had to be a dreadful mistake. It simply had to be.

Mrs Pilkington didn't seem to share the same opinion. "Don't kid yourself, girl, he's as guilty as they come. There was a room full of witnesses who saw him do it. That's boy's lucky they've not hanged him."

"That's what his aunt said. Perhaps I should go and visit him? It must be dreadful being locked up like that.

Do you know which prison he's in?" If only he could talk to her, tell her what happened, perhaps she could try and do something to prove his innocence.

"That isn't a good idea. Forget him. If he thought anything of you, he would have been in touch by now. The fact that he hasn't means he doesn't want you involved. Now drink up, don't let your tea go cold."

They sat in silence whilst Beth mulled over Maisie's words. Perhaps Maisie was right. That would be typical of him, shielding her, trying to protect her. But all the thinking and opinions in the world couldn't change the fact that she believed him innocent, and unless he admitted it to her that he had indeed done it, she would never believe. One way or the other she just had to find out the truth.

"I've been thinking," Maisie spoke after several minutes, interrupting Beth's thoughts. "I could use extra help in here during the week some days. And I suppose while the baby's still small and sleeping a lot, you could bring her in. Keep her out back like, in the stock room where you can keep an eye on her. That's if you want your job back, that is?"

Beth's eyes widened in delight. "Oh, Mrs Pilkington, could I? I would be *ever* so grateful. And Molly's no trouble, she's really good. You won't know she's here."

"Well, we'll give it a try, shall we? See how we get on. Come in tomorrow morning at about nine-thirty and we'll take it from there."

As Beth strolled home pushing Molly, there was a spring in her step. Even if she could only work in Maisie's two mornings a week, it would give her a little extra money, and she'd be meeting people instead of staring at four walls all day long as she washed and ironed, cleaned and changed horrible nappies.

Things were finally looking up, of that she was sure.

Chapter Nineteen

Up to her armpits in steaming water and soap suds as she scrubbed and rubbed, squeezed and wrung out their laundry, Beth heard a loud, double knock at the front door. That must be the rent man, she thought, drying her hands swiftly. He always called on a Monday. She looked up at the clock before picking up the rent book and money from the kitchen table, thinking he was early today.

The formidable man took the proffered rent from Beth's hand without a please or thank you. Not even a good morning when he asked, "Is your mother in?"

She pulled her cardigan tightly around her, for the November wind was keen, whipping up the fallen autumn leaves from the pavements, sending them in a swirling mass along the road and gutter.

"She's not here."

"Your father then?"

"No, he's away, working."

"I see. When will he be back?"

"I don't know. He's away weeks at a time."

The rent man stiffened as he handed back the rent book. She glanced at it, checking he'd written in the correct amount and date.

"We'll be in touch," he said sharply then turned, and walked away back down the path to the gate.

Beth shut the door, thinking what a nosey old man he was. None of his bloomin' business where her parents were as long as he got his money each week. Without giving the matter another thought, she put the rent book away in the bureau drawer in the front room, and returned to her chores in the kitchen.

On Wednesday, a letter arrived from Mike, telling her that he'd made up his mind to stay in the army, claiming he was used to the army life, found it suited him, saying he could understand now why David had enjoyed it so much. They were going out to the Suez Canal soon and he was looking forward to feeling some sunshine on his back. He told her about hearing from Janet Collier. How she'd found someone else and that it was finished between them. That snippet of news cheered Beth, glad two-timing Jan had let him down gently. But his other news about staying in the army caused mixed reactions. She wanted him home. She needed his support, but at the same time it meant she didn't have to worry about him quite so much.

The letter went on to express her brother's bitter disappointment in their father's continued attitude, and that her priority was in taking care of Molly. He would be on leave the last week of October, he told her, when he would visit their father and again try to talk some sense into the old fool. Meanwhile, he would continue sending money each week to take care of Molly. If she needed more, she only had to help herself to his share of Gran's money, and what she didn't use to deposit into a bank so he had savings for his future and a rainy day. He finished his long letter by telling her she wasn't to worry about him, and to keep her hopes up about Dad. It would all come right in the end. She wished she could believe him.

Since that first day in coming home with Molly, she had hoped Dad would turn up on the doorstep as if nothing had ever gone wrong, or be sitting in the front room, feet up, paper in hand as he waited for her to arrive home. Mike kept the hope going, as had Mrs Pilkington, Mrs Coombes, and everyone else who knew what had happened. Autumn had already dissolved into winter yet still she hoped, but with each passing day that hope dwindled.

On Friday, a letter arrived in the post addressed to her father. She put it to one side on the kitchen table so she wouldn't forget it. On her way to work she would pop it back into the post box, redirected to her father at Clackett's Farm.

As she fed Molly, her eyes kept wandering across to the letter. There was something serious about it, official looking, but then all typed brown envelopes looked official to her. This one screamed to be opened. *Read me. Read me now*, it seemed to shout at her from across the room. Should she open it, she wondered. Unable to contain her curiosity a moment longer, she picked it up and opened it, telling herself if it was that important, she could always put it in a new envelope before sending it on.

The letter was from the council.

"Dear Mr Brixham," she read. "It has been drawn to our notice from various parties that you and your family are no longer residing at 23 Busch Lane and that you have not been at this address for ten months despite the rent on the property being paid each week. This is in breach of your tenancy agreement, the terms of which stipulate full occupation by yourself, your wife and your immediate family. Therefore, unless the council receives by return confirmation that you are in full residency the agreement will be terminated and the council forced to evict those persons at the said premises."

"*Evicted!* But they can't do that," Beth cried aloud. "I pay the rent. How can they throw us out? This is our home."

At a loss for what to do, she decided to show the letter to Mrs Pilkington. She was knowledgeable about this sort of thing. She would be able to tell her what she should do to stop her losing her home.

Beth had always admired Maisie Pilkington. Her independence. Her ability to run the teashop with such acumen. She possessed a charm and poise that made Beth wish she would teach her the same tricks, but she knew that abilities such as hers came naturally. Secretly, she was a little jealous of the woman owning her own business. She could quite see herself running such an establishment, thinking it would be such fun. If only… But these were pipedreams far beyond her reach. She would never, ever be able to afford to run her own shop.

Maisie handed the letter back and shook her head.

"I don't know, Beth. The council must know what they're doing. I suggest you go along to their offices and speak to them direct. Ask for the housing manager, and explain your situation to him. I can't believe they would just throw you out onto the streets, not with a young baby."

"I do hope you're right," said Beth. "I've nowhere else to go. They can't throw me out. They just can't."

"Oh, but I'm sorry miss, we can," the officious clerk at the council office told her on Monday morning. "We have lots of families waiting for three-bedroomed houses such as yours. Families of six or seven or more, who are cramped together in just one or two rooms at the moment. New houses aren't being built quick enough to keep up with demand, we've families waiting, so we cannot let a young girl like you continue living in such a large house on your own. There was what, five, six of you living there? The council has more important families to consider."

Beth slammed her rent book onto the counter. "But I

pay the rent on time, you only have to look, and I paid up all the arrears in one go. What about when my brother comes home from the army? Are you going to throw him out as well? I demand to speak to who's ever in charge."

"My dear, it isn't a matter of money. When your brother is demobbed we can consider his case, but not until. And unless he's married, I don't expect we can help him then either. We do not give houses to single men. Or women. It's the rules. I'm sorry, but there's nothing I can do."

"But can't you find somewhere smaller for me and the baby? What would you have me do, walk the streets with a young child in the middle of winter? We'll catch our death."

"There is a mother and baby home over in Baron's Court where you might be able to find a place. It's not up to the—"

"But I keep telling you, she isn't my baby. She's my sister." Beth was almost shouting now, thinking the stupid woman couldn't have been listening to her properly. "Look, I can show you her birth certificate if you don't believe me." She rummaged in her handbag for the folded slip of paper that registered the child, naming Alfred and Constance Brixham as Molly's parents, and pushed it across. "See for yourself."

The woman glanced briefly at it then gave it back. "Look, love, I can see you have the best intentions at heart for the child, but I really think it is too much responsibility for you, looking after such a young child. Where are your parents?"

Beth explained.

"If your father wants nothing to do with the baby, then I really do think you should consider putting her up for adoption. Other than that, perhaps you could take yourself off to live with your father? You two are his responsibility after all, not the council's. And the clean fresh air in the countryside would be far, far healthier for the baby."

The condescending remark made Beth seethe. They had no right to treat her like this. No right whatsoever. The stupid woman couldn't possibly have a clue what life was like in the country. She'd probably been no further south than Kingston to buy her tweedy suit.

"No! I won't give her away. How could you be so heartless? And I'm never going back to the farm. Never! You've no idea what it's like. I'm doing my best for her. Surely you have somewhere else I can stay? It's not as if I don't have the money to pay rent, and I do have a job. I don't see how you can just throw me out like this. It isn't fair. Or right."

"This is all about being fair. Being fair to those families whose needs are greater than yours. Sorry, but we cannot allow you to continue staying in that house. Apart from which, you are still classed as a minor in the eyes of the council, and the law. We cannot rent properties to people under the age of twenty-one. It's against council policy."

"Then the council's policy stinks and it's about time it was changed. This is nineteen-fifty-three we're living in, not the eighteen hundreds. Families have changed. Priorities have changed. What about all those women during the war whose husbands were killed? You didn't throw them out onto the streets." Tears of frustration were welling in her eyes at the unjustness of it all, but she held her head up haughtily, determined she wouldn't break down in front of this supercilious woman. She had to handle the situation as an adult. Be mature in her manners and calm in her argument.

"No, because they were women with their own children, their responsibility. Those women's husbands had given their lives for this country's freedom. If it wasn't for those men, we'd all be speaking German now. It was the least the council could do. No, it was entirely different in wartime; you cannot compare the two. This baby isn't yours. She's not your responsibility, and neither of you are ours. She'd be far better off being looked after by foster parents. Don't you see, child—"

"I'm not a child! I'm seventeen and old enough to get married. Old enough to have my own babies but not old enough it seems to take responsibility of running my own home, according to your stupid council rules. I'm not giving up on Molly. I made a promise."

"All very commendable, Miss Brixham, but I'm sorry, it is out of my hands. I'm only obeying the rules."

"Can't you just transfer the tenancy to me, then? That's got to be straight-forward enough, surely?"

The clerk studied Beth for several silent moments before saying, "At seventeen? No, dear. By law you have to have come of age to sign a tenancy agreement. Perhaps your brother; is he twenty-one?"

Beth sighed, lowered her eyes, shook her head. The situation seemed hopeless.

"Look, I'll see what I can do for you. See if I can find somewhere else for you both, but I really don't hold out much hope. I'll make some enquiries to see if anyone knows of any rooms to let. Meanwhile, I suggest you go home and start packing and looking for somewhere else yourself." She shuffled up the papers on her desk, wrote a few words on the corner of the top page Beth couldn't make out then looked up again.

"I can allow two weeks from today's date for your father to prove to us he is still in residency, otherwise we have to deem he has terminated the tenancy agreement. After that, we have no alternative but to move you out. Forcibly if needs be. But we don't want it to come to that, do we? Now, if you'll excuse me…"

Two weeks? How was she supposed to find anywhere in two weeks? It would be impossible. Dejected and disillusioned, and feeling at a total loss what to do next, she put Molly back into her pram and began the long walk home.

Why was life treating her like this? What had she done to be cast aside, treated like a child when all she was trying to do was make a home for her sister, and for Mike to come back to, keeping the home together in case her father ever did decide to come back? Which she doubted. Why was she always made to feel she was the one out of order? It wasn't good enough, and she wasn't moving out without a fight. She'd fight it every step of the way.

That evening, after she had settled Molly down for the night, she took out the lined notepaper from the bureau, and began to write to her father, thinking once he knew what was happening, he would surely come home now and sort it all out. And after, she would write to Mike. Between the three of them they had to find a way to stop the council from carrying out its threat. After all, she thought, wasn't that what freedom was all about? The right to live in your own home. What her father and all the others had fought for.

The spark dimmed from her life as she tried to cope with the awful day forever looming closer, each day nearer without a word from Dad. She had bought all the local newspapers, studying all the advertisements for rooms to rent.

To her surprise, there were plenty of rooms available,

it seemed almost everyone had a room or two. At first, she wondered why this should be, then realised there was probably a plethora of war widows desperate to make ends meet and so offered accommodation. Be it box room, bedroom, attic, or a whole basement or second floor — far too large for her to afford. No pets or foreigners. Well, she thought, she fitted in to that requirement. Suit professional person. She worked, so that must count? Only one way to find out, she thought, and ringed yet another advertisement in pencil.

Newspaper in hand, she gathered up Molly, well-bonneted and wrapped up against the cold, strapped her into the pram, slipped on her own coat and scarf, and went in search of the addresses, hope in her heart and fear in her stomach of what yet another day's hunting would yield.

It yielded only disappointment. Everywhere she was greeted by the same shaking of heads.

"Sorry, no vacancies."

"Sorry, you're too late, the room was let yesterday."

"Sorry, I don't take in children."

"Didn't you read the sign? No babies."

"I don't entertain unmarried mothers."

"But I'm not an unmarried mother, she's my sister," Beth argued.

"Yeah, that's what they all say. Now clear off! We don't want the likes of you around 'ere."

She walked to the shops on Busch Corner and further afield, scanning all notices offering rooms for rent, but no one was interested. Doors slammed in her face. She and Molly weren't wanted. Her feet ached from so much walking, and her heart ached from the weight it carried. Perhaps everyone was right, she began to think. Perhaps she should put Molly into care. But then what? She'd still be without a home.

Without Molly, she could work full-time, better herself. But without Molly, she would be lost. It would be like giving up. Giving in and giving up Molly was something she wouldn't do, defeat not something she was prepared to contemplate.

She cuddled the baby tightly to her chest.

"No one and nothing is going to come between us, little Molly. I'll make sure of that," she vowed into the baby's soft hair. "We're in this together. Something will turn up, I promise no one's going to take you away." She had to hold on to that last vestige of hope. It was all she had left to cling to.

The hatred she felt for her father grew treblefold in that moment, detesting him with a vengeance for putting her through all this when he was the one person who could put things right. Not once had he written to ask how she and little Molly were doing. It was as if they didn't matter any more. As if they never even existed.

But they *did* exist. They were alive, and she would fight tooth and claw to keep them together, and be everything to Molly that their dad wasn't. And when Mike came home for good, they would show the world that the Brixham children were not a family to be messed with.

In desperation, she went to see Annie Coombes.

"Would you consider letting out your spare room to me? I'll pay you a good rent. I'll help around the house for you. Anything you want."

Mrs Coombes pinned back the stray strand of grey hair falling out of its roller on her head as she kneaded pastry on the kitchen table.

"Sorry, ducks. Mr Coombes wouldn't like it, not a baby in the 'ouse. 'E's far too old to be messin' 'bout with nappies hangin' around dryin' and the extra washin' and cryin' an' all. And he ain't well. Got a nasty chest infection."

"But I'd see to the washing. There wouldn't be extra for you to do. And she's ever so good. She doesn't cry a lot, and she sleeps all through the night. You know how good she is."

"Just you waits till she starts teethin'. No, sorry, girl, as much as we'd like to 'elp. What about your own family? You got uncles. Aunts. They're the ones who should be 'elpin' you out, like."

Frank and Joan both shrugged and said no, as did Uncle Bert and Aunt Vera. Aunt Ethel said much the same thing.

"You ain't our responsibility, girl. That good for nothin' father of yours should be takin' care of her. Of you both. He can't expect us to be doin' his job."

"But I only want a room to rent," she pleaded, not that she wanted to be under the same roof as lecherous Uncle George, but she was that desperate she would put up with anything. Even him.

"Then next you'd be wantin' us to babysit while you're out gallivantin' about. The novelty'll soon wear off, you mark my words."

It seemed every one of the family had an excuse not to help, no matter how feeble. Huh, so much for Dad's pontificating about the families helping each other out, because the Brixhams certainly don't. But there was one last hope – Maggie and Don. They weren't Brixhams. They'd help, she was sure of it. With increased determination, she pushed the pram on along Brentford High Street, on her way to see her last hope. Auntie Maggie always did have a soft spot for babies.

"Sorry, but Uncle Don's ill. That's why we never made

it to your mum's funeral. He was ever so upset."

"None of you made the effort to come," Beth threw back. "If you or Uncle George or Aunt Vera had, you would have seen how our Dad was. You could have made him see sense, then I wouldn't be in this predicament."

"'Ere don't you go blamin' us, girl. We didn't know until it was too bloomin' late. If we 'ad of them telephone's like, it would 'ave been different. Anyway, I've enough on me plate lookin' after Don. What with 'im and with three of your cousins still livin' at home, there ain't the room to have the two of you 'ere. You know I would if I could, pet," Aunt Maggie said as she rocked Molly in her arms, cooing of the child. "But you're always welcome to come an" visit. There'd always be a 'ot meal for you and a cuddle for Molly."

"But Mum was Uncle Don's sister. Her only family. Isn't there any way? I don't mind sharing a room."

"I wished there was, girl. Oh, but isn't she delightful."

For a moment she thought her aunt was about to relent, but that wasn't to be. Her reasoning and advice the same as all the rest of the family as she handed Molly back.

"Go home to your father, Beth."

At every turn, her plight went unheeded. She felt she didn't have a friend left in the world to turn to next.

Except Maisie Pilkington.

There were empty rooms above Maisie's, she remembered. Surely Mrs Pilkington wouldn't object to her living there? And it would be so much more convenient. She could leave Molly upstairs, out of the way, whilst she worked in the teashop. She could put in more hours. Be more useful. Keep an eye on the place when it was closed. She thought it a wonderful idea. Why hadn't she thought of it before, she asked herself, pushing down on the handle of the pram to lift the front wheels up over the front step of the teashop.

Maisie smiled apologetically. "I can't let you have the rooms, love, as I won't be here much longer. I'm putting the teashop up for sale."

Beth's smile dropped from her face. "Selling? Why? I thought everything was going fine."

"It is. Business is very good, but I'm getting tired of it. It's hard work and now I have enough money put by, I can move to the coast as I've always planned. I've found a nice house in Margate I'm going to run as a little bed-and-breakfast place during the summer. Find myself a nice young man and settle down again. I don't want to be the merry widow for ever."

"I always thought you and Mr Chiselhurst might get together. You always seemed so friendly with him."

Her comment made Maisie laugh.

"Good gracious no. Henry's a fine man, he'll make someone a darned fine husband one day, but he ain't my sort. Not with that bulging beer-belly of his, and he's not exactly what you would call good-looking, is he?"

Beth couldn't argue with that observation.

"He may have a fine house down by the river," Maisie continued, "and no doubt he'll make a good father too some day, but Henry isn't my idea of a good time. I need a young stud, someone who's handy with his hands, who'll show me a good time between the sheets, if you know what I mean?"

"What happened to your first husband?" She hoped Maisie wouldn't think her nosy or being too forward.

A far away look appeared in the older woman's green eyes. They seemed to mist over with sadness.

"Harry was killed in the war. He was in the RAF. He got himself shot down on a mission over Germany, on his way to Dresden. Oh, but he was a handsome lad. I'd only met him a few weeks before he was called up. We married in a hurry, spent one night together and then he was off, never to come home again."

"How dreadful." Beth wished now she hadn't asked.

"It happened to a lot of us girls back then. We were all young and all in such a rush. Still, it was a long time ago now and I'm ready to move on with my life. Ready for another husband, although why I want another man in my life is beyond me sometimes. They ain't nothing but trouble. Always bossing you about. Telling you what you can and can't do. What you can wear, clipping you round the face if they don't like something you say."

"A bit like dads," Beth commented with a wry grin.

"Worse in some ways, but lots better in others. And like dads, you get good ones and bad ones. Henry Chiselhurst, now he would be a good one. He's a real gentleman, as you know, but somehow the thought of his naked body crawling into my bed makes my flesh creep. I'd rather be a nun. But whoever marries him won't go without anything. He's well moneyed." Maisie beckoned Beth closer across the table, and lowered her voice. "I've heard tell he's got a house in the country as well as the house he lives in near Richmond Park, and that he owns a boat."

"Wow! That *is* rich."

An idea was slowly forming in her head. What if she were to buy Maisie's Tea Room? If only she could get the money up together somehow. There must be ways. She still had some of Gran's money left, and it would mean she would have somewhere to live, right above the shop, and it would be somewhere for Mike to come home to. He could become part of it. She could then have her dream, her own little business, just like Maisie.

"Mrs Pilkington, how much are you asking for the teashop?"

Maisie shook her head. "Far more than you have, I'm sure. Nine hundred pounds."

"Oh, as much as that." In as quick an instant as the thought had materialised, her idea was snuffed out, as she realised the dream was just that – a dream. She didn't have that sort of money. Her money had dwindled down just helping her live from day to day, paying out the rent and on bills and food.

But what if she borrowed Mike's share to help buy Maisie's? She would have to ask him, of course. She couldn't just use his money without his agreeing despite his saying she could use it for Molly. This was different. It wasn't the same. So far, she'd not had to dip into his legacy, it hadn't been necessary, and wasn't that what Gran intended? For their futures to be secure, money for their own homes. This would be their home. She'd be doing it for all three of them.

Then seeds of doubt crept in. What if she was an abject failure in running a business? What if she should lose every brass farthing they owned? She did some rough calculations in her head. Payment for the shop. Redecorating. Rental of a jukebox. And that was just for the things she could think of, there were bound to be other costs involved.

The sums didn't add up. Even if she used Mike's share, it still wouldn't be enough, and how was she supposed to make up the difference? The pittance she earned wasn't enough. Her bright sparkle of a future with a hope, a dream, was dimmed by stark reality. The likes of her were never going to be able to afford to make something of themselves. Be someone.

"How soon are you selling?"

Maisie shrugged. "Just as soon as a buyer comes along. It could be a few days, a few weeks or months even. Who's to say? Don't worry, I'll have a word with the new owner and ask them to keep you on. Tell them you're my best waitress and how reliable you are. You never know, they might even let you have those rooms upstairs."

"But what if they don't keep it as a tea room? What if they turn it back into a betting shop, or change it into a greengrocers or something, or use upstairs themselves to live in? What then?"

"Then it's out of both our hands. I'm sorry to disappoint you, Beth."

That, she thought sadly, was the story of her life. Life was one disappointment after another. Every plan and every hope squashed flat by other people's wants and wishes and ideas, leaving her with no say in the matter. Always other people ruling and dictating how her life would run.

Well, all that was going to have to change, she decided. It was her future. Her life. And she was jolly well going to start right now and show the world that she wasn't going to be stepped on. The young had rights. The youth of today was tomorrow's future even if they didn't have the vote yet. Teenagers were going to have to band together and lead the revolution. Youth was king.

Great fighting talk, Beth, she told herself, but how are you going to start a revolution with no home, little money and possibly no job, and a baby to look after?

Pushing Molly home brought reality tumbling swiftly back into her footsteps. There was going to be no revolution.

Unless, that is… Yes…, why not? It was worth a shot. She would ask the bank for the money. Simple. With business at Maisie's thriving, she could repay a loan in no time, and no reason she could see why she should be refused one. Tomorrow, she would go along to the bank in the High Street and demand to see the manager. He would see she was serious and that she had savings towards it, even if it wasn't much. She just needed that little extra bit of help to set her on the road to success.

Her lips pursed in determination. She was going to buy Maisie's and re-open it as a coffee shop especially aimed at teenagers. Put in one of those fancy, new-fangled jukeboxes. Redecorate and... and... become the guiding light of the rebellion. Move over stuffed shirts and bureaucracy, youth culture is about to take over. Let the revolution begin.

Chapter Twenty

The revolution was quashed before it had even begun. Across the large, dark mahogany desk in the bank manager's office, the leader of the resistance sat po-faced, his fingers enfolded under his chin.

"I'm sorry, Miss Brixham, but we cannot consider a loan for three reasons. One, you are under age to take out such an agreement. We would need your parents' signatures to guarantee the loan. That is the law. Second, you have just told me you are about to be evicted. That doesn't instil faith in you. With no fixed abode, the bank cannot lend money on a whim. That is also the law. Third, and to my mind, more importantly, I do not think that a young lady such as yourself with a child to look after, is capable of taking on such responsibility. What I would strongly suggest is that if you have cash at home, you deposit it in the bank for security. If you get broken into, you will lose it. Having money lying about the house nowadays is not safe. Meanwhile, you have no collateral with which to offset a loan."

"But if I have the café, that will be your collateral."

The bank manager shook his head dismissively. "I suggest you go home and forget all about this idea. Find yourself a husband and settle down. Then come back in a few years' time and he can take out a loan if necessary, if this idea of yours is still about, though I very much doubt it. These coffee shops are never going to take off. They're nothing but a five-minute wonder, you mark my words. I've seen it all before. All these fancy schemes and plans all come to nothing. People are too anxious to bail out when the going gets rough."

He rose from his brown leather chair and made

towards the door. "Good day, Miss Brixham. And thank you for thinking of Barclays Bank."

Beth remained seated, totally dumbfounded. How could anyone be so condescending and pompous? Who was he to say that coffee shops were not going anywhere? What did he know? What gave him the right to tell her to go away and get married, do what all other little women do?

Every right, she supposed with a shrug of her shoulders. He was the one holding her future in his hands and obviously wasn't prepared to yield one inch. Realizing she wasn't going to get anywhere with this man, she gathered her things and strutted out of the building, head held high, inside feeling completely rejected and despondent. Thwarted at every turn no matter how hard she tried, it seemed no one had faith in her, a mere child, as they all referred to her. No one seemed willing to help.

She pushed the pram along Isleworth quay. At least today the wind had dropped and despite it being cold, the weather was pleasant enough for her to take the longer way home, blow the cobwebs and fugginess out of her head. Coffee shop indeed. Whatever was she thinking of? Ideas above her station, Mum would say.

The tide was up, the brown water lapping noisily against the quay steps in the wake of a passing boat heading upstream. A pair of swans swam gracefully over to her, seeking food, but she had none. They gave up and glided away towards the island in the middle of the river. She walked on towards the London Apprentice, stopping to rest at one of the wooden table and chairs always left outside the pub. What was she going to do? Where was she to go? What a merry Christmas hers was going to be again. Perhaps she should give in and go back to her father. Life just wasn't worth all this hassle.

It was nearly noon and she could hear the sounds of bolts being thrown on the doors to the pub. Opening time, but she couldn't even go inside and buy a shandy to quench her thirst – she was under age.

Hearing male voices, she turned her head to see a group of young men approaching around the side of the building. They were laughing and chattering to each other. They must have noticed her for one of them called out, "'Ere, wanna drink, darlin? Come wiv us, we'll soon warm you up."

She ignored them, her attention firmly attached to rocking the pram gently.

"Come on, 'Arry, she's got a sprog. You don't wanna be messin' in there."

"Nah, guess you're right, Tommy. No bird's ever worth a punch up with her old man."

They all laughed rowdily then disappeared inside the public bar.

It's all right for them, she thought, bitter. Men can do what they want. They aren't the ones left at home holding the baby and trying to make ends meet all the time. Instead, they're out enjoying themselves and calling the shots, telling us women what to do all the time.

Molly stirred and whimpered; time to move on.

Passing a newsagent, Beth stopped to read the notices in the window, in the hope of finding rooms to rent amongst all the other things for sale. One card advertised two rooms and a shared bathroom in a "respectable" neighbourhood at the far end of Brentford High Street. With nothing to lose and all afternoon free, she decided she would go along and enquire, but first she'd better get Molly home. It was almost time for her feed and the whiff of air as she tucked the blanket tighter around her told her Molly also needed changing again.

*

From the address on the card, Beth found the house in a back street off the main road. A quiet, pleasant place but the houses didn't look particularly grand, just ordinary two-up-two-down Victorian terraces with fancy brown and black tiled paths leading up to the front door. She knocked and waited.

It was opened by a large, plump woman, hair in curlers, and wearing a stained and grubby floral cross-over pinny. Beth wrinkled her nose. There was an overriding whiff of cooking fat about the woman, and an equally unpleasant smell of cooked cabbage drifting down the hallway. The woman wore dirty tartan slippers with grubby beige fur around the edges. The left one had a gaping hole in it, a big toe poking out, the nail ragged and dirty. From the woman's mouth hung the thin stump of a half-smoked cigarette. At its tip, held in place by a miracle or sheer determination, the grey ash bent towards the ground, defying gravity. It seemed standard attire for landladies, Beth thought grimly, repelled by the of sight this one.

"I've come about the rooms," she said, putting on her poshest voice and smiling as best she could, for the woman's stance, hand on hips, made her feel nervous.

The landlady eyed her up and down then looked over Beth's shoulder to the pram left outside the gate. She sniffed very loudly, her fat face creasing into an ugly scowl.

"We don't want no sluts around 'ere. This is a respectable 'ouse. So bugger off!"

Before Beth could utter another word, the woman slammed the door shut, its tarnished knocker clattering noisily against the tarnished, unkempt brass plate.

The indignity infuriated Beth. She hadn't even given

her the chance to explain her predicament. Why did people automatically assume Molly was her baby? She went back down the path, leaving the gate open on purpose. The curtain at the bay window twitched. Sensing the horrible woman watching her, on impulse, Beth stuck out her tongue. That'll teach the old cow.

Time was running out rapidly. In a few days the bailiffs would be knocking on the front door, ready to throw her out on to the street, and there seemed nothing in the world she could do to prevent it. Worse, was the fear that if she didn't have anywhere to live, the authorities would take Molly away. She also knew if she couldn't find somewhere to live soon, she only had one other choice. One she didn't relish.

Her feet felt as if they had walked to Bristol and back, such was the throbbing in her toes and heels from walking so far already today, knocking on doors and finding them closed in her face the instant the pram was spotted. It had just turned four o'clock and getting dark. She needed to sit down and rest before continuing in her quest, although she had started to wonder whether it was all worth it. It seemed so futile, so soul destroying.

Maisie's Tea Room was close by, so she dragged her aching feet on, the weight of the pram aiding her weary footsteps. Perhaps she'd feel better after a cup of tea and a toasted teacake.

Walking along, deep in thought, she couldn't get the idea of running her own café out of her head. It had seemed such a brilliant idea. The perfect solution. Why couldn't everyone else see that? She would be keeping herself, providing a service, somewhere for the kids to hang out instead of messing about on street corners. There was nothing complicated about it. All she needed was a bit of help to get her going. So why were people so frightened of helping?

Leaning her weight against the heavy glass door to open it, she was surprised to see Henry Chiselhurst seated at his favourite table near the door. She hadn't seen him at all since the day she left his employment.

When he looked up at the sound of the bell tinkling above the door and recognised her, he smiled such a wonderful smile of welcome, her heart lifted. At least someone was glad to see her.

"Well, look who's here. Maisie said you were back. Are you well? You look bonny. I take it that's your little sister outside in the pram? Don't leave her there in the cold, lass, bring her in so we can take a look at the little bundle of trouble. I do so love children. Wanted lots of my own but never got married to have any. Always too busy trying to make a living. Sad that, really. My big one regret. My own fault."

"Molly's asleep at the moment, she's quite safe outside, and well wrapped up. I'll soon know when she wakes as the pram shakes with her movements. You can come outside and take a peek at her, if you want."

At Henry's invitation, she sat down at his table.

"What would you like, lass? My treat."

The waitress gave her a curious stare as Henry gave his order for a pot of tea for two and two currant buns. Beth guessed Gillian was probably wondering what she was up to, fraternizing with the customers, something Mrs Pilkington always discouraged. She smiled at her, amused at the look of consternation on her co-worker's face. Whilst she had tried to strike a friendship with Jane in the last few days, she'd reached the conclusion that Jane was a little snooty, much too aloof. They would pass the time of day as they worked together waiting tables, but shared little gossip. She couldn't remember ever hearing Jane laugh.

"I used to work for Mr Chiselhurst, as his secretary," she explained for Gillian's benefit. Gillian strutted away with a dismissive shrug of her shoulders.

"Beth, would you like your old job back, lass?" he asked. "You were a good one, you know, one of the best. The other girls... well... no one seems to match up to your abilities."

The question took her by surprise. "Why, Mr Chiselhurst, you flatter me. I only worked for you for a few weeks, how can you say I was so good? I left you in the lurch."

"That wasn't your fault. You left with the best intentions in your heart. No, I'm serious. Do you want to come back?"

She looked out of the window towards the pram. Working full-time would certainly solve a lot of her problems, but how could she work all day with Molly to consider? Who would look after her?

"That's good of you, Mr Chiselhurst, but I would have to find a babysitter for Molly, and they don't come cheap. None of my family will do it, I've already asked before. So I couldn't come back, even if I wanted to."

Henry looked wistful. "Oh dear, yes. Maisie told me about your mother. I am so sorry. It must be doubly difficult, what with your father leaving you to cope like this. He must be beside himself with grief."

"Oh, Mr Chiselhurst," she blubbered, blowing hard into the handkerchief pulled swiftly from her coat pocket. "I'm about to lose my home, and not because I can't pay the rent. No one will rent me rooms because they all think I'm an unmarried mother and want nothing to do with me. And now Maisie's selling the shop. I want to buy it from her but the bank tells me I'm not old enough to have a loan, and that I should be more concerned in finding a husband who can keep me. It just isn't fair, Mr Chiselhurst, it just isn't. I don't know what I've done to deserve all this."

Henry shuffled uncomfortably on his seat, at which point Gillian arrived back and plonked the tray of tea things down without so much as a smile or a thank you. She glared at Beth before strutting away from the table.

"She's a bit of a madam, that one," he said with a smile.

"Yep, not a bit like Kate, is she?" she laughed. "I do miss Kate, Mr Chiselhurst. She warned me about Terry, and I ignored her. He was good in respect of trying to help me and the family, but she was right about one thing: Terry was trouble. He abandoned me out in the sticks and now he's locked up accused of murdering his old man. I can't believe he would do that, but it seems that's the way it is."

She sniffed again and smiled, knowing he didn't like girls who cried. "So here I am, all on my own with nothing to look forward to. Thanks for the job offer, but as you can see, I've got my hands tied. And sorry for that little outburst of mine. Sometimes it all gets on top of me. I'm not normally like that."

He raised his eyebrows. "Nay, nay, lass, say no more. You've a right to kick and scream a bit with what life's chucked at you. You're a good lass, I'll give you that. There's not many that would stand up for themselves and the things they believe in as you have. And as for that Terry. What he did was bad and you're better off without him. At least you weren't hurt by him in the worst way."

"I was thinking of going to visit him."

"Whatever for? You mark my words, it'll do no good and will only go upsetting you further. No, best leave things as they are. Forget him. A lovely young lass like you will soon find yourself some other lucky fellow."

"But—"

"Look, lass, what that boy did was wrong regardless of what you think. You don't want to be messing with him, holding no torches, because he's going to be in prison for a long, long time. You've got your whole future to look forward to. Best leave things as they are."

"Huh, some future I've got. I've got nothing to look forward to. It's only my little sister out there and my brother that keep me going."

She pushed her half-drunk tea away and reached to the floor for her bag. Nice as it was talking with Mr Chiselhurst, it was wasting precious time. Time when she should be out knocking on doors, and scouring advertisement boards. Or visiting more letting agents, despite the fact that they took her money but never came up with the goods.

"I really ought to be going, I've some more rooms to look at this afternoon, not that anything's going to be offered. They never are as soon as they see the baby. Before I know it, it'll be time to be getting Molly back home. She'll be waking and will want feeding again. It's all my life is at the moment, bottles and formula and soapsuds and shitty nappies. Thanks for the tea. It was nice seeing you again."

He beckoned her to stay where she was. "That can wait. Now, tell me, what's this I hear about you wanting to buy the teashop?"

She stared wide-eyed at him, unable to believe he was actually interested, so she told him her grand plan to start a revolution and run Maisie's as a modern café for teenagers. And all about how her ideas had been crushed by the bank's refusal, pulling the crumpled letter from her pocket, the one from the council explaining how she must to find somewhere else to live soon. Like today. He listened without interrupting.

"So you see, I guess I've no choice but to move back to Gloucestershire to my dad, but I don't want to do that. I hate him, Mr Chiselhurst, I really do. I know I shouldn't but this is all his fault. He was the one to get my mum pregnant in the first place, knowing the consequences. She would still be alive if it weren't for him. He could have found a job here instead of dragging us away to the middle of nowhere. If he hadn't, I might still be with Terry, and he might not have ended up in the clink. And it's all Dad's fault I'm lumbered with Molly. It's as if me and the baby don't exist, as if we're nothing to do with him. How can he do that to us? If I go back there I think I might do something stupid, like kill him."

"Now that is daft talk, lass. You'd end up in the same place as Terry. I'm sure given time your father will come round. The way I see it, he must be lost in grief and a whole lot of guilt. Us men are no good with emotions and sickness and death. We're brought up to be big and strong and brave, and so hide our tears when deep down we cry like you lasses, probably a darned sight harder, too, because we aren't allowed to show it. You have to be patient with him."

"For how long?" she all but shouted. "He hasn't considered mine or Mike's grief. And what am I supposed to do while he gets his act together? I'm past waiting. In fact I'm past caring. I don't think I can ever forgive him now for what he's done to this family."

They sat silently for several minutes, finishing their tea, Beth deep in her own thoughts, wondering where she could try next for a room. As she put down her empty cup she had a brainwave, at least she thought it one, but whether Mr Chiselhurst would consider it so was another matter, but unless she asked, unless she put the proposition to him, she would never know. What was it Gran said? "Those that don't ask, don't get, those that don't ask, don't want".

"Mr Chiselhurst, would you ever consider buying the tea room from Mrs Pilkington?"

Henry looked at his companion in a mixture of surprise and amusement.

"Whatever would I be wanting with a teashop, lass?"

"As an investment, like. Mrs Pilkington said that business was good. You're an accountant, I'm sure if she showed you her books, you'll see for yourself. But what I was thinking was, if you bought it and put me in charge, it would be an investment for you, and solve all my problems as well. You see, there are rooms above the shop, rooms that Molly and I could live in."

Henry leaned back in his seat, his large girth pushing against the table. "No, lass, I'm not prepared to buy it, certainly not just as a case of charity for you."

"No, no, I realize I haven't explained myself too well, have I? I don't want you to buy it all outright, see. I thought perhaps you might consider buying half of it, coming in with me like. I have some money I can put towards it but not enough. Perhaps you would consider buying up the remainder."

He leaned forward. "What, like a partnership?"

She nodded rapidly. "That's it, a partnership. And then, when I'd made enough with the profits, I could pay you back your share."

"With interest added, of course."

"Oh, of course. I wouldn't expect you to see nothing on your investment. I don't know much about money and loans and things but I know about interest rates and…

and you would have a share of the profits too, fifty-fifty."

"Seventy-thirty, in my favour. After all, I'd be putting in the bigger proportion."

Such an amount sounded far too much, even by *her* sums. She tried to calculate the figures in her head, at the same time studying his face, trying to gauge his reactions. Was he treating this as a joke? A game? Was he being serious or just teasing her? It was difficult to tell from his expression but there was a glint in his eyes behind those thick-rimmed spectacles, a twinkle of something.

She sighed, slumping back into the chair. "I know, it'll never happen. I'm just being stupid. It's just a dream of mine to help bolster up my spirits and give me something to fight for. But I have to do something. And soon."

Henry folded his hands under his treble chin, elbows on the table. "The idea is sound in principle, lass, but buying into a business isn't straight-forward. There are lots of things to be considered and worked out. Sitting from where I am, it's not a sound investment, but it is one we can talk over." He grabbed her hand. "You know, I admire you, Beth. There's not many young girls would give up their lives to look after their sisters or brothers like you're doing. You're young. You should be out partying and enjoying life, have loads of friends. The whole world's out there for you youngsters to take and shape into your own futures."

He let go of her hand, pulled off his glasses and wiped them on a linen napkin, polishing the lens until they sparkled before putting them back on.

"Let me think over your proposition," he said, "but I'm not making any promises mind. I'll tell you what, call into my office on, let's see... let's say on Friday. Come in at noon and I'll buy you lunch, and bring the baby along as well. Make sure she's awake so you can introduce me properly."

"Thank you, Mr Chiselhurst." She picked up her bag then held out her hand. "Until Friday. And thank you for the tea."

It had been a long week trying to guess what Mr Chiselhurst would say. Building up her hopes, trying not to build them too high. She peered through the front room window. The rain poured down in slanting stairrods, bouncing off the pavements and running in streaming torrents along the gutters and into the drains. Oh dear. She was going to get soaked walking out in this.

She picked up the duster and continued cleaning the windowsill and its few ornaments, then looked out at the rain once more. Oh well, what was the point in going anyway? Owning the café was just a frothy dream. He wasn't going to accept her offer, she could tell. He was just stringing her along, giving false hope to her fantasy.

On the dining table lay the letter she'd received the day before, from the council, warning of its imminent plans to take possession of the house. It seemed nothing was going to prevent it short of her father walking back in the front door, and miracles didn't happen in Beth Brixham's life, she thought dismally. Nothing good ever happened any more.

But she would fight the bailiffs. She'd barricade herself in. Drag the bureau in from the front room and block the front door. Pile the kitchen table and chairs against the back door – anything to prevent the indignity of being thrown out onto the street, with all the neighbours watching and pointing. And, with no roof over her head, the authorities would take Molly, of that she was sure. They would shove her in a home somewhere and she'd never see her little sister again, just like what had happened to Terry's sisters and brother.

If she didn't find somewhere soon she'd be spending Christmas walking the streets. Either that, or she would have to give in and go back to Clackett's Farm. The last resort! She had tried everything she could think of. And even if Mr Chiselhurst did agree to buy Maisie's, things couldn't be sorted in a week, she'd still need somewhere to live meanwhile.

As she returned the cleaning rag and dustpan and broom to the cupboard under the stairs there came a loud rap at the front door.

"Why, Mr Chiselhurst! What are you doing here?"

"I couldn't expect you to walk out in this awful weather, could I, lass? So I thought I'd come here to talk. May I come in?"

She showed him into the front parlour, thankful she'd only just given the room its weekly clean and polish. The room was rarely used now. There wasn't much point on her own so it never got that dusty or dirty nowadays, but she liked to keep up her mother's standards, make sure the best room in the house was always presentable to guests.

Henry settled his bulk onto the sofa and looked appreciatively around, admiring the yellowing painting hanging on the wall opposite, of mountains reflected in a lake, and commenting on the fancy etched mirror over the mantelpiece.

"A fine house this, lass. Such a shame to have to be leaving it."

Not content with small talk, she was anxious to get down to the real reason of Mr Chiselhurst's visit.

"Have you thought about what I said?" she asked anxiously.

"Aye, I have that, lass, and I don't think it's such a

good idea. It's not a sound investment. As Maisie's accountant... Yes, I know I didn't say anything before. Takings are good, profits sound, but I don't think a young lass like you should be spending her fortune on something that could turn up tail and perish under competition or mismanagement."

She opened her mouth to express her indignation at his intimation she might be a bad manager before even given the chance to prove otherwise, but Henry continued speaking, refusing her the opportunity to interrupt.

"No, I'm not going into partnership on the café with you. Instead, I have a different proposition to put to you."

Her curiosity roused, she wondered what this might be. If he didn't think she could run a café, what did he think she was capable of doing? What could he be suggesting that would counter her ideas?

"I have a very fine house alongside the river. Four floors and a basement, with lawns leading down to the water's edge. Why I need such a dirty great place for is sometimes beyond me, but there I am."

"I heard you also had another house in the country. Why don't you live there then?" Her words didn't mean to sound as rude as they came out.

He seemed not to be offended. "That is nothing more than a beach hut on the coast. And if you've heard tell of my yacht as well, that's another false rumour. I used to do a lot of fishing. The boat's nothing more than a skiff. Hardly Rule Britannia and hey ho, blow the whistle, the Captain's on board, hoist the mainsail. Where was I? ...Oh yes... the house in Richmond. It takes a lot of looking after and—"

"And you want me to be your housekeeper?" she

interrupted, presupposing his offer.

"Nothing of the sort. I already have a perfectly good housekeeper and a very fine job does Mrs Potter too. No, what I mean is the house is empty. It needs a womanly touch, and it needs to be filled with the sound of laughter and children. It gets lonely in there with no one to share a meal with, just me at my dining table with nothing between me and the flock wallpaper. No, lass. I'm asking if you would consider marrying me."

Her jaw dropped in disbelief. Marry him? Good God no. Just the thought made her stomach heave.

"But you're…" Fat, ugly, grotesque, a complete turn-off, she wanted to say but checked herself, "…too old for me!"

He laughed. "I'm only thirty-seven. Still, to you young things I suppose that is old. But I'm fit and strong. Look, lass, I'm not asking you to bed me. What woman would want to roll in the sheets with a fat walrus like me?" He patted his bulging stomach. "I'm asking for companionship. With me, you'd never want for anything. You'd never have to wonder where the next meal is coming from, only when Mrs Potter is going to serve it and, as you can see, I like my food. I'm also a wine connoisseur. You'd eat and drink like a queen. You'd have a wonderful house to live in, need never go without anything, nor that baby. In fact, I'm even willing to adopt the child. Treat her as my own."

"But Mr Chiselhurst, I—"

"Henry. The name's Henry."

"Mr Chisel… Henry, I don't know what to think. I can't marry you. When I marry it will be for love to the man of my dreams."

"And when are you going to meet him, eh? Tonight? I don't think so. Tomorrow? Doubtful. Next week? Next year? It'll be too late then. You'll be on the streets, the baby with foster parents, and then what? I might not be much to look at, old according to your books, but I'm honest, I'm faithful, and I'd never let you down. You'd have your own rooms, mind. You wouldn't have to share my bed, if that's what you're thinking. And you'll not be wanting for money. Think of it as security for Molly. She'd be well cared for. Spoiled. She'd have everything you could never give her and more besides."

Beth shook her head, dismissing the whole idea as complete lunacy. Utter madness. The man must be crazy to think she would ever consider marrying him.

"If you'd agree to marry me, lass, it would be a marriage of convenience, nothing more. I vow not to touch you. And if you did consent to be my wife, I would buy you Maisie's as a wedding present. Yours to do with as you want. The profits all yours. I certainly wouldn't expect you to sit about the house all day with nothing to do more than lording over the manor and twiddling your thumbs. No. This way we both get what we want. I get a beautiful young wife to keep me company and a ready-made daughter to dote on. You get your coffee shop and a lovely home and security. What more could be better?"

He reached out and took her hands. "Look at these. They're so sore and rough. Old hands for one so young. Delicate fingers such as yours shouldn't be buried in water and soap all day, lass. They should be soft. Displaying pretty rings and be beautifully manicured. I could give you all that. Mrs Potter would see to the washing. She would be doing the horrible jobs, like wiping pooey bums and clearing up sick, not you."

The sound of Molly crying caused them both to look towards the door. She pulled her hands away from his grip. "I'd best go and see to her."

"May I come too?"

She nodded her agreement.

Molly was lying on her stomach in her pram parked in the kitchen, pushing herself up on her arms, her blue eyes full of tears peering over the side. Her tiny face was contorting into another impending yell of impatience. Henry moved towards the pram.

"May I pick her up?"

"She's probably wet. I expect that's what's woken her." But she didn't prevent him from reaching in to lift the baby out of the pram.

Instantly, Molly stopped bawling, instead staring up at the stranger's fat face gazing fascinated back into her own. Beth stood back and watched. He seemed so gentle with her, so natural. Even his big clumsy-looking hands possessed a delicateness with the infant that she found difficult to fathom. It was if he was a natural to handling babies, and as she watched them, she could swear Molly smiled at him.

Would being married to this man be such a bad thing, she wondered. A mad thing, yes, but… well, there were advantages. Security. A home for them both. But could she trust him to keep his word?

She studied him silently as he cooed and talked baby-talk to the child. There was no doubting his immediate affection for her. Molly would be well catered for, probably spoiled rotten, as Henry had said, which was more than she would ever be able to do for her sister. Then there was that big house to consider. Most tempting of all, she would have Maisie's. But what a price to pay!

Her mind was in turmoil, thinking of all the pros, the cons. All the things that could go wrong. It seemed the perfect answer to her prayers, but was it the *right* one? There couldn't be many men willing to take on another man's child as Henry had just offered. And who would want to marry her with a child in tow? And as Henry had rightly pointed out, when would she ever be in a position to even meet another man?

All thoughts turned suddenly to Terry. He had wanted to marry her, but he'd clearly pushed her to the back of his mind. But what if he was innocent? What if he was released? What if it hadn't been his fault she'd not heard from him? Should she wait, find out the truth before jumping at the first viable solution to her current predicament? When she married, she thought it would be for love, not need. So many questions spiralled in her head, she felt dizzy. Oh, what a decision to have to make, she thought, totally confused and bewildered.

"Where would my brother live when he comes home?" she asked finally, wondering what Mike would think of it all.

Henry turned, holding Molly over his left shoulder and gently rubbing her back; Molly obviously enjoying the sensation, gurgled in contentment as she sucked on her fist.

"There are enough rooms at the house for Michael to have his own there, if he wants. Or else you could always do the rooms up over the coffee shop for him instead."

Henry had it all worked out, it seemed. He must have spent ages figuring out all the answers, pre-empting every worry or doubt she may have.

Could it work? Was it right? What would Mike say? Her father? Would he even care? And what would others think of her, marrying this man? The neighbours? The family? They'd not shown any interest in her or Molly's welfare so far but they'd all say she was only marrying him for his money. There would be gossip, tongues wagging, fingers pointing. Could she cope with all of that?

Of course she could. She didn't care what others thought about her now. It was her life. Her future. It didn't concern anyone else. But she wasn't going to rush into it. There were so many things still to consider.

"I need time to think about it, Mr Chiselhurst. But remember, if I do agree, I'm doing this for Molly."

"Fine. Just don't take too long."

Chapter Twenty-One

Beth read the label on the next record in the box then put it down in the reject pile. Too old fashioned. Teenagers don't want to listen to Eddie Calvert trumpeting *Oh Mein Papa* over espresso. They want the new stuff.

"Ahh, now that's more like it," she said aloud, spying *Such a Night* by Johnny Ray. She pulled the record in its red and white paper sleeve out of the box. "Now, he's a real heart-throb."

Other records were already stacked in piles of ten along the table. Before putting Johnny to join them, she quickly recounted the last pile – six, seven, eight. Oh, and we simply must have the number one, *Cara Mia* by David Whitfield, she decided. Right, one more to go and it just has to be *Broken Wings* by Dickie Valentine. It was a particular favourite of hers. The way he crooned always sent a shiver down her spine, made the hairs on the back of her neck quiver.

As she rummaged through the records remaining in the box, she could feel a tingle of excitement creeping over her, bubbling up ever closer to the surface. Coffee-A-Gogo was due to throw open its doors tomorrow. The Big Day less than twenty-four hours away. A day she had waited and worked so hard for. July the tenth, nineteen-fifty-four – a date she would never be able to forget. She could hardly believe it was almost here.

A loud knocking on the door made her look up. Henry stood outside, his face pressed close to the glass, making his fat jowls look even more grotesque as he sheltered the sun from his eyes to peer in.

"What, no music on, lass?" he asked cheerily as Beth opened the door to let him in. She stood on tiptoe to greet him with a light kiss to his cheek. In return, he planted a wet kiss on her head. "I'd have thought you'd have it playing full blast by now."

She laughed. "I'm spoilt for choice. I thought it would be easy choosing music for the jukebox. It's not. It's far more difficult than I'd imagined. I didn't expect to see you here today. You said you were going to be too busy."

Henry pulled at his tight collar and went across to inspect the new Seeburg M100B delivered that morning.

"Thought I'd drop by and see it before the storm hits. There's something I want to discuss."

He ran his hand over the smooth, chromium top of the jukebox before stooping to peer through its Perspex front, inspecting its innards, stabbing a finger at several buttons along its front. "Well, if your customers don't like the selection, you can always get them changed. I hope you've picked some Rosemary Clooney. She's a little belter, that one."

Beth joined him by the machine. "The delivery man who left the records said they come around every week to see which I want added or taken off."

A bright shaft of sunlight glinted off the top, blinding her for a moment. She squinted.

"Are you sure putting it by the window is the right place? With all the money in it, you might tempt fate and get robbed. It'll be easy for some hoodlum to put a brick through the glass and get in."

"I've put it there on purpose, Henry, so everyone passing can see it and realize what a lively, modern coffee shop old Maisie's Tea House has now become. Hopefully, it will tempt them in. The money in the machine will be emptied each day, so even if anyone did break in, they wouldn't get much."

"Let's hope the kids use it a lot, then, the price of this

thing. I could buy a flipping new car for how much it cost."

Remembering how Henry's complexion had changed from ruddy to grey when she'd first handed him the price list, Beth said laughingly, "I thought you were going to have a heart attack the way you choked until I reminded you I was only renting it."

"And if it breaks down, they will come and replace it straightaway?"

Beth nodded. "And I can swop it for a newer model over time. But it looks such a complicated contraption. I'm not even sure how it works yet, even though the man did show me several times. Thank goodness he's calling by later to load these on and slot in all the title cards."

Henry appeared satisfied with the jukebox and patted its top.

"Don't worry, lass, the kids will soon figure out where to put their money in, have no fears. That's all that matters. And with the building next door derelict, you won't have the worry of upsetting the neighbours with music blaring out all day." He turned and gazed about the room. "I'll give you your due, lass, it's a grand job. I didn't agree with the colour scheme at first as it seemed almost sacrilege to paint over all that lovely wood panelling, but it's turned out fine. It's hard now to even remember what the old place looked like."

"That's the whole point," said Beth, enthused. "The pale mint green on the walls has given the room a fresh look, makes it feel clean and… and… What's that word I'm looking for? … Cool! Yes, that's it. Cool. Cool and modern."

She tapped her foot lightly on the floor. "It was worth all the arguments, don't you agree? This industrial lino makes a difference, too. It's brilliant how the green and white marbling pattern complements the paint and the green leather upholstery on the bench seats along the wall." A wall now adorned with pictures, prints and posters: Frankie Laine sporting his famous cowboy hat, Perry Como and Al Martino, glamorous photos of Kay Starr and Jo Stafford, and others Henry had acquired through his many contacts.

Looking back over the past six months there had been many hectic, fraught times, what with the delay in the transfer of the lease, and then interminable waiting whilst the decorators and shopfitters came in and did their bit. Hold-ups when the wrong things had been delivered, or one of the painters overslept. A regular occurrence. Henry had said workmen were always like that, it was part of the game. But, to give them their due, they had always made up their time when they were running behind by working on an extra half-hour here and there or putting in a few hours on a Sunday morning. At the time there seemed to be frequent arguments with them, and with Henry, but now, on reflection, she realised they were more like inconveniences. Minor hold-ups that always got resolved one way or another.

Henry scowled. "We didn't argue, just had different opinions, that's all. I only gave my advice when I thought it necessary, and stopped you every now and again from getting too carried away with yourself and my chequebook. The only real fight was convincing me about having these tables made to order. They look good, mind, I have to say. Very good. They fit into your scheme perfectly."

He bent to inspect the underneath of the nearest table, shook the white Formica top, checking it was secured tight enough to the central chromium pillar. The tables and chairs were copied from a design Beth had seen in a

National Geographic magazine. It was the idea of the central support that had appealed most to her, getting rid of the usual four legs that always got in everyone's way. The gleam from the chromium matched the shine from the jukebox and the shimmer from the glass and mirrors around the counter. Maisie's was finally transformed, and Beth couldn't remember ever feeling so happy.

With much effort and puffing and blowing, Henry hauled himself up from his crouched position. Watching him, she was sure he had put on even more weight in the seven months they had been married.

"Did I tell you I had to buy Dickie a very large drink when he signed that one for you?" he said, pointing to a black and white photograph of Dickie Valentine hanging in a silver-coloured frame near the counter. "You take care of it, lass, it'll be worth a fortune one day. Dickie's going places. Said he might even pop in and say hello and see where you've hung him. Pride of place, I told him, pride of place. He lives nearby, lass, so he just might."

Beth doubted the singer would, but Henry was obviously proud of her; that was all that mattered. Looking around once more, she knew all those worries and frustration, the setbacks and delays, disagreements and arguments, all those times she'd had to gently persuade Henry to sign yet another cheque, had been worth the time and effort.

Her plans had finally come to fruition, and it felt good. But crawling amongst all these good feelings and the excitement, another emotion wormed itself around, tying her stomach in knots and sending her pulse racing. An even greater feeling of trepidation and fear of what tomorrow might bring.

"I'm nervous," she admitted.

He turned from the picture of Kitty Kallen he'd been

admiring. "What of?"

"Whether anyone will actually come in. What if the kids don't like the place? Or the pictures? What if they loathe the pick of the music to play and hate the taste of the coffee from my Gaggia?" Her hands were shaking so she clenched them into tight fists but still they shook. "What if they want food served? I'm only providing biscuits, chocolate bars and ice cream."

She couldn't be messing with all that cooking for Coffee-A-Gogo was to be just that. A coffee shop. A meeting place where they could be as rowdy as they liked, within reason. Somewhere where they could relax without upsetting the oldies. She didn't want middle-aged ladies out for afternoon tea or suited businessmen, like Henry, coming in to read their newspapers and smoke cigars, moaning to turn the music down.

"Then you change things until you get it right. You don't give up. If they can't stand the shape of those glass cups and saucers you've bought, you get something else. If they want egg and chips, you consider doing egg and chips. If they want sandwiches, you make sandwiches. It's all about supply and demand. The biggest thing in your favour is that you're roughly the same age as those kids you're hoping to attract. And, at the end of the day, if they dislike things that much, tell them to go somewhere else."

"There isn't somewhere else, least not around here."

He grinned broadly, his eye sockets almost losing themselves behind his swollen cheeks. "Then you've got a captured market." He gave her a hug. "You'll be just fine, lass, just fine. After all, isn't this what you wanted? And you wouldn't be normal if you weren't just a wee bit scared."

Normally she would have recoiled from his clutches,

but today she needed his support. A show of confirmation that she had done okay. His reassurances were comforting. Over the intervening months he'd become her backbone, her pillar of strength, and her path to a future now assured. She was grateful to him. What man would have done more for her in the pickle she was in? But underneath the surface, she was still a little in awe of Henry, unsure of where that future might lead.

It hadn't been easy reaching the decision to marry him. She'd spent several long nights tossing and turning in bed, unable to sleep, wondering what she should do, for in her heart the candle for Terry still burned, not brightly but the flickering flame wouldn't go out nonetheless. She knew waiting for him was hopeless, even if he were let out early for good behaviour. If she didn't marry Henry, what would have happened to her and Molly? A question she had asked herself over and over again. If she waited to fall in love and marry someone else, they certainly wouldn't be able to offer all the things that Henry had done. She probably would have spent the rest of her life scrabbling to make ends meet. By the time she was ready to tell Henry she would accept his proposal, she had convinced herself it was the right thing to do.

Today, with the coffee shop ready to fling open its doors on the world, that decision was confirmed as the correct one. Mum would be proud, she thought. Dad too, if he'd bothered to make the effort. If only he would come, just once, that would be enough, she thought wistfully as she brushed a large fleck of fluff from Henry's jacket. Suddenly, she remembered it was Thursday. Mrs Potter's day off. She pulled away.

"Where's Molly?"

"Don't panic. Mrs Potter's gone to visit a friend. She's taken Molly with her. Said the time together alone would do us good without having to fuss about the little one. I swear the woman regards that child as her own some days."

Beth relaxed, relieved. Adjusting to her new comfortable lifestyle was something she still found difficulty getting used to. A life in which Mrs Potter took over all the nursery duties whilst she was out all day tending to the emerging coffee shop. She found it hard to get out of the habit of making beds and changing sheets; many a time being told off by Mrs Potter shooing her away. Likewise doing the ironing and the shopping and cleaning the house. She couldn't deny Mrs Potter kept Hanbury House spotless.

When she had first moved in with Henry after the wedding, she had felt totally out of place. An intruder in Henry's well-kept house. At first too timid to touch anything, too scared to move and nervous to enter a room, unable to accept all that stood within Hanbury House and its vast garden was now hers. And as the new lady of the house, it felt uncomfortable giving the housekeeper orders. It didn't seem right somehow, so it had been easier to let Mrs Potter carry on the way she always had looked after Henry, choosing what food they ate and tending to Molly as she saw fit, and Molly seemed happy in the housekeeper's care.

Busch Lane seemed a lifetime away. Indeed it was, but her roots lay firmly back there. Living life as Mrs Chiselhurst seemed but a dream; one she was frightened would burst into nothingness when she awoke in the morning. Thrust back into reality and a life of poverty once more. Scrimping and saving, mending and washing.

"Well, you have to admit they do spend a lot of time together," Beth commented, adding, "I regard Mrs Potter as her surrogate grandmother. It's comforting to know

Molly's in safe hands all day. I've neglected the child so much lately I'm beginning to feel guilty."

"There's no reason why you should. After all, you're not her mother, and you are doing the best for her. The wee thing's too young to even notice you're not there half the time."

Beth shrugged. Henry was right. She wasn't Molly's mother just as much as he wasn't her father, but that didn't stop her caring for the child like one. Wanting to be there when she took her first tottering steps unaided, finding the first jagged little tooth to break through, the first utterings of a word. All these things she'd missed whilst she'd been busy overseeing the evolution of Coffee-A-Gogo rise from the rubble of Maisie's.

"And seeing as it's nearly lunch-time, lass, I've come along to take you out. Thought you could do with a drink. You've earned it." Henry looked around the coffee shop once more with admiration. "You've done well, lass, a grand job. I didn't think you had it in you."

"Oh ye of little faith, Henry Chiselhurst." She nudged him playfully in the ribs. "Well, I certainly showed you then, didn't I? And the rest. Us women can do just as good a job as you men. It's a pity you don't all give us the same credit. You men forget who kept this country running during the war whilst you were off playing guns and soldiers."

"Aye, and you young things forget we did it so you all could live in peace and have the freedom to open up coffee shops and enjoy yourselves."

"You're beginning to sound just like my father."

"I feel like him some days when I look at you. Your youth. Your beauty. When I look in the mirror of a morning as I shave, I sometimes wish I did have a daughter like you, with your strength and courage, and then I look at little Molly and think perhaps she is that daughter and I've been blessed. That's what I want to talk to you about." He reached for her left hand and admired the thick gold band and sparkling sapphire ring she wore.

Beth watched him curiously, studying the look on his face, the way his brown eyes were sparkling. Was he in love with her? Her brow furrowed, remembering the words Henry had spoken the day she'd tried on the engagement ring.

They had been in the jewellers opposite the Bell on the corner of Hounslow High Street. She remembered how expensive everything in there was. "The blue matches your eyes in the firelight," he had said, making her blush with embarrassment at such a compliment. More so because the salesman had been standing right by them on the other side of the counter and had heard every word. He must have thought her a proper little gold-digger, carrying on with a man old enough to be her father. Now she was beginning to wonder if Henry's motives were more than he'd admitted the day he'd suggested marriage. She shuddered at her own thoughts.

"Come on, grab your things. Let's go eat," Henry said. "I'm getting hungry. And I want to talk about young Molly."

"You'll have to wait a minute whilst I lock up out back. I still find it hard getting used to dining out in good restaurants. Drinking the best wines. The taste of good-quality Scotch beef instead of stewed mutton or sprats, although there's nothing wrong with either, and some days I could just fancy a big bowl of them, all lightly floured and fried."

He waved his arm about the air in gesture. "If Madam wants fried sprats then she shall have fried sprats. I'll tell Mrs Potter to get some for tomorrow night's tea. And if you want eels, pie and mash, we shall eat eels, pie and mash."

"You spoil me," she told him, laughing, thinking if she wasn't careful, she would grow as fat as him with such good living.

He was certainly generous. She could go out and buy whatever clothes she liked, never having to worry if there was enough in her purse, juggling the wants against the needs now a thing of the past.

Molly no longer had to wear hand-me-downs and faded, well-worn matinee jackets. Her nursery was full of the new clothes and toys Henry had generously bought. Spending money seemed to be no problem for him.

Despite his seemingly always open chequebook, she didn't go mad spending. Each item was valued and judged for its need and purpose, but it was such a wonderful feeling to be able to have her hair permed properly in the latest style by professional hairdressers, instead of having it cut at home. The pleasure at being able to search through the clothes rails at Dickens & Jones in Richmond, able to choose the latest fashions and colours, have shop assistants fetch and carry, helping her to do up zips on full-skirted dresses. Now they suggested alterations to make a dress fit her slim figure better, the use of their own tailors all part of the service. And nothing could match the thrill of being able to say, "Just put it on Mr Chiselhurst's account." It made Beth feel she was royalty. Someone special.

She also valued the way Henry treated her with affection in a fatherly sort of way. He showed respect for her own wishes, needs and opinions, much more than Dad had ever done, and whilst Henry might not have always agreed with those opinions, argued them sometimes, he accepted them regardless.

Perhaps it *is* love for me he feels, she thought, as she went through to the back of the shop to lock the back door and pick up her crocodile-skin handbag. But it certainly wasn't love she felt in return. Not the same kind of love she had felt for Terry. Her feelings for Henry were more of gratitude, and as time had moved on, she'd come to regard him as her best friend. Possibly her only friend after Mike, and he didn't really count as being a friend seeing as he was her brother. This was different.

Could friendship be a form of love, she wondered. That special kind of love with no physical contact other than the exchange of delicate kisses on cheeks or head, the squeezing of a hand, the touch of a shoulder? Could their marriage last being nothing more than a friendship? A convenience?

Marrying Henry had been her salvation and, true to his word, he had kept to his side of the bargain. In every aspect. Not once had he tried to force himself upon her, instead showering her with money and fine jewellery, even persuading her to have her ears pierced so he could bestow more upon her. Thinking about that now made her wince at the memory of that sudden shot of the ear gun when the process was carried out at the jewellers. She twiddled at her earlobe, unable to get out of the habit of checking the delicate golden butterflies were still in place securing the fine-engraved gold hoops she had put in that morning.

"Come on," Henry bellowed impatiently. "Pub'll be shut by the time we get there at this rate."

"I'm coming, I'm coming. Hold your horses," she retorted jovially, pushing her way through the beaded curtain dividing the back room from the main shop. "I'm ready now."

As they made their way out of the door, she suddenly

knew how Cinderella must have felt, finding her Prince Charming, turning from rags to riches. Only her Prince Charming was no fairy tale, and whilst Henry hadn't presented her with a glass slipper, he had presented her with a comfortable home. There may have been no true-lover's kiss to awaken her from the depths of despair and imminent destitution, but there was life in the man and she did enjoy his company. Happy ever after as long as he kept to his side of the bargain, and his side of the bedroom door.

The Star and Garter on Kew Bridge wasn't one of the better public houses they frequented, but it wasn't very far to walk from Coffee-A-Gogo, and the sandwiches they served were excellent. She waited and watched as Henry spread a thick layer of yellow mustard onto his ham.

"Do you want some, lass?" He offered her the small, brown earthenware pot.

She shook her head, not wanting to spoil the taste of the ham sliced fresh off the bone.

"You said you wanted to discuss Molly. Is there a problem?" She dreaded Henry's answer. Was Mrs Potter about to leave? Did she not like the child, because Molly had certainly taken to her and appeared more than content?

Henry took a large mouthful of sandwich and chewed, as if mulling over how he was going to phrase himself. Finally, he swallowed.

"Not a problem, lass, no. A proposition. I want to adopt Molly. Make her my own daughter, all official and legal like. I want you to write to your father and tell him."

The idea of adoption didn't come as any surprise. Henry had mentioned it on many occasions, saying how much happier and settled their relationship would be.

How it would be best for the infant, seeing as how he was doing everything a father would do for his child.

With each day that had passed, it had been obvious Molly had grown more and more attached to him. He had proved to be a good, caring father figure, but all the while she kept thinking it was wrong that he should be looking after her little sister when their own real dad was still alive and kicking up the mud in deepest, dullest Gloucestershire. It wasn't right.

"I'll write to him, but you know Dad. He probably won't even bother to answer. He never does. He's had nothing to do with us since the day we first left." Her eyes filled with tears. It still hurt being abandoned no matter how hard she tried to hide it. It was like an empty void inside her heart.

Henry picked up his glass of whisky. "I have to have his permission. It would be different if we didn't know where he was, but we do, and the courts won't grant custody or sign an adoption order without it."

"And if he doesn't?"

"Look, lass, I love Molly. How's she going to feel as she gets older and starts school? She's going to wonder why you and she have different surnames. She's going to ask all sorts of awkward questions. And she's going to get teased something rotten. Bullied. I know kids. They can be right bastards to others who are different. What are you going to tell her then? That I'm not her real dad and the person she'll regard as her grandfather is, in fact, her real one. That isn't any way to grow up. If I adopt her, the problems will not be there and she need never know the truth."

"But I *want* her to know the truth, Henry. She has a right to know her real father even though he never looked at her or held her. You can't bring a kid up in a world surrounded by lies. That isn't fair. Anyway, the truth is bound to come out sooner or later. Think how she would feel then?"

"Aye lass, you have a point, but she needn't be told until she's older. Much older. When she's twenty-one. You seem to be finding excuses for me not to adopt. Don't you want me to? I thought that was part of our agreement."

"No, Henry, it wasn't. We only spoke of the possibility. Look, it's not that I don't want you to, far from it. You've been more of a father to her than any child could wish for, and it's marvellous the way you look after her. And me. It's just, well..."

"Well, what?"

She shifted uncomfortably on the red leather bench. "It's just I know he won't reply to any letter. It'll be a wasted effort. He'll just bury his head in the cabbage patch as usual and ignore me, so what's the point? It was the same when I wrote about wanting to marry you. No response. No permission. Not even a card to wish us well. Let's be fair, Henry, it's over seven months since I last wrote. What makes you think he'll answer now? He might even be dead for all we know."

"Those people at the farm would have told you, you daft ha'p'orth. Look, lass, if he doesn't answer then we drive down to Gloucestershire and force him, face to face. We'll even take my solicitor along if necessary. By your father's continued refusal to acknowledge Molly as his own and his persistence in ignoring you adds further weight to our argument. The more he thinks this is all going to go away, the more it's going to persuade the courts in our favour. If he's relinquished all his responsibilities for his children, no court in the world is going to refuse Molly's adoption."

Beth watched him over the top of her schooner of sweet sherry. "Is it really that important to you?"

He put down his glass and looked directly into her eyes. "Yes. I want a real family. I want the world to acknowledge I have a wife and a lovely daughter. And I don't want to have to forge his signature a second time. Not where Molly's concerned. It was different for you and I getting hitched, we're adults, but Molly's only a child. It could lead to all sorts of complications later on if we don't do it properly."

"Okay, have it your way. I'll write tonight." But first, she would write to Mike and ask his advice, she decided. After all, Molly was as much his sister and responsibility as hers. At least she knew she would get a reply from him.

When she'd written to Mike telling of her impending marriage to Henry, he'd sent a telegram wishing her good luck, shortly followed by a long letter expressing his surprise that she should be marrying a man many years her senior, and in such haste. He'd asked how she had managed to persuade their father to give his permission.

The truth was she hadn't. After waiting several weeks for his response, Henry had become impatient, unwilling to wait any longer and so had forged her father's signature on the consent form.

It was wrong, she knew, but she had little choice. It was either that or no marriage. Dad's consent was immaterial, Henry had said. In another few years, her father's signature on a scrap of paper wouldn't matter anyway as she would be twenty-one. Of legal age to marry without parental consent. She had wanted to wait but Henry had been very persuasive.

At least Mike had sent his love and given his blessing. That was all she wanted from her father. Just a little something to prove she and Molly still existed in his eyes.

Chapter Twenty-Two

"Giss a nuvver cuppa coffee, darlin'. Ain't you got nuffin' more wiv it on that jukebox? That Alma Cogan's doin' me head in. Ain't you got that Bill 'aley fella?"

Beth regarded Dave Smith, one of her regular customers, standing on the other side of the counter. He was looking at his reflection in the big mirror at the back of the shelves behind the counter, admiring his long, grey jacket with its red-piped collar and cuffs. He straightened the Slim Jim tie at his wing-collared, blue shirt.

"Like the suit, darlin'? Only got it yesterday out of Burton's."

She didn't have to look over the counter to know he wore matching drainpipe trousers with his suede shoes. The way all the kids liked to dressed now. The style had rapidly become the fashion for this generation with liberty taken from the Edwardian era, except now they also wore colourful, bright socks.

The Teddy Boys. The newspapers had daubed them with the nickname and the name had stuck. Their clothes and hairstyles and their music set this new breed of teenager apart, and hanging about the coffee bars was the new hip thing to do.

She was happy to be part of the culture and, whilst she couldn't join in their social life as much as she would have liked, running the coffee bar was the next best thing. She was in the centre of things, able to enjoy the banter and music and atmosphere as much as her customers on the other side of the counter. They were of her own age, her own thinking and she loved the music. Her music. Fun, lively, foot-tappable rhythms and beat that made you want to shout and sing and move with freedom and happiness. Much better than that classical rubbish Henry always played at home.

"The records get changed on a Friday, you should know that by now, Dave," she said. "Someone in here obviously likes it though. It keeps being played."

"Nah, it's only Nobby over there keeps puttin' it on. 'E only does it to wind me up like, know wot I mean?" He turned to his mates sitting in a blue haze of cigarette smoke at a table next to the jukebox. "Don't you, Nob?" he shouted across. A roar of laughter issued forth from their corner.

"I'll make sure it comes off on Friday for you, and get *Shake Rattle and Roll* loaded instead. Great for making you get up and dance."

She'd lost count of how many times the music on the jukebox had been changed since opening a year ago. Only *Broken Wings* remained of her original selection, and she was adamant that was staying there. It was her favourite. Her song. A pleasant reminder of back to the beginning, that first day. How, shortly after turning the sign over on the door, a lad of about eighteen came jigging in, wolf-whistled at the décor, then sauntered over to the jukebox where upon he exclaimed, "Cor, dig this great music." Her first customer and he approved of it all. He'd been followed swiftly by more and more eager customers coming in as word spread over the next few days, and she hadn't looked back since.

"Yeah. I bet you and your old man do a mean jive." Dave gave a cheeky wink, pulled out a packet of Weights cigarettes and offered one across the counter. "Wanna fag?"

She shook her head. "Thanks, but I don't smoke."

He looked taken aback. "Don't smoke? But everybody smokes." He lit one up, inhaling deeply then flicked the spent match into a blue tin ashtray on the counter.

"Me and my old man prefer waltzing," she told him with a smile as she refilled his glass cup and pushed it and the saucer back across the counter. "He's a bit doddery on his feet on account of bunions."

That bit wasn't quite true, and she didn't have a clue how to waltz either, but what concern was that of Dave's? Small-talk was all part of her job. Part of the fun and one of the many reasons why the Teds loved coming in here, she guessed.

"Cor, he sounds just like our dad. He's always complaining of his aches and pains."

Clamping the cigarette tightly between his teeth, he pulled out a metal comb from his jacket pocket, flashing the brightly-coloured paisley silk lining, and began fussing with his Brylcreemed hair, checking his appearance again in the back mirror.

"Your DA's just fine, Dave, only please, not over my counter, there's a love." She rebuked him with a friendly smile, one that said no harm done but don't do it again or you won't get served. Her regulars knew the score – step out of line and you're barred. They all respected her wishes.

"Sorry, darlin'." He put a tanner down on the counter. "About time you kept this place open a bit later an' all. We ain't got nowhere else to go of an evenin'. There's nuffin' else round 'ere."

"Nonsense. Why, there's plenty. You've got the cinemas, the youth club. There's the bowling alley and even Hammersmith Palais just up the road. What do you want to be hanging around a coffee bar for all evening? There's loads of other places."

The idea of keeping open for longer of an evening had been something she'd thought of already, and had been pushing the idea to Henry, only he'd been reluctant to even consider the idea. Couldn't see the sense of it, even if it did mean more clientele. And more clientele meant more money in the till. It was still a big bone of contention between them.

Dave shook his head. "Blimey, you don't get about much then do you? Look, Friday nights is Palais night. Pick up a new bird night, like. Sa'urdays you always takes your bird to the pictures, usually the Regal near the bus depot. The youth club only opens two nights a week and they don't want us lot in there. We all got kicked out the other week. The gaffer said we was a bad influence an' troublemakers. As if? So where else are we expected to go? Out drinkin' all night? We can't afford that. Anyways, we all likes somewhere to meet up before'and or for a coffee after. You know, somethin' to round the night off wiv. At the moment, if we wanna do that we 'ave to go up Chiswick High Road or 'Ammersmith Roundabout, and that's a bloody long walk at the end of the night, I can tell you." He picked up his coffee and went to join his friends.

"Did you ask her, Smiffy?" Beth heard one of them ask Dave as he sat down.

She was right about his drainpipe trousers and the nancy-boy shoes, as Henry referred to the coloured suede shoes all the Teddy Boys wore. Another epithet the press had conferred on them. She hated the term.

Hers were good kids, no trouble at all. They were all polite and never gave her any hassle. There were two lads in particular who always watched out for her if there seemed the slightest inkling of trouble from anyone. Her bodyguards, she called them.

Johnny Suthren, one of Dave's friends, strutted up to the counter. He, too, wore the required uniform to be part of the gang. His drainpipes were navy today, his long jacket piped in black velvet. And like Dave, his hair also slicked back with Brylcreem. His sideburns reached down almost to his chin. A good-looking boy, one who normally came in around five-thirty with his girlfriend, Sue Calloway. They often helped at closing time by collecting the dirty crockery and sweeping the floor, in return for a couple of bottles of coke or a free coffee.

"'Ere Beth," Johnny said, plonking his elbows down on the counter and propping up his chin. "I gotta big favour to ask you."

"Such as?"

"Me and Sue's like gettin' 'itched. Five weeks next Thursday, it is. We was wonderin' like, if we could 'ave the reception 'ere?"

"A wedding reception? What, here?"

Johnny nodded, wide-eyed and hopeful.

"But why here? Surely you'd be better off having it in a proper hall or down the pub. The Apprentice along the river has a lovely function room upstairs, and the—"

"It ain't gonna be that sort of weddin'," he interrupted. "Me and our Sue, we only wants our mates wiv us. Me Mum an' Dad ain't comin', on account they don't like Sue. They thinks she's too young for me, and her parents can't afford anythin' posh. It's only goin' to be in a registry office. We was kinda hopin' you could lay on a few sandwiches like, and coffee, and we could have a bit of a dance to the jukebox. We don't want no booze nor nuffin' like that. Only we was hopin' you might keep the gaff open all evenin'. We'd pay you, of course."

She was so taken aback by his request she was at a loss what to say. All the weddings she'd ever been to normally ended up in a punch-up. Fists flying and hair pulling over something so totally stupid, usually because everyone got themselves so drunk. But she'd only been to family weddings. Weren't all family do's like that? She pondered the request. If, as Johnny was suggesting, there were to be no alcohol and no family present then maybe there wouldn't be any fights. And, seeing as this was their own place, somewhere where they all liked to hang out, then perhaps they would respect it and not cause any trouble, like Johnny said.

She was still mulling it over when Johnny confirmed, as if reading her mind, "Look, there won't be no trouble, I promise. It's only me mates. You know most of 'em 'cos they all comes in 'ere. They all thinks it's the best place for it."

"I'll think about it," she replied, refusing to be pressed into giving an immediate answer, "but I'm not making any promises. It all depends on what the governor thinks tonight when I put it to him. He doesn't like me working late." But this might be just the impetus needed to help make him change his mind, she thought.

"I thought this was *your* place, not your old man's?" Johnny retorted, standing erect.

"It is, but he is my husband and what he says, goes."

Johnny laughed. "I'd best send my Sue round to you to 'ave a chat like then. She thinks she's gonna rule the roost after we's 'itched. Perhaps you can tell her like it really is."

Beth laughed with him. "Yeah, right. My old man might think he's the boss but us girls have a way of wheedling what we want from our men. Special little ways of turning ideas around so as to make them think they thought of it first. In the end, we always get our own way."

A smile lit his face. "Good, so that means you gonna do the reception?"

"Like I said, Johnny, I'll think about it. I'll let you know by the weekend."

Hopefully by then she would have convinced Henry staying open longer was the right move forward, and he would wonder why he hadn't thought of it sooner. She would put the suggestion to him later that afternoon, when she took the accounting books across to his office.

The climb up the narrow staircase leading to Henry's office was as intimidating as the first time she had climbed these well-worn wooden treads, remembering the fear, the trepidation, the pain of that first day.

A steady clonk, clonk, clonk resounded down the stairwell. The sounds of someone typing. Henry still hasn't got around to changing that old monstrosity of a typewriter yet, she thought with a wry smile, recognizing the noise. So much had happened to her since that cold December day back then when she'd first sat down at it. What a difference in her life since then, far more then she'd ever dared thought possible.

She took the last few steps to the top landing with pride and, ignoring the Please Knock Before Entering sign on the outer office door, walked in.

The stale odour of dust and aged paper assaulted her nostrils. She wanted to sneeze. Things hadn't changed. Glancing swiftly around the room the only real difference she could see was the typist. Yet another in Henry's long line of secretaries. None of them seemed to last very long. Couldn't take the pace he worked at, nowhere as up to the job as you were, he kept telling her whenever one left.

This one was a slip of girl, wearing too much lipstick and rouge for Beth's liking, sitting at the desk she had once occupied. So, which one was this? Annie? Susan? Shirley? She couldn't remember, there'd been so many she'd lost track. The girl stopped typing and looked up, brushing her long blonde fringe away from her eyes as she spoke.

"Yes? Can I help?"

Her strong, efficient voice impressed Beth. The lack of a smile or word of welcome didn't, nor her clipped, abrupt tone.

"I'll go straight through, Mr Chiselhurst is expecting me." Beth made for Henry's closed door. Through its frosted glass panel, she could see his broad outline – he was standing, talking to someone on the telephone.

Swiftly, Joanne stepped around the desk, blocking her path. "Excuse me. You can't go in. Mr Chiselhurst is talking to a client."

From the other side of the door, Henry could be heard saying goodbye. This was followed by the clunk of the telephone receiver being put down.

"That's all right, he won't mind me. I'm Beth Chiselhurst."

"Oh!" Joanne's quick hand shot to the bakelite handle and with the other, rapped on the glass pane.

"Your daughter's here, Mr Chiselhurst," she announced, opening the door.

Henry's face reddened rapidly.

Joanne shot her a steely glare before moving out of the way to let her pass.

Beth felt herself blanch. Why did everyone automatically assume she was his daughter? And surely Henry had told her his wife was coming in with her accounts?

"I'm Mrs—" Chiselhurst, she was about to inform the girl but Henry butted in.

"Thank you, Joanne. Please bring in two teas and hold any phone calls." When the door closed, he pointed to the two black books Beth clutched to her chest. "I see you've brought the ledgers."

She handed him the accounts books as she sat down. "Well, it's almost a year to the day since Coffee-A-Gogo opened and trade's good, even you have to admit that. The café's invariably full no matter what time of day. I think you'll find everything is in order in those. I've managed to balance all the columns like you showed me, and according to my calculations, I'm actually in profit."

He smiled. "And according to mine and the laws of accountancy, I very much doubt it, lass. It will be at least three years before we see a return on my investment. I thought I explained all that before. You're forgetting the actual costs of all the decorating and equipment have to be deducted first. Once we have recouped those costs, then we can start to see where we're going."

"Oh dear. Yes, I'd forgotten about that bit." Beth shot him a meek smile. "Still, with your guidance and expertise I'm sure all is well. There can't be many café owners that can boast their accountant having more than a vested interest in their business. But Henry, bookkeeping is so boring. Isn't there another way we can do this?"

"Boring, is it?" he guffawed. "It keeps you well, my dear. To me, boredom would be standing behind a hot counter all day serving cups of coffee and listening to wretched music blaring out. To me, figures are king. They tell no lies, hide no secrets."

He opened the sales ledger to the appropriate page and began to run his index finger down the right-hand column. Beth knew he was adding up the totals in his head, and marvelled at how he could do it without jotting down little sums and calculations in the margin as he went. It took her long enough to add up two totals in her head, how he could do a complete page and carry it over to the next, was beyond her.

Joanne crept in and put down two cups of tea on the desk.

"Thank you," Beth mouthed so as not to disturb Henry whilst he concentrated. Joanne stared intently at her for a moment, not even a glimpse of a smile before slipping back out, closing the door without a sound.

Well, Joanne was certainly efficient, Beth thought, taking a sip of the weak tea, but she did need to work on her client communication skills a bit.

What bothered her more was why Henry hadn't corrected Joanne's mistake in thinking she was his daughter. It was almost as if he was embarrassed to admit it. Why, for God's sake? It's not as if it's illegal or anything for an older man to marry a younger woman. Look at all those film stars. They did it all the time.

Henry picked up a short, stubby pencil and made an alteration to one figure then continued his silent adding up. Beneath her last entry he finally wrote a total, drew two black lines underneath with the aid of his wooden ruler and then closed the ledger.

"Not bad, lass, not bad, but you must write with more clarity. It's too easy to misread a one for a seven with sloppy handwriting. Even easier to switch numbers around in error. The Germans have it right, putting a line through a seven so it isn't mistaken for a one."

"I've seen that," Beth commented, "only to me that looks more like the number's been crossed out."

"No, lass, errors should be crossed out with a slash and rewritten alongside, certainly not overwritten like some of yours. You can't tell which is the correct figure when you do it like that. Now, the most important point is adhering to double-entry bookkeeping principles. These are strict. For every debit out of your sales ledger there must be a corresponding balancing credit in your purchase ledger..."

She tried to concentrate on what Henry was advising, but the matter of her introduction was niggling, wheedling its way through her brain like a parasite.

"Then why don't you do it all? I'm no good with figures," she said crossly. "I was always useless at arithmetic at school, especially divisions and subtractions. And I could never see the point in knowing how many times eleven divided into a hundred-and-twenty-one, or how many degrees there were in a right-angled triangle."

"Or how many cups of coffee you could get out of a two-pound bag of fresh beans," he interjected with a lighthearted laugh. "Now you can see why. Anyway, running the coffee shop was your idea. That includes the bookkeeping, right? Now, let's go through the bought ledger and see what that throws up."

He opened the other book and looked down. His tea had gone cold, she noticed.

When she left Henry's inner sanctum a short while later, Beth stopped alongside the desk watching Joanne engrossed in trying to scrub out a mistake using a pencil rubber on several sheets of paper sticking out of the typewriter. The black from the carbon paper had marked her fingers and left inky carbon smudges on the back of each white sheet. As she rubbed away, the tip of Joanne's tongue poked out. Then Joanne drew a deep breath and blew away the fine filaments of pink pencil rubber, sending them scattering through the metal workings of the typewriter. Becoming aware suddenly of her standing there watching, Joanne jumped in her chair in surprise.

"A bit of advice," Beth proffered, "ask Mr Chiselhurst to buy you a proper typist's eraser when he next gets stationery. It doesn't tear the paper or smudge so much.

And by the way, I'm not Henry's daughter, I'm Mrs Chiselhurst. His *wife*!"

Joanne's jaw dropped.

Mmm, thought Beth, making her way back down the narrow staircase, Henry clearly hadn't told Joanne anything about her, judging by the astonished look on the girl's face. Why? And why had he blatantly avoided correcting the mistake? Was he ashamed of her? Of himself? She shook her head in disbelief. That didn't sound like Henry at all. He was always saying he wanted the whole world to know he had a wife and a daughter, even if Molly's adoption was still in debate.

As she strode back across Richmond Green heading for home, the whole puzzling episode in the office buzzed around and around inside her head like a wasp looking for something to sting.

Chapter Twenty-Three

From the way Henry crunched the gears of the Jaguar, Beth knew he was not happy with the idea of her catering for a wedding reception.

"I see little of you as it is," he grouched, glancing quickly at her sitting stiff-backed and upright on the soft leather seat, hands clasped firmly in her lap. Screeching away from a set of traffic lights by Heathrow Airport, he slammed the gearstick into second, accelerating fast.

She winced at the noise, her teeth on edge. She despaired if the way he was driving today they would even arrive at the restaurant in Virginia Water.

Normally, she enjoyed riding in their car. It was much smoother to travel in and didn't bounce and rattle over any bumps like Terry's car used to, remembering how, whenever Terry turned a corner, she had to hold on to the dashboard or brace herself against the door.

She bit the inside of her top lip, wondering why she should suddenly think of him after all this time. He'd not crossed her mind even once since the day she had accepted Henry's marriage proposal, putting him to the deepest reaches of her memory in the hope that they would disintegrate with time and crumble away to nothingness. Any feelings for him she thought were well and truly buried deep in her past. Yet here he was now, in her head, the night he'd kissed her goodbye outside the cottage gate at Clackett's Farm and driven off into the darkness. Like some phantom ghost reappearing to haunt her.

She gave Henry a furtive glance as he concentrated on overtaking a Bedford van crawling along, and realised the flickering in her heart wasn't nerves of Henry's bad driving, it was the flame of emotion burning inside for Terry making her feel uneasy. Unsettled.

Staring out of the passenger window at the houses and gardens flashing by, she tried to shake the image of Terry from her head by wishing all those mean, dreadful landladies who had slammed their front doors on her, turning their noses up at her, could see how respectable she had now become.

It was her aunts and uncles that should be shamed for refusing to help her and Molly when they needed it most. Rejection made all the more cruel by the knowledge that her father would have helped any one of them if they had been in trouble. Yes, let them *all* see her now. See how she'd managed without them. How she'd clawed herself up in the world and made something of her life despite the odds. But knowing her family as she did, they would only think she had come to show off and gloat.

There was only one person who wouldn't think that way of her. Annie Coombes. Mrs Coombes wouldn't look upon her visit as showing off; she'd be delighted to see how well she and the baby were doing. Perhaps Henry would take her there at the weekend? She turned to him to ask, but instead studied his face, his brow set in a frown, mouth closed tight, concentrating on his driving whilst chewing his thoughts angrily in his mind. No, perhaps now wasn't the best time to ask, she decided. Not in the mood he was so obviously in.

Henry must have felt her eyes on him for he turned his head slightly towards her.

"What?"

"Nothing," she said with a shrug.

"Then why are you glaring at me in that way? You always do when you're angry with me."

"I'm not angry with you, Henry, I just wish you'd slow

down a bit. Your driving's making me nervous. Calm down."

"Well, how do you expect me to feel? We don't spend a lot of time together now as it is, without you working extra hours in that flaming café. It's taking over your life."

"I don't recall our marriage arrangement mentioning anything about having to spend time together," she retorted, a little unkindly she realised the moment the words were out.

"Henry, we do spend time together. Look at us now, all dressed up and going out to dine. Why, only last week you took me to the theatre. In any case, you often have your head buried in the newspaper or pawing over ledgers, bringing work home. And where are you every Tuesday night?"

"At the office working, as you well know."

He indicated right and pulled into the car park beside the restaurant, turned off the ignition and turned in his seat to face her, one elbow on the back of the leather upholstery, the other on the wooden steering wheel.

"Beth, I worry that you don't enjoy your time with me. You always look tired. You fell asleep in the Odeon the other evening."

"That was because I found the film boring. Gangsters and guns or cowboys are not my scene, particularly when they start fighting and brawling as if using fists is the only way to settle an argument. If it isn't cowboys and Indians, it's horrible war films. I don't enjoy them."

He patted her knee. "Your penance for forcing me to take you to see James Dean last week. Look, I don't want you doing this wedding because it's too much extra work and you don't have a licence for dancing."

"It's a private party, I don't need one," she reminded him.

"There'll be trouble. There always is with these kids. You read about it in the papers all the time. It'll end in a fight and they'll wreck the place, and then where would you be? Kids these days don't respect anything."

She sighed. "Oh, Henry, you really have no idea, do you? You don't know these kids at all. They're not vandals, layabouts and good-for-nothings. I know my customers. They wouldn't do that. They know if they wreck the joint they'd have nowhere else to go. Coffee-A-Gogo is like a second home to them. It's not as if the door will be open and anyone can just walk in."

"And it's about time you wrote to your father again. My solicitor's written several times and he's ignored him. The adoption can't go ahead until he agrees. I'm running out of patience." He got out of the car, slamming the door.

"It's nothing more than expected. He's not interested in Molly no more than he is in me. He's never going to answer," she said when he pulled open the passenger door to help her out.

"Then next week we drive down and have it out with him. We should have done it months ago, not all this pussy-footing about. Molly'll be grown up and married the rate things are going."

"Henry, even Mike's tried to get him to make a decision. Apparently, he won't discuss it. Or me. I think you should seriously give up on this adoption idea. We're never going to get anywhere."

Henry's nostrils flared. "Never! Henry Chiselhurst never gives up; you should know that by now. I always get what I want."

Inside the restaurant, he pulled out a chair at a table for her, then seated himself down opposite before beckoning the waiter to bring the menus. As usual, he ordered for them both.

"I still can't understand why those kids can't have a proper do. Hire a hall or a room at the Star and Garter like most normal people do for weddings," he said when the waiter had gone.

"Because they want something different. Teenagers don't want to do things the way their parents or their grandparents did. They want to do it their way. This isn't a conventional wedding. As a matter of fact, I feel quite honoured to be asked. It shows they trust me, that they like me and the café. I can't refuse."

"You'll be worn out, what with running the place all day then making up masses of sandwiches and rolls, and then on your feet all evening."

"Stop trying to find excuses for me, Henry. I've decided and that's that. I will shut the shop in the afternoon to prepare. A couple of the girls have volunteered to help me with the food."

"What about a cake? They have to have a cake. All weddings have cake. It's tradition."

Beth glared at him, dumbfounded. "Ours didn't."

"That was different."

She sat back in her chair, indignant. "No, it wasn't. We just happened to have an unconventional marriage. Well, Johnny and Sue's wedding is going to be unconventional too. I can't see the difference." She thought for a few moments then smiled across to Henry and picked up her soup spoon. "I shall ask Mrs Potter to make them a cake as our wedding present."

"*Our* wedding present? Oh no. You keep me out of this," he said, his voice rising by several octaves. "I don't know the kids. There's no 'our' about it."

"Ssshhh. Stop shouting. Everyone's looking. You know, you could come along and join us that evening. It'll be fun. Johnny and Sue won't mind." The thought of Henry jiving and gyrating across the floor of Coffee-A-Gogo to Bill Haley or Tommy Steele filled her with mirth, all those rolls of fat wobbling around. Mr Roly-Poly man.

"What's tickled your fancy?" he asked, noticing her amused expression.

"Nothing, Henry. Finish your soup before it gets cold."

When Sue and Johnny arrived from the registry office, Beth effused how stunning she thought Sue's outfit looked. The white, full skirt with layers of stiff petticoats, and the white frilly blouse she wore were set off by a bright, wide red belt around her trim waist. She wore white bobby-socks and white pumps and had her long, auburn hair pulled back into a ponytail tied with a scarlet ribbon intertwined with gypsophila. A happier and prettier bride Beth couldn't remember seeing.

Johnny wore his grey Ted suit, edged in red velvet trimming. His black hair was slicked up into a quiff with the front pulled down into a single curl over his forehead. He looked so smart and so proud with Sue clutching his arm, it brought a tear to Beth's eyes.

At least Johnny and Sue had married because they loved each other and had all their friends around them, celebrating a day they would remember all their lives, she thought wistfully, looking enviously from behind the counter as a stream of guests almost tumbled in behind them. The girls were kissing Sue, pushing pretty paper-wrapped parcels decorated with bows and ribbon into her hands. The lads, too, were kissing Sue, some a bit too familiarly for a new bride, she noticed with amusement.

It was all so different from her own wedding; that brief, sombre moment, with two passing strangers persuaded in from the street to act as witnesses because Henry had no family, and she had no one she wished to invite. No friends. No gifts. No cake. Not even a honeymoon. Nothing at all like the wedding she had imagined or wished for.

The jukebox burst into life as Bill Haley started what was going to be a busy time for him and all the other records on the machine. Already the noise of the music and voices and laughter were deafening, and a long queue had formed at the counter.

"Set 'em up, Beth, we're gaspin'," Dave Smith yelled out. "Cokes all round, on me!"

When Beth carried in the square, white-iced cake Mrs Potter had baked, a burst of applause broke out, and loud cheering resounded around the room. Freddy Suthren, Johnny's elder brother and best man, had brought along a brownie box-camera and was busy taking photographs of the bride and groom holding the carving knife, poised in the act of cutting the cake. Snapping pictures of everyone enjoying themselves until the film ran out.

Whilst everyone ate their slice of fruitcake, complimenting the cook and praising Beth on such a good bash, Beth emptied the money from the jukebox then set it to free play for the remainder of the evening.

The notice that had been taped to the door had fallen to the floor. Someone had trodden on it for the Closed–Private Party sign now had a dirty footprint of a brogue across the neatly handwritten words. Picking it up, she managed to catch Johnny's attention, beckoning him over.

"Is everyone here now who's coming?" she asked.

Johnny shrugged. "I think so, but some of me mates were gonna drop by later."

"Okay, I'll leave the door unlocked. I'll just put this

notice back on the door. Hope it sticks, I'm out of Sellotape. It's turning into a good do, isn't it?" She smiled widely at him, pleased it was all going so well.

"Oh crackin', Beth. The best. Thanks a million. We owe you one."

On her way back to the counter she wiggled and jigged in time to the music, the money in her pocket jangling and clanking as she moved. Peggy and Linda, who had helped her so much already with preparing the food, were behind the counter and shooed her away.

"Take a break, Beth. We'll hold the fort here for a bit. Go on, go have some fun. Where's that Doug? He promised to show you how to jive, didn't he? Doug, Doug, over here," Peggy called out, waving the tea towel in the air to catch his attention.

Doug sidled over to Beth, bowed, took her hand and pressing it to his lips, kissed the back of it delicately.

"Would madam care to dance?" He'd spoken in an exaggerated, fake posh voice that sounded so funny Beth couldn't help but giggle.

"Yes please, young man."

"Right then. Come on, sister, let's show this party 'ow to swing. Trev, Trev," Doug shouted above the din to the lad standing at the jukebox choosing records, "put on number thirty-two and let's teach the little lady 'ow to rock-n-roll."

Beth was enjoying herself, picking up all the steps easily but the money jingling in her pocket was a distraction. She pulled away.

"Hang on a moment." She dashed over to the counter and thumped down the handful of coins onto the top. "Here, Linda, put this in the bottom of the till for me."

Returning to her dance partner, they picked up mid step where they had left off, to the sound of much laughter and clapping.

"Cor, you're a bloomin' natural," said Doug, changing hands behind his back as Beth sashayed around him. "You wanna get that old man of yours to take you up the Palais on a Saturday night. It's a lotta fun."

As she swung under his arm, she saw Peggy was having a hard time keeping up with supplies of fresh-perked coffee, and Linda was busy scraping out the last vestiges of vanilla ice-cream into an empty glass. Beside the glass stood an opened bottle of coke waiting to be poured on top of the ice-cream. The ice-cream would foam and overflow the glass, trickling down the side in a thick, brown sludge. Served with a straw and a spoon, it seemed the in thing to drink today, proving very popular with all the girls.

When the record ended, she thanked Doug with a kiss on the cheek, amid a chorus of cat-calls and whistles.

"Aye up, Doug. Looks like you're in there!" Someone pushed him from behind. He stumbled, almost knocking into her. He spun round and glared at Chris.

"Ah shuddup, Spikey, 'fore I knock the livin' daylights outta you."

"Now, now," said Beth, "no fighting." It was all said in good jest, and she knew Doug didn't mean it, but the smug expression on his face as he lit a cigarette with a match and winked at her, told he had enjoyed the dance as much as she had.

"Thanks, girls, now go on back and join the others. I can manage from here on." She ushered Linda and Peggy away from behind the counter.

"Well, if you're sure."

"Go on, go enjoy yourselves. You've done enough today."

The floor was so packed with people rock-n-rolling,

there was very little room for them to do it properly. Certainly not enough space for the girls to be swung between legs and lifted on to the hips of their partners, or rolled around the man's back, but everyone seemed to manage and only a few toes were trodden on.

Looking around the room as she wiped down the counter for the umpteenth time, Beth could see girls sitting on boy's laps, lads perched up on tables, their legs swinging to and fro in time to the music. Groups of girls were doing the hand-jive and, above it all, hung the blue fug of cigarette smoke. For the moment, everyone seemed occupied, either dancing or chatting, so she took the opportunity to slip to the back room and get another box of crisps.

She hadn't been gone more than a few moments when the sound of breaking glass and a shrill scream from the shop filled the air. Dropping the box, she reached for the broom and dustpan.

"Oh well, it was bound to happen. Something was bound to get broken," she muttered, hurrying back to the front of house.

"Stop it! Gerryeeee."

Beth recognised Peggy's voice yelling out. As she stepped through the white beaded curtain, a cup flew through the air and crashed at her feet.

"What on earth...!" she shouted.

Two lads, one of whom she didn't recognize and couldn't remember seeing there earlier, were fighting. He was about to swing a punch at Dave Smith. A bright band of metal glinted about the stranger's hand. Her heart lurched. Knuckledusters. A heavy blow landed on Dave's jaw, sending him reeling backwards.

"Why you fuckin' little..." Dave was pushed back towards his assailant, fists clenched in a boxer's pose.

"Yeah, come on then," the other goaded.

"Stop it, all of you," she ordered in her loudest voice, coming swiftly around the counter and forcing her way through to them, but someone pushed her aside. It was Johnny.

"Keep out the way, Beth, we'll 'andle this."

He caught hold of the boy who had punched Dave, holding him by the lapels of his leather jacket, and head-butted him. The boy fell to the floor, blood trickling from his nose.

Johnny stooped over him, hands on hips. "Want some more?"

Sue grabbed hold of Beth's arm. "Call the police. Quick. The bastard's spoilin' me day. Johnny'll kill 'im."

She turned to see Linda already talking on the telephone by the till. Good girl, she thought, and was about to tell Sue when all hell appeared to break loose around her. Like something straight out one of those Western films Henry so loved.

Boys were fighting, punches and arms flaying in all directions, a sea of angry faces she didn't know. Gatecrashers, all intent on ruining the party. She must put a stop to it before they wrecked the place. Girls were screaming, crying, trying to pull the men apart, glasses and cups and saucers flying.

There was a loud grating sound, then the noise of the needle scratching over Elvis Presley. Someone had been pushed into the jukebox. It would have to have taken considerable force to make it move like that, she knew, reprimanding herself for not thinking of putting the lock on the door.

Out of the corner of her eye she glimpsed a flash of metal. One of the troublemakers had pulled something from inside his leather jacket.

"He's got a knife," a girl screeched out.

Suddenly scared, Beth ducked for cover, grabbing Sue's arm and pulling her down underneath a table with her.

"Grab 'im," someone shouted.

"Hit 'im!'

"Nobby don't."

"Shuddup, Jules, this is between us men."

"Men? Huh, you're all ruddy wimps. I'm gonna teach you a lesson, mate," someone shouted back.

"Yeah? You an' whose bloody army?" Johnny's voice.

"S'all right. I'm gonna knock his fuckin' light's out."

Sue leapt out from under the table and lunged at the boy who was throwing the knife from hand to hand menacingly.

"Leave 'im alone, you bastard." She grabbed a hold on the guy's hair, pulling and yanking at it. "Grab him, Johnny. Watch out!"

Johnny, his nose bloody and what looked like the beginnings of a black eye forming, grabbed his assailant by the shoulders, pulled his leg up sharply and knee'd the other in the groin. The boy collapsed on his knees to the floor, clutching himself in agony. A loud cheer went up from the girls.

Beth rushed over and dragged Sue away. "Come on, out of here." She turned and caught hold of Peggy's hand. "And you. All you girls, behind the counter and into the back room quick before you get hurt." In the distance she could hear the faint wail of a police siren.

There came a sound like an explosion. A piercing scream, followed by the sounds of showering glass. Beth turned to see the front window had been smashed and everyone was gathering around it, looking out. She forced her way through, Sue right behind her pushing and shoving with her elbows.

"Get out of my way."

Outside on the pavement, Johnny lay spread-eagled on his back, his face covered with blood. Someone had pushed him through the glass.

Sue screamed, rushing out of the door to him.

"Johnny! My Johnny! What have they done to you?"

Beth looked on horrified as Sue knelt beside him, her white skirt dirty and blood splattered. She could see the tears streaming down Sue's face.

Johnny didn't move.

Chapter Twenty-Four

Peggy swept the floor, pulling the debris into a pile in the middle of the room, her head hung low as she went silently about the task. Seated on one of the benches, Beth watched, grateful Peggy and Doug had stopped by this morning offering help.

"Linda was gonna come as well, but she's too upset," Peggy said quietly as Beth lifted her feet from the floor. Peggy reached under the bench with the broom, gathering a pile of broken glass.

"It's okay," Beth replied in a hushed voice. "I didn't expect anyone to come after yesterday."

"Well, we couldn't just leave you on your own to clean up this mess, could we? Look at it."

She had, several times, and still couldn't believe the chaos around her. The damage was almost total. Only the counter top remained intact although the Gaggia machine sported a large dent in its stainless steel backplate.

She watched as Doug, helped by Henry, shifted a tabletop away from the wall where it had been hurled during the fight. They lowered the laminated top gently to the floor. A large gouge indented the wall where the table had struck. Beth wondered how the thugs had managed to yank it from the metal base. It must have taken at least four of them to do that, she thought, judging by how heavy it looked.

The tables and chairs had all been bolted down, but somehow even they had been pulled away and thrown at people. Benches had been dislodged. All were slashed. Ruined. She poked idly at the padding spilling out of the leather beside her, knew it was pointless, but she couldn't help trying to push it back in, her brain unable to function properly this morning. Total disbelief in what had happened had numbed her senses.

The subdued, quiet manner in which the others worked told her they, too, felt the same sadness and shock. The way Peggy kept sniffing a sure sign she was crying again.

"Does anyone know how Sue is?" asked Beth.

Peggy stopped sweeping and looked at her, face white, bloodshot eyes puffy. "She's with her parents, poor kid. The police were round there first thing."

"I'll go round later, offer my proper condolences. Take some flowers."

"You'll do no such thing," Henry growled, brushing plaster dust from his trousers. "Stay away. There's nothing you can do."

Beth stood defiantly, hands on hips. "It's the very least I can do. Gawd Almighty, Henry, what's up with you? The girl's just been made a widow on her wedding day. In my coffee shop. Of course I've got to go and see her. See if there's anything I can do."

Tears stung her eyes thinking of Sue, unable to imagine what could be going through that poor girl's mind. She saw Peggy and Doug look at each other, Doug's eyebrows raise. Peggy shrugged then turned away and began sweeping again.

"I don't think now's the time to be discussing this, Henry. We've made Peggy and Doug feel uncomfortable. We shouldn't be arguing. Not over this."

Henry smiled apologetically at Doug. "Sorry, mate. This has upset us all."

"S'all right, gov. We're all on edge. Here, cop 'old of this end and we'll take it out back."

"Leave it there, son. No point straining ourselves and giving us a hernia." Henry bent over to retrieve a silver picture frame led amongst the fallen plaster. As he picked it up, large shards of glass crashed to the floor. He turned the picture over. "Look at this. They've even managed to spoil Dickie."

Beth glanced briefly at it but wasn't really interested in the photographs. They could all be replaced, Dickie could always sign another. It was the rest of the things that bothered her more. The ripped and torn upholstery. The smashed crockery and glasses, the broken tables.

"It looks like a bomb's gone off in here," she muttered. "Why did they do it? They've ruined everything. Including Sue's life."

Henry propped the picture frame against the wall and came across to where she sat, clasped one of her hands in his.

"Because they're nothing but bloody hooligans and troublemakers, that's why. All of them. I did warn you."

She pushed his hand away. "It wasn't my kids' fault. They didn't start it. It was all going well until those gatecrashers arrived."

"'Ere, Mr Chisel'urst," Peggy spoke out, "don't you go blamin' any of us for this. It was that Gerry Connor's mob that started it. Him and his mates. They're the troublemakers. Doug 'ere warned Johnny that Gerry was out gunnin' for 'im, didn't you, Doug?" She turned to him for confirmation. Doug nodded.

"Why? What had Johnny ever done to him?" Beth asked.

"Johnny pinched 'is girl, that's why," said Doug. "Sue 'ad been going steady with 'im for nearly six months before she went off with Johnny. Gerry didn't like it, see. Threatened to cause trouble all along. We'd all kept the weddin' quiet like, on account of Gerry, but somehow 'e must 'ave found out. Me and the boys will get 'im, have no fear, and when we do we'll cut 'is fuckin' balls off for what he's done to Johnny."

Henry scowled. "Very noble, but you must let the police deal with it. You have told them all this, I hope?"

"Sure we 'ave, gov, but Gerry's scarpered, ain't he. The law won't find 'im. And if they do, they'll only chuck 'im in the Scrubs. He deserves to be hanged, but even that's too good for the likes of Gerry Connor. Nah, what we'll do to 'im will be much better justice."

"If you knew this Gerry was going to cause trouble, why didn't you stop him getting in? Surely you could have stopped the fight? Protected Johnny," Henry protested.

Beth listened silently, horrified that it all could have been prevented, and feeling very much to blame. If only she'd locked the door...

"'Cos we was outnumbered, see. And we didn't 'ave knives. It was a wedding, weren't it? We might be thugs and 'oodlums to you, Mr Chisel'urst, but we do 'ave 'earts. We weren't goin' out to spoil Johnny and Sue's big day, were we? We didn't know they were gonna kill 'im."

Peggy uttered a loud sob and rushed out the back.

Beth hurried after her. "I'll go see to her. You two carry on here as best you can. Whilst I'm out there I'll see if I can find some cups and make us all some coffee. That's if there's any left in one piece, that is."

"Ah, thanks Mrs Chisel'urst, I am bit parched." Doug wiped his arm across his forehead, leaving a streak of clean skin across his grubby face, then wiped his hands down his jeans. "Some of the guys said they'd come by and give us a 'and later."

"Hadn't you better wait until the insurance assessor comes?"

Startled, Beth spun to the direction from where the familiar voice had come. A voice that sent a chill of magic and memory dancing up and down her spine. Surely it couldn't be…?

"Terry?"

He stood on the pavement outside, leaning against the doorframe, taking a long drag on a cigarette. With his back to the bright sunlight, it was difficult to see his face in full. All Beth noticed were his dark eyes in the momentary red glow from the cigarette as he inhaled.

"I heard you had some kind of trouble. I've come to help." He flicked the remains of the cigarette into the gutter and stepped into the ruins of Coffee-A-Gogo.

He was the *last* person she expected to see, least of all today. What was more disturbing was the effect he still had on her. On her heart as it pounded rapidly. On the spark of emotion that so readily burst into flame, burning her ribs, catching her breath. She could feel herself shaking from head to foot.

"Bloody hell," Henry exclaimed.

"Mr Chiselhurst! What are you doing here?" Terry looked equally surprised to see him there.

"Well, it is my place," Henry replied curtly. "News obviously around here doesn't travel on some things as fast as others. When did they let *you* out?"

"I thought the café belonged to Beth. At least that's what I was led to understand. I also heard she got married."

"I did," Beth said. "To Henry here. He's my husband."

Terry's jaw dropped. He gulped. "Blimey, Beth. Now there's a turn up."

"Don't look so shocked. Henry's a good man. I'm the one that's in shock at seeing you again. I thought you were in prison."

"I was. Been out some time. Almost a year now."

Henry picked his way across the rubble towards him, a finger pointing. "But you went down for murder. I heard for life. So how come you're out?"

"Manslaughter, Mr Chiselhurst, and I didn't do it. The real person owned up."

A large gasp of air expelled loudly from Beth's mouth. "I knew it! I knew you weren't guilty. I said that all along."

About to rush across and throw her arms about him, the sudden elation and happiness fell away. Joy replaced by anger. Anger directed more at herself for allowing him, after all that had happened, to still hold her heart in his grasp. She remained where she stood.

"So why have you never bothered to come and see me before? Why now?"

"I've been away working, over near Dagenham since I got out. I got digs over there with a mate. We've been doing up a riverboat for some toff who wants to live in it. They're all the rage nowadays, apparently. We towed it in to Isleworth quay last Wednesday to finish the job off." He stared around what was left of the coffee bar. "Blimey! They've certainly done a good job here, trashed it good and proper. Any ideas who did it?"

"I was here when it happened," she started to explain. "There was a whole gang of them. The ringleader, this Gerry Connor fella, has done a runner. No one knows where he is. The police are looking for him. I'm sure they'll find him soon enough."

Terry scoffed. "They won't try that hard, Beth, believe me. Fights are always ten-a-penny, happen all the time."

"This was more than a fight. Someone got killed here." Peggy had reappeared looking noticeably calmer and composed, her face washed, hair tidied and pushed off her face with a bright-blue Alice band.

Terry let out a low whistle. "Jesus! How? Was he knifed?"

Peggy shook her head. "He was thrown through the window. I'm sure the police will find Gerry sooner or later, and even if they don't the boys here will and give him what for, mark my words. Won't they, Doug?"

"Yeah. Johnny had a lot of friends. We'll make fuckin' sure Connor gets his comeuppance, know what I mean, mate?"

"So you can understand if we don't want you to stay, don't you Terry, my boy?" said Henry dismissively. "There's nothing you can do here. I suggest you move on. No need to hang about. We've got it all covered."

Ignoring him, Terry tilted his head in the direction of the jukebox. Pulled away from the wall, the Seeburg lay on its side, the Perspex front cracked where someone's boot had landed a hard kick. The records inside had spilled out onto the floor. Many were broken.

"It's going to take more than the two of you to move that thing," Terry said to Henry. "Come on, let me give you a hand. I expect they've forced the back and took the money."

"There was no money inside. I'd emptied it before setting it to freeplay yesterday for the party." Beth said this more for Henry's benefit.

Henry raised his arms in jubilation. "Well, thank heaven for small mercies. Where did you put it?"

Was that all he could think about now, thought Beth. The bloody money. It wasn't as if there was lots of it; about four pounds, if that.

"It was in the till. Now don't go rushing over to check, Henry, I took it all out last night along with the takings. It's all quite safe. Now, either make yourself useful by making the coffee, or else give Doug and Terry a hand."

"I'll do the coffee," Peggy volunteered and disappeared back through the beaded curtain.

Terry scooped the scattered records up in his arms and dumped them unceremoniously on a nearby table.

"How's your mum and the baby? Was everything okay in the end?" he asked.

"Mum died after the baby was born, didn't your aunt tell you? I'm looking after little Molly as Dad couldn't cope." It still hurt when she spoke of her mother, the pain still intense.

"Gawd, I'm so sorry, Beth. I didn't know. Aunt Edie never said a word. Then again, when I came out of nick she didn't want to have anything to do with me. I think she thinks it was all my fault anyway. Regardless, she still seems to blame me. So, how are you managing?"

"I *was* managing fine. Until this morning... You let me down badly, you know that, Terry, don't you? I should hate you for dumping me in the middle of nowhere on your uncle's farm like you did. You'd obviously ended it between us but couldn't be bothered to tell me. You could have at least written and said. You never even bothered to answer my letters. Not one! And I wrote lots."

"What letters? I never received any letters." Terry hung his head, looking ashamed suddenly, then looked back, holding her gaze. "Actually, I know you wrote to me. I also know you gave the letters to Freda to post. She didn't. Freda didn't post any of them. Your father told her to destroy any letter to me you might write. They were all in on it, Beth. Your father. Freda. Aunt Edie. The lot of them. Anything to prevent you getting in touch with me after your father warned me off."

She glared. "What do you mean, 'warned you off'?"

"Your dad. That day we all drove down to the farm

and moved you in. He caught me alone outside as we were unloading the van. He told me you were far too young, and that he didn't want me messing around you any more, grateful as he was for me arranging the stay. He told me if I didn't back off and leave you alone to get on with your life, he would make sure I did. Said he had ways and brothers that would make sure of that."

"He said *what*? I don't believe it." She felt her body crumple, could see the floor looming up. All the pain and heartache, misery and despair. All so unnecessary. Then she stiffened, held her head up. "Wait a minute. Yes, ...actually I *do* believe it. It's just the sort of mean, evil thing Dad would do."

She looked intently into Terry's eyes. "I'm so sorry, I didn't know he'd done that to you. But that still doesn't explain why *you* didn't write. I would have thought if you really loved me, you would have stood up to him. You would have ignored his threats and not let anything stand in our way. Or was it all just a big lie, telling me you loved me? All that talk about wanting to marry me. Was that all lies and pretence as well?"

"No, it was the truth. I did love you. I still do, and I suppose I always will. I don't know what I'm supposed to do to convince you of that. Anyway, that's all too late now, but you were special to me. Very special." He shrugged. "I was a nobody with nothing to offer you. A boatbuilder who worked greasing engines and hammering and corking planks at weekends, trying to claw my way out of the cesspit of poverty I lived in by wanting to become a lawyer. Saying I loved you and wanting to marry you was the truth. But they were right. All of them. You were better off without me. Then, after what happened with my dad, I knew I had to let you go. You didn't want to be associating with criminals and killers. I had to let you get on with your life without me."

"What did happen with your father?" She needed to know; she wanted the truth. Without it, none of them could move on in their lives. She'd always be wondering.

Looking sad, Terry said, "You don't want to hear. I just want to put the last few years behind me. When I came back and heard about you owning Maisie's, I was going to come and say hello. See how you were. But then I changed my mind. I'd heard you'd got married, so I thought it best if I stayed away. Then this morning, Billy Jones, he's the guy working with me on the boat, he said something about there being a big punch up here last night, so I just had to come and see you were okay."

Terry tilted his head slightly in Henry's direction, lowering his voice to almost a whisper when he said, "Whatever possessed you to marry him? He's twice your age. Look at him!"

For some inexplicable reason the comment riled. Henry might be old and fat but that didn't mean anyone could insult him. Not after all he'd done for her. Least of all Terry. Just who did he think he was, waltzing in here, today of all days?

"That, Terry Gibbs, is none of your flaming business. So what happened to your great ambitions of being a lawyer. Give up, did you?"

Inside, she seethed, angry with pain and hurt that he'd never come back to find her when he came out of prison if he really loved her. She should hate him for that. So why was her heart still yearning for him? Aglow and trembling like it did now.

"One, I couldn't afford to. Two, having a criminal record. Even though the sentence was quashed, they would never let me go into law now. Christ, they wouldn't even let me become a copper if I wanted to.

Not even traffic cop on point duty, let alone a barrister or solicitor. I had to make a living somehow and eat, and seeing as boats and barges is all I know, I went back to that." He looked towards Henry, who stood with his hands on his hips watching his every move, before turning back to Beth. "You got any kids?"

"No."

He stepped closer. She could feel his warm breath on her skin, smell that alluring mixture of aftershave and Brylcreem she had once so yearned to smell again. That intoxicating allure that could only say Terry.

He winked. "What's up, can't the old codger do it? Ouch!" He caught hold of her hand before she could slap him again. "What was *that* for?"

"How dare you! How dare you come in here out of the blue and start making snide comments. Get out. Go on, clear off. I thought you'd come to help not to insult my husband."

Rage boiled inside her like a kettle ready to whistle and the mood she was in, it wouldn't take much more to make her blow steam and fury. She didn't need this. Him turning up like this, stirring and mixing up all her emotions and feelings she had for him. Feelings she thought she no longer possessed.

"Here, what's going on?" Henry rushed over, rolling up his shirtsleeves.

Terry backed away, hands held up in surrender. "Whoa, Mr Chiselhurst. I'm sorry, I said the wrong thing." He looked at Beth, pleading with his eyes, imploring her to forgive him. "I only came round to see what I can do. You've obviously got it all under control. I am sorry, Beth."

"What's that supposed to mean?" asked Henry, his face flushed with anger.

"Don't!" she cried out. "Stop it. Just go, Terry. *Please.* We don't need you. I don't need this."

Terry was at the door. "It's okay, I'm out of here. But I'll promise you this, Beth. And you Mr Chiselhurst. I'll find the bastard who did this. He isn't going to get away with it. I've contacts. We'll get him, and when we do we'll beat seven bales of shit out of him before turning him in."

"Hear, hear," Doug shouted loudly. "We're with you, mate. We all want a piece of that slimeball's flesh."

"Yes, and end up straight back in prison," Henry sneered.

As Terry walked away, she dropped her head into her hands and sobbed, no longer able to prevent the tears from coming.

Henry was at her side in an instant, cradling her shaking body in his arms.

"There, there, sweetheart, it's all right. I'm here. It'll be all right." He reached into his trouser pocket and pulled out a handkerchief, passing it to her. She blew her nose then forced her head up to look at him.

"Oh, for us maybe, we can rebuild all this. Start again. But what about poor Sue? She'll never get over it. What happened here yesterday will haunt her for the rest of her life."

"She's young. Given time she'll get over it, find someone else. Time heals."

But time hadn't healed her heart for Terry. As she had watched his retreating figure walk away and disappear out of view, she knew she was still in love with him.

"Are you sure you want to rebuild this place?" Henry was asking her now. "I can't see the point. Another fight, another argument with those kids and it will all be wrecked again. It's happening all the time, everywhere."

She stood firm. "I won't be defeated, Henry. I've put too much into this place. It's all I want. It's my dream."

"She 'as to rebuild it, Mr Chisel'urst," Doug interrupted. "She's good at what she does. Us kids love 'er and we respects 'er. We loves this place. If she needs help bringin' Coffee-A-Gogo alive again, we'll help. We'll all help. The whole bloomin' gang. We'll help with all the paintin' an' cleanin'. Nobby's a dab 'and with a drill an' a saw, and my mate, Al, can fix up the plasterin' good like. She's got to reopen it, Mr Chisel'urst. We ain't got nowhere else to go if she don't. Don't let this one setback spoil it all for her. Or us."

She smiled an appreciative thank you to Doug.

"I'd hardly call the place being wrecked and someone killed on the premises 'a setback'," Henry said.

Peggy came and stood by her side. "Doug's right, Mr Chisel'urst. We want this place as much as Beth does. It's gonna be hard comin' in here again, 'cos every time I look out of that window now I see Johnny sprawled out on the pavement covered in blood, but we owe it to him. He wouldn't want to see this place close. He'd want us all to carry on without him. This was his second home. It's our second home, too. In fact, to the likes of Smiffy and his brother it's better than home. Least here it's clean and warm and friendly, not like his gaff. No, Mr Chisel'urst, this place is as much ours as it is Beth's and we want her to reopen it." She put her arm around Beth shoulder. "We're all with you."

Who could resist such a heartfelt plea. She had to rebuild. She *had* to open up again.

"I just don't want to see you get hurt again, Beth." Henry spoke with tenderness.

"She won't Mr Chisel'urst," said Doug. "We'll all make sure of that."

"Well, that's reassuring to hear but I have my doubts reopening the place is the right thing to do. We've thrown so much money at it already and it's going to take a pretty penny or two to put it to rights again. I don't think it's worth it."

Beth wasn't going to be defeated. "I *do*. With or without you, Henry, I'm jolly well going to do it. As soon as possible, before all my best customers find somewhere else."

Doug and Peggy cheered, Doug leaping up and punching the air. "Good on you, Beth."

"Right then. Let's get cracking," she ordered with renewed enthusiasm. "Henry, you go find some wood and help Doug to board up the window for the time being. Glaziers can't get here until tomorrow. Peggy, where's that coffee you were making?"

"Comin' right up!"

Henry offered his hand to Doug. "Thank you, son. I appreciate you both coming over this morning. It couldn't have been easy for you after what's happened. I'll see you're paid for your trouble."

"We don't want payin'," Doug said crossly. "We ain't expecting nothin' an' we don't want nothin'. This is our place. We likes it 'ere and Beth's our friend. There ain't many people treat us as equals. They normally look down their noses at us an' tar us all with the same brush as Gerry Connor. We ain't like that, Mr Chisel'urst. You keeps your money an' use it to pay the best fuckin' lawyer you can find to put 'im behind bars, where he belongs."

Chapter Twenty-Five

Weeks had gone by since Terry had walked into the coffee bar. Now, every time she looked at Henry, Beth knew marrying him had been the single-most, stupidest mistake she'd ever made. If only she'd been more patient and not rushed into it so quickly.

She pushed the plate of uneaten eggs and bacon away and reached for the tea pot. It was pointless thinking about all the ifs, buts and maybe's. No way to change the past. Watching Henry slathering marmalade over his toast, she wondered where it would all end.

He caught her eye as he lifted the bread to his mouth.

"You've not eaten. You have to have something. It's no good starving yourself."

"I'm not hungry. A cup of tea is enough."

"It's shock, lass, over that lad getting killed and the mess they made of the coffee shop. But fretting over it isn't going to help put it right."

She resisted enlightening him the loss of her appetite had nothing to do with Johnny's death. It was Terry. The last time she'd mentioned his name in conversation, Henry had been vociferous.

"Forget that no good Terry Gibbs. He's nothing but a waste of space. That boy's all talk. He only said he'd help to make you feel better. Honestly, lass, what could *he* do that the police couldn't? Let's be fair, that boy's got a criminal record. Even if he did find out anything, the police aren't going to take him seriously."

Well, that might be Henry's opinion; it certainly wasn't hers. Henry didn't know him like she did. Terry would never say things he didn't mean. If only he hadn't turned up like that. He should have stayed away. Seeing him again had fired up all the smothered longing, the wanting. Now she craved the feel of his arms around her, the remembered taste of his soft lips against her own. She wanted to be loved. Proper love. The love that makes babies. She wanted her own baby to nurse and feed and cherish. Molly wasn't the same thing.

But with Henry, she would never have these things – the bitter price she'd paid for marrying him, something she didn't understand or appreciate before, too concerned with her situation at the time with no real thought to what future really lay ahead. What a fool she'd been.

Henry rattled the *Financial Times* as he turned the pages. The sound took her back to the little house in Busch Lane. Back to her father. Back to the past. The good old days to where her life was beginning to emerge from the chrysalis of childhood. To Mum. To Gran... and... She sniffed. This wasn't how it was meant to be.

Oh, Henry was kind enough, generous to a fault, in fact. Look at all she'd gained, she told herself. The grand house. The flashy car and the comfortable, secure lifestyle that came with it all. Wasn't that what she'd always wanted? Well, it might have been once, but not any more. It wasn't enough. Not now. She shook her head wearily.

Oh why did Terry have to come back? Didn't he realize what it would do to her? How it would turn her heart and world upside down. She'd been fine up until then.

Now everything had changed. Henry may have done nothing but good for both her and Molly, treated them both with love and kindness yet, try as she might, there were no feelings for him other than gratitude and friendship. Staying with him wasn't the future she wanted, but she had made a vow, for better or for worse, and she couldn't just walk away from it. There was Molly's future also to consider.

She turned to the child sitting up at the table with them, propped up by two cushions so she could reach her breakfast bowl. Darling Molly, with her cheeky smile and bright blue eyes, always questioning, always teasing. A contented little soul whose very presence in the room gave it light and life, and Beth adored her.

"Want more," Molly said, pointing at the pile of toast on the table.

Wordlessly, Beth buttered another slice then scraped on a thin layer of Marmite and began to cut the bread into soldiers.

"No, me do it," Molly whined. "I can do it."

Reluctantly, she gave Molly the plate and the knife and watched as the child ripped at the bread.

"Not like that, sweetheart. Look, let me show you." She covered Molly's hand with her own and helped her saw through the thick slice. "You have to cut like this. Gently. See?"

Triumphant, Molly grinned as she picked up a finger of bread, pushing the whole slice into her mouth. Beth ruffled the child's blonde hair and smiled back.

"Have you written to your father yet? We can't move any further with the adoption until he responds. We *need* his permission." Henry asked brusquely, shaking the pages of the newspaper as he folded it in half, put it down.

"I wrote to him weeks ago, but you know as well as I do, he isn't going to reply. Couldn't we just tell them my father's dead? I mean, he could be. They wouldn't know any different."

"And you've got a death certificate to prove it, have you? These people do have ways of checking up, you know. Without one, we'd have to wait seven years before the authorities deem him dead. Seven years! I don't want to wait another four."

Beth rested her chin on her hand. She didn't want this adoption lark. She didn't want Henry having any further hold over her. If it went ahead she knew there would be no escaping from him.

"Write to him again," he ordered. "If he doesn't answer by the end of the month, we're driving down there to see him, face to face. Don't look at me like that, Beth. It's got to be done."

She sighed heavily. "I'll write to Mike. See if he can persuade him one final time. He's been all right with Mike. Still talks to him apparently. It's me he ignores."

"Whatever. Just do what's necessary. Oh Molly, you've got Marmite all round your cheeks, you messy little moppet."

Molly jumped down from her chair and ran to Henry.

"Lick it off, lick it off."

Beth couldn't help but laugh as Henry picked up the child and made a great play of pretending to lick the sticky, brown mess off Molly's cheeks. Those two were certainly friends, the love between them totally unbounded by their history, she thought, watching them together. He idolized Molly. Spent every moment he could with her playing or reading stories. Everything a normal, loving father would do. He never lost his temper, even when she'd been particularly naughty, which wasn't often; Molly was a good kid. Usually, just a certain look from Henry was enough to discipline her. There were never shouts or smacks. He'd never raised a hand to her, and Beth knew he never would.

"There, all clean."

Molly touched her cheek. "No, Daddy, you've missed a bit." She put her sticky finger on Henry's nose. "There, now you all dirty too." He made to bite her finger. She squealed with laughter.

"Don't Daddy, don't!" Molly yelled helplessly as Henry now had her yellow dress raised over her head and was blowing wet raspberries on her naked belly.

"I gives in. I gives in," she pleaded breathlessly amongst shrieks of delight.

Beth stood. "Put her down, Henry, she's just eaten. Come on madam, let's go and get you cleaned up."

Henry put the child to the floor. "Go on, you monkey. Go wash your face. You're supposed to put the bread in your mouth, not on your cheeks."

Molly took Beth's outstretched hand and turned back to Henry, a wide cheeky grin across her face.

"You didn't do a good enough job of licking me clean. Now I've got to have a cold, wet flannel."

Henry playfully smacked Molly's backside. "Be thankful you don't have a wet flannel there."

Molly looked up at Beth, her eyes wide. "He wouldn't, would he, Beth?"

"He most certainly would," Beth teased.

Molly giggled and skipped out of the door.

"Don't forget that letter, Beth," Henry called out.

Beth straightened the photograph of Elvis Presley on the wall then stepped back to check the frame was aligned with others hanging on the freshly painted walls. New tables and seats had been obtained at large expense. The jukebox replaced. The plate glass in the window new and gleaming in the sunlight.

Coffee-A-Gogo had resurfaced from the mess of virtual destruction ready for re-opening. She was well-pleased with the result. In three days' time the Closed for Refurbishment sign would come down from the window.

In its place she would put a large poster announcing Open for Business.

New beginnings. A fresh start for the coffee shop, this time with a slice of hindsight on the menu. She knew which suppliers she could rely on, which brand of coffee her customers preferred, and knew what could go wrong.

She should have been feeling excited, but she wasn't. Instead, a thousand questions buzzed about her head. Was everything ready? Would her customers come back? Would the atmosphere ever be the same again? What if there was another fight? How would she cope?

Without seeing what lay on the other side of the window, she stared through the glass. All she could see were broken shards and blood and Johnny's blank stare looking up at her, as Peggy had seen. Beth screwed up her eyes to blot out the awful vision. When she opened them again it was the litter-strewn grey pavement, the road, the green Bedford lorry parked up against the kerb with its rear doors open, she could see. Life outside continuing as normal.

Images of the fight often haunted her. At night she could still hear Sue's screams. If it was this bad for her, she asked herself, how much worse must it be for Sue?

She picked up the cleaning rag from a table and gave the glass on Elvis Presley's photograph another quick wipe to remove her finger marks. Only it wasn't Elvis she saw, it was Terry's face floating into view in her mind's eye. He was smiling, calling to her. Always there. She just couldn't get him out of her head. She threw the cloth across the room. This was all Dad's fault. If only he hadn't interfered it could have all worked out so differently. She certainly wouldn't be trapped in a marriage of convenience. He might have thought he was doing what he thought best, warning off Terry, but he didn't know what was best. Certainly not for her.

She had to find him again. She had to see him. Tomorrow. She'd do it tomorrow. Tomorrow morning. She'd go to the quay at Isleworth to look for him. They needed to talk.

A glance at her watch told her it was almost time to leave. Henry was expecting her at his office so they could go over the accounts books once more now that the cheque from the insurance company had finally arrived. On her way, she needed to stop at the bank to pay it in. She would have to rush. Time was ticking on, and Henry didn't appreciate tardiness.

Letting herself out of the café, she stood in the doorway, gazing back around the shop. It looked all in order. All spick and span and clean, waiting for the first customer to come bounding through the door. Yet she couldn't help feeling detached from it, as if looking at it for the first time, and not seeing what was really there. She locked the door and walked away.

As she turned a corner, Terry came towards her. Seeing her, he waved and broke into a run. Her heart jumped into her mouth.

"Beth, I was just on my way to see you."

"You were?"

"I've come to tell you there's no sign of Gerry Connor. No one's seen him since that day. Sue told me where he lived. I've been round there, but his dad said he'd gone off to work up north somewhere. Said he was fed up with the police bothering him. Said he didn't know where his son was."

"And you believed him?"

Terry shrugged. "He seemed genuine enough. I don't know what else I can do. The Old Bill's still making enquiries, as they put it, but I don't hold out a lot of hope. He could even be out of the country by now."

"Poor Sue, she's taking this hard. How do you ever get over seeing your husband killed before your eyes, and on your wedding day too? I sometimes feel it's all my fault."

He put a comforting hand on her shoulder. "How can you say that? It was nothing to do with you."

"Yes it was. If I hadn't agreed to hold their reception, there wouldn't have been any window for him to be thrown through. If I hadn't had the coffee shop, there wouldn't have been a reception. He'd still have been alive."

"Beth, that's silly. That fight was going to happen no matter where Sue and Johnny were. You can't go blaming yourself."

She knew what Terry said was true but it didn't stop her thinking these things. Thoughts that had gone through her head a thousand times over since that tragic evening. Always reaching the same conclusion.

"No, it's Dad I blame."

"What? He's nothing to do with this."

"Yes he is. He's everything. It's *all* his fault. If he hadn't gotten Mum pregnant in the first place, I wouldn't have had to look after Molly, consequently I wouldn't have had to marry Henry, and thus wouldn't have had the coffee shop for Johnny to go and get himself killed in."

"But that's ridiculous thinking."

"Is it? It makes perfect sense to me. Dad's not only destroyed Mum's life, and mine and Molly's by shunning us, he now has Johnny's death on his hands. As good as throwing him through that window himself."

"Beth, it was a matter of circumstance. You're being irrational."

"Am I? I don't think so. Think on this. All this is a chain of events set in motion by the act of one man. One man's selfish act of lust that has snowballed. Cause and effect. Four lives ruined. Five, if I include what happened to you. Six, if we include your dad. Don't you see? If Dad had let us be together as we had wanted, you wouldn't have been in the wrong place at the wrong time. God. My father is a mass murderer! I hate to think who else has been affected by his stupidity."

Terry looked at her dumbfounded. Finally, he cocked his head to one side, smiled sympathetically.

"He's really hurt you, hasn't he?"

"More than you could ever understand."

"Come on, let me buy you a drink. You look like you need one."

"I can't. I was just on my way to see Henry. I'm in a hurry, but you could walk with me, if you like. What happened to that old banger you used to drive?"

He fell into step alongside. "Roger never came back. The car got parked up in one of the old sheds by the quay. Billy and I have been doing it up in our spare time. The engine was clapped out and the steering seized after being in a lock-up so long. A bit like me," he joked.

"Was your friend doing his national service then and decided to stay in, like my brother, Mike?"

Terry laughed. "What, Roger? No. He was what you might call a conscientious objector. He thought conscription was against the freedom of the nation, so he refused to go, and scarpered. Last I heard he was bumming his way around the Greek islands."

"Oh dear, that's not very patriotic, is it? Did you do yours? You never said."

"I did my turn. You know, Beth, I'm surprised you've never learnt to drive. With all that money Henry has, you could afford to have your own little runaround, surely. Especially to-ing and fro-ing to that coffee shop. When's it opening again?"

"Friday morning. As for learning to drive, Henry and I discussed it once, but I didn't think I could master that clutch thingy or know when to change gear. I could see myself making a right pig's ear of it."

"Tosh. That's what they teach you, how and when. It's all to do with the engine revs. You'll soon learn when the engine makes the right noises. It sort of tells you it's time to shift up a notch. Lots of women are driving now. I could teach you, if you like."

She turned slightly and laughed. "I'm sure Henry would have a lot to say about that idea."

"Do you know, Beth, I still can't understand why you married that old goat?"

"He's actually very sweet when you get to know him, and he's ever so good with Molly. Treats her like his own daughter."

"So, he's the blesséd saint of Richmond, but that doesn't answer my question. Why did you marry him?"

"I wasn't in love with him, if that's what you're implying. We made this arrangement. I was on skid row, about to lose my home as the council said I couldn't stay there. I couldn't get anywhere to rent. People slammed their doors in my face, called me all sorts of names. And with Molly to look after, I couldn't get a job. You see, they all thought Molly was my daughter and that I was the wicked girl from the gutter. Henry offered me a way out so I took it. For Molly's sake."

"Very noble of him. But there has to be something in it for him?"

She didn't like the implication in Terry's voice. She stopped and grabbed his arm.

"Now look here, Terry Gibbs, I don't know what you're inferring but Henry's been very good to me and

Molly. I won't have you talking about him like that. Without Henry, goodness knows where I'd be now. Molly probably would have had to go into care. You of all people should understand how horrible that would have been, so don't knock him."

"Oh, I'm not running him down, Beth. I think what he's done is bloody marvellous. But I can't help thinking—"

"Thinking what?"

"That he has an ulterior motive. I don't know how to put it, but I just don't trust him." He slipped his arm through Beth's as she continued walking again, her pace a little quicker.

At the merest touch of his body against hers, her heart somersaulted with a yearning that couldn't be quelled.

"He says much the same about you. Actually, he wants to adopt Molly. There's not many would be willing to take on another man's kid like that. And Henry's not daft. He knows he's no oil painting and would never have married otherwise. This way, we both benefit. There are no strings."

"But you can't love him. I mean—"

"No, not in the way you're thinking, Terry, I don't. But I do care for him. You can't live under the same roof with someone and not have feelings."

Good feelings once, she thought miserably. She didn't wish Henry any harm but did wish he wasn't part of her life. Terry's arm on hers felt so different from Henry's firm grasp. With Terry there was a tenderness she couldn't explain. A comfort in being so close to him.

"You can't be happy?"

"I'm certainly not unhappy," she told him, but it was untrue. She felt desperately unhappy. Unsettled and unnerved by events that had seemed to turn her world once more into uncertainty.

"Henry cares for me," she continued, trying to keep her voice calm and composed. "He treats me as an equal, as a friend. He spoils me. And Molly. Showers me with fancy clothes and jewellery. He's—"

"He's treating you like a kept woman!"

"Well, that's what I am, aren't I?" she answered.

Terry shook his head and laughingly said, "Oh Beth, at times you are so naïve. Do you know what a kept woman is?"

She shrugged.

"Beth, a kept woman is another name for a mistress, a man's plaything. A fancy name for a prostitute! Are you seriously saying that's what you are?"

She shook her head rapidly, mouth agape in indignation. Flustered, she said, "No, no, not that. I don't... sleep with him, if that's the inference."

"That's exactly what I am saying."

"It's nothing like that. I earn my keep from the coffee shop. From the business. It's all my own hard work that's gone into Coffee-A-Gogo. For your information, Terry Gibbs, he's never laid a finger on me. Not one. It was part of our agreement. I have my own separate bedroom."

Terry looked relieved. "It's just I couldn't imagine you with him... You know...? The thought turns my stomach."

"As it does mine."

They walked on in silence, stepping across the road and along the path that cut Richmond Green in two.

Eventually, Terry asked, "Are you content with that sort of marriage, Beth? A young, beautiful girl like you should be made love to. Frequently. Cherished and caressed into old age, not doomed to a life of celibacy."

She felt herself blush. "You shouldn't be talking like this to me. I'm a married woman."

"A married woman who's still a virgin."

"Terry!"

"Well, it's true, isn't it?"

She could only nod. It was true, but talking about things like sex to another man was embarrassing. It was different discussing intimate things with Gran, she was a woman, but not with Terry. He was… what? Hardly her boyfriend any more. Even she and Henry didn't speak like this.

Terry pulled her to a halt then stroked her cheek lightly, the way he used to. The way she'd craved for so long.

"You know, you could divorce him. You must be set up by now, have some money behind you. You could just walk way from him."

Leaving Henry was precisely just what she wanted to do. There was no future in their relationship. Her father was never going to allow Henry to adopt Molly. What reason did she have to stay with him? There was only one she could think of. The only thing Henry had really represented all along. Security. But how could she leave, she asked herself. She had nowhere else to go.

Instead, she said, "Why should I want to leave him? Henry's a good man. There are no grounds for divorce. He doesn't hit me or Molly, he isn't cruel and sadistic. He doesn't sleep with other women."

Terry frowned. "How do you know? Do you know where he is every minute of the day? Does he never come home late from the office? Don't you see, Beth, you have the one reason for divorce that every judge in the land would willingly sign the papers for. If the marriage hasn't been consummated, there is no marriage."

"Consummated?"

He rolled his eyes. "Do I have to spell it out? If he's never made love to you the marriage hasn't been consummated. It's what marriage is all about, Beth, making babies. You can't be that naïve. Look, if you haven't done it, and they can prove you're still a virgin, then that's it. End of marriage. An annulment. It's that simple."

Her head was a swirl of emotions, spinning and tossing. A life without sex hadn't been a consideration. It wasn't relevant at the time. But now, here in Terry's presence, close to him, touching him, the need and urge to kiss him were as strong as ever. Yearnings flooding through her, all-pervasive. Demanding. Tugging at her. She was scared in case she let them loose. She had to keep control of herself. She stepped back.

"Terry, don't. Please don't do this to me."

"Do what?" he asked, brushing the hair away from her face, his breath warm and close. "I'm only saying I still love you and—"

"Stop it. This is lunacy. I have to go…"

She pushed his hand away sharply and moved to walk away, but Terry caught hold of her arm, pulling her back. All at once his lips were upon her. She tried to resist, to pull away, but his hold was fast, the kiss hot, and with a hunger that was frightening in its intensity, she could feel herself responding. She wanted this. Wanted him. Abandoning all sense of loyalty to her husband, she closed her eyes and allowed herself to be swallowed into Terry's passion.

"I can make you happy, Beth," he whispered when the long kiss was over. "I love you so much. Okay, I can't shower you with gifts or offer you a flashy house to live in, but I can rain love down on you like you'd never imagine. Walk away from Henry and come with me now. Divorce him. I'll look after you both."

If only he knew what he was doing to her, she thought, fighting against what her heart truly wished. "Oh Terry, I can't. It's not that simple. No, I really must go." Reluctantly, she let go of his hand and hurried away.

"When can I see you again?" he called out after her.

She looked back, knowing it was foolhardy, that she should have just kept on going.

"Come to the coffee shop on Friday."

Chapter Twenty-Six

Joanne looked up from the typewriter, acknowledging Beth with a slight smile.

"He has a client in there at the moment, Mrs Chiselhurst. Do take a seat. May I get you a coffee?"

"No, thank you."

A vast improvement with her welcoming technique since last time, Beth thought, sitting down, observing how neat the girl looked this morning in a black twinset jumper and cardigan, and around her neck a single row of white pearls. To her untrained eye they looked real.

When Joanne removed her spectacles to rub at the bridge of her nose, Beth noticed her eyes were red, as if she had been crying.

"Are you okay?" she asked, concerned.

Eyes downcast, Joanne nodded and continued striking at the keys. The desk shook at each stroke.

"You know, you really must get Henry to get you a new typewriter. That thing is so ancient, even Noah had a better model."

"Who's Noah?" Joanne asked, without looking up.

"Never mind, it was meant as a joke."

It was evident she wasn't going to get anywhere making small talk with Joanne, so Beth gave up. In between the clunk, clunk, clunk from the typewriter she could hear Henry's muffled voice and that of another man's coming through from his office. She unbuttoned her coat, crossed her ankles and waited.

A few moments later, Joanne stopped typing and pushed the typewriter away from her.

Beth couldn't resist saying, "You want to push it a bit harder, make it fall off the desk. That way he'll have to buy you a new one."

Joanne stared at her intently. "May I ask you something?"

"Yes."

"Are you really Mr Chiselhurst's wife?"

"I'm Henry's wife, yes," she confirmed, puzzled. "Why do you ask?"

"Well, I mean, you look so young. He said he's got a three-year-old daughter. I can hardly believe that."

"Molly isn't our daughter, she's my baby sister. I take care of her. I've had to since our mother died." Not that it was any of Joanne's business, she thought, but she did wonder what precisely Henry had told the girl.

"Oh, I am sorry," Joanne said. "That must have been dreadful, your mother dying. Sorry, I don't mean to pry or anything. Is it hard looking after your sister?"

"Sometimes."

Joanne typed a few more words then stopped again. "So how come you're married to Mr Chiselhurst? There's such an age difference between you. You can't really be in love with him, he's so... so..."

"Fat? Ugly?" Beth finished for her. "Is that what you mean? Don't let's beat about the bush here."

"Old, I was actually going to say." Blushing, Joanne shifted nervously in her chair. "I'm sorry, it was very rude of me to suggest that—"

"It's all right, I'm used to comments. So what did Henry tell you about us?"

"Well, ...nothing really. That's the point. I didn't even know he was married until that day you first walked in here. He'd told me he lived alone. He said he was looking for someone to keep him warm in bed at nights."

Beth could hardly believe what she was hearing.

"To be honest," Joanne continued, "I feel

embarrassed at times, the way he talks. And he touches me."

Beth's brow creased. "Touches you? How?"

Joanne shrugged. "He'll brush past me sometimes when it isn't really necessary. Makes out it's accidental, like, but I'm not so sure it is. And sometimes, he'll pat my bottom as I walk by. Or pinches it, playful like. He's always got his hand on my shoulder when he's talking to me by my desk. He makes me feel uncomfortable. It's got to the point where I'm actually thinking about leaving."

Somewhere from the back of Beth's mind came a vague memory of Henry doing the same to her, how he used to squeeze her shoulder whenever he stood behind her, dictating letters. And, thinking about it, looking back, she began to wonder how it came about she had come to be working for Henry. The girl she'd replaced had so-say taken a day off, leaving him stranded? Was that the real excuse, she wondered now. Or had that girl quit and not gone off as Henry had claimed? She had no way of knowing. She'd had no cause to question him at the time, she'd been so anxious to have the job. Was this why his secretaries never seemed to last long? The one before Joanne had left at very short notice too, if she remembered right. Unease settled over her. Abruptly, she stood, eyes burning into Henry's door as she stomped towards it, ready to barge in. How dare he do these things?

Something made her stop. Best not, not with a client in there, she thought. That would be just too embarrassing for all of them. She stepped across to Joanne's desk.

"Then why do you put up with it? Tell him to keep his hands off you." Beth kept her voice calm. Gentle. She certainly didn't want Joanne to feel any way to blame, and she may be jumping to conclusions with no proof.

"I like the job. Believe it or not, I actually like working here, and the pay's good. I couldn't earn this sort of money anywhere else. Only I don't know what to do. I was kind of hoping you might have a word with him. You see, Mrs Chiselhurst, your husband's got wandering hands." Joanne pulled off her spectacles once more and rubbed at her eyes. "Do you think you could speak to him about it? Tell him I don't like it, the way he keeps touching me."

This was a side of Henry Beth never knew existed – a lecherous beast who liked touching-up his secretaries. She clutched at her stomach, sick at the very thought. Terry's words about not trusting him echoed loudly inside her head.

"I most certainly will, but you must as well. Next time, tell him to keep his sweaty paws off you."

"If I do that, Mrs Chiselhurst, he'll sack me, I just know he will."

Anger rose in Beth's chest, a tightness gripping at her ribs as if the very breath were being squeezed out. "Joanne, you don't have to put up with that sort of behaviour—"

"But it's just men, isn't it? They all do it."

"No they don't! Nor should they. Whatever gives them the right to think they can manhandle us like a piece of meat? We have rights. Unless we stick up for ourselves they'll go on doing it. Have you told anyone else about this?"

"My friend, Gail. Her boss does it to her too. She says it all goes with the job."

Beth shook her head in despair. "What about to your parents?"

Joanne laughed. "Don't be daft. My dad will come

round here and deck him one."

"There you are then, doesn't that prove that it isn't all right? That Henry shouldn't be doing these things?"

Before Joanne could answer, the door to Henry's office swung open and out he blustered, behind him a puny little man in a grey suit that appeared three sizes to big for him.

"Don't you worry, Mr Connelly," Henry's voice boomed around the office. "I'll have this sorted out in no time. Now, you know your way out. Ah, Beth, my dear. Do come on through."

She followed him into his office and slammed the door.

He indicated for her to sit down. "You look cross, my dear, whatever is the matter?"

"Cross is putting it mildly," she told him and repeated what Joanne had just divulged. When she'd finished, Henry gaffawed loudly as he leaned back in his chair, his chubby hands clasped behind his head.

"The stupid girl's making it up. She's living in a fantasy world. Surely you don't believe her?"

She tapped a finger rapidly on his desk. "Yes, as a matter of fact, I do. Particularly as you never even bothered to tell her you were married. You blatantly told her you lived alone. Why? Hoping she'd feel sorry for you? What were you after, Henry, a cheap thrill? Or is it some sort of intimidation? Whatever it is, it has to stop."

"Oh, calm down, lass, for goodness sake. This is getting totally out of proportion. It was just a bit of harmless fun. Nothing wrong in slapping a girl across the arse occasionally. They love it!"

"No we bloody well don't," she shouted. "It's a ruddy insult. I'm warning you, Henry, you touch that girl once more and I'll walk out and take Molly with me."

Henry leaned forward over the desk, his face almost touching hers until she could feel his warm breath on her face.

"You wouldn't dare. You know what side of life your bread is buttered on, my girl." His eyes and tone carried implied threat. Determined she wasn't going to be intimidated by him, she held his gaze.

"Try me. So help me, I will not put up with you groping your secretaries. You're a married man, for God's sake. It's no wonder they don't stay long with you running your grubby little hands up their legs. It's a wonder you haven't been sued or thumped by someone's father or boyfriend." She stood. "I'm going. We cannot discuss what I came to talk about now, I'm too angry with you. Think on it, Henry. And I'm warning you. Don't you dare fire that poor girl sitting outside or take this out on her."

Henry pulled himself out of his chair. "You'll not be the one giving *me* orders around here, lass. Just who do you think you are?"

"Your wife. Remember?" she snapped. "It seems like you don't like admitting that fact. Why? Afraid of being accused of cradle-snatching? I thought you were proud of me and Molly? So glad in fact, you wanted the whole world to know we existed, else why all the fuss about Molly's adoption? I can't see much evidence of that around here."

"Yes, and a wife does as her husband tells her."

"Not any more. In case you hadn't realised, things have changed. Women will not put up with being threatened and beaten like stray dogs. We have rights. We don't take orders lying down any more."

Henry's faced turned red, the veins in his neck pulsing, throbbing. "You don't do anything lying down. If you behaved like a proper wife, I wouldn't have to go elsewhere for pleasure."

Taken aback, she glared at him. "What the hell is that supposed to mean?"

"Proper wives sleep with their husbands. Men need a good woman in their beds at night, not some young virgin who they can't get near. You might be willing to open your mouth and say something, but you're never willing to open your legs."

He'd never spoken to her like this before. Their non-existent sex life was never mentioned. Never an issue. She could only stare at him open-mouthed, unable to answer, and wondering if Joanne was listening; if she could hear.

As the shock of his outburst faded, she stepped towards his desk and said softly, "You seem to forget that was the agreement when I married you, Henry Chiselhurst. I had no intention of sleeping with you. I did it for Molly, as well you know. I didn't love you then, I don't now."

His face softened. "Perhaps, lass, but I love you. I thought you the most fascinating creature to have walked on this planet." He hung his head. "Go home, Beth. We'll talk later."

"Just remember what I said, Henry. You leave Joanne alone."

As she walked through the outer office, she stopped beside Joanne's desk.

"Don't worry. I don't think you'll have any more trouble with my husband. And if you do, I want to know about it. Okay?"

Joanne's smile of gratitude showed her relief. "Thank you, Mrs Chiselhurst. I didn't want to cause any trouble between you two. I just thought you ought to know."

Henry was late coming home which, in itself, wasn't unusual. He often worked late on Tuesdays and Thursdays. Nor was Beth surprised considering their argument in the office earlier that day. He had probably stayed late on purpose. Either that or drowning his sorrows in the Rose and Crown. Henry liked to have a drink on his way home from work, but it was now a-quarter-to-nine. He wasn't normally *this* late.

With Molly tucked up in bed fast asleep and Mrs Potter retired to her rooms on the top floor, she sat alone in the sitting room of Hanbury House, flicking through last month's *Good Housekeeping* magazine without really taking much interest in the recipes and articles therein.

In the quietness of the room her thoughts wandered back to what Terry had said. Did she ever really know where Henry was? What he was up to? Joanne's revelations and her husband's unexpected outburst had proved he was a womanizer, led by frustration and temptation, and it seemed she was the cause of his behaviour. Had it really come down to this?

Bored with only the company of a ticking mantel clock, she got up and crossed the room to turn on the television. It stood in the corner between the fireplace and bay window. She still marvelled at this wonderful piece of modern technology. Radio with pictures. The tiny grey screen nestled inside the mahogany cabinet flickered into life, the streaks of white lines fading eventually to reveal a grainy, grey and white image of Robert Dougall's face reading out the news. On her way back to her comfortable armchair, she picked up the *Radio Times* from the glass coffee table, turning to the day's listings to see what was on next.

Ten-thirty and Henry still hadn't returned. Tired, she turned off the television, watching intently at the black screen until the little white dot in the middle finally disappeared, before going up to bed.

Wrenched back into reality from the depths of sleep, she sensed someone was in the bedroom as she rolled over beneath the blankets. Henry stood framed in the doorway, the landing light silhouetting his bulky outline. Alarmed, she sat up.

"What's wrong?"

"Nothing." He staggered into the room and kicked the door shut, plunging the room into darkness.

She turned on the bedside lamp to see him standing over her bed in his shirtsleeves, slipping the braces of his trousers off from his shoulders. The smell of alcohol on his breath confirmed he had been drinking. Swiftly, she pulled the blankets around her neck.

"Then what are you doing in here? Get out and go to bed. You're drunk."

"Not so drunk as I don't know what I'm doing, lass."

Suddenly afraid, she held the blankets tighter and demanded he leave at once. Ignoring her, he yanked the covers back, revealing her body in her flimsy, pink silk nightdress.

"My, you're a pretty sight. Let me have a proper look at you, *wife*."

His emphasis on the word wife cut through her head. She grabbed the covers, pulling them swiftly up again but Henry caught her wrist, holding it in a vice-like grip.

"What are you doing? Get out. Get out," she shouted, panicking.

With his free hand, he unbuttoned his shirt, swapping hands in a deft move, giving her no chance to break free as he shrugged out of the shirt, letting it fall to the floor in a crumpled heap.

"Henry, no. Please. Please don't."

She turned her head away, heard the sound of his trouser zipper undoing, so struggled even harder, fighting against his grip, but his hold was too tight. With her free hand, she flayed out, hitting him but he ignored her blows. Then he caught hold of her chin and forced her to look at him. She tried to knock his arm away, but it was no use. He was too strong for her to fight against.

He was naked. She'd never seen him fully undressed and the sight repulsed her. His hairy chest. Those long, wiry black hairs making him look like a gorilla. Rolls of wobbly flesh hanging down in folds below his waist. Her face was level with his erect penis. She shut her eyes tightly, screwed up her face. She didn't want to see, but Henry held firm.

"Look at it, lass," he ordered. "Look it at and admire what you are getting whether you want it or not."

He pulled her hand to him. "Go on, hold it. Touch it."

"No, no, you're horrible. How could you?"

As he forced her hand to him, she tried to pull free but the urge to scratch and claw at him was too great so opened her fist, bent her fingers, ready to attack. As if reading her thoughts, he pulled her hand away sharply.

"Don't you bloody dare," he yelled.

Meanwhile his other hand had pulled up her nightdress, exposing her naked body beneath as she flayed out with her free hand, kicking the covers but succeeding in only pushing them off the bed, exposing more of her body. She knew he stared down at her and in vain tried to wriggle and dodge out of his way, but within seconds he was upon her, forcing her legs apart with his knees and pinning her down with his weight.

"No! No! No!" she screamed out. "You promised."

"It's my right, you're my wife," he demanded. "And I shall have you. Ouch!"

She had sunk her teeth into the hot flesh of his shoulder, the taste of blood in her mouth. She had hurt him. Good, she thought, expecting any second for him to lash out and strike her. Instead she could feel the tip of his penis trying to fight its way inside her, and she could do nothing to push him off. His mouth now was on her nipple, sucking and pulling with his teeth, his tongue flicking back and forth across it.

He lifted his head. "See, you're enjoying it. Can you feel how hard your tit's getting?"

His breathing fast, great rasps of whisky-tainted air wafting around her face as he moved closer to kiss her mouth. Thrashing her head from side to side, she tried to keep out of the reach of his slobbering lips looming ever closer. If only she could raise up her leg a little, knee him hard where it would hurt him most, but she was no match against his weight advantage and she could not move.

"So help me, I'll bite you again, you bastard," she uttered between clenched teeth. Her mouth was dry. There was no saliva there to aim at him.

"That's it, lass, keep struggling. I like it when they struggle."

She froze at his words. *They?* God, how many women had he forced himself on? The question echoed around her head in an explosion of terror and hatred. The instant she stopped moving, it seemed to spur him on. Suddenly, he rammed hard into her. She screamed out as pain seared through her abdomen, feeling as if she was being ripped apart.

"I've never taken a virgin," he boasted in between short gasps of breath. Already his body ran with sweat from his efforts as he pushed and pushed himself inside her.

She wanted to die. No, she screamed in her head, he's

the one who should die. I'll kill him, so help me, I'll kill him!

"If I can't have Molly as my daughter then we make our own baby," he spoke loudly into her ear, his hot tongue flicking in and out. She felt wet spittle on her skin, but still she wouldn't move, thinking she must stay still. Stay still and it will be over soon.

"I'll get rid of it." She hurled the words at him in contempt.

"Then we'll keep on doing it until you make me a father," he snarled back.

Within a few moments she felt his body shudder and he sank down, the full weight resting on top of hers. She had survived, but the deep hatred and loathing she felt for him reached such a height, she knew if she'd had a knife or a pair of scissors close at hand, she would have rammed them into his sweating flesh.

Slowly, Henry lifted himself up from the bed, the perspiration sticking his skin to hers, making a shlooping sound as he pulled away. She tried hurriedly to cover herself with her nightdress. Henry's hands stopped her.

"Don't! I want to look at you and savour this moment."

"Take a good hard look then, because it will be the last. You're never going to do that to me again."

He laughed. "Oh my dear girl, that was just the beginning." Without warning, he pushed her over, forcing her face into the pillow, one arm held tight behind her back. The mattress dipped and groaned as he climbed back on to the bed.

Chapter Twenty-Seven

The house sounded unusally quiet when she awoke and eased her aching, sore body to the bathroom to run a hot bath. What time Henry had gone back to his own room, she had no idea, but as she had lain awake in the darkness, she had vowed no man was ever going to subject her to that ordeal again. Least of all Henry. She would rather die than give up her body to the vile, lurid demands he had subjected her to. Tears welled with anger and loathing. She fought them back.

As hot water filled the tub, she sprinkled in some Dettol, hoping the disinfectant would take way the smell of him on her skin and soothe the soreness between her legs. His abuse of her body was tantamount to rape, she reckoned, thinking of the indignities he had put her through. As she lay wallowing she was tempted to sink beneath the hot water and stay there forever. A fleeting thought that evaporated instantly in the steam rising from the tub when the image of Molly flashed through her mind.

Looking into the dressing table mirror, she pulled and tugged at the tangles in her wet hair with her tortoiseshell brush. The mirror reflected back the swollen redness around her eyes, the anguish written on her face, as the realization dawned. After last night, there could be no simple annulment of her marriage. Henry had ruined any hope of that.

The only way she was likely to get a divorce now was if Henry deserted her, and she was certain he wasn't about to do that. Or unless she could obtain proof he had been unfaithful. Concrete evidence. Just because he said he liked them struggling didn't necessarily mean he had.

And groping a few secretaries could hardly be classified as adultery. Henry would also demand she kept to her part of the agreement. If they divorced, he would lose any claim on Molly, and she would lose Coffee-A-Gogo. Of that much she was sure. Well, he could have the shop, as far as she was concerned. It was spoiled. Everything was spoiled now. Every hope, every dream, every wish. Gone, swirled away like water down the plughole.

She flopped down onto the crumpled bed then sprang up quickly, the memories of last night flashing through her mind. He was here, defiling her on this very bed. How could she ever sleep on it again and feel safe?

Somehow she had to get herself and Molly away. But where? If she wanted a divorce, it seemed to her that she must be the one to leave. Be the guilty party. The adulterer. Her reputation smeared. All the more reason for not running to Terry, she thought, despite his promise he would take care of her and Molly. Terry would have his name dragged through the courts again. That wouldn't be fair on him, she thought, when neither of them had done anything wrong. With so many thoughts and questions rushing around her head, she could feel a violent headache coming on. An evil worm of turmoil let loose by Henry's actions, throwing her world into chaos once more.

She stared at the bed still in disarray and pulled away the covers, revealing a bloodied stain on the sheet. Would Mrs Potter be able to tell what happened when she came to make it this morning? Mrs Potter was fully aware of the sleeping arrangements. What the housekeeper's opinion of them were, she had no idea but she wasn't prepared to change Mrs Potter's understanding of the relationship. Embarrassed by the evidence, she yanked the sheet off the bed, bundled it into a ball and tossed it to the floor.

Next, she flung open the wardrobe doors, searched through the row of clothes hanging there. All expensive. All well made. Norman Hartnell suits with black piping, Dior dresses cut in the latest Y fashion; designer clothes that once upon a time she'd only dreamed of ever owning. This morning she hated them, each and every one a reminder of the world she was trapped in. Pushing beautifully-tailored creations and smart tea-dresses out of the way, rifling through the hangers until she found a plain navy, cotton skirt, she stepped into it then pulled out a cream silk blouse, put it on. Her fingers didn't seem to want to work as she fumbled with the pearl buttons.

Men! She hated them all. Apart from Mike, of course. He was one of the few good ones. But a fat lot of good he was at the moment, he'd become a virtual stranger. He much preferred shouting orders at men to fight. A sergeant now, abroad for months at a time, he could never appreciate she lived in constant fear that he, too, would be snatched away, like David. Taken by some cruel hand, some foreign soldier wielding a rifle. Some mindless fighter who didn't care where his grenade landed. Why were men so determined to crush the very things they believed in? There had to be better ways of resolving things than fighting battles. Always, it seemed, the only way men knew how to deal with something was to resort to violence. Ever since Cain and Abel, men had used their fists or weapons to end their differences. Look at what happened to poor Johnny! Put a woman in charge, she'd soon put an end to it. Make her Prime Minister; that would show them. She laughed at her thoughts. Huh, the men in this country would never vote in a woman to run the place. What? And have a woman show them how it's done? Never in a million years, they would say.

From a drawer she pulled out a dark-blue cardigan, factory knitted, each precise stitch small and neat. It felt soulless. Characterless. There was no love knitted into each row as there had been in the things Gran had made. She studied it for a moment before putting it around her shoulders. She hadn't thought of her grandmother in such a long time. How she wished the old lady was there with her now. Gran would know what to do. Beth bit her lip, knowing all the wishing in the world wouldn't bring her back. Nor Mum. Nor David.

For the first time since marrying Henry, she realised with a mixture of regret and sadness, she was all alone in the world. There was no man beside her. No one to support or help; only to use her. Apart from Terry. But would Terry still want her now she was no longer a virgin? Would he be able to tell just by looking at her that she'd been forced to do licentious acts by a demanding husband? And did she really want him now? If he deserted her once, he could do it again, so why hope. There was only one comfort and reason for being, one reason for living. Molly. Darling Molly.

It was no use feeling sorry for the mess she was in, she told herself. She'd made her bed and now had to lie in it, as Dad would say. No one else was going to help her, so she would just have to get on with it and sort out her own life. No one to blame. No one to scream and shout at. No one's fault but her own. Why did she let the men in her life walk all over her? What a fool she'd been.

Well, not any more, she decided resolutely. She was making the decisions about her life from here on. Never again would anyone, not man, woman or child, dictate to her what she could or could not do.

With controlled, determined movements, she put on a

dab of bright red lipstick and pressed her lips tightly together. A pat of rouge, a light dusting of face powder. Trying to look normal, as if nothing had happened. Then she would pack. She needed to be ready as soon as Molly came home from nursery school at lunchtime, collected by Mrs Potter. They must be gone long before Henry returned home. Each step of her planned escape fell easily into place in her head.

They would go to the coast. Anywhere a train would take them where Henry would never find them. Southend or Brighton. She'd never seen the sea. Never made sandcastles or splashed in the ocean. Molly would love it too.

Or they could go to Margate. Yes, why not Margate, she thought. She could search out Maisie Pilkington's B&B perhaps. Take rooms there until she found somewhere proper to live. Then, remembering Henry also knew Maisie, they were old friends, he probably knew where she now lived. For all she knew, he might still be Maisie's accountant. No, Margate was too risky.

Up north somewhere, then? To Scarborough. Even Scotland. She would have to find work, she realised as another thought occurred. She had no money she could actually call her own. No means of support. What was left in her purse was all she had. She didn't have her own bank account – that was in Henry's name. Any monies paid out for the coffee shop had to have both hers and Henry's signature on the cheques, and she couldn't sell it without his agreement. *His* name was on the lease. She couldn't even draw money out from the account without Henry's say so.

He had promised it would all be okay, he would take care of everything. Back then, she thought everything would be all right; she never dreamed something like this would happen, that she would be on her own again. No home. No money. How could she have been so foolish not to see Henry had tricked her?

If she thought she hated her father, the vile abhorrence she felt for Henry was treblefold, and she tugged at her wedding band and engagement ring on her finger, anxious to be rid of the ties that bound her. She hesitated, stopping herself. The rings were expensive. Valuable. She would pawn them. And her gold and diamond watch. All her jewellery, in fact. She tipped the contents of her jewellery box into her handbag. What did she need flashy, fancy bracelets and necklaces for where she was going? Wherever that was to be.

And what was she to say to Mrs Potter? She thought for a moment before the answer came. She would say she was taking Molly to visit their father. Hopefully, Henry would think she'd gone to plead with him to allow Molly's adoption. He would never think to follow her there after the way he'd treated her last night if he's an ounce of sense, she reasoned. He wouldn't risk the confrontation that might ensue. Plus, she realised with a sense of satisfaction, Henry had no idea where the farm actually was.

From downstairs came the sound of the brass frontdoor knocker.

"You've a visitor," Mrs Potter called up the stairs.

Her heart leapt. Terry! It had to be. At least he could help her get away. But how did he know where she lived, she wondered. Had he been following her? Oh, but what did that matter, he was there now; he would help her get away. As gracefully as her aching body would allow against the discomfort she felt, she descended the stairs.

"Where is he?" she asked Mrs Potter.

"I've put him in the sitting room with a cup of tea. I'm

off to do a bit of shopping and then I'll pick Molly up on my way back."

Beth breathed in slowly, composing herself before pushing open the sitting room door. The man standing by the window, his back to her as he looked out over the garden, turned around.

"Dad!" She felt her legs buckle with the mixture of shock, stunned surprise and relief.

His hair had turned almost white and receded to almost a bare crown, his face tanned and heavily creased. He looked far older than she would have expected. Suddenly, the past didn't matter. He was here now. Everything now was going to be okay. He would make things right. With arms outstretched, she ran to him, resentment and hate falling away in teardrops of relief.

"Dad, you've finally come."

He shied away from her advances. "Where's the baby?"

She halted, staring at him in incredulity. He'd not even said hello.

"Do you mean Molly? She's hardly a baby now, Dad."

"I've come for my daughter," he said, keeping his distance. "I want the baby."

She took a step backward, resting hands on hips, all elation at seeing him evaporating to nothingness. He'd come for Molly. Not her. Not both of them. Just Molly. She couldn't believe it. Nothing, it seemed, had changed.

"She's not here. She's at school?"

Alfie let out an impatient sigh. "I'll wait then."

He gazed about the room, at the same time rubbing his foot in the deep pile of the cream carpet.

"See you've done all right for yourself. Landed a good job 'ere by the looks of it. What are you, the housekeeper? The cook? You always was good at that cookin' lark, I'll give you that. It's a bit posh for you though, ain't it?"

Well, at least he was talking to her, Beth thought, the tension within her body easing; but what was he on about, the silly old fool?

"Job? …Dad, I don't work here. I live here."

"Watcha mean, live 'ere? You mean you rent rooms?"

"No, I mean, this is *my* house. Dad, you did get my letters, didn't you? They explained all this to you. Mike has spoken to you about it, surely? He kept saying he has."

Alfie rubbed his forehead. "Yeah. But he never said you lived in whoppin' big house like this. So, you just live on this floor then or somethin'? One of these fancy conversion things, is it?"

She rolled her eyes, unable to believe this discussion was taking place. Had living in the country puddled his brain? He wasn't talking sense. He knew all of this. Surely that was what had prompted him to come?

"Dad, I own the whole house. Well, at least my husband does. This is mine and my husband's home. The whole of it. Every brick, every window, every roof tile."

He let out a long, low whistle. "He must be well off then. What is he, a banker or something?"

"Actually, Dad, it's Mr Chiselhurst. You remember him, don't you? The accountant. My old boss. The job you made me give up to go to Gloucestershire with you. Yes, Dad, don't look so shocked. I married him." She couldn't help the sarcasm in her voice; there was a perverted pleasure in seeing her father's discomfort. "But you knew all this. I wrote, asking your permission, not that you bothered replying."

"I got your letter, yeah, but I never read it. When I saw it was from you, recognised your neat handwritin', I tore it up and burnt it. Mike did tell me what was goin' on, but to be truthful, I didn't take a lot of notice. I didn't really care what you did, you see. I ain't read any of your letters. It was that Sally who made me open the last one, and I thought, I ain't havin' that, so 'ere I am. Come to take 'er 'ome with me."

"But not me. Which only confirms what I thought of you all along. Do you really hate me that much as not to give a damn about me? Bloody hell, I must have been really wicked in the last world to suffer the loathing and treatment I've suffered since from you."

She felt as if her soul was being wrenched from her body, the hatred and venom she felt for Henry and her father was slowly turning itself inside out and gnawing at her from the knees up. It took all the effort and courage she possessed not to cry. She didn't know how much more of this she could take. How could any father ignore his own daughter like this? She hadn't brought scorn or shame on the family. What was the matter with the man? Why was he being so cruel? So heartless?

She'd heard enough. She wanted him out of her house. Now. Out of her life for good. He hadn't changed one bit, not even after all these years. Nothing there but rejection.

"Dad, I want you to—"

Alfie put the figurine he'd been looking at back down on the mantelpiece.

"But hang on a mo'," he said, turning to look at her. "That boss of yours, he was years older than you. Must be my age at least. Whatever in the world possessed you to marry 'im?"

"I married Henry because of you. Now, if you don't mind—"

"*Me?* What the flamin' hell did I have to do with it?

363

I've never met 'im."

"You gave me no choice. You rejected us both, remember? I had no job, no money and my baby sister to look after. Nor were you the slightest bit interested I was about to be thrown out of our house in Busch Lane. You didn't care tuppence." She clicked her fingers at him. "Not that much. It was either marry Henry or Molly got put in an orphanage. You spurned me and her from the moment Mum died. You blamed me although it wasn't my fault. Her death was your doing. If you hadn't—"

"'Course it was your fault. If you hadn't 'ave run off like you did, Connie wouldn't have been tryin' to do things herself. You should have been there helpin' her."

Head held high, she took a step closer to him, unwavering in her fervour.

"No, Dad, it wasn't *my* fault. Don't you dare keep trying to put the blame on me. You were there with her. You were her husband, for gawd's sake. You should have made sure she wasn't doing anything she shouldn't have been doing. I wasn't her keeper. I wasn't the skivvy either, but you certainly treated me like one."

"You were her daughter. It was your duty to look after your mother," he snapped back.

"I was also your daughter too. I still am, in case you'd forgotten."

Alfie held her gaze for a moment then turned away, hanging his head as if in shame. Beth hoped she'd struck something within him, some tiny chord.

"'Course I haven't, Beth, but, well…" He turned, half-smiled and took several steps closer. "Let me explain things, how it was. You keeps shoutin' it's all about you, you, you, but there was more to it than that. I can see that now, but—"

"You've had years to explain things, Dad. Years when

you did nothing, just let the two of us rot for all you cared. Not one word. And now you come here expecting to whisk Molly off as if nothing has happened."

"It's not like that, Beth. I had hoped after all this time you and me——"

The door to the sitting room burst open and in skipped Molly, her long, blonde hair tied in bunches on either side of her head, red polka-dotted ribbons trailing out behind her. She stopped short as she saw the stranger then sidled up to Beth, wrapping her arms about Beth's legs and hiding her face.

Beth reached down and picked up the child, hugged her tightly and kissed her forehead.

"Don't go all shy."

"Is that...?" he muttered.

"Molly." She set her little sister down to the floor, thinking the child seemed to be getting heavier by the day.

"Who's that funny-looking man?" Molly whispered up at Beth.

She turned Molly to face their father, his mouth open, watching the two of them.

"Molly, say hello to your father."

Molly stared intently at him, her blue eyes wide, a frown on her forehead. Beth could almost hear the cogs and chains in the child's brain whirling around and around, trying to make sense of the words.

Finally, Molly looked back to her and said, "No, silly. He ain't my daddy. My daddy's at work. He'll be home in a minute. He's coming home for his lunch today. He said so. I'm going to wait for him."

Molly pulled herself away from Beth's grip, gave Alfie another long, curious stare then skipped out of the room.

"Trouble is, Dad, Molly's right. You aren't her daddy.

Not in the sense she knows it. Henry's the one who's looked after her all these years. Clothed her, fed her, bought her toys, read her bedtime stories, rubbed Vic on her chest when she's had a cold. Henry's her real daddy, the one that's been here for her."

"I'm her real dad, not some pounced up jerk who thinks a few bob in his pocket gives him the right. I'm takin' her back home with me, back where she belongs, and that's that. I ain't havin' her adopted."

A cold icy chill ran down Beth's spine. "But you can't do that. You can't just come swanning in here and demand to take her home. *This* is her home. This is where she belongs. What can you offer her in that grotty little hovel in the middle of nowhere? You haven't even got a bathroom."

"Fat much you know. Did you ever think to come and visit me? See if I was all right? No. I wasn't good enough for you, so you married a rich man and thought sod the old man, he don't need me."

"And where were you when I needed you?" she whispered.

"Grievin' girl, grievin' me heart out. And what do you do? Bugger off and leaves me to it. Some daughter you turned out to be."

"That's not fair, Dad."

"Life never is. No, the kid's comin' back with me. End of story. She'll have the love of her father, somethin' she should have had all along. I can see that now, but I was so cut up about your mother, I couldn't cope with seeing a young sprog. In some twisted sort of way she was the cause of it all. Her and you."

"Don't you think I was grieving too? I'd only just got over Dave and Gran, where was your love and support then? I needed you Dad, but you turned your back on us.

You can't have her back."

"And you can't stop me." His voice rose. "She's my daughter and she belongs with me. Now, I suggest you go and pack her things 'cos I ain't leavin' 'ere without her."

The front door slammed. Henry had arrived home.

"We'll see about that," she retorted.

A moment later the door to the sitting room swung open again and there stood Henry, his arms full of the most beautiful flowers she had ever seen. A mass of red roses, orange lilies, pink carnations, frothy fronds of white gypsophilia, all sorts spilling out from his arms.

"Seems like I've interrupted a birthday or somethin'. An anniversary, is it?" Alfie asked.

She went to Henry's side and slipped her arm through his. "No, Dad, my husband often brings me flowers. Henry, I'd like to introduce my father."

The flowers were Henry's way of apologizing for last night, she knew, but all the flowers in the bulb fields of Holland couldn't make up for the way he had treated her last night. She would never forgive him, but for now, she needed his support. They had to show a united front because no one was going to take Molly away from her. Especially Dad. She gathered the blooms into her arms and reached on tiptoe to kiss Henry's cheek.

"Thank you. I'll just go and find a vase whilst you and Dad get to know each other, I'm sure you have a lot to discuss. You really have excelled yourself this time, Henry."

She wasn't sure who was more stunned – her father or her husband – as she hurried away into the kitchen, where she dumped the flowers into the sink so hard, it was as if one of the blooms had jumped out and bitten her hand. She wanted nothing to do with them. They could rot in the dustbin of hell for all she cared.

"Oh, what lovely flowers," cooed Mrs Potter. "I'll put them in some water for you straight away. I'd best lay the dining table. I'm all behind today. Will your visitor be staying for lunch? It's only cold meats and salad, will that be okay?"

"No, he most certainly won't be stopping, Mrs Potter," Beth snapped. "And never, *ever*, let than man into the house again."

The mortified look Mrs Potter gave made her feel guilty. She'd never spoken in that manner before to their housekeeper, but she couldn't help it. No way was he going to take Molly back to that dreadful place. She had to get her away from here. Sneak her out in secret somehow. The difficult bit was going to be getting Molly and two suitcases out of the house without Henry or her father noticing. She hoped Henry would keep him occupied for long enough.

"Where's Molly?" she asked Mrs Potter, looking around the kitchen, expecting to see her sister "helping cooking".

"Upstairs. Playing."

"Good. Mrs Potter, I need your help. I want you to go up and help her change into something suitable for travelling, and pack a suitcase for her whilst I see to my things."

"Travelling? Why? Whatever's going on?"

"I'm taking Molly on a little trip, a short break to the seaside. Just for a few days. The sun and sand will do us good. I'm all washed out what with all the extra work I've had to do to get the coffee-shop up and ready again."

"What a lovely idea. You do look all done in, this morning, if you don't mind my saying so. Shall I put some things out for Mr Chiselhurst to take?"

"No. Henry's not coming with us. In fact, he doesn't

know we're going."

Mrs Potter stared curiously at her. "Oh! Here, you're not running out on him are you? I don't think I can be colluding with you if you are, you know."

"No, Mrs Potter, I'm not running away," she lied. "Now please, I haven't much time, I've a train to catch."

Looking confused and shaking her head as she wiped her hands down her apron, Mrs Potter obeyed, following her up the back stairs.

"Are we going away?" Molly asked excitedly as she was being buttoned into her red coat. She wouldn't stand still, and kept trying to take the coat off. "It's too hot for a coat. I don't want it on."

Beth tried to keep calm. The last thing she wanted now was for Molly to throw a tantrum that would bring Henry rushing up the stairs to see what was going on.

"Be a good girl, now. It's getting chilly outside, the wind's getting up. You don't want to catch a cold now, do you?"

Beth glanced out of the window. The midday sun blazed down, the leaves on the plane tree outside the house hardly stirred. But Molly needed a coat; it would be windy by the sea, and Molly wearing it now meant one less thing to carry.

"But where are we going?" the child pestered. "Is Daddy coming too?" Coat buttoned up, Molly dived onto her bed to reach her favourite dolly, a floppy, rag-stuffed one with long, yellow pigtails and red-and-white striped legs. A present from Henry last Christmas. "Can Loopyloo come?"

"Of course she can," said Beth, looking anxiously around the room, making sure she hadn't forgotten anything.

"We're not going away with that funny man

downstairs, are we?" Molly whispered. "I don't like him."

She pulled Molly to her and gave her a big hug. "No, poppet. We are definitely not going away with that horrible man downstairs. You and I are going to the seaside."

"Yippee!" Molly shouted, excited. She began running around the bedroom, singing loudly, "I'm going to the seaside. I'm going to the seaside."

"Ssshhh," pleaded Beth, fearful. "Calm down. If Daddy hears us, he'll be cross and stop us going."

Molly stood still. "Why? Doesn't he know? Doesn't he want us to go?"

"No. It's a secret. We have to be very, very quiet and tiptoe downstairs. Now, have you got everything?"

Molly cuddled her doll. "Yup, I got Loopyloo."

Beth carried a case in each hand as they slowly crept down the stairs. Mrs Potter stood by the front door and opened it as they reached the bottom. Outside in the street, a black cab waited at the gate, its engine running.

"Thanks for ordering the taxi, Mrs Potter. I thought I was going to have to walk to the station." She spoke quietly, eyes fixed on the sitting room door, praying Henry and her father hadn't heard or suspected what she was up to.

"I didn't. It's just pulled up." Mrs Potter answered.

The sitting room door burst open and there stood her father.

"Ah, good. Glad you've got her ready."

Before Beth could do or say anything, Alfie swept the child up into one arm, grabbed the two cases, and was out the front door and climbing into the cab, Molly screaming and kicking.

Chapter Twenty-Eight

"Stop him, Henry!" Beth screamed as the cab pulled away. She could see Molly frantically banging on the window.

Mrs Potter was already running to the phone. "Oh my goodness. He's kidnapped Molly. Quick, quick, I'll call the police. Oh dear, this is all my fault. I shouldn't have let him in," she sobbed, dabbing her eyes with the hem of her white apron.

"Henry, do something," Beth yelled.

"I can't do anything, Beth. We can't stop him. Put the phone down, Mrs Potter, we won't be needing the police." There was no emotion in his voice.

Beth leapt at him, thumping his chest for her life's worth. "How could you? How could you just stand there and do nothing? You should have stopped him. I hate you, Henry, I hate you. I thought you loved Molly."

Henry caught hold of her wrists, gripping them tightly. "I do. I do love her like my own, you know that, but he *is* her father. He has every right to take her."

She collapsed in tears against his broad chest.

Beth's fury hadn't abated. "Don't just stand there, Henry, go get the car. We're going after them. He can't get away with this. Molly's scared out of her wits."

"I left the car at the office. It was such a glorious morning, I walked home."

"Then wave down a cab. Sod it, I'll do it myself. We're waiting precious time. We have to go after them."

"You can't do that," said Henry.

"Why ever not?" she shouted back.

"Because you're my wife, and I'm ordering you not to."

She scowled at him and, ignoring the shocked Mrs Potter, said accusingly, "You only married me because of Molly, didn't you? Well, Henry, looks like you've lost her. And after last night, you've lost me too. It's over. Finished. When I find Molly, we're not coming back."

He reached out to put a hand on her shoulder, "Beth, about last night—"

She pushed him away, stepping back further and further from his reach.

"Don't touch me," she screamed. "Don't ever lay a hand on me again. So help me, I'll kill you." She meant every word.

"Beth, you're getting hysterical. Now, please, let's discuss this in a civilized matter. Privately. Not in front of Mrs Potter, you're embarrassing her."

She lowered her voice an octave, thinking she might be furious with Henry but she certainly wasn't hysterical. She was in complete control of herself, and right now she didn't care if the whole world heard what she was about to say, least of all their housekeeper.

"Civilized? Do you call what you did to me last night civilized? No, let Mrs Potter hear. Let her know what an animal you are. Let her know what kind of man she's working for. You weren't content with touching-up your secretaries, were you? No. You had to abuse me. Hurt me. No, Henry, there's nothing civilized about rape."

Mrs Potter gasped and ran into the kitchen, slamming the door behind her.

Beth waited for the expected slap across her face. It never came. Instead Henry stood, massive hands on his wide, protruding stomach, and laughed.

"She doesn't believe you."

"I don't care what she thinks. Now, if you don't mind, I need to get to Molly. At least I know where he's taken her. Back to that dump in the sticks."

She had to go to her. Molly needed her. She would be frightened, all alone with a strange man. The child wouldn't understand he was her real father. She rushed outside, ran down the path and at the gate stopped, buried her face in her hands and cried. Everything had gone horribly wrong, and without Molly, her world had suddenly collapsed. Pulling her hands away from her face, she looked up into the cloudless blue sky and shouted at the top of her voice.

"I hate you, Dad. I hope you rot in hell some day for all you've put me through!"

The sound of her anguish sent the starlings and sparrows spiralling up out of the trees in a noisy squabble.

Henry's heavy footsteps resounded behind her. She flung open the gate and began running, stumbling, almost tripping over as her tired feet and limbs pounded the pavement. How could he just let Molly go like that? How could he? Terry wouldn't of stood back and let it happen. He'd have fought and chased after him. If only she could drive, she thought, she'd have taken the Jag and gone after them.

No, but Terry could, she suddenly remembered. He'd help fetch Molly back. She had to find him.

She ran faster, needing to put as much distance between Henry as she could. He wouldn't be able to catch up; he couldn't run more than a few steps without stopping for breath. And all the while, the distraught, frightened face of Molly screaming at her through the cab window flashed in her head.

When the discomfort of a stitch in her side prevented her running any further, she stopped, doubling over and gasping for breath. Henry was nowhere in sight. As she straightened, still breathing heavily, she saw how far she had come from the house, already half way across the footbridge spanning the weir. The quay was still some way further ahead on the other side of the river, but she had to keep going, she told herself. She broke into a run again, pushing herself on.

She could hear men working long before she reached where the boats were moored along the brick wall shoring up the river's edge. Booms of heavy banging, shouting, the screech and grinding of metal filled the air. All around her she noticed the grime and dirt, the layer of brown dust coating the path, the leaves on the trees hanging limp with the weight of it.

The noise appeared to come from a large, straight-sided barge, its rusting hulk above the waterline full of holes of decay. A blue flash caught her eye. It came from inside the hull. Another flash. Someone was in there working.

Breathless and wheezing from running, she stood for a few moments, hands on knees, trying to get her breath back. Eventually, she had the strength and puff to call out.

"Hello!"

She could hear voices, movement, but no one answered.

She cupped her hands around her mouth and called out louder. "Hello in there!"

The metallic scream of metal against metal was deafening. Beth clapped her hands to her ears and stepped back, waiting for it to stop. After a few minutes, silence ensued before heavy banging from inside the boat started again. Bang. Bang. Bang.

"'Ere, Fred, toss me that crowbar," she heard a man's voice shout from inside the barge. There was a loud clank that seemed to echo all around inside it.

"'Ere, watch wot you're fuckin' doin'," the same voice yelled out again. "That was nearly me fuckin' foot!"

Suddenly a male face popped up over the top of the hulk, making her jump.

Seeing her, he said, "'Ello darlin'. You lookin' for someone?"

Shielding her eyes from the sun, she stared up to him. His hair was matted with bits of rust, and his face so dirty with sweat and rust powder, it made the whites of his eyes stand out.

"Yes, I've been calling out but you couldn't hear me."

"Who you lookin' for? The gaffer? Or Tommy Maddocks? Girls are always chasin' after Tommy."

"No, I'm after Terry. Terry Gibbs. Do you know him?"

"What, Terry? Yeah, everyone round 'ere knows 'im." The banging from inside the barge continued, making it difficult for her to hear what the chap was saying.

"Do you know where he is?" she shouted up.

"Who wants to know?"

"Pardon."

He shouted again, louder this time. "I said, who wants to know?"

"I do. Come on, I'm in a hurry."

"And who are you, when you're at 'ome?"

Beth cupped one hand to her ear and looked at him. She could hardly hear a word he said over the incessant noise from inside the barge.

The man turned his face away and yelled, "Fred! Stop that fuckin' bangin' a mo', will you? I can't 'ear meself think up 'ere."

Instantly, the banging stopped. "Sorry, boss," someone, presumably Fred, yelled back.

The grimy face turned back to Beth. "Sorry about that,

darlin'. I said, who are you?"

"A friend. Look, this is urgent. Is Terry here or not?"

"Nah, 'aven't seen 'im this mornin'."

"Does he work here, with you, on this boat?"

"Nah. 'E's normally over at the quay, doin' the finishin' like." He pointed towards a barge moored a little further downstream. "'E prefers paintin' to gettin' his 'ands mucky, know wot I mean?"

"Okay. Thanks."

"Hold on. That looks like him over there now."

She followed the line of his pointed finger. A little further along the towpath she could see Terry chatting to someone. He seemed to be nodding a lot, the other one doing most of the talking.

Relieved, Beth turned back up to the man on the boat. "Great. That's him. Thank you."

"That's all right, darlin'. Any time."

At that same moment, Terry looked her way, and recognizing her, waved out. The man he'd been talking to walked away in the opposite direction. Terry broke into a run.

She wanted to run too, but her feet hurt from doing so much already. The aching stiffness in her body proved too much so she was forced to walk slowly to meet him. Each footstep seemed to wear her down further to the ground. When he finally reached her, she almost collapsed into his arms.

"Oh, Terry. You must help me? Where's your car? We need to—"

"Whatever's up? What's happened to you? You look dreadful."

He guided her to a wooden seat set back on the grass bank overlooking the swirling, murky water racing downstream on the turning tide. "You're not ill, are you?

You look absolutely worn out."

That was hardly surprising, she thought, considering all she'd been through since yesterday.

"Oh, Terry, it's awful. My dad came and snatched Molly. He grabbed our two cases as we were coming out of the door. Just scooped her up then drove off with her in a cab. He's kidnapped her." She couldn't keep the tears from cascading again. She wiped her eyes with the back of her hand and sniffed, burying her head in Terry's shoulder.

"But if he's Molly's dad, it's hardly kidnapping," Terry said. "It ain't no crime to take your own daughter away."

"But Molly doesn't know him. She'll be petrified."

"Do you know where they've gone?"

She nodded. "He's probably taken her back to the farm. Terry, she'll just die there, I know she will."

"Don't be daft, she'll love it with her proper dad. All that fresh air and fields to run about in and the animals to play with. And Sally. Aunt Edie will see she's okay, comes to no harm."

"You don't understand. She needs me. She'll have no one to read her bedtime stories, or dress her, or wash her. Watch television with her. I bet he hasn't even got one. Who's going to sit with her during Andy Pandy or the Woodentops?" She wasn't making sense, she knew, her mind in a turmoil of confusion. "He might be our father and, yes, maybe he hasn't done anything illegal, but it doesn't make snatching her away like that any more right. It's a terrible thing to do to a child. A child needs a mother. I might not be Molly's mum, but I'm the nearest she's ever going to get to one. I can't let her grow up with a man who thinks his daughters are only there to nursemaid him and run errands. What's going to happen when she gets older and he's incapable of taking care of himself? Is she expected to nurse him, feed him, look after him in his old age? What sort of life is that for her?"

"It might never come to that."

Unshakeable in her resolve, she pleaded, "Don't you see, I have to get there and bring her back? You have to help me. Please, Terry. I just don't know what else to do."

Terry rubbed his brow. "I don't understand, Beth. Why isn't Henry chasing off with you in his car to get her back? Where is he? Does he know?"

"Henry let him do it. Said there was nothing he could do to stop him. I just can't believe it of him after all he'd said, all that talk about wanting to adopt."

He looked puzzled. "Hold on a minute. You said your dad took both your suitcases. Why? What were you doing?"

"I was taking Molly up to Scarborough."

"Why?"

She hung her head, hoping he wouldn't see the hurt inside. "For a little holiday."

He lifted her chin. "Come on, that's not the real reason, is it? Were you walking out on him?"

She nodded slowly.

He threw his arms up into the air in jubilation. "Hallelujah! You've finally seen the light." She sensed a glimmer of hope in his dark eyes as he asked, "You were walking out on him for good? You weren't planning on going back?" He studied her face. "That's not all though, is it? I can tell. So come on, out with it. What else has happened? He's not knocked you about, has he? If he has, I'll kill him, so help me—"

"Henry's never hit me." She didn't want Terry to guess what had happened. She didn't want to tell anyone, it was simply too horrid.

Terry smiled widely. "But that's great, Beth. You can

divorce him and then, once it's sorted, you and I can… Oh Beth, please don't look so worried. It'll be all right. I'll take care of you, I promise. And Molly. Get shot of old Henry. It'll be easy, like I told you." He lowered his voice. "Do you remember before you all went off to my uncle's farm, that night on Waterloo Bridge? I asked you then to marry me. The offer still stands."

He pulled her to him, holding her close, his lips almost touching hers. "I love you Beth. I always have." The words were a whisper, his breath caressing her face so delicately Beth felt her knees go weak, despite the fact she was sitting. "Say you'll marry me, Beth."

Haunted by what had taken place the previous night, Beth covered her face with her hands. "No, Terry, I can't. I can't divorce Henry."

He looked hurt. "Why? If he's not slept with you, the marriage will be declared null and void."

She pulled away from him. "That's just the point." Tears brimmed her eyes. How was she going to explain this without him thinking the worst of her? What would he think? Would he blame her?

Terry frowned, a wounded look upon his face. "You lied to me."

"No, no, I didn't lie. You see…" She hesitated. It was so difficult to know where to start. More worrying was the fear that Terry wouldn't believe her. She drew a deep breath before speaking.

"Last night Henry raped me."

"Oh, my darling Beth." He pulled her back into his arms, letting her weep on his shoulder as the tears fell faster than the waters over Richmond weir, her whole body racked with sobbing.

"The bastard." He stroked her hair, comforting as her body shuddered.

"I feel so ashamed," she sobbed into his shirt.

"The bastard," Terry repeated, shaking his head. "The dirty, rotten bastard."

"I thought if I go away, go somewhere where he wouldn't think to find me, at least that way he could divorce me for desertion."

"But there's no need for that. You could stay with me. We could—"

She held up her hand to stop him. "No, Terry. Don't you see? If I did, it would drag you into it. I don't want that. I don't want you getting involved in this. Henry can be ruthless when he wants something, and he wouldn't hesitate in dragging you through the courts. It would play straight into his hands. He would claim he's never laid a hand on me, say I wouldn't do my wifely duty. He would shame me. It would be my word against his. Against yours. If I stayed with you, we would be living in sin, and then I might never get Molly back."

This morning she couldn't bear the thought of any one touching her, yet in Terry's arms, the fear had vanished. But would it stay hidden? Could she trust him?

"Beth, this is ridiculous. It makes it seem as if you're the guilty one, this running away and having to hide. You shouldn't have to be doing this. There must be another way."

"If you can think of a good one quick, I'll be happy to listen, but there isn't. I've spent all morning trying to come up with an alternative. And then Dad turns up out of the blue, says he wants Molly and whisks her off. Oh, Terry, why is my life so complicated? What did I do that was so wrong to deserve all this? Why did he take her?"

Terry held her close. "You did nothing wrong. Don't take it all on yourself. Listen, I've been thinking. Henry forced you to marry him, right?"

"Well, no, not forced. He offered me a way out of the pickle I was in, so I took it. I thought I knew what I was getting myself into. I trusted him. How wrong I was."

"But you were young. How old were you? Seventeen? Eighteen? Too young to marry without your father's consent. Or did he agree? Do you see what I'm getting at? If you married without your father's permission, with Henry pressuring you, kind of blackmailing you, your marriage would be illegal. Henry could find himself in a lot of deep, dirty water."

Her eyes lit up. "Henry forged my father's signature on the forms, said it would be okay, no one would ever find out." Then the dreadful truth struck her. "But *I* knew. I agreed to it. Oh, but that means I'm just as guilty. I'll also be in trouble."

"No, no, Beth. That's my whole point. He *forced* you to do it. He made you." He pursed his lips, a spark of mischief in his eyes. "I'm sure I'm right. I didn't study law for a while without learning a few things. Perhaps it's come in useful after all."

"It all sounds so messy. I could say he raped me, have him arrested. That would be grounds for divorce, wouldn't it?"

Terry shook his head slowly. "A man can't be accused of raping his own wife."

"But if we're not legally married then I'm not legally his wife, and therefore it must be rape, surely?" To her, it made perfect sense. A logical assumption.

"Oh, I wish that it were that simple, Beth. He believed you were his wife. There's a possibility that would let him off the hook. I don't think there's a judge in the land that would convict Henry on that score."

"Then the law's bunkum. Stupid laws made up by men to keep us women down. It's all for one and let's keep the women chained to the kitchen sink. Barefoot and preferably pregnant, isn't that what they say?" A dreadful thought entered her head. "Gawd, what if I'm pregnant? Then what am I to do?" She stood abruptly.

Terry pulled her back down onto the seat. "Whoa, calm down. Worry about that later."

Easy for him to say, she thought, getting impatient now. Each minute they sat here meant Molly was being taken further and further away.

"Look, will you help me get her back, or not? We're wasting so much time."

"Of course I will but, Beth, my car's off the road still. It ain't going nowhere today."

She was crestfallen. Now what was she to do? They could hardly go back and take Henry's car.

Terry put a reassuring arm around her shoulder. "Look, I'll go and ask Billy. See if he'll let me use the van. It's a bit grubby though, not like the stately charabang you've probably been used to riding around in."

She jumped up from the wooden seat again. "I don't care, as long as it's got four wheels and goes like the clappers."

He grabbed her hand. "Come on, then, what are we waiting for?"

Chapter Twenty-Nine

Heaving her weary body up from the step to slide on to the seat, Beth climbed back into the van parked on the grass verge in the lane opposite the row of cottages at Clackett's Farm. Every muscle in her body ached.

"There's no answer," she said to Terry, sliding the door closed.

"Perhaps he's taken her elsewhere. Didn't you say you had lots of aunts and uncles? He may have gone to one of them."

She shook her head. "I wouldn't have thought so. Perhaps we've beaten him here. He was in a taxi, which means he would have had to catch a train to Bristol. Then they've got to get out here. They'll be here sooner or later. We'll wait."

The van windows were open, the late evening sun slowly slipping down, its red glow lighting the high clouds with scarlet. Beth leaned forward, staring ahead at the row of neat cottages. They looked different in some way from how she remembered them. Brighter. Almost welcoming. Then she realised all the front doors were now painted a bright white. The glass in every window sparkled, lacy white net curtains hung at every one. There were solid paths leading to each door flanked by flowerbeds, each a riot of colour from roses and dahlias, clumps of lavender and blue delphiniums and showy lupins. The lawns were mown in neat, straight rows of light and dark green stripes. Someone had certainly been busy, she thought.

The gate to her father's cottage was arched by a pergola festooned with honeysuckle and saucer-sized purple clematis. A vibrant red rose scrambled up the cottage wall and tumbled over the porch roof.

The farm and cottages had brought such hopes to her when they had brought her mother here that dark, freezing winter's night, but had wrought nothing but sadness and grief. And yet they looked so peaceful now, so tranquil nestling on the hilltop, bathed in the setting sun's last rays, turning the honey-coloured stones to a golden glow.

As she studied the buildings, a barn owl glided silently past the windscreen, its white face and underwings so close, she could almost see each feather, see the van's reflection in its black eyes. She watched the magnificent bird land on a nearby fencepost for a moment before it flapped its wings and took off, flying in the direction of Clackett's Wood. She couldn't recall seeing owls here before.

"Penny for them?"

Startled, she turned to Terry. "What? Oh, nothing. I was just thinking."

"About what?"

"This and that and nothing. Mike. David. Mum. The past."

"Hardly nothing."

She shrugged. "No, but it's all things I can't change. Being here, seeing this place again, has brought it all back. All the memories."

"Don't dwell on them, Beth," he suggested kindly. "Let them be. It's the future you should be planning."

"How? I don't even know where I'm going to go once I've got Molly. Up to Scarborough, I suppose. Like I planned."

"Do you think that's wise, dragging the child up north? And to what? And what if he refuses to let you take her? Wouldn't it be better to let her stay here?"

"Why? There's nothing here for her. No shops, no

cinemas, no theatres, or restaurants. Nothing. Deadman's Gulch in the back of beyond."

Terry dismissed her comment with a shake of his head. "Those are for adults. Kids aren't interested in that sort of thing, apart from Saturday mornin' pictures. They do have them down here, you know. Just have to travel a bit further to get to them, that's all."

"Dad's a stranger to Molly. Think how unsettling that's going to be for her. She'll be crying for me. He doesn't know the first thing about looking after a child so small. Mum was always there to do it. I bet the poor thing's screaming her head off as we speak. She took an instant dislike of him the moment she saw him this morning."

"She's with her father; how much safer can she be? He doesn't mean her any harm from the sound of it. She would have sensed that by now, I'm sure. Even babies can sense who's kind and caring and who doesn't like them. We don't give kids enough credit."

"All right then," Beth protested, "what if Molly has an accident running about the fields, falls in a ditch and breaks her leg? How long before someone finds her, let alone gets her to a hospital? Back home we've got the West Middlesex right on our doorstep, and doctors and everything. Here, there's nothing for miles."

"How do you think people living here all this time, for generations, have coped? It's not like they're living on the moon. Gloucestershire *is* civilized. It's not all country bumpkins and pigsties."

A door of one of the cottages opened. Two young boys bounded out, one not much older than Molly, the other by several years. They were laughing and throwing a ball to each other, having fun.

"Looks like she'll have plenty of friends here to play

with," said Terry, watching the older boy climb over the gate to retrieve the ball that had gone over the dry-stone wall of the garden and into the lane.

"She'll have plenty of friends back home. Lots of children to play with and plenty of adults about to keep an eye on them. And parks with swings and slides and roundabouts."

"Yes, and smog and dirt and grime. Cars and lorries to get knocked over by, and gangsters and gang fights. Is that what you want Molly to grow up in? I bet this place is screaming with kids in the summer, she'd be making friends all the time."

"And saying goodbye to them a week later. That's not friendship, Terry, not proper friends you keep for life. And what about during the winter? What about Molly's education? A poxy village school that's miles down the hill, probably falling to bits and been there since the ark. And goodness only knows where the secondary schools are."

"And they're not like that in London?" Terry asked sarcastically.

He did have a point. Worple Road had been a very rundown and old-fashioned school building, a Victorian edifice that sadly had missed being bombed during the war. It would have been a blessing.

"Okay," she conceded, "but think on it from Molly's view. She's going to be lonely and isolated, and she'll grow up resenting it and hating Dad for dragging her here, just as I did."

"You don't know that. You're only seeing this from your side. Okay, so you hate the countryside. I can understand that. I used to hate coming here as a kid myself. We used to come often when we were small because Mum was always having to go into hospital.

Looking back, I expect it was the old man who put her there. When I was here I hated the smells and the insects, and I missed my friends. But if I'd have been born to this way of life, I wouldn't know any different. I'd probably love it just as much as Freda or Sally, or any other kid hereabouts. Look at those boys over there. I bet they'd give their eye-teeth to stay here all the time."

Beth couldn't agree with his argument. "But Molly wasn't born to it. She's a Londoner, the same as you and me and Mike. Molly's been brought up in that city, in a warm house with schools close by and the river and, and… plenty of things to do. Safe things."

"And she's young. She'll forget today and everything else that's gone before. Let her stay and make up her own mind when she's older."

He pulled her to him across the engine cover that separated the two seats.

"Sweetheart. I know it's hard. You've had a rotten time of things and you've done your best for her, the very best any parent could have done, considering the circumstances. I'm proud of you. Your father should be proud, too. I expect he is in his own way. Don't you think it's time to let go and start enjoying your life now? You've done your bit for her. It's not as if you won't see her again. Not if you make it that way. Not if you patch things up with your dad. Now. Today."

She pulled away and looked at him, perplexed. "Just whose side are you on? I would have thought with all you've been through with your dad, you would be with me on this."

"I'm on Molly's side. Think on it, Beth. Did it ever occur to you that your father could be blaming himself for all this?"

"Never. He's not the sort."

"At least give him the benefit of the doubt. You two have been wrenched apart by tragedy. Just as you had hopes and dreams for yourself, I bet he and your mum had theirs." He nodded towards the cottages. "Probably of a little house just like those over there. For all we know, your father may feel he's let everyone down. Went off to war the conquering hero, and came back with less of his body than he went out with. Then, when your mum died, a part of him died too. I'm not defending his actions or the way he treated you, not for one moment, but I suspect he's the sort that doesn't know how to say sorry either. Can you understand what I'm trying to say?"

She tried to imagine what it had been like for her father, see things from his point of view, but her vision was masked by feelings of betrayal and desertion clinging to her heart.

"In some ways you're just as stubborn as he is." Her mother's words filled her head, reminding her suddenly of the promise she'd made. *"Be kind to your father. He's been through a lot."* But was it reason enough to forgive him? She wished she knew the answer.

"I want to forgive, I really do," she said, "but, I'm scared we'll just argue and hurl accusations at each other again just as we did this morning, and I'll lose Molly forever in the process."

"Handle it right and you won't. We all get scared sometimes, and say and do things we regret when we're angry or upset, but we have to move onwards. And it is hard. I know how you feel. I know how I feel over my two sisters."

She hung her head, eyeing the floor before looking back up at Terry's face. "I'm sorry, I'd forgotten your family's been ripped apart as well. Have you ever been able to see them since they were put into care?"

"I've no idea where they are, the authorities refuse to tell me. They say it's better that way, that they be allowed to forget their own flesh and blood and grow up not knowing their past. I don't know if they're still in a home or fostered out. They could even have been sent abroad for all I'm allowed to know. I've heard rumours that a lot of the kids in orphanages have been shipped out to Australia to have a better chance in life."

"But Australia's wonderful. All that warm sunshine and blue seas."

Terry shot her a look. "Yeah! And full of poisonous spiders and killer jellyfish and snakes and convicts. Bloody wonderful country."

"But surely your sisters are allowed to write to you?"

He shook his head. "The letters stopped when I got sent down. Apparently I was a bad influence."

"Oh, Terry, that's so sad. And all so wrong."

She would hate it if she lost contact with Mike. He might not be a frequent or good letter-writer but at least they were in touch, and she knew where he was. The same with Molly, but she couldn't just abandon her because, if she went away today leaving her behind, she'd feel that's exactly what she would be doing. Deserting her. Terry had certainly had it rough, she thought, more so than she had considering all he had been through with his own father. She still didn't know what happened to put Terry behind bars, and could contain her curiosity no longer.

"You know, you never did tell me about going to prison. What happened?"

"You don't want to hear."

"Yes I do," she said indignantly.

"There was a fight."

"Yes, with your dad. I know that. But what I can't

believe is that you would hurt anyone, not even him, despite all he'd done to you. It's not in your nature."

He looked her directly in the eyes and said slowly, "I didn't kill him. I said it was me. I took the blame to cover for someone else."

She sucked in a long breath, aghast. "Who? Why?"

"To protect someone."

"But you could have been hanged."

He sighed heavily. "Look, Beth, the fight happened, I took the rap and I didn't get hanged. I'm still here. In the end, the real person confessed. They let me out and he got a suspended sentence because of mitigating circumstances. It's all in the past now. Finished. Forget it."

He sounded exasperated but she wasn't going to let it end there. She couldn't. If they were to have any future together, she had to know.

"Terry, who were you protecting?"

He remained silent. She kept glancing across to him, willing him on, wishing she knew what was going through his mind. She didn't like not knowing, didn't want any secrets between them.

"Please tell me. You can trust me."

He turned away, drew a long breath, took a cigarette packet from his top pocket, tapped a woodbine out and put it to his mouth then lit it. After inhaling several times, he blew a cloud of wispy grey smoke out of the side window before speaking.

"Okay, if you must know… it was my kid brother, Joe."

Her hand shot to her mouth. Not knowing what to say, unable to look at Terry, she stared beyond the hedge at the field of barley swaying like rolling waves on a sea.

Many the time she'd wanted to kill her own father, but

that had all been just fanciful thoughts. Just an expression brought on by temper or frustrated anger; she would never actually harm him. She'd never want to harm anyone. Then, remembering Henry's vile attack on her last night, how, given the opportunity, knew she would have gladly stabbed him to death had she the weapon to hand, she turned back, smiling at Terry. She now understood. Terry's father had been a man far, far worse than her own, she considered. That man had been a drunk, a bully; her own was just lonely and bitter. She knew which was the better and knew in that instant what she had to do.

"Seems like both our fathers were tyrants in their own individual way. They've both made our lives hell."

Terry continued smoking in silence. Finally, he took one last draw on the cigarette and flicked it out of the window into the hedgerow.

"What made you take the rap for Joe?" she asked.

He sighed. "Joe wouldn't have been able to survive in prison. He'd a family to think of. His girlfriend had just told him she was pregnant, they were going to get married."

She touched his arm. "It was very brave of you."

"Or foolish. It's a very thin line between both."

"What made him confess? A guilty conscience?"

Terry laughed slightly. "Something like that. Actually it was Julie, his girlfriend, persuaded him. Said she couldn't marry a man who couldn't stand by his convictions. I'm actually proud of my little brother doing that, it wasn't easy for him. Thankfully, the court was merciful once they'd heard how my old man used to knock seven bales of shit out of us kids, including the girls, and how the old man had thrashed him with his belt that very night when he found out Joe had got Julie into trouble.

"What, just for getting a girl pregnant?"

Terry nodded. "Dad came looking for him in the pub, see. Started mouthing off about what a useless lump of nothing Joe was in front of all his mates. Dad was drunk and pulled a knife on him. Said he was going to cut Joe's tackle off and throw it to the fish in the Thames, shouting that no one in his family was going to bring shame on him. Joe went for him. I tried to pull him off, but the fight got out of hand. The next minute the law was wading in. I was bending over Dad on the floor. I'd just pulled the knife out of his stomach. He was bleeding all over the place. The coppers naturally assumed I'd done it and put two and two together, and I didn't argue. In fact, to be honest, I wished it *had* been me that had stuck that knife in his guts, such was the hatred I felt for him for what he'd done to Mum and my sisters and Joe. I was glad he was gone."

"Oh, Terry, how dreadful." She shook her head in despair. "But it was really Joe who'd stabbed him?"

Terry nodded. "In self defence."

"But if it was self defence, why in God's name didn't your brother own up at the time? Why did he let you take the blame?"

"I made him. I owed him one for saving my life once, so I confessed to doing it. He'd pulled Dad off me one night when he was giving me a thrashing over something, can't remember what. Something trivial no doubt. Apparently, I'd already passed out and Joe feared Dad was going to kill me. Anyway, he pulled the bastard off and knocked him out. Sparko. He was only a kid at the time. I don't know to this day where he got the strength from, let alone swing a punch like that. See, the old man wouldn't have stopped hitting me. He never knew when to stop. So I reckoned I was returning Joe the favour."

"Why didn't someone there come forward and tell the police what went on? Surely someone must have seen? Known?"

"With so many people in the pub that night, Beth, it was all confusing. No one really saw what actually happened, so it was easy. They all saw what they wanted to believe. I couldn't let Joe go down for doing something I'd been wanting to do for years. The old man deserved it. I'm surprised you never read about it in the papers, it was plastered all over them at the time."

She shook her head. "I never was one much for reading the newspapers. Dad always used to, but once we came out here he didn't seem to bother buying them much. It was as if he was trying to block out the real world. He changed so much here, you see. Mum reckoned it was because he had work to do and had found an interest in tinkering with your uncle's tractors."

"Or they kept them out of your sight so you wouldn't read what I was up to and come rushing back to save me," Terry offered.

"Knowing what I know now, I expect you're right. Yet, during all this, you never gave a thought for me. Did you never think what it was going to do to us? Wasn't I that important to you that you could have least written and told me these things?"

"Beth, darling, how am I going to explain so you understand? I loved you but I knew there was no future for us. Your old man would have stopped me any which way and how. It would have made you unhappy and turned you against your family who were good people. I envied you the love of your parents. Your mum was poorly. I would have made things worse. So I thought—"

"You did make things worse. By deserting me. If I'd had known you were still there waiting for me, I'd have coped. It was only a matter of months. I wouldn't have conned them in letting me go up to see the Coronation, when in truth, I came home to try and find out where you were. If only you had written, just the once. Told me. I hated deceiving them, but I was worried what had happened to you. That's when Mum died. Whilst I was in London looking for you."

"Any letter would never have reached you anyway. They would have intercepted it. And even if you had been here with your Mum, do you think it would have stopped her dying? No. Beth, she was ill. What happened, happened."

"I know that, but Dad doesn't see it that way. He blames me totally for Mum."

"Then try to put it right. For Molly's sake, if not your own. I'd bet my last tanner your dad's aching to make things up with you but just doesn't know how or where to start. The longer he's left it, the harder it's become to say sorry. He knows he's hurt you, done wrong, but doesn't know where to start asking for forgiveness. I bet his taking Molly like he did today was the only way he could think of to get both of you back. He knew you wouldn't just let her go, would follow him."

"He's had plenty of opportunity to patch things up over the past few years."

"Perhaps your dad's been waiting for *you* to do it."

"And it's not like I've tried? All he had to do was tell that to Mike."

Terry squeezed her hand. "Make it up with him, Beth. Somehow. Families are precious and life's too short to be hating each other for the rest of it. It doesn't matter who's right and who's wrong, because you both are. And I can't help feeling I've been the cause of a lot of it, hearing what you've just told me.

"I am not blaming you, Terry. You tried to help us. It just all went wrong somehow."

He kissed her cheek lightly. "What are you going to do when this is over? You're not going back to Henry, I hope?"

She shook her head vehemently. "Never. I'm never going back to him. Oh, he'll kick up a fuss; it wouldn't be Henry if he didn't. I'll just have to lie low for seven years and then he can divorce me for desertion, or however long it takes. You should know, you're the expert in holy matrimony." There was a sardonic laugh in her voice.

"You mean I have to wait seven long years before you can marry me?"

"Who says I'm going to marry you? Terry, look—"

"Oh dear, sounds like the big put-down coming."

"No, listen to me," she pleaded. "Try to understand. Last night, I went through the most horrendous experience. I hurt inside and out. My marriage is in ruins, not that it was much of a marriage anyway, and I've just had Molly snatched screaming from my arms by a father who ignores me. I have a lot of thinking to do. There's a lot I want to do. I never realised until this morning just how much us women are suppressed. Half of what's happened to me is because of stupid laws that are so antiquated and out-of-date. Young women, especially teenagers, are suffering because of it. We can't get mortgages in our own name. We can't sign this or do that, go here or there without our husband's or father's say so. And it's always the man of the house people ask for when they knock. They don't want to speak to the little woman."

"But that was just Henry keeping you down. You had your own business."

"No, it's rife. It's everywhere. Yes, it's Henry who

holds the purse strings on the coffee shop but that's the way these things are. Unless you're a woman with your own means, born into money, or inherit a fortune, you're kept down or put down, controlled and manipulated from every corner. Just look at your mum and the way things were for her." The moment she said the words, she wanted to kick herself.

"But it's not like that in every family," Terry countered.

"True. In many, the men have to hand their pay packet over to the wife else he'll gamble or guzzle every last penny. But it's more than just that, Terry. Why shouldn't the council give me a house just because I don't have a husband if I can pay the rent? Why shouldn't I be able to buy things on hire purchase on my own, without my husband's, or my parents' say so if I earn the money? Why shouldn't I be able to vote for whom I please, instead of who my husband dictates I should? This country fought wars for freedom. Where's the freedom for young women? I can't see any of it happening. It's okay for men to go out boozing and playing darts and dominoes of an evening, but the good little woman must stay at home and look after the kids. She can't go out for a drink with her friends, she'd be classed as a tart. Men can voice their opinions about politics and the Government, but we're told to shut up because we don't know what we're talking about, that we don't understand these things. That it's men's business. Well, we *do* understand. We *do* know what we are talking about, and our opinions about our future matter. It's high time women stood up and were counted, not be the ones walking in our husband's footsteps, doing as he commands. We have to get the laws changed, Terry. Men can't go on treating us women like slaves. We have rights.

We have a right to our own money, a right to a say in our own affairs, our own lives. We need to stand together and demand change. I'd chain myself to the railings like those suffragettes did to get women the vote in the first place, if it meant women could be their own bosses, choose their own destiny. Well, it's time they gave the vote to younger people. If you're old enough to work, you should be old enough to vote; have a say in how this blooming country's run. It's time to start the revolution, Terry." She took a sharp intake of breath and stared at him. "Gosh, did I say all that?"

He laughed. "Yeah, you sure did. I didn't know you had so much spirit in you. But before you go taking on the world, you have to think of your priorities, which at this point in time, I thought was Molly."

She shot him a look of indignation. "This *is* all about Molly. It's about her future. Her wellbeing. It's about the wellbeing of all kids."

"And what about *your* future? Your wellbeing? You always were a fighter, Beth, but how are you going to get this revolution started on your own?"

She slumped back into the seat, winded. "Oh, I don't know. There has to be something I can do."

"Don't you think you've done enough fighting? You've spent the last few years making sure that little sister of yours had a roof over a head and was well cared for, and look at how much it's cost you. More than anyone should have to pay in a lifetime. Let your dad take over his responsibilities again now he's willing. Molly's safe here. No harm's going to come to her. It's time you started thinking about yourself for a change. Think of your future and what you want to do with it. It's high time you started enjoying life. Having fun."

"What with? I've no money, no home unless I move

back here, and no job. Some fun!"

He pulled her back across to him so she was nestled against his shoulder.

"Married to me, you would have fun, Beth. Lots. I'd make sure of it. Jobs are easy to come by and we could soon find a nice little place of our own. I'd never let you down. You'd never go without anything. What do you say, Beth? Marry me."

"And Henry?"

"He's ancient history. So, we may have to wait a few years, so what? We wouldn't be the first couple living in sin. Say it, Beth, say it. Just one little word… Just nod your head if that's easier. Either way, say you'll marry me, Beth. I've never stopped loving you. I never will."

She nodded. Slowly at first, then rapidly as he wrapped both arms around her and kissed her. In that moment, all her heartbreak and pain melted away.

As their lips drew apart, Terry glimpsed out of the windscreen.

"Look," he said, "here's them coming along now, walking up the lane."

Beth looked out of the side window. Backlit in a fire of light from the death throws of the setting sun, Molly and Alfie were strolling along hand in hand, heading towards the cottage. Molly, skipping along beside him, clutching Loopyloo, seemed as happy as anything. She was wearing different clothes from what Mrs Potter had dressed her in earlier, Beth noticed.

"She should be in bed by now. I wonder where they've been." She turned back to Terry, not expecting him to know or answer. A quick glance back at her father's face told her he was sad, deep in thought, but at the same time he looked to be enjoying his little girl's company. He was laughing now at something the child was saying, quite what she couldn't hear from inside the van. Molly appeared equally at ease with him.

"You know, Terry, I actually feel sorry for him. He's missed so much of Molly growing and developing into the fun-loving, teasing joy she has become. You can't be sad when Molly's around."

"Then let him enjoy the rest with her. Don't take the next precious years of her life away from him."

Just then, Alfie looked towards the van. Swiftly, Beth ducked down out of sight behind the door. She didn't want either of them to see her. Not just yet. She wasn't ready. She hadn't worked out quite what she was going to say to him.

"It's all right. They've gone inside now," Terry whispered.

She sat upright.

"What was all that about? I thought we'd come all this way to get Molly and you chicken out. I was half expecting you to leap out the van, grab her and come back yelling, 'Drive, Drive', like some bank robber."

"That was my intention when we arrived, but in sitting here talking to you, I've come to realize taking her away isn't the right thing to do. I have to go in and confront him. Talk to him. Rationally. I have to give him one last chance. No, that isn't enough," she said, shaking her head. "I have to *keep* trying until between us, Dad and I repair the damage we've done to each other. I might never forget all the suffering I've endured over the years because of his thoughtless actions, but I have to at least try and forgive him. And not all those years were bad with Henry. I wasn't exactly on skid row and I had the coffee shop, which was always one of my dreams. Just because I hated it here, that's not cause enough to deny Molly the chance to get to know her real father. No, you're right, Terry. She has to reach her own conclusions about him. And who knows? He might be totally different with her."

Terry clasped her hand, pulled it to his mouth and kissed her fingers. "Do you still want to go in? I could just start the engine again and we drive off, go back home."

She shook her head. "I'm certain. I need to talk to him. Only, come in with me, please, as I don't think I can do it alone. Perhaps with you there, we might both stay calm and start talking again like two rational human beings."

"Your dad might not welcome me after all this time. What if he slams the door in my face."

"Then we keep on knocking until he opens it. You get used to doors being slammed on you, I should know. You wouldn't believe the number of times it happened to me when I was looking for somewhere to live for me and Molly."

"She looks to be a happy little girl, your Molly. Reminds me of my kid sisters at that age."

"She's wonderful, Terry. I adore her."

He took the keys from the ignition. "Well then, come on. Best we go and say our peace before you change your mind."

"I won't," she said, already climbing out of the van.

As they walked down the path to the cottage, Terry kept her hand tightly clasped in his.

"Are you positive you want to do this now? We could wait until morning."

"No, Terry, I wouldn't sleep. Let's get it over with. Whatever happens, whatever he says, I'm going to stand up to him. He's not going to treat me like I don't exist. I'm real, I'm here and he's going to listen to me. I'm his daughter; he can't go on like there's nothing between us. I should have done this years ago. In fact, now I think about it, I think it's what he was trying to do this morning in his own way. I think he wanted to explain things, but I wouldn't let him."

The door to the cottage stood slightly ajar, as if waiting for them. From inside came the sounds of Molly and her father's laughter.

Terry winked at Beth and nodded towards the door. "They sound happy. Come on, let's do it. Don't forget, I'm right behind you, every step of the way, Mrs Gibbs."

"Mrs Gibbs?"

Terry laughed. "You'd best get used it, because that's who you are from now on, whether there's my ring on your finger or not."

Beth pulled him to her, wrapped her arms about his neck and kissed him. He had come through for her. This time, she wouldn't let him step out of her life again. He had captured her heart and she would never release it to another. Even if it took seven years or a whole lifetime, Terry was hers. Confronting Dad, trying finally to make peace and pick up the pieces of their shattered family wasn't going to be easy, but Terry there with her. Supporting. He was all the strength she needed.

She pushed open the cottage door, flooding the stone porch with yellow, welcoming light.

About The Author

Kit Domino grew up in West London, England during the 1950s and 1960s, in the areas and places she so vividly brings to life in *Every Step of The Way*, and can well remember the pea-soupers dominating much of her early childhood, leaving her a lifetime legacy of chronic asthma.

In 1972 she moved to Gloucestershire. Unlike her character Beth Brixham in *Every Step of The Way*, Kit loves the West County, not missing London in the least, and has no intention of moving back there.

A trained secretary, her working career has always involved books, copy-editing, proofreading and typesetting, and for 10 years ran her own word-processing agency. During this time she began writing her first novel as well as poetry, several of which were published. Later, she became office manager and company proofreader for a large planning consultancy near Bristol, and continued to write in her spare time.

In 2004, Kit was shortlisted for the Harry Bowling Prize for a London novel with *Every Step of the Way*. Fifteen years later, following redundancy in December 2010, she fulfilled her dream of being a published author, having already written five books in various genres, with another under way.

Not content with writing, Kit is also a semi-professional internationally-selling artist working in acrylics. Learn more about Kit and her work at: *www.kitdomino.com.*